Edited by Laura Jorstad and Chris Barcellona

Cover Art & Design by Kate O'Hara
Interior Design by Kevin Miller
Published by Nikota Publishing House Incorporated
Distributed by Riyria Enterprises

ISBN: 978-1-943363-83-4

THE ETHER WITCH

VOLUME 3:

THE DIVINING OF A DEVIL

by

Delemhach

DEDICATION

To Kevin and the cats. The days are better because you all are in them.

Even if Kraken does try and occasionally succeed in stealing food from my plate.

CHAPTER 1

AN INTERRUPTED INTERMISSION

"One would think that after battling a daughter of the Gods, a dragon, and—to a lesser extent—an emperor, the valiant heroes would get a well-deserved rest. Instead they were given half a day off.

Tam woke from a deep sleep with a jolt, though it wasn't immediately clear why.

A mind-numbing headache made his skull feel as though it had just been cracked open with a mallet.

The night before, during his battle against a group of witches and the sea monster plaguing Zinfera that he had learned was a kraken, he had received a blow to the head that resulted in a concussion. He was not enjoying its effects.

As Tam drove his knuckles into his temples, wishing there was some sort of reprieve from the pain, his wake-up call thundered again. It was the sound of wood splintering under the assault of an abnormally strong fist.

Tam stumbled out of bed, careful not to wake Eli. They were in the Zinferan palace that he'd almost managed to burn down the previous night with some help.

He crossed the guest room, nearly vomiting from the agony of the movement. Wrenching open the door, he braced his forearm against the frame and glowered down at his sister as colored dots danced around the edges of his vision.

"What?" he growled.

Katarina Reyes, queen of Daxaria, stood outside his chamber with her familiar, Pina, lying on her shoulders. Luca's and Penelope's hands were clasped in hers.

She stared at her brother's disgruntled state with a raised eyebrow, her golden eyes flitting to his bare torso. "Gross."

Tam made an animalistic snarl. Then he felt a gentle tug on his pants, and his attention fell to his son, Luca, peering up at him. Luca's face was pale, but he still spared a smile for his father before wrapping his arms around Tam's waist.

Tam had learned that his son was, in no uncertain terms, the devil. Not that Luca remembered who he was in his child state.

"Time to grab your stuff and get out of here, sunshine," Kat informed her brother airily. "The emperor is going to be a real pain in the backside about Eli staying in Zinfera. You lot have to leave. Now. And take Mum."

By this time, Eli had risen from the bed and made her way over to the door, her short hair full of cowlicks. She, too, stared blearily at the Daxarian queen. Penelope perked up at Eli's arrival. The young girl, whom Tam and Eli had saved from a pirate ship, was only a year older than Luca. It had been an incredible coincidence that the Troivackian child was not only one of the few remaining seers in the world, but also Tam and Kat's distant cousin.

Tam frowned, resting his hand gently atop Luca's head as he spoke to his sister. "What about you and Harris?"

"We have to do damage control here. The emperor is right to be concerned about the dragon returning, and the first witch probably won't stay in your void forever. Plus there is the whole matter of the Coven of Giong and Coven of Wittica now rebelling… It's a mess. We can't leave them high and dry. All the kingdoms need to be united, and Kezia only just woke up. She's pretty disoriented, so she won't be traveling for a while, and I'm not leaving her and Sir Cas here alone."

Tam nodded along as he was reminded of the Troivackian princess, who'd been gravely injured mere days earlier. The action pained him, so he closed his eyes and pinched the bridge of his nose.

He felt Eli's warm hand rest on his upper arm. "We'll grab some painkiller tea as soon as possible."

Kat scoffed. "Pfft. I can't believe what a baby you're still being. A little concussion has you in such a state."

Tam shot her a narrowed-eyed look.

She stuck her tongue out at him, but then seriousness overtook her once more. "There's something else you should know before you go… I finally was able to get my hands on the letters that have been sent to me from Daxaria." Kat paused, anguish filling her eyes, making Tam straighten. "Shortly after you left, Antony's magic surfaced. I knew this before leaving, but you wouldn't have heard the news. He's a weather witch."

Tam's eyebrows shot upward. That was an incredible power.

Kat continued, her tone still grave. "But in his letters, Eric says that Antony's not handling it well."

Tam felt his own anxiety lurch forward at the thought of his eldest nephew.

"Antony's upset because he knows now he can't be king, and his emotions are affecting the environment back in Daxaria. Eric is struggling to figure out what's going on here, and Da… Mum saw Da in one of the magic visions after we were attacked at Soo Hebin's palace. He probably thinks Mum is dying. You need to go home and tell everyone what is happening. We won't be able to have reliable messages even if we send hawks. Not with the witches at large. The majority of both the Giong and Wittica Covens have scattered. Nowhere is safe."

Swallowing, Tam once more peered down at Penelope and Luca. "Alright. We'll steal a ship and head home to Daxaria."

Kat's serious expression melted away as she shot her brother a wry smile. "Steal a ship? Look at you, you little vagabond." She reached up and tried to muss his hair, but Tam dodged her hand with a grunt. Cackling, the Daxarian queen added. "Jiho is giving you a ship. No thievery required."

"Aw. It was kind of fun setting the fire that one time!" Luca contributed while dropping his head back to stare at Kat upside down.

Kat snorted. "Gods. Four Ashowan boys… and the oldest has already set a pirate ship on fire and punched a foreign prince in the crotch. I'm going to miss when Mr. Howard hears the news."

Ignoring his sister's musings, Tam turned back to the spacious room and spotted his black tunic on the floor.

Barely stifling a yawn, Eli asked, "Where is Duchess Ashowan?"

"Ah, I believe the last I saw her she was—"

"BUKAA!"

The herald of a chicken echoed from the hall, making everyone turn—including Tam, who had already reappeared with his tunic on, albeit untucked, and found the duchess strutting down the marble hall, making the dome of feathers around her head bob.

Thanks to a mutated witch from the Daxarian coven named Henrietta, Duchess Annika Ashowan had been transformed into a black-and-white chicken the night before. At present, the duchess was perched on the back of none other than Kraken, her husband's familiar, as he trotted toward the group.

Kat nodded at the animals. "Right. That works. Now, Kraken, it is up to you whether you leave with Tam or stay here with me."

Kraken chirped.

No one knew what that meant, but his decision would become apparent when they departed.

Eli leaned farther out of the doorway and glanced down the long hallway, which was adorned with jade-encrusted pillars and gold filigree. "I'm surprised no one is coming to get us."

Kat grinned. "Oh. That'd be because I may have taken some inspiration from my children and oiled the stairs and most of the main floor."

Tam and Eli gaped in silence at the redhead, who stared unabashedly back.

"How… did you do that with no one noticing?" Eli said dazedly.

"You're asking a lot of questions when you should be grabbing your things and leaving," Kat retorted glibly.

Tam gave a disgruntled noise before turning back to the room. He hurriedly gathered the few belongings they had, including the red dress Eli had stolen from the shrine the night before.

"Alright. Our remaining things are at The Opulent Opal, and everything else should already be in Daxaria. We shipped a lot from Junya," Tam explained.

Kat jerked her chin down in understanding before her eyes moved to the corridor. "I recommend leaving out the window. The guards may be in an oily heap on the ground at the bottom of the stairs, but they are a spiky heap, what with the swords and spears."

Tam glanced at the window. "I guess it's a good thing that everyone will be disorganized and exhausted from the chaos yesterday."

"Mm-hm. Now get going. Give my love to my boys, snap Antony out of his bad mood, and tell Eric I'm fine."

"Did you write a letter you'd like me to pass along?" Tam ventured before attempting to stifle a yawn. He still felt like he could have slept for another week.

Kat stared blankly at him. "Right. A letter… That probably would've been good…"

Being the responsible adult present, Eli once again weighed in a little more briskly. "Would Harris like us to say anything to his wife and sons?"

At this, the Daxarian queen perked back up. "Yes! He said to tell her in as much detail as possible about the fires, and explain that he dedicated the palace one to her."

Eli, Tam, Luca, and Penelope took a beat to stare at the queen in silence.

"How will we find the ship we need to take?" Tam asked—without commenting on the odd, but fitting, message from the duke—while gesturing Penelope over.

"Bong is waiting for you all at the docks. And to get to the docks, there is a hackney one street north of the palace," Kat explained while following her brother and his group toward the window in his chamber.

Tam took a moment to stoop down and pluck up his mother, the chicken. Kraken then revealed his decision about whether he planned on going or staying by leaping up onto the windowsill and peering down from the second story to the street below.

"Penelope, Luca, hold my hands. Eli, if you could take my mother and my arm, we can go into the void and I'll get us over to that dark alley without people seeing us. Kraken, did you want to come with us into the void to get down, or—"

The fluffy feline leapt nimbly onto one of the carved stone dragons that lined the walls, then proceeded onto one of the elaborate balcony ledges below before he found his way into an ornamental tree, then the palace wall. He disappeared behind that.

"You'd never guess he was almost thirty years old," Kat stated, openly impressed.

Tam gave a half smile in agreement, then locked eyes once more with his sister. "Don't get yourself killed. Your husband's grumpy enough."

Kat sighed. "Yeah… Yeah, I know. Now get on with it. I want to see this magic of yours that *everyone* has been dying to know about for decades!"

Rolling his eyes, Tam passed his mother to Eli, then seized both of the children's hands while Eli laced her free arm through his. "Penelope, the void is a little bit scary, so feel free to close your eyes."

The little girl's mouth wrinkled stubbornly, but Tam noticed she gripped his hand a little tighter nonetheless.

"See you soon." Tam tilted his head with one last smile to his sister, then allowed his black-and-silvery aura to sweep himself and everyone that touched him into the dark embrace of his void.

Kat stared dumbly at the space where her brother, Eli, and the children had just been standing, then stepped forward and peered down toward the alleyway that Tam had just mentioned. It took another moment or two, but eventually, she watched them file out of the alleyway and head north as per her directions.

Letting out a low whistle, she shook her head in disbelief. "How the hell was he so bad at hide-and-seek all those years?" Sighing, Kat made her way out of the room, but not before pausing thoughtfully beside the tousled bed Tam and Eli had shared.

"Pfft. She'll probably be pregnant next time I see her, knowing our family's talent for procreation." Kat laughed to herself. "I'll take bets with Harris over when it'll happen. Though I wonder if they actually are married like Harris was saying. I really couldn't tell before. I'll feel bad for Da if they are." Clasping her hands behind her back, Kat planted a kiss on Pina's fuzzy cheek. "Come along. I think I'm going to have to ask you to work your charms on the emperor and see about making him less of a royal arsehole."

The familiar purred, her lips curling upward in a smile.

"If you end up being the one to rule over Zinfera, don't gloat to Kraken too much, hm?"

While Pina was far quieter in every sense than Kraken, she was known for being magnificently daring in her own way. And despite the fact that Pina and Kraken had learned to respect each other, there was still a bit of a rivalry between them, according to Kat's da, who could speak with Kraken.

The Daxarian queen and her familiar proceeded out of the room and down the abnormally quiet palace hall. Kat knew she might wind up spending a bit of time in a Zinferan cell for impeding the emperor's orders, but she planned on pointing out that she wasn't much use fighting dragons when hungry and tired from poor accommodations.

"Hopefully this stupid war can wrap up soon," she murmured to both herself and Pina. She slipped a leg over the long wooden banister, which she intended to ride down to avoid oiling the bottom of her boots.

Pina mewed in agreement and sank her claws a little more deeply into the dark-blue jacket that Kat had donned that day in preparation for sliding down the stairs via banister. And then the witch and her familiar whizzed down in a most improper fashion to check on the state of the emperor's armed guards, feeling a mixture of weariness and sadness at having to say goodbye to her family yet again.

CHAPTER 2

ODDLY NOT OUTRAGEOUS ODDS

Tam craned his neck to peer over the crowds filling the dock. He knew it was a matter of time before imperial soldiers would be sent to find them.

They needed to leave quickly.

"Kraken, do you happen to see or smell where we should be going?" Tam glanced down at his side, where Kraken sat watching the dock activity. The fluffy cat's eyes kept being drawn to the barrels of fish that were currently being unloaded from a nearby fishing vessel while Annika the chicken clucked quietly at his side.

Sighing, Tam resumed his search. Kraken was too preoccupied to help.

"Hello again, friends!"

Whirling around, Tam found Bong standing a short way down the dock wearing a deep-blue coat and white pants, his hands clasped behind his back as he smiled handsomely at them.

"Bong!" Luca burst out and darted over to the elder Ryu son, throwing his arms about his waist.

Bong wrapped an arm around Luca's back. "Goodness, Luca! I think you've grown two whole inches since our time together in Junya!"

Luca beamed as he released the Zinferan and turned to Penelope. "This is my friend Bong that I told you about! He's really nice! Are you coming home with us?" Luca asked as Tam moved forward with Penelope and Eli following behind.

Bong raised an eyebrow at Penelope, who was holding Eli's hand. This was to ensure she didn't get lost in the throng of sailors and merchants flooding the docks—and no other reason, of course (she had been quite adamant on that point).

"Penelope?" Bong lifted a questioning look to Tam, who took in a long breath.

"We found her on Captain Woo's ship shortly after we left Eusa," Tam explained while gently clasping Luca's shoulder to stop him from getting swept away by the crowd.

"Ah." Bong nodded slowly. "I must confess, as much as I am dying of curiosity to know just what all has happened since we last met, I'm afraid that there isn't much time to spare. Your boat is ready to launch. You all simply need to board the vessel located at the end of the dock."

Tam smiled appreciatively as they all moved as quickly as possible, with Bong leading the way.

"It's good you were able to get home safely to Haeson," Tam said conversationally.

"It was an exceptionally easy journey, thank the Goddess. Jeong had a tougher time, I'm afraid to say, what with the imperial soldiers becoming desperate. However, we received notice that he is home a few days ago," Bong assured as they moved.

"Thank Gods." Tam breathed in relief. "Are you and your father alright after last night, by the way?"

"I confess it was a lot more terrifying than I could have imagined. But I must thank you again for saving us. We had thought we were prepared, given that we already knew that there would be a poisoning attempt."

Tam shot him a serious glance. "I'm glad we got there in time as well."

The two shared a meaningful look as the weight of what had nearly happened settled over them. Tam and Eli had interrupted their would-be execution the night before at the orders of the corrupt concubine Soo Hebin, who had also managed to poison a number of guests attending her son's birthday celebration.

"Will your father be in trouble with the emperor for helping us?" Eli interrupted as they neared the end of the dock.

"Maybe a little. Truthfully, the emperor has always had a bit of a soft spot for my father, so we are not worried. Not to mention I've no doubt your sister the queen did something to help you escape that would earn a significant portion of the emperor's attention and frustration."

Tam chuckled. "You're not wrong."

Grinning, Bong at last drew to a stop, faced them, then gestured elegantly to the last ship at the dock. Distracted by their conversation, Tam hadn't paid much attention to the boats they had passed, and so he was more than a little taken aback by the ship that sat bobbing in the water.

It was massive. And there were odd hatches lining both sides.

"Erm… This isn't exactly a discreet ship," he ventured as he gaped.

"That is true, but its defensive prowess is incomparable. It carries weapons my father has been a key figure in developing." Bong added the last part in a discreet whisper before continuing. "In part, we're sending this ship with you to show your father and the Daxarian king. We must see to more being built, to help with the beast that troubles Zinfera and the terrible pirate problem. To do so, however, we will need more investment."

Tam nodded slowly. "Alright. Are the designs and details on board?"

Bong gave a slight bow in acknowledgment, then procured a silver key from his pocket. "They are. I have set them in the chest in your quarters."

Tam accepted the key and stowed it away in his own pocket. "I'll pass this along to my father and the king. Hopefully we can figure out what to do about the covens soon."

Bong released a long breath. "It would be good if we could find out a way to settle it all without a war, but I confess that I do not believe we can."

Tam grimaced, his gaze dropping down to Luca, who was evidently struggling to follow the conversation.

Pushing away his anxieties about war, he tried to buffet the morale of the conversation by saying, "Who knows? Maybe my father has a trick or two still up his sleeve."

Bong's smile widened. "Maybe he can be the one to bake those miracle cookies Jeong was requesting."

Tam laughed and clapped a hand on Bong's shoulder before pulling him into an embrace. "Be safe."

Bong gave Tam's back a hearty thump. "You as well, friend."

As they all continued their farewells, Tam, Eli, Penelope, and Luca approached the gangplank. A steward waited at the top. It would seem the days of keeping Tam's identity a secret were over.

Sighing, Tam lifted a foot to move forward when he stopped abruptly.

"Something wrong?" Eli paused to look up at him.

Tam cleared his throat and reached up to rub the back of his neck. "Everyone, head on up. Eli and I will be there in a moment."

Luca and Penelope blinked. Then, looking at each other, they shrugged and darted up the gangplank excitedly, leaving Tam and Eli behind. Kraken gave a lone meow before he, too, trotted up after the children. The duchess, having fluttered onto the cat's back moments before, bobbed along as he went.

Once they were out of earshot, Tam turned to face Eli fully and moved both hands into his pockets.

"Eli… You wouldn't happen to be… Erm. It's just because of the previous times that I—"

Eli's attention snapped over to where the children were just stepping aboard as a particularly loud giggle escaped from Penelope.

"Tam, whatever it is you are trying to say, could this not be done on board? We need to leave."

Tam flushed. "Eli… I'm two for two. So I'm sorry if this isn't something you want to talk about with me, but I at least have to ask…" Tam let out a long, steadying breath. "Is there any chance you're pregnant?"

Eli's eyes went wide, then relaxed as she opened her mouth.

Tam could see in her face that she was about to assure him that was not the case, but then she froze. "Oh… Um." Concern filled her expression. She dropped her attention to the dock with a manic glint in her eyes.

"Are you serious?" Tam felt a wealth of emotions overtake him. Panic, excitement, disbelief—maybe just a little bit of an urge to laugh at his weird karmic bond with ships and finding out about children that would fall under his care.

"You think I would joke about this kind of thing?" Eli's voice was already rising in volume.

"Well, it's only been what… a few weeks? A month? Since we started doing that… that kind of—"

"I need to count, and I need to find out what moon phase we are at right now." Eli surged up the gangplank, leaving Tam to rush behind her in an equally fretful whirl.

Completely lost in his thoughts, Tam was caught off guard when he and Eli stepped onto the ship and discovered tidy rows of sailors and their captain already bowing.

"Lord Tamlin, it is an honor to travel with you on this voyage," the men chorused in unison.

Eli had halted right in front of Tam. She, too, was stunned by the sight.

"Ah, yes. Thank you all for… agreeing to lend us your talents for this voyage," Tam managed awkwardly.

The crew righted themselves, and the captain strode forward.

He was a Zinferan man in his early fifties with a short salt-and-pepper goatee and a shaved head. Clad in a white coat with gold buttons and white trousers, he cut a striking figure against the brilliant-blue sky.

"I am Captain Sun, my lord. It is good to meet you."

"Ah. Right… Right. This here is—"

"Lady Elisara Ashowan, I am told," Captain Sun interrupted. He bowed to Eli, stunning both of them into silence.

Jiho must have repeated Harris's announcement that they had married.

"Uh… Yeah. Yes." Tam cast a nervous glance at Eli. He worried that she would be upset about this news, but at the moment, she was staring blindly at the ship railing as if struggling to remember something.

Presumably the date of her last courses.

Tam swallowed with difficulty.

"This is Luca, my son, and Penelope," Tam finished introducing the children, careful to keep Penelope's tie to them ambiguous.

"It is a delight to meet you all." The captain smiled affably at the children who, during the introductions, had casually sidled closer to Tam and Eli. "Now, I am given to understand that we are in a great hurry to reach Daxaria, and I assure you, my lord, I will do my utmost to see you all arrive there safely as quickly as possible. The witch named Henrietta has already been secured belowdecks as per Lord Jiho Ryu's orders."

"Thank you, that is appreciated." Tam lifted the corners of his mouth. "I'm afraid my… my wife is not feeling well. I'd love to make your acquaintance better along with the rest of the crew soon, but might we be shown to our quarters now?"

"Mom, you're not feeling well?" Luca peered up at Eli fretfully.

It took a beat, but Eli eventually blinked herself back to the present. "I just need a bit of time. I'll be fine, Luca."

The captain gestured toward the stairs that would lead belowdecks gracefully. "Not a problem, my lord and lady. Men! Prepare to cast off!"

Eli sat scribbling at the large, heavy desk pressed under the impressive bank of windows that made up most of the back wall of her and Tam's quarters.

"Alright, so… your last cycle was… ?" Tam paced the large expanse of the cabin, his steps cushioned by the sprawling cream carpet that covered most of the floor.

"It had finished that day in Eusa when I drank with the old couple."

Tam swung around in alarm. "That was ages ago!"

Eli's glare snapped up. "It was not. It just *feels* like ages ago."

"Well, a few days after that your parents came, and another day or so after that was when we stole the pirate ship. That was our first night together," Tam argued.

"Yes, but it was still too early! It shouldn't have been a risk for another week, and we didn't do anything for a while afterward because the children were with us and we were steering the ship in shifts."

Eli leaned back in her chair, looking a little more confident, but not entirely at ease.

"With the time sailing and then two or three weeks in the mountains, though? You should have had it since then!"

Tam watched her eyes fall back to the page as she gnawed on her tongue.

"We were intimate quite often during the week I trained with Wixim," she recalled warily. "But I should have been close to my—" She stopped talking and instead made an aggravated noise as she leaned her forearms against the desk.

Tam rubbed his face with both hands before driving them with great force through his hair. "There is no chance that you had it and forgot, is there? I know that sounds like a stupid question, but we *have* had a lot happening." He approached the desk.

Eli's eyes fluttered closed, and she inhaled deeply. Tam could tell that this question was trying some very sensitive nerves.

Deciding to lighten the mood, he risked speaking again. "I mean… I did warn you that my family is pretty—"

The withering stare Eli gave him when her eyes opened encouraged Tam to close his mouth in a timely manner. After a careful moment of staying perfectly still, he decided to move despite the narrow-eyed look Eli kept giving him. It was not unlike a cat debating swatting something irritating.

Tam knelt at Eli's side, prompting her to turn toward him, and gently clasped the hand that remained curled into a fist on her lap.

"We're going to be fine."

She didn't say anything.

Tam forced himself to come up with perfectly reasonable reasons for her missed cycle. "It's possible you aren't… expecting… and it's just the stress of everything."

"Even when I was starving and enslaved, I never fully skipped one," Eli muttered, her gaze homed in on the page of notes she had made.

"Do you even feel as though something is different, though? Maybe it's just a bit late."

Eli didn't look convinced.

"What if the hard training in your beast form with Wixim changed things?"

At this, Eli's eyebrows rose, and her expression lightened. "That *would* explain it!"

Tam smiled. "See? No need to stress."

Sighing, Eli at last relaxed back into her chair.

Tam, still holding her hand, raised it to his lips and pressed a kiss against her knuckles.

"You seem more terrified of pregnancy than you did fighting a dragon," he observed softly.

Eli tensed at the reference of the battle she'd almost engaged in with the golden dragon named Wixim. They hadn't wanted to fight, but his loyalties remained with the first witch at the time of their last confrontation.

Tam could see that she wanted to snap at him, but when she locked eyes with him the combativeness ebbed away.

"Tam, now is really not the time for me to be in any kind of altered condition."

"I know. But just as you wisely said that first night we had together, we can handle it if that happens."

Eli arched a wry eyebrow at him. "Are you pretending that you weren't about to faint moments ago?"

Tam continued smiling, though he forced a good deal of innocence into it. "While I'm good with children, I'm… admittedly… quite nervous when it comes to pregnancy."

"It does kill a lot of women," Eli agreed somberly.

Rising back up, Tam pulled Eli into his arms and gently rubbed her back.

"Let's not assume anything. I know there is a physician aboard, so if you really need to know, we can go to him."

Eli said nothing in response, but her arms gripped him a little tighter.

Tam hoped she couldn't feel his heart hammering in his chest. The truth was, he hadn't been entirely forthcoming with his suspicions. Between his family's history and his odd fate with boats, an overwhelming sense of inescapable destiny nipped at the back of his mind.

But Eli didn't need to hear that. So he bit his tongue and made the silent decision to start paying close attention to Eli's well-being for the voyage.

CHAPTER 3

THE DRAW OF THE DARK

A long, long time ago…

Her feet were caked in dirt.

Every inch of her trembled.

She doubted that this humble little cottage was where she'd find him.

Whispers sounded from all around her, but they didn't sting her the way the wind did through her chemise and the thin shawl she'd manage to grab before she'd started running.

While her eyes watered, she wasn't necessarily crying. The tears had yet to fully come, but they would.

Her hands were red and swollen from the cold. Moving them hurt, but she needed to knock or at least open the worn wooden door to the cottage.

"Brother…" Her voice rasped as a warm tear escaped her eye. The trail of water down her cheek chilled instantly.

Using the side of her shaking hand, she pounded the door twice. The tremors grew more violent, making her hunch over. He probably wasn't here. Some cottar's wife would probably open the door and tell her to leave. She'd probably be called a horrible name or three.

The door grunted as it lifted and then opened with a whine.

"Aradia?"

Her eyes snapped up.

She should hate him.

She should shout and bring down every righteous bit of fury imaginable. He was the reason she was powerless and hurt.

Instead, seeing his familiar face staring down at her reduced her to sobs.

She crumpled into a crouch as she cried. Her fingers grabbed uselessly at the shawl around her as she wept. Strong hands grasped her upper arms, trying to help her stand, but her knees gave way.

"How long have you been outside?" she heard him ask softly.

His gentleness made her cry all the harder.

He scooped her into his arms and turned back to the warmth of the cottage. She was aware of the door closing against the blue evening, the smell of coming snow sharp in the air.

She felt herself set on a rough woven carpet before a hot hearth. A soft blanket was thrown over her shoulders. She heard the noises of a kettle being set over the fire.

"What happened?"

Aradia squeezed her eyes shut. Her fingers were throbbing in the warmth, but they still clumsily tried to tighten her hold on the shawl.

"What do… they call you in this life?" she managed through a tightened throat.

"Daniel."

Aradia nodded and rocked back and forth on the carpet. Her emotions surged in the face of her safety.

"I'll deal with the ones who did this."

Aradia's eyes snapped up to meet her brother's dark ones. She saw his somber sincerity and his pain on her behalf.

"I can't feel fear. Not since our battle… What is this… What is… this feeling?"

"Grief. Anger. Despair."

Aradia felt the soft blanket slip from her shoulders as she stared at her brother vulnerably. "Why?"

"It's normal to feel this way after something horrible happens. A lot of people go through it. I didn't know you were nearby." He slowly seated himself on the floor a short distance from her side.

Instead of explaining how she had come to find him, all she could manage was, "Why… would you do this to me?"

Her brother stilled.

A century ago, his face had been filled with ire and hatred. They had battled. They'd almost destroyed an entire continent doing so… Lobahl had once been a lush jungle. Now eighty percent was desert because of them.

"I wanted you to understand a fraction of what I was feeling. Do you know that in this village, two-thirds of the women have endured what I believe you just have? There are even men who have been hurt this way."

The fact that her brother seemed to already know exactly what had happened to Aradia made her throat close to the point where breathing became a struggle.

"I feel your pain. I feel all of their pain. Aradia, the cruelty of these humans… It's capable of destroying any good that could have been." He paused and visibly weighed his next words. "There is good. I never said otherwise. But humans do not deserve this beautiful world our parents have made. Can't you see that now? Can't you see how they will destroy everything?"

"What about those who have been hurt? Don't they deserve every scrap of goodness so that they can heal?" Aradia argued, but unlike in the past, this argument was desperate, and even to her own ears it sounded broken.

"Good might win out for a little, but the evil of them, Aradia…" Her brother shook his head, his grief palpable. "Aradia, I'm scared for the good humans just as scared as I am for the ancient beasts. The evil will spread more and more. It is beyond my ability to solve. Our parents were wrong. No one can help the humans."

"There has to be a way to stop them. To stop the evil in humans from growing more powerful!"

It was her brother's turn to grow misty-eyed. "I'm not strong enough for it, Aradia. I can't even… I can't even be raised in my child years without suffering. How can I help people when they fear me because they fear their own darkness? Rather than face it, they say I'm the root of evil. When really, they're too afraid to see that the root is in them. I don't even hate them for it. I hate them for looking for someone to blame. For ignoring it. For embracing it because it is easier for them than to be humbled."

Aradia listened, her tears quietly falling.

Her brother's words... She could tell that if she were capable of feeling fear, she would have felt it then. The sentiment rattled around in some vacant space where her heart used to be.

"Why couldn't we try to fix it together?" she whispered. "Like Mother and Father told us to?"

Daniel stared at her, a tear of his own escaping. "Because you don't feel and see what I do. Just like I will never know the strain of summoning a tidal wave or building a mountain the way you did. Aradia... What you have been asking of me this entire time is the equivalent of a master looking at its beaten, starved dog and saying, Why can't you go hunt for my family? Why can't you try?" He took a shaking breath, his gaze falling to the carpet as the fire used its shadows to cut the truth of his feelings into his face. "I can't do it anymore, Aradia. And it was cruel of our parents to expect me to."

Aradia stared at her brother.

There was nothing she could say. These were discussions they'd had before. But she had to silently confess to herself that in the past, she never could have imagined how wretched powerlessness could be. How soul-shattered she felt when she had been attacked earlier that very day.

Something hot and uncomfortable sparked in her chest as she looked at her brother. "If you know how horrible this kind of thing is... why did you wish an eternity of it for me? Why do I deserve to be tortured? I just wanted to help."

Her brother's agonized eyes found her own. "Because you were torturing me. And you were torturing the ancient beasts without knowing what you were doing."

When Aradia spoke again, it came out choked. "I never wished harm on you."

"I didn't want you to be harmed, either, but it was the only way."

Tears fell more quickly down Aradia's cheeks. "If this, in your eyes, is the only way to help me understand, then you aren't any better than them."

Her brother flinched as if her words had hurt him, but his expression was accompanied by acceptance. "I never said I was better than them. I know I'll pay in the Grove of Sorrows. But one day, Aradia, I think you might realize that sometimes there are no good choices. You must simply make the decision you believe to be best for as many people as possible."

Tam woke with a start, sweat coating his brow, his stomach roiling.

He located the chamber pot under the bed and retched.

Shivering, he clambered out of bed to sit on the floor. The ship rocked more than it had during the day, and it was making Tam's head spin.

Grabbing his discarded tunic from the floor beside the bed, he launched himself at the door of his and Eli's cabin. Next, he pushed himself out into the corridor and proceeded blindly until his stiff legs clambered up the stairs.

The frigid sea air struck his face as soon as his head crested the main deck.

He welcomed it and gulped down a clear breath, which in turn made his vision whirl even more aggressively. His hand clasped the banister as his knees buckled.

"Lord Tam, are you alright?" A sailor's voice called from somewhere on the main deck, but Tam couldn't respond as he sprinted up the rest of the stairs, crossed the deck, dove for the railing, and heaved all over again.

"My apologies, Lord Tam! I will retrieve a coat for you!" The sailor's footsteps scampering off sounded distantly behind him.

A dull throbbing entered Tam's head as he raised an unsteady hand to his forehead. "What the hell was that dream?" He remained glued to the railing as the waning moon shone brightly overhead.

Eventually the sailor returned with a coat that Tam slipped on with a quiet mutter of thanks. He didn't want to return downstairs yet. The longer he was above deck, the better his stomach felt. Bit by bit, his head managed to clear. Though the haunting dream he'd had of the devil and first witch was still sharp in his mind's eye.

The devil really did look like him.

Something soft brushed against Tam's ankles, jolting him in surprise. When he glanced down, however, he found the familiar shining green eyes of Kraken. Stooping over, he swept up his father's familiar into his arms. He could feel Kraken's soothing purrs rumble beneath his fluff, and it calmed Tam's erratic heartbeat.

"I had a bad dream," Tam explained softly. "But it felt more than just a dream… And with everything going on, I suspect it has a lot more meaning and truth behind it."

Kraken didn't make a sound, merely flicked his head to the side to look out over the shadowed water before them.

Tam's shoulders eased as the cause for his nightmare appeared in his mind in a sudden rush. "I think I… I did something."

Kraken turned to peer up at him.

"You can't tell anyone, Kraken. Promise?"

The fluffy familiar slowly blinked at Tam.

"I started telling people I was the devil. I even told it to the first witch."

Kraken gave a chirp of alarm.

"I felt something in the air when I decided to start doing this. And I think… I think something is happening to me because of it."

A low rumble sounded in Kraken's belly.

Tam chuckled quietly. "Are you really growling at me?"

Kraken's growl increased in volume.

"Yeah. I know. But I did it for Luca. He's my son, and everyone kept targeting him. It wasn't my best idea, but it seemed like the only way I could keep him safe."

Kraken let out an exasperated huff.

"I'll figure it out. I'm an Ashowan, right?" Weariness filled his body like an iron weight. "I've known for a long time that there is something off about me. As if darkness was always ready to eat me. Hunting me, even though it felt attached to me like my shadow."

Kraken's tail twitched.

Tam tilted his head, his thoughts drifting. "My da and sister always seem like they are in this other world. A world that's warm and whole. A world filled with light, and hope, and… good. I've never felt like I could be in that world."

With his breaths quickening, Kraken nuzzled Tam's bicep.

"I used to think it was because I was scared of my magic. But I'm not scared of it anymore, and I still feel this way. It's one of the reasons I'm so uncomfortable around the Troivackian king. He's always been able to see it in me somehow."

Kraken's grumblings and twitches stilled as he listened.

Tam lifted his gaze to the stars. "Mum says that you only have to look up at the stars to see an example of infinite possibilities." He cast a melancholy smile to the sky. "I wanted to believe that maybe one day I would live in the light, too."

Tam lowered his face to Kraken. A sharp prickling started behind his eyes, but his smile remained fixed in place, though it was harder to hold. "I'm starting to think I was never meant to be in the light. I think there's a chance that I was always supposed to become the devil."

Kraken extended his right paw and gently brushed it against Tam's chest in a clear attempt at comforting him.

Tam returned his attention to the stars. "I'm probably being dramatic after a bad dream. Don't worry too much, Kraken… But if someday the darkness does get me? Please keep my family safe for me?"

Kraken pressed his head even more firmly against Tam's arm This time, when Tam gazed into his soft face, he saw a tear gleaming on the feline's long lashes. It made Tam feel even worse, but at least he was a little less alone for a moment.

CHAPTER 4

THE CONNIPTIONS OF A CAT

Kraken padded into the cabin. He'd left the duchess chicken strutting around the upper deck. After promising Tam that he wouldn't tell anyone his secret, Kraken reluctantly decided to keep it. But that didn't mean he couldn't do something about it.

He rounded the end of the bed. On the other side he could smell the new familiar. Leaping onto the bed with a chirp, he noted that Tam had already risen for the day, but his familiar slept.

Kraken's eyes narrowed. He clambered over her limbs, then up her torso until he could sit on her chest.

He stared down, waiting.

His tail twitched impatiently when she still didn't wake.

Giving a huff of annoyance, Kraken took matters into his own claws. Lifting a paw, he slapped the familiar woman across the face. He didn't use his claws, but he rather hoped the powerful blow would be enough to stir her.

Evidently it was not.

He slapped her again. Still nothing. A low rumble sounded in Kraken's chest. He proceeded to repetitiously slap the familiar's face until her eyebrows twitched and her eyes fluttered open in confusion.

She stared blankly at Kraken.

"You are far softer than I realized," she announced bluntly.

Kraken wished he could roll his eyes as dramatically as some humans could.

"Of course I'm soft. I have the best fluff in all the world. Now, get up. We need to have a chat," he meowed. He knew she couldn't understand him in her human form, but he still felt the need to retort.

"Can you please get off me?" Eli requested evenly.

Kraken's tail twitched again.

Then he raised his paw and slapped her across the cheek once more.

She blinked. "It feels like a fluffy caress when you do that."

Occasionally, Kraken's divine softness worked against him. He growled again.

"Is something wrong?" Eli slowly pushed herself to sit up, forcing Kraken to move off and to the side of her.

"Yes, there is a big problem. Your witch is floundering. It's your job to help him," Kraken chirped.

Eli raised a confused eyebrow and sighed. "I can see about changing into my other form on the deck if you need to talk."

Kraken blinked in confirmation.

"I'll be up in a bit. I have to change and wash up."

Despite wanting to complain, Kraken knew there was nothing else he could do for the moment to hurry this familiar along, so he moved out of the cabin and headed for the stairs.

In truth, he hated being belowdecks. His balance wasn't what it should be.

Upon darting up the stairs, Kraken very nearly crashed into the chicken, who also happened to be his witch Finlay's mate.

"Where have you been?" Duchess Annika clucked.

Kraken sighed. He already missed the days when she couldn't understand him. *"Minding my own business. How are things here?"*

The chicken's beady eyes glared at him.

His chest fluff remained unruffled.

"*Fine. It is a sunny day, and the winds are still coming from the south. It is annoying having to avoid being stepped on.*"

Kraken chuckled. "*Yes, it is a feat cats are better at, to be certain.*"

The pair turned and started sidling down the center of the main deck.

"*I'll be having a private discussion with your son's mate when she eventually comes up,*" Kraken announced briskly.

"*What about?*"

"*Did I not say the word 'private' loud enough for you to hear through your feathers?*" Kraken drawled without a single glance to his right where Annika strutted.

He was not entirely surprised when he felt the peck at his shoulder.

Swinging around, Kraken slowly moved until he sat perfectly straight with his tail wrapped around his feet. "*That was a bold move for someone who tastes like dinner.*"

The duchess gave an indignant "bok" before adding, "*I knew you were difficult even when I didn't understand you. However, what you will tell me is if everything is alright with Eli.*"

Kraken turned and surveyed the bustling ship. His gaze eventually found Tam, who leaned against the ship's railing nearby, looking out blindly toward the horizon. Even from where he sat, Kraken could see the smudges under his eyes.

"*Your son's mate is fine. Your son, however, needs her assistance.*"

"*What's wrong with Tam?*" Annika asked in alarm.

Kraken looked back at her with slitted eyes. "*That is, again, a private matter.*"

"*Does it have anything to do with how she was feeling unwell when she boarded the ship? Gods. Did Tam get her pregnant? Is that why he's stressed?*"

Kraken's claws flexed into the wooden planks of the deck in irritation. He really wished he *could* eat the chicken duchess. He'd have to go deal with the witch who could turn her back soon...

"*I do not know, nor do I care right now if there are more grandkittens in your future. This is a matter regarding familiars, and I will be saying nothing else on the matter.*"

Annika's head jerked to the side. "*That isn't a no to her being pregnant.*"

Kraken could already tell she wasn't going to let the matter rest, but he was fortunately spared from the duchess's needling by Eli's appearance. He turned without bothering to mew another word and sauntered over to Tam's familiar.

By the time Kraken reached her, she already had the boy Tam called his son latched to her side, while the little girl prattled on about one thing or another.

Kraken meowed up at Eli.

She didn't look away from the little girl.

Kraken chirped.

Still, nothing.

With his calm turning rapidly to furious indignation, Kraken opened his mouth and let out a long yowl that sent several heads turning in his direction.

Eli looked down at him, sighed wearily, and patted Luca on the back, prompting him to release her. She said something about talking or playing later to the two children, then pulled away.

At last alone, Eli addressed Kraken. "I'll go ask the captain about changing forms."

He let out a very long meow. He wanted to go nap, and this was taking far too long!

As Eli climbed up toward the stern of the ship and approached the captain, Kraken watched their exchange. Then, striding past him, making his fluff rustle, he noted Tam ascending the stairs before joining the conversation.

What little patience Kraken possessed disintegrated. Bolting up the steps, Kraken sat directly behind Eli's legs and proceeded to bat at her calves—with his claws this time.

"Okay! Okay! Ow—Stop that!" she chided.

Kraken glared guiltlessly up at her.

Did she think he wasn't busy, just because they were aboard a ship in the middle of nowhere? To see her meander and trod around while he, an empurror, waited? The nerve!

"Kraken, don't do that," Tam chastised.

Kraken hissed at him.

Tam's eyebrows rose toward his hairline.

It was rare that Kraken became this annoyed, but it was Tam's fault that he was so stressed to begin with!

Bending down, Eli scooped Kraken into her arms and stepped away from both the captain and Tam to head back down to the main deck.

"I don't know that there will be enough room, and it will most likely affect the speed of the ship while I'm in my other state. So this needs to be quick."

Kraken let out another loud yowl. *"DO YOU EVEN KNOW WHAT THE WORD 'QUICK' MEANS?"*

"Alright! Alright!" Eli finally reached the middle of the deck. "Back up!" she ordered tersely.

Kraken didn't stop grumbling.

He watched as she shifted into her beast form, noting that just about every sailor on board stumbled back in shock. There was a shout or two of alarm, even though they would have been informed of her abilities beforehand.

As it turned out, the deck was a little more cramped with the familiar named Kasha taking Eli's place.

"There! Now, what in the world is it?" Kasha demanded.

"You have been slacking on your familiar duties," Kraken bit out. *"Your witch is in over his head, and it is up to you to manage things better."*

"What are you talking about?" Eli snapped.

"He has sworn me to secrecy, but your witch is toying with a fate bigger than he can fathom! Something even the Gods will most likely take exception to!"

"And what am I supposed to do?"

Kraken slapped her whiskered snout. *"SOMETHING! ARE YOU OR ARE YOU NOT A FAMILIAR?"*

"Pardon me." The cool cluck of Annika Ashowan joining the conversation had Kraken rounding on her.

"I SAID THIS IS PRIVATE, YOU UNDERCOOKED SNACK!" Kraken snarled in the chicken's face.

The duchess pecked him smartly on the nose. *"Gods. I owe my husband a lot of sympathy if this is how you are."*

Kraken lifted a paw, wrapped it around Annika's neck, and pulled her closer. *"Ask yourself this. If I'm worried, just what has your kitten done?"*

"I'd love to know, but you aren't telling me," Annika fired back before jerking upward to stare at Kasha. *"Are you pregnant? I don't know if you know this, but our family is rather susceptible to—"*

After overcoming her visible shock of hearing the duchess speak while a chicken, Kasha closed her eyes and dropped her head with a pained moan.

Tam stood beside the captain with Luca and Penelope in front of him.

They were all captivated by the very unusual meeting of animals on the ship's deck.

Kasha looked vexed, Kraken sounded angry, and his mother…

He had no idea.

But she was in a sort of scuffle with Kraken, who kept jabbing her with his paw while she pecked him in retaliation.

"And you say they are having a conversation… ?" the captain asked delicately, his usual primness audibly fragile.

"Allegedly. Eli will tell me more once she turns back."

The captain nodded. "Ah."

Out of the corner of his eye, Tam could see the strain between the man's eyebrows.

"Dad?" Luca peered up at his father.

"Mm-hm?"

"Can we go play now?"

"Nope. Now that Eli's awake, it's time we get you both caught up on your studies."

"Aw!" Luca whined.

Even Penelope's nose bunched up in dislike at the idea.

"After lunch we can play a game together. Sound good?"

Luca's eyes sparkled. "What game?"

"I'll tell you later. I know you're stalling. Go head down into Eli's and my cabin, and I'll meet you there soon."

Letting out laments, the children gradually dragged their feet over to the stairs, leaving Tam to stare after them with a tired smile.

"They'll appreciate it when they're older," the captain said, his voice full of fondness.

As Tam turned to ask the captain if he had any children of his own, he noticed Kraken slapping Kasha's face again. This time, he did so over and over while his mother flapped her wings and kept trying to grasp Kraken's fur as though to pry him away from Kasha.

"Apologies, I'll be back in a moment."

Tam darted down the stairs, stalked over to his father's familiar, waved off his mother, who was still beating her wings, and snatched up Kraken by the scruff.

"Slap Kasha again and I will chuck you overboard," Tam informed the fluffy cat sternly. "I don't know what this is about, but I've never seen you in such a bad mood in your whole—"

Kraken slapped Tam across the face, silencing him.

Tam gaped at the cat. "That felt oddly nice. But I feel the insult that was behind it."

Kraken tried to slap him again until Tam changed his grip on the scruff then held Kraken out over the ship's railing.

The fluffy familiar went perfectly still.

"I know you're going to take a dump in my bed or shoes for this," Tam guessed, "and I accept that. But you do not slap Eli—even in her Kasha form—again. Unless she asks you to. Because again… that was strangely pleasant."

Kraken's eyes slid sideways. The familiar was unable to move, but Tam caught the brief huff of acceptance, so he set the cat back down on deck. Kraken fluttered his tail upward and sauntered off, giving a spectacular view of his haunches.

"Is the discussion over? Kasha, you haven't eaten yet." Tam raised a stern eyebrow in her direction.

A great whoosh of hot breath came out of Tam's familiar, as though she were as irked by him as the children had been. With a shudder, Eli shifted back into her human form. She remained kneeling on the deck, her eyes lost in thought.

Meanwhile Annika scurried off after Kraken.

"Everything alright?" Tam asked, his brows lowering in worry.

Giving her head a shake, Eli rose to her feet. "Yes, everything is fine. And I don't need you nagging me to eat."

"Oh, so you aren't hungry? I shouldn't have told the cook to prepare you a plate with some tea?"

Eli scowled at him, evidently unable to disagree. He grinned back at her.

She had no less than three cowlicks in her hair, and she looked adorable.

Which was why Tam decided to spare her nerves a little and instead of teasing her further said, "Come on. The kids are already waiting for us in our cabin, ready to start studying again." He swung around, hands in his pockets as he headed toward the stairs.

He was only a little surprised when Eli's arm slipped around his and her head gently rested on his shoulder.

"Thank you," she mumbled.

Tam chuckled. "Not sure why you're thanking me exactly, but you're welcome."

"You'd tell me if something was wrong, right?" she asked suddenly, tilting her face up to him.

Tam balked. Maybe it had just been too long since he'd been able to relax in any capacity, but he was finding his assistant's loveliness distracting. "I'm sure I will eventually."

Her sweet expression dropped, and Tam was forced to laugh as she resumed her more typical grumpy countenance.

She continued to pester him as they went belowdecks, and while Tam had a hunch about why she was suddenly asking him questions, he decided he would delay bringing forward his concerns about taking the devil's fate for the time being. He wanted to put off any dark thoughts of the future... if only for a little while.

CHAPTER 5

AN AIR OF ALARM

Inspecting her nails, Kat marveled at how adept the maids at the Zinferan palace were at removing every speck of dirt from under the whites. They were even filed into a lovely shape.

Kat had never been all that fussy about nails. She knew her mother on occasion would pay extra attention, and her father was highly regimented in ensuring his remained cut practically to the quick to ensure the food he handled would be unspoiled. Nails just hadn't seemed relevant to Kat aside from keeping them short enough to not bother her when she wielded a sword.

But now she had to admit, it really *was* quite elegant looking.

Someone cleared their throat, drawing Kat's golden gaze upward.

A long table of Zinferan officials and nobility stared at her where she sat farther down their ranks. From the head of the table, the emperor practically glowered at her.

"Well? We wait, Queen Katarina," the emperor rumbled.

"And I think," she answered bluntly, dropping her hand to her lap.

The mood descended even further into unease. Were it not for the summer heat, some of the attendees might have shivered.

The emperor looked down his nose. "We are all aware you went against my orders and aided Princess Elisara in leaving Zinfera."

Kat raised an unbothered eyebrow at the ruler. "You went against *my* orders that my brother and his wife should return home."

The two officials nearest Kat leaned away from her, as though they worried that the emperor might throw something in her direction and wanted to avoid the possibility of getting in the way.

"You harmed my soldiers."

"They were holding my brother and his family prisoner," Kat returned shortly. "And they were also the ones who held *me* hostage, if you recall."

The emperor pressed a hand on the table in front of him, the gold designs and threads of his fine cream coat catching the light. "You are in my empire, Queen Katarina—"

"If I'm not welcome, I can return home and you can deal with your coven and the dragon by yourself, then." Kat rose to her feet, her hand resting on the hilt of her sword.

The guards at the doors stiffened.

She didn't bat an eye. She could see the fear in their faces.

A few nights ago, she had effortlessly slain a number of men without sustaining so much as a scratch. Two guards weren't going to slow her down much, if worse came to worst.

"You impeded matters pertaining to the royal family." The emperor's voice filled the room, giving no indication of the several months of coma he had experienced.

"I believe Elisara already addressed the fact that she has not been a member of the imperial family here for over a decade, as it was your own concubine who sold her. Which means she has been relieved of any and all responsibility to this empire for many, *many* years. And with her marriage to my brother, she is now firmly tied to Daxaria and is my sister-in-law," Kat volleyed, her own volume spiking in response.

The emperor's eyes glittered with displeasure.

She met it unflinchingly. "The world does not bend on the whims of a man. Even if that man is an emperor. My family has offered aid and saved Your

Excellency, and we are being repaid with a tantrum. Get over yourself. Your kingdom has fallen into chaotic disrepair."

The emperor's cheeks flushed, and the air filled with ire that seeped from every official present.

Kat swept her gaze over all of them, leveling the attendees of the meeting with her golden eyes that she ensured glowed with magic. "Piss me off and I will leave. I've no interest in helping people who are too busy whining about power to save their own citizens."

The emperor opened his mouth and Kat growled, her grip on her sword tightening as her aura flared, silencing him.

"I suggest you all sort yourselves out. If you want to declare war with Daxaria, you are welcome to give it a try. Though I will also remind you that your army is in disarray all over the bloody empire, and your ships are few and far between what with the kraken and the pirate problem that you also have." Kat moved toward the doors. She could feel Jiho Ryu's eyes boring into her, but she didn't spare him a glance. "I'm going to go for a walk. If you manage to pull your heads out of your arses long enough to actually realize you have bigger fish to fry, feel free to send a messenger to summon me and we can all stop wasting time."

"Katarina Reyes," the emperor rasped, his palpable outrage making Kat turn with a snarl waiting. "Your brother came onto Zinfera's shores without proper notice. Don't think I'm not aware that he came to spy on my empire."

"That isn't the case at all." Kat's voice was low, her conviction unwavering. "We sent my brother as one would send a friend to check on a partner. We had heard of your people's suffering. Of a dragon. Your Excellency had been asleep for months. We would not be your allies if we allowed your empire to fall under these threats."

The sharpness of the murderous sentiment in the room dulled ever so slightly. It seemed the emperor was mollified by the reference to the long-standing partnership between the kingdoms and by Kat's continued use of the emperor's formal title.

"The ones you should be challenging and questioning are the men still seated at this table, Your Excellency. *They* were supposed to be the ones you could trust to keep your great land prosperous. Not only did they fail, but they went the opposite fucking direction and attacked your people because of their own greed."

The ferocious emotions among the Zinferans returned swiftly.

Kat lifted her chin, unapologetically. "So again. Stop being a giant arsehat to the Daxarians that actually saved you, and start dealing with the people who created this Godsdamn mess in the first place."

Stalking forward, Kat reached the doors, where the two guards jolted. "Move."

The two men should have looked to their emperor for permission, but both were trembling violently, and their knees had buckled. Rather than move out of the way, they tilted. It was enough space for the Daxarian queen to shove the doors open and take her leave.

Shutting the doors once more behind herself, Kat let out a long breath.

She cracked her neck.

It hadn't been the worst council meeting she'd ever been a part of—not by a long shot. She got to swear at people and leave early. If it weren't for the fact she couldn't go eat a whole pie and spend time with her children and husband now, it would've been a good day.

Sighing, Kat turned her sights down the long walkway that was open on the right to a palace courtyard. She felt listless. At least with her mother around she'd had a bit of fun and someone to talk to.

"KAAAAT! You're out early!"

A loud, slurred voice hollered behind Kat, making her turn round to find Duke Oscar Harris stumbling toward her with a bottle of moonshine clasped in his hand.

"Hey, Harris. I see you're enjoying a bit of a break."

The Daxarian duke snapped and pointed his finger at her. "You bet your bottom I am! I spent weeks starving in the woods with your brother and Elisara. I'd say I've earned the right to some debauchery."

Kat scoffed knowingly. "You're missing Mackenzie and your boys a lot, aren't you?"

Harris's goofy grin faded. His shoulder sagged against the wooden panel beside him and he let his head thump against the wall.

"Yeah… Yeah, I really do. It helped being around your wonderful nephew and soon-to-be-niece Penelope, but now that all the fun little people are gone, it hits much harder. I don't like not knowing when I can go home."

Kat gave a grim half smile of sympathy before reaching for the bottle in the duke's hand, uncorking it, and taking a prolonged drink from it herself.

When she'd finished, she smacked her lips and proceeded to start walking in the direction the duke had originated from. "Come on. I might as well join you. I'm missing my own boys."

The duke belched, then moved unsteadily to join the Daxarian queen. "How did the meeting go?"

Kat allowed a rueful smile to rise before she took another gulp of moonshine. "I was in an unsupervised council meeting with a bunch of officials who tried to complain about me. I'll let you imagine how it went."

Harris burst out laughing. "Aah, Your Majesty. I've always felt like we were kindred spirits."

"Well it *was* you I modeled my political approach after."

"And you will take that fact to your grave, or your mother will use a soup spoon to gouge my brain out through my eye sockets."

Kat slid an amused look at the duke. "Colorful."

Harris shuddered. "Your mother has threatened me with those words verbatim before."

Caught between surprise and amusement, Kat was forced to ask, "What were you doing that warranted such a threat? You've already been responsible for destroying parts of our keep and traumatizing farm animals, and she barely batted an eye."

"I may… or may not… have at one point tried to give you coffee when you were a toddler."

Kat sprayed out the mouthful of moonshine she had just taken and stared at the duke in awe. *"Why in the world would you have tried to do that?"*

"You had been sick! And your parents were all worried because you were being sluggish," Harris replied heartfully.

"I was still the fastest toddler in the entire kingdom in a weakened state!"

"Yes! I know! Your mother brought that to my attention!"

Kat burst out laughing as the two fell into familiar stories of their loved ones and kingdom. It helped to be reminded that she was not entirely alone in an empire of strangers, and at the very least, they did both share the same troublesome sense of humor.

The fourth day of their journey from Zinfera, Eli woke before Tam.

He had been acting more or less like himself, if perhaps a little distracted.

Eli had done her best to prompt him to share whatever was on his mind, but every time he'd managed to deflect her efforts by catering to some need or perceived desire of hers instead. If it hadn't been such an apparent ruse to avoid bringing up whatever was troubling him, Eli would've been more annoyed.

She still wasn't certain if she was expecting or not, and if Tam had started doting on her because of that, she would've most likely lost her temper with him already.

It was easier for Eli to accept that there was something else bothering Tam, as it also helped her avoid her own anxiety about the possibility that she was pregnant. Though she did wonder what Tam had said to Kraken that had gotten the familiar's fluff scruffed.

Rising from the bed they shared, Eli stretched and yawned.

Luca had stopped sleeping with them once Penelope started teasing him about it.

While Eli knew that it was most likely for the better that he was starting to find his independence, she had to admit she missed the family nap times.

Looking out through the bank of windows, Eli was mildly surprised to find that it was not magnificently sunny like all the other days since they'd been aboard the ship. Rather, the sky was overcast, with a strip of bruising dark clouds on the horizon that hinted at a storm.

Taking a moment to briefly grip the bedpost and tap her finger, Eli cast her mind about for ideas on how to distract the children from getting too frightened should a storm hit.

Wandering over to the chest that was filled with clothes for her—a thoughtful bit of cargo provided by Jiho Ryu—Eli tugged off the sleep tunic she'd been wearing. Technically it belonged to Tam. She hadn't gotten used to sleeping in anything other than men's clothes yet.

As soon as the garment hit the ground, awareness prickled at the back of Eli's neck, making her glance over her shoulder.

Just as she suspected, Tam had woken from a dead sleep.

He grinned at her exposed torso, his eyes only half open.

She lifted a wry eyebrow at him. "I swear you are getting far too good at sensing when I'm taking my clothes off."

Slowly propping himself up on his elbow, Tam responded with, "I'd like to think of it as being attentive and loving to my *wife*."

Eli grimaced and stuck her tongue out in disgust over the sickly-sweet voice he'd used. "Stop that. Or I will take great efforts to never take my clothes off in front of you again."

Tam's mischievous expression sobered instantly. "Yes, ma'am."

With a huff, Eli returned her attention to the task of getting dressed for the day. Still, she was unable to resist a smile.

Once she was ready, Tam held out a hand.

She gradually made her way back to the bedside. Tam grasped her hand, then kissed her palm.

The move made two things happen.

First, a rush of tingling started in Eli's belly. Second, her own gaze slipped over Tam's bare, muscled torso.

"You know you don't have to rush off just yet…" Tam pointed out suggestively.

Eli grumbled. "We're in the middle of a pregnancy scare and you still want to be intimate?"

Tam shrugged ambiguously, then grinned in a way he *had* to know made Eli a little too susceptible to his whims.

Leaning over, Eli brushed a chaste kiss over his lips. The warm musk that hung around Tam was starting to draw her in when shouts from above deck rang out.

Looking at the ceiling, Eli listened. Several thumps followed the voices, and she turned to the door.

"Never a moment of peace—even in the middle of the sea," Tam lamented as he rose behind Eli and hastily pulled on his pants from the previous day.

Eli had already reached the door. "I'll go see what's going on. They might just be preparing for the coming storm."

Tam sighed. "I never wanted to live a life when I actually prayed for the mild danger of getting caught in a storm on a boat, but here we are."

Giving a chortle of agreement, Eli slipped out of their cabin and set off toward the stairs.

Hopefully it really was just the threat of bad weather. It would be a nice break to have something so mundane be all that troubled them.

Alas…

She quickly learned that was not what the fates had prepared.

CHAPTER 6

DANCING WITH DANGER

Tam joined the line of sailors that had gathered at the starboard side of the ship as Captain Sun and his first mate shouted orders.

Not wanting to disturb the men as they navigated whatever trouble was afoot, Tam squinted at the boat that seemed to be causing a commotion.

Was it the Zinferan emperor?

Had he sent a ship to catch them?

But the longer Tam stared at the boat, the more he realized that it didn't look like a Zinferan or a Daxarian boat at all.

It had a long bow that curved upward, even more so than Troivackian boats. It was also long and narrow, with only two large white sails.

Tam tilted his head, puzzled, until he noticed another boat on the other side of the strange one. It was Zinferan, and the flag told him that it happened to be a pirate ship.

"I really should never get on another boat. It's a safety risk for everyone at this point with my luck…" he muttered while turning to find the captain.

Captain Sun got to him first. "Lord Tamlin, I'm afraid we have come across a Lobahlan ship in distress."

"Lobahlan!" Tam looked back over his shoulder in surprise at the vessel.

No wonder he'd never seen the design before!

"Yes. They are being assaulted by pirates. This might be a good time to show you the weapons Lord Jiho Ryu has funded and helped design. The only issue is that we will need to get closer to the pirate ship and come up and around them. So we will most likely lose half a day of travel."

Tam's interested expression hardened. "Is there a more expedient way of helping the Lobahlans? It really is important that we get back to Daxaria as quickly as possible."

Captain Sun paused. "This is the safest means of intervention. Otherwise, we could leave them to fend for themselves."

Tam's lips pressed together. As much as the delay would cost, he couldn't just turn away from an entire vessel of people.

"Alright. Where is Eli?"

Captain Sun gestured with his chin toward the ratlines. "Lady Elisara insisted on climbing upward. She said if she can transform and take to the air, she can get a better idea of what is happening from above."

Tam nodded. He moved to cross the deck and climb up after her, but he was too late.

He watched, his heart stopping for an instant, as Eli took a flying leap off the crow's nest toward the water.

She transformed midair, flapped her wings once, and continued to plummet toward the water. Tam flushed with numbing panic. At the last moment, Kasha held her wings out and caught an air current that helped her glide right over the surface of the Alcide Sea, her front paw scraping over the waves.

She's trying to kill me, Tam sputtered in his mind as he watched Kasha rise into the air overhead.

He stood with his hand on the ratline and waited. Kasha circled the two ships overhead, then dared to drop a little lower.

Tam's grip on the rope tightened. "Not so close," he whispered.

Sure enough, his heart seized as he saw an arrow streak into the sky.

His hands flying through his hair, Tam turned away momentarily, struggling to watch Kasha flirt with death.

Gods… And she might be pregnant. Holy hell…

Luckily, Kasha only made two more swoops before rounding back toward their own ship—though Tam had been a moment away from disappearing into the void and attempting to reappear on one of the ships and take care of the archers. He had never traveled that far to somewhere he hadn't seen before, but right then he didn't give a damn.

By the time Kasha's wings flared out, pulling her to a stop over the ship's deck, Tam was almost ready to lock her in a cabin for the rest of the trip.

Then she crouched and shifted back into her human form, prompting her to drop down on a hand and knee to catch herself on the deck.

Two sailors moved forward as though to assist her, but Tam beat them to it, offering a hand and helping her stand. He was about to share the wide array of anxiety-induced speculations he'd just endured when Captain Sun approached.

"Lady Elisara, what is the situation?"

"It doesn't look as though the Lobahlans are sailing with a full crew for the size of the ship they're on, so they are at a severe disadvantage. The pirates haven't boarded yet, but they will soon unless they decide to wait and see what we do."

"A large flying cat would make a lot of people change plans," Tam pointed out drily.

Eli shot him a quick frown before turning back to the captain.

Captain Sun nodded. "They most likely will prepare for a fight. Hopefully this provides the Lobahlans some time to escape."

Tam moved his hands to his pockets as he fought against the blind panic he was still wading out of. "Were you able to see how many pirates were on deck?"

Eli raised an eyebrow and considered the question. "At least fifteen."

"A smaller boat, then." Captain Sun's shoulders relaxed fractionally at this discovery.

"Do you think I could dispose of them myself?" Tam asked, his tone light.

Both the captain and Eli stared at him dumbfounded for a moment.

"Tam, just because there were fifteen on deck doesn't mean there aren't more belowdecks."

"It'd put a dent in their plans, and they may retreat," he argued.

"That's dangerous," Eli countered evenly.

"Oh, and I suppose what you just did was simply a fun stretch of the wings?" Tam stared at Eli, who crossed her arms.

Evidently sensing the tension between the couple, Captain Sun hesitated before continuing. "Lord Tamlin, it is not necessary to risk yourself. The weapons that Lord Jiho Ryu has armed us with really will not leave the pirates much choice but to flee."

"If you are talking about the weapon called the cannon, I reviewed its design in my cabin." Tam's attention swung back to the Zinferan. "From what I was reading, it is entirely possible that the Lobahlan ship could receive damage from a missed shot."

The captain gave a slight grimace. "I'm hoping the Lobahlan ship will have been able to pull far enough away by that time."

"Then why bother attacking?" Tam persisted.

He was beginning to get the impression that the Zinferan captain was maybe just a little too excited to showcase this new cannon invention.

As they'd been talking, however, their ship had been making its way closer to the pirate and Lobahlans. When Tam eventually realized this, he fixed the captain with a flat look, then made his way back to the railing to see if the pirates had started boarding the Lobahlan ship. As he squinted, the captain appeared at his side and handed him a spyglass. Taking the brass instrument without a word, Tam lifted it to his eye.

"They're launching flaming arrows at the Lobahlan vessel. It doesn't look like they've boarded, and... They are already starting to pull away... Oh."

"What?" Eli asked from his other side.

Tam lowered the spyglass. "I think what is happening... is the pirates saw you, and decided that to avoid getting eaten, they'd cripple the other boat."

Tam cast a sidelong glance at Eli and watched her cheeks pinken.

"They do seem to be pulling farther starboard to loop around and escape," the captain agreed, sounding a little too glum as he took his turn peering through the spyglass.

A particularly large flare of flames drew everyone's attention. The Lobahlan sails were swiftly swallowed in a cloud of smoke.

Sighing, but also feeling relieved that they would not be entering into combat, Tam turned his back on the Lobahlan ship and rested against the railing. They would soon be able to rescue the Lobahlans, who were already boarding their lifeboats—of which they had many in excess due to their smaller crew size.

Eli, still facing the blazing vessel, eventually noticed that he was watching her. "What?"

Tam tilted his head. "Why didn't you talk to me before you ran off to check over there?"

"Why would I need to? They needed help, we needed more information."

"Because it was dangerous?"

"We're always in danger." Eli pushed away from the railing, her right hand still resting on the wood. The way she stared back up at Tam told him that she was damn well ready to fight him on this.

"You could've been shot." Tam lowered his voice as more members of the crew passed by them and Captain Sun left—most likely to talk to the purser about room and provisions for the Lobahlan survivors.

"I was high enough in the air that they would've missed."

"You dipped closer, though—and for all you know, one of them could have been a witch."

"Tam?"

"What?"

"You're smothering me."

Straightening, Tam gazed down at Eli as she moved her hands to her hips. "And what if I'd just vanished on over there? What if I appeared on the pirate ship and said, *Oh hello, don't mind me, just taking a head count?*"

"Again, I was higher up in the air! There was a lot less risk. I could see what they were doing—why are you not trusting my judgment?"

Tam made an aggravated noise and turned away. He took a beat to calm himself.

When he looked back at Eli, she was quite obviously gnawing on her tongue as she practically steamed with anger.

Letting out a long breath, Tam then said, "I trust your judgment, but sometimes a heads-up would be nice."

"Oh, like you gave me a heads-up when you went to break into a nobleman's house?" Eli shot back. She was referencing a time months ago when Tam needed to search for evidence at Lord Guk's residence as he was hosting Lord Yangban—the concubine Soo Hebin's cousin and one of her most influential allies. They'd been gathering information on the corruption in Zinfera, which Tam had been tasked with doing before leaving Daxaria.

Tam blinked in surprise but collected himself again quickly. "We weren't a couple then."

This managed to make Eli even more incensed. "So you've never valued my opinion and judgment. Perfect. It isn't just because I'm sleeping with you."

Tam felt a ball of prickly anger churn in his own chest. "Your opinion always has mattered to me. But back then when I was only your *employer*, it was well within my rights to be making decisions for everyone."

"Like *that* never had bad repercussions for others! It's not like you'd *disappear for days* or anything!"

"I came back and saw everything through! Eli, just what the… Do you really not think that before you went charging off toward a pirate ship, you maybe should've checked in with me?"

"If someone had been in a life-or-death situation, I could have saved them! Time was important, and I didn't want to waste any!"

Tam fell silent for a moment. "You don't see a life-or-death situation as dangerous to *you*? And—I'll ask this again to be sure I'm clear—that I shouldn't be told about it at all?"

It was Eli's turn to go quiet. "We're going to argue in circles."

Just as Tam was opening his mouth to make another scathing remark, Luca and Penelope bolted up to them.

"Dad, are we fighting more pirates?" Luca asked excitedly.

After giving a final, lingering stare at Eli, Tam slowly lowered his attention to his son. "No, they are already leaving."

"Aw!" Luca's shoulders slouched dramatically.

Tam looked at the sky. He needed to teach Luca that violence and conflict were wrong. His plans on how to make that happen, however, were interrupted when Penelope chimed in to address Luca.

"That would have been a *bad* thing, dummy." She gave a very grown-up sigh, folded her arms, and stared up at Tam. "So what's happening now?"

Unable to help himself, Tam glanced back at Eli, then back down at the little girl watching him impatiently. "I'm starting to have a vague inkling of what my future home life might be like, and I'm not sure I'm okay with it."

Ignoring Tam's comment, Eli answered Penelope. "The pirates set fire to a ship belonging to some Lobahlans, so we are going to see about helping them."

"Oh! I've never met any Lobahlans!" Penelope perked up.

"I've met one or two. They're nice. They don't like talking about Lobahl much. But Dad's met and talked a lot with one! Remember? He talked about Mr. Kasim Jelani!" Luca burst out eagerly.

Unable to remain unaffected by the children's exuberant reactions, Tam smiled. "Well, we're going to talk to a few of them today. But they're probably a little stressed after the pirates set fire to their boat, so I think the adults will meet them first and introduce you kids later, to be safe."

"Aw!" This time the lament was made in unison by both children.

Reaching up to rub the back of his neck with a long sigh, Tam couldn't help but think, *I can't seem to say the right thing at all today.*

CHAPTER 7

COLLECTING CHAOS

Tam and Eli stood at the front of the crew facing the group of Lobahlans that had boarded their ship.

In total there were thirty of them, including the two wealthy-looking charges. It was not nearly enough to properly crew or defend the size of ship they had been on. The emptied vessel continued to crackle behind the Lobahlans as the Zinferan ship pulled away. Only a few belongings and supplies belonging to the passengers and crew had managed to make it over. At present, they were leaning against the railing of Tam and Eli's ship while introductions were made.

A young man and woman, former passengers of the burning Lobahlan vessel, stood in front of their own sailors dressed in clothes the likes of which Tam had never seen before.

The man, with his dark skin, eyes, and short black curly hair, wore a long, robe-like coat with billowing sleeves that ended at the elbows. The garment was the most brilliant deep azure blue Tam had ever seen. Finely embroidered gold ribbons lined his coat, cuffed pants, and flat hat. A deep-purple silk shirt and black shoes, worn without stockings or socks, were the only breaks in the astounding blue and gold.

The woman's clothes were no less beautiful. Delicate threads of gold shot through her olive-green dress, matching the necklace and earrings that caught the afternoon sun. The garment's wide sleeves hid her hands, which she clasped in front of herself. Her thick, straight black hair draped over her shoulder in a heavy braid, and she kept her heart-shaped face downturned.

The young man swept into a deep bow, his right arm extended dramatically. "Kind seafarers, you have our heartfelt thanks for your timely rescue." He rose with a gleaming white smile.

The young woman at his side kept her expression schooled as she also inclined herself during her companion's greeting.

The young man continued. "My name is Hamil of Judge Mago the Third, and this is my friend, Bes. Daughter of Tyre, Counselor for the People."

Tam took in the introduction, his mind already whirring with interest.

Even though Kasim Jelani and his sister Adamma had been more forthcoming than most Lobahlans ever were, they were still incredibly tight-lipped about the details of their land.

"I am Lord Tamlin Ashowan, this is Lady Elisara and Captain Sun," Tam introduced while lowering his chin as etiquette dictated. "We are happy to offer assistance, though we are in a hurry to return to Daxaria. To ensure we have enough supplies for yourselves and crew, we will be landing in Rollom."

"Thank you. We offer our apologies for the inconvenience," the woman, Bes, said serenely.

Captain Sun stepped forward, laid a hand over his heart, and bowed as he spoke. "It isn't your fault that the pirates found you. They've been a problem in Zinfera for some time now. Even though we are more than a day's sail away from my kingdom's shores, they have been venturing farther and farther out in the Alcide Sea to find helpless merchants to prey upon."

"Pirates taking over Zinfera? How interesting!" Hamil replied breathily, his eyes glittering with excitement as though he hadn't nearly been murdered by an entire ship of said criminals.

Tam raised an eyebrow at Hamil. He would have guessed his age to be around twenty-two… likewise with Bes. But he seemed more immature.

Tam moved his hands to his pockets and did his best to don a polite smile. He was a little tense about having strangers staying with them for the rest of the voyage, and anxious that saving them had eaten up nearly an entire day of travel. "It is rare for a Lobahlan ship to be seen far from its own shores. What brings you out west?"

Hamil swung around to stare at Bes. He squinted, openmouthed, in a comical display of a youth caught doing something he shouldn't.

Bes's eyes rolled toward the sky when he did this, but she reclaimed her former smile quickly with a very deep inhale—though she looked a more stressed than she had before.

"We—Hamil and I—decided to see some of the other lands we have only heard rumors and stories about."

Hamil clamped his mouth shut, grasped his hands behind his back, and nodded sunnily in agreement.

It wasn't hard to guess that these two had left against someone's wishes. Most likely both sets of parents. While not much was known about the government or monarchy of Lobahl, Tam could also guess that given the introduction they'd given, they came from prominent families.

Well. At least neither of them is in need of adoption, Tam thought dully.

Tam shared a quick glance with Eli before addressing the newcomers. Her pursed lips told him she had come to the very same conclusion he had about the nature of their trip. "I'm afraid we don't have any hawks to help you send a missive to your families, but once we arrive in Daxaria, the harbormaster will be able to point you in the right direction for registration and accommodations."

"Registration?" Hamil's face was once again rife with intrigue.

Tam paused. "Yes. All foreign visitors must register their stay with a magistrate assigned to the port."

"Oh! That makes sense. In Lobahl that process is handled by a division called jamar. The jamar see to—" Hamil's words were cut off by the sharp elbow Bes drove into his ribs.

Bes kept her eyes lowered despite the violence of her move. "Thank you for your guidance."

Tam started to form the vague worry that these two young people would cause him even more problems than he already had. However, there was nothing he could do at present, so he gestured toward the stairs belowdecks. "We have managed to secure separate rooms for you, Hamil, and you, Bes, as you requested. Your men, on the other hand, I'm afraid, will be rather cramped with our crew for the next week and a half of our journey."

The first mate of Tam's ship stepped forward and proceeded to guide their new passengers down to show them around, leaving Tam and Eli above deck to stare after them.

Once the last of the Lobahlan crew had disappeared from sight, Eli turned to Tam and folded her arms.

"Runaways?" she speculated aloud.

"Most likely. They probably left wanting adventure. I imagine it is rather difficult to leave Lobahl, given how few people do," Tam said. He turned toward the rail and sidled over.

Eli followed.

"They aren't siblings, and they aren't married," Tam continued.

"They act like siblings. So I doubt they are running off to elope," Eli added.

"Mm-hm. My concern is whether or not they stole that boat, and whether or not misunderstandings will take place when they try to get in touch with their families. If we don't handle the situation carefully, we could be named as accessories to their antics if they did anything outrageously illegal."

Eli cringed.

Tam said nothing else as he allowed his attention to wander to the pale-blue sky. The temperature was already cooling considerably, and he wondered if Eli was warm enough.

"I'll talk to the physician in the morning."

Eli's sudden announcement made Tam's neck snap round to stare at her. Her face was perfectly still.

So, keeping his tone as neutral as possible, he said, "Alright."

She peered down at the water, her long fingers fluttering against the railing. "I feel fine. But not knowing is making me look for symptoms and overthink. It's annoying."

Tam leaned his forearms on the railing and nodded silently.

"Are you ready for the news?" Eli ventured on, resignation thick in her voice.

Tam raised his eyebrows at her with a closed-mouth smile. "Who is ever ready to be a parent?"

"Apparently you. All the time. Anytime. Especially on a boat," Eli reminded him glibly.

Tam laughed while turning back to look out over the water. "You know better than anyone I've been fumbling my way through with a lot of help from everyone around me. Yourself included."

Eli gave a half shrug of concession to his point. "Are you going to be unbearably protective if we know that I am?"

"That depends on what you think is unbearably protective. Though if you're trying to resume our fight from earlier, I'd keep it timed out. You know we need energy to deal with the kids when we go belowdecks. They'll be pinging off the walls wanting to hear about the Lobahlans."

"Mm," Eli conceded, nodding.

"What pregnancy symptoms do you think you've been experiencing?"

Eli shot him a wry look. "I keep getting angry and wanting to fight with you, for one."

Tam *could've* chosen his next words carefully, but he didn't. "I certainly would *like* to think that isn't how you normally are."

He could feel Eli's eyes bore into the side of his face.

He glanced back at her innocently. "Any other symptoms?"

It took a few tense moments, but Tam could see Eli opt to let him off the hook for the previous comment. "I'm craving milk in my tea and jam on toast."

"It could be that just because you're heading back to Daxaria, you're thinking about that more. Jam and toast weren't common as breakfast food in Zinfera—"

"I know," Eli snapped.

Tam blinked and watched as she pinched the bridge of her nose. He gingerly rested a hand on her back.

She let out an aggravated huff that made him remove it.

"When I'm Kasha, your mother keeps asking me whether or not I'm pregnant."

Tam recoiled. "Oh. I'm… I am *very* sorry about that."

Eli grunted. "She also repeated your family history of virility."

"Aah!" Tam backed away, his hands coming up as though to cover his ears, his expression horrified.

"*How do you think I felt about it?*" she asked, her eyes rounding.

Shuddering, Tam resumed his position beside her. "Maybe don't change into Kasha anytime soon. Unless it's an emergency."

"I'm fine with that," Eli agreed grimly.

Tam suddenly frowned. "Come to think of it, I haven't seen my mother or Kraken in a while…"

Tam and Eli looked at each other.

"Do you want to pretend that we didn't notice?"

"I'd like that," Eli confirmed while they moved away from the railing toward the stairs.

As they walked, Tam allowed his mind to drift toward the next morning. Were they going to be parents to an infant in the near future?

Before, he had been nervous because he'd been worried about Eli's reaction to the news of expecting a child of her own flesh and blood. Now memories of when his sister had been pregnant with the Daxarian princes resurfaced. Tam started feeling a little afraid for himself in the coming months, should the physician confirm what he was already suspecting…

He decided that, come the next morning, ensuring Eli got to enjoy her tea with milk and toast with jam had just become his utmost priority.

Deep in the hull of the ship, Henrietta stared through the bars, her eyes wide.

The chicken duchess clucked ominously.

Kraken, the infamous familiar, sat beside the duchess and stared straight through Henrietta's soul.

"I-I'm not turning her back! It's—It's for the greater good! Daxaria needs to… The king needs to agree to annex the coven to rule on its own! Witches aren't like humans! We should be more in tune with the Gods and should have our elders leading a temple for all our kind! It would be better for Daxaria, too, if—"

"Bok bok, bok bok bok bok bok. Bok bok bok, bok." The chicken duchess tilted her head and blinked once. Her beady eyes glinted in the dim lanternlight.

"So?" Henrietta whimpered softly.

"Bok bok bok bok. Bok bok bok bok. Bok. Bok. Bok."

Tears pooled in her eyes. "What will you do to them?"

The chicken duchess poked her head through the bars, leaning closer to Henrietta's manacled feet.

"Bok bok bok bok, bok bok bok. Bok bok bok bok bok bok."

Kraken emitted a short low growl, making Henrietta's eyes snap over to the emperor.

"Y-you wouldn't! You're Duchess Ashowan! Finlay Ashowan is a good man, and a witch who—"

"BKAAAAAW! BKAW! BKAW! BKAAAAW!"

Henrietta was reduced to sobs.

The chicken duchess withdrew her head from the bars. "Bok bok, bok bok bok bok bok bok bok bok bok."

Shivering in her cell, Henrietta dropped her head to her knees. Out of the corner of her eye, she vaguely saw the animals' shadows stretching larger and larger as they strode away from her cell.

While Henrietta couldn't hear them climb the stairs, she could sense that she was once again alone in the rocking, damp bottom of the ship. In her renewed solitude, she was forced to question just how long she could keep refusing the utterly terrifying duchess… and she didn't think the answer would bode well for the coven.

CHAPTER 8

CONVERSING OVER COFFEE

Tam sat on the deck of the ship in the cool morning air. He was enjoying a rare moment of peace alone. Eli still slept, and the children had gone to request some breakfast from the ship's cook so that they could eat on deck with him.

The sun had barely finished cresting the horizon, revealing that it was going to be a stunning day. The wind was brisk, and so Tam had donned a thick, Daxarian-style navy-blue wool sweater.

He hadn't often worn such a garment—it was a style that usually graced the wardrobes of the lower-ranked sailors—but Tam rather enjoyed its practicality. He wondered idly why Jiho had thought to pack it for him, but he wasn't one to complain.

Wrapping his hand around the warm, white porcelain cup of coffee on the small round table, Tam felt the warmth chase the chill of the sea air from his fingertips, bringing a flush of goose bumps to his arms. A particularly strong gust of wind tousled his hair, casting a spray of strands into Tam's eyes. As he sipped his coffee, he tried to rake a hand through it and pull it back.

I might have to look into tying back some of this now...

"Good morning, Lord Tamlin!" The jubilant voice almost made Tam flinch.

Turning slowly, Tam watched as Hamil stepped spryly over to him. The young man's hands were clasped behind his back, and he wore a long mint-green coat with loose white pants and a matching shirt.

Bes walked behind him in a far more demure manner. Her brilliant-blue dress was similar in color to what Hamil had been wearing when they'd first met.

"Mind if we join you this fine morning?" Hamil asked brightly.

Tam lowered his head and gestured toward the two seats that had originally been set up for Luca and Penelope.

Hamil proceeded to drop himself into the chair while flaring out his coat dramatically.

Tam raised an eyebrow and stood to offer his hand to Bes so that he could help the young woman sit.

Her eyebrows rose in surprise, but she then smiled at him in appreciation. "Thank you," she said while settling herself down. "It is good to see that it is only Hamil who is without manners in this world."

The young man ignored her jibe as he peered around at the crew members changing shifts.

"Don't you just love the way the cold, fresh wind whisks away that dampness in the morning? Pair that with the salty air and you just get this smell…" Hamil paused to inhale deeply, his eyes closed. "You really can't get it anywhere else than the open sea."

Tam nodded distantly but moved his attention back to Bes. "Do either of you have any family in Daxaria you might be able to stay with while you arrange for another vessel to take you back home?"

Bes's shoulders rounded almost imperceptibly. Tam could see the thread of guilt tugging at her conscience.

"We… We do not. We had been intending to visit the vineyards of Troivack, then circle back around the north and east coast of Lobahl, but a storm blew us off course, and then Hamil… Hamil suggested we sail around the west of Troivack to get back on course, only we weren't as prepared for the extra time it would add to our journey, and—"

"And here we are!" Hamil finished cheerfully.

Tam could feel the disgruntlement simmering off Bes.

Clearing his throat, he indulged in another mouthful of coffee and decided not to probe.

"Is that coffee you're drinking?" Hamil asked interestedly.

Tam hesitated, then confirmed the young man's guess.

"Ah! Splendid! I've often wondered how the beans fare when they have to travel so distantly." Hamil raised a hand. One of the Lobahlan aides bowed to his employer then disappeared belowdecks, presumably to fetch more coffee.

"Is coffee common in Lobahl?" Tam kept his tone mild. The Lobahlans he had met were always skittish about revealing anything about their kingdom.

Hamil snorted, but a sharp look from Bes had the young man pretending to cough instead.

"Yes, we have coffee," Hamil responded while giving a cheeky look to Bes.

Tam's brows lowered. It would seem there was more to that answer than they were going to let on.

Hamil smiled charmingly. "Would you mind telling us about Daxaria, Lord Tamlin? We hear all sorts of interesting tales. Of course, we aren't sure how much is true and how much is made up for the sake of a good story."

Tam set down his cup as a light spray of seawater wafted up and over them. "That's a broad question. Mind narrowing it down?"

Interestingly, it was Bes who shifted forward in her seat, curiosity bright in her eyes. "Is it true that witches used to be hunted there?"

Tam nodded slowly.

"Truly?" Hamil's eyes widened in awe. "How barbaric!"

Tam gave a passive shrug. "Those laws were changed over seventy years ago, so we aren't in danger anymore."

"We... ?" Bes trailed off as she stared quizzically at Tam. "Are you a witch, Lord Tamlin?"

It was Tam's turn to quirk his mouth up in amusement. "Yes. I am."

"Fascinating! In Lobahl, witches are usually in their own sect, so—"

An apparent kick under the table had Hamil clamping his mouth shut as Bes gave a strained smile.

Sensing that the young man was the one who was most likely to blab kingdom secrets, Tam redirected his attention to Hamil with a question he had been needing an answer to for quite some time.

"I'd been planning on trying to speak to your kingdom's coven before I had some complications on my own journey, truth be told," he began while ensuring he maintained a relaxed air.

Regardless of his efforts, Bes shifted back in her seat warily.

Tam pretended not to notice. "My nephews are the princes of Daxaria—"

"Truly?" Hamil interrupted with sparkling eyes. "My word! The sons of the Sun Queen are your nephews?"

Tam balked. "Sun… Queen? Are you referring to Kat—Katarina Reyes?" he corrected himself.

Both Hamil and Bes nodded excitedly.

"Huh…" Tam blinked and cleared his throat. He had never heard of that nickname for his sister. "Well, her eldest son, Prince Antony, is a witch."

"Oh, how exciting! What is his magic?" Hamil leaned his forearms on the table eagerly.

Tam kept his expression smooth as marble. "I'm not at liberty to say. My question," he persisted, the edge in his tone discouraging any more interruptions, "was how Lobahl handled witches who were in line for the throne. The Daxarian coven is of the mind that witches should not be leading humans when they are meant to be a representative of nature."

Despite being the more cautious one, Bes seemed unable to help herself from contributing to the discussion. "It never would become an issue in Lobahl because our 'king' is not exactly a king. He represents a sect of our government. Witches have their own sect with an elected councilor that sits on the ruling panel."

Surprisingly, it was Hamil who shot a nervous look at Bes, but unlike his travel companion, he seemed hesitant to cut her off.

"Wait… Everyone I know is taught that Lobahl a kingdom. Is it not? Is it a country ruled by a democracy?" Tam couldn't stop his eagerness overtaking his tone. It was far too interesting a topic.

Bes nodded. "Yes. The people vote in representatives from each sect, and they run for varying lengths of terms. In the event a witch is born to non-witch parents, however, they can attend school and seek employment in the witch sect of the city, but they can also choose to grow up in their parents' sect. If later they want work that involves using their ability, they have to—"

"Ahem." Hamil raised his eyebrows at his friend.

Bes ducked her head, her embarrassment palpable.

Deciding that the best way to receive advice was to avoid seeming like he was pressuring them for answers, Tam took a slightly different approach when he spoke next.

"The Daxarian queen has already been ejected from the coven. That was the agreement for her to be allowed to rule beside her husband. However, if the next king is a witch, the worry is that resentment will build in the citizens. So whether or not Prince Antony can inherit the throne has now been brought into question. Introducing a vote on the matter would open up a lot of scrutiny for His Highness. That said, I know the Zinferan emperor had no qualms naming a supposed witch as the next heir to the throne. So there is a great divide of opinion."

Surprisingly, after a beat of silence as the pair absorbed Tam's story, Hamil leaned forward to speak. "You are ridiculously honest about the private affairs of your monarchy to a pair of strangers."

Tam stared at the young man flatly, while out of the corner of his eye he noted Bes pressing her lips together and avoiding looking directly at either of them.

With a casual shrug, Tam responded, "You are the runaway children of high-ranking members of government in your land. And at present with the coming wars, one can't be too picky about where sound advice comes from."

"How did you know we were runaways?" Bes squeaked.

Tam sent her an apologetic smile while Hamil shrank back awkwardly. "Lobahlans don't often leave their land, and when they do, it's on a fully crewed ship. I've only met perhaps four or five Lobahlans who were born there in my entire life. Then there was the way you introduced yourselves… I have something of an eye for rebellion thanks to my sister."

While their darker complexion made it difficult to tell, Tam had the keen sense that both Hamil and Bes were blushing.

"Look. This advice I'm asking for is most likely a moot point anyway with the current state of both Zinfera and Daxaria, but I want to do everything I can to help my nephew."

This bit of sentiment seemed to soften Bes and even made Hamil relax a little.

"Well… I don't think Lobahl would be able to offer any sort of helpful advice—though neither Hamil nor I is a witch. It sounds like the entire structures of our governments are too different," Bes explained carefully.

Tam sighed. "Fair enough."

"Now… What was that you said about wars, plural?" Hamil asked, idly scratching his earlobe.

"Ah. The daughter of the Gods, Aradia, has managed to turn both the Coven of Giong and the Coven of Wittica against their crowns. There is a rebellion taking place to instate a temple that would act independently of the kingdoms."

Both Hamil and Bes sat up straighter.

Bes shot a wary look at her friend. "That sounds similar to Lobahl's history, which makes sense. The first witch and her brother, Muta, were the ones that formatted our government before the great battle—"

"SSSH!" Hamil shot a desperate look at Bes, who cringed upon realizing just how much she had just revealed.

"The battle that left most of Lobahl a desert?" Tam guessed, trying to sound easygoing, though the new information about Lobahl had his scholarly mind buzzing with questions.

Hamil and Bes snapped around to stare at him.

It was during the silence that their manservant set down a fresh, glass pot of coffee.

The trio waited until the servant was out of earshot once more.

"How is it you know of the battle?" Bes asked seriously.

Tam shrugged ambiguously. "I'm honestly surprised that neither of you is alarmed to hear about the first witch being alive, not to mention what she is aiming to do."

It would seem the time for letting details slip about their land had finally passed, as neither Lobahlan answered.

Before the discussion could turn uncomfortable, however, the sound of approaching small footsteps drew everyone's attention.

Tam turned to find the expected sight of Penelope and Luca barreling toward him, their gazes homed on the Lobahlans with hungry curiosity.

"Ah…" was all Tam had to say before the children reached them.

"Morning, Dad!" Luca called with a smile.

Penelope stayed quiet as she eyed the Lobahlans intently.

"And who might these fine tuts be?" Hamil wondered with a theatrical wave of his arm.

"This is Luca." Tam rested a hand atop Luca's head briefly before reaching around him and tugging Penelope's sleeve. "And Penelope."

"I didn't know you were traveling with your children! How fun!" Hamil gushed while leaning closer toward the kids, making Penelope casually sidle closer to Luca. "Are you two twins?"

"No, I'm older," Penelope informed Hamil coolly.

"Well, I'm eight now, so not much older!" Luca interjected cheerily.

Tam sat up in alarm. "Luca, we missed your birthday?"

"It's okay, Dad! We were busy and I never usually celebrate my birth—"

"We shall have a party!" Hamil crowed, pointing his finger into the air as though he'd just had the most brilliant of ideas. "Jort! Come! We must plan!"

The manservant from before rushed forward before Tam could get a word in edgewise. His attention was torn between wanting to check in with Luca and telling Hamil to give them some privacy, when Penelope spoke up.

"Oh, I almost forgot... Eli says you can be with her while she talks with the physician. They're in your cabin."

Tam's thoughts sputtered to a stop.

Apparently Eli wasn't going to be wasting any more time.

Taking a steadying breath, Tam clasped Luca's shoulders. "We are absolutely going to celebrate your birthday. Tonight. I'm so sorry I missed it."

"That's okay! You asked me to write it down, but I forgot, and I'm not even completely sure what day it was on anyway."

Tam winced, feeling guilty that he should have missed something so important.

"I'm going to go see Eli, and we're going to talk about how we're going to celebrate, alright?"

Luca beamed and nodded.

"You call your mother by her name?" Bes asked Penelope suddenly.

The child narrowed her eyes in response, and, in true Penelope fashion, answered with an abundance of attitude. "Mind your own business."

Tam dropped his chin at her rudeness. That was another parenting matter he'd have to take care of… but it'd have to wait.

So, muscling up a contrite smile for the Lobahlans, he stood.

"Is everything alright with your wife, Lord Tamlin?" Bes tilted her chin up with an innocent, concerned frown.

Tam moved his hands to his pockets, already turning away from the table while saying, "Probably… I just have to go find out if I'm now three for three."

CHAPTER 9

TOUGHING THINGS OUT
TOGETHER

Sprinkling rosemary into the mortar, Fin plucked up the pestle without needing to even glance its way. Driving it down into the stone bowl, he ground vigorously over and over, until his arm throbbed.

He didn't even notice the pain.

"Fin?"

At last, his attention snapped up to none other than Hannah and Captain Taylor. The pair stood in the doorway to the castle kitchens.

Were it not for the fact that both of their faces had grown lined, and their hair (what remained of it in Captain Taylor's case) streaked with white, the sight of them felt like no time had passed since Fin had first started as the royal cook.

Fin did his best to push a half smile in their direction as they moved into the dimly lit castle kitchen, both eyeing the worktable where a bowl of fermenting yeast already sat waiting to be turned into dough. It was nearing the middle of the night, not a usual time for him to be dallying in the kitchen.

"I heard about Annika," Hannah said softly. She slipped into one of the tall chairs positioned across from where Fin worked.

The captain did the same.

Fin set down the pestle and pressed his palms into the cooking table's worn surface. "Ah."

Hannah's mouth twisted. "I'm sure if she were… If she weren't alive, you would have heard something more."

Fin's mouth lifted grimly. Though he felt his gaze remain gentle, he knew it revealed his weariness. "I know."

"Her Majesty will take good care of her mother," Captain Taylor added confidently.

Tapping a finger on the table, Fin's eyes fell back to the scored work surface. "I know that, too."

The trio fell into silence as Fin then plucked up the mortar and dumped the ground herbs into a bowl already a quarter of the way filled with flour. He whisked that together, poured in the yeast water, and started kneading the mixture into a heavenly smelling dough.

"I haven't felt this powerless in a long time," Fin began. "Both my children and wife are in danger, and I can't go help them. I don't even know where Tam is… And even if he were to feel true fear, I still wouldn't know. When that happens to him, all I see is darkness." Fin's throat tightened painfully. "I'm scared."

The humbling admission resulted in both Hannah and the captain sharing an anguished look.

"He'll be alright. Tam's smart, and Kraken and Pina should be with everyone by now," Hannah reasoned. Her confidence seemed forced.

Fin kept working the dough without responding.

When that task was completed, he rinsed his hands in a basin of water on the table, then transferred the dough to an oiled bowl before covering it with a red-and-white tea towel and setting it beside the fire to rise.

Turning back around, he wiped his hands on his beloved old apron, which had an embroidered broom and pan handle crossing on its corner. Fin leaned his back against the side of the fireplace.

"Sir Andrews is heading to Rollom, and Sir Lewis is nearby in Xava. He's keeping an ear out for new arrivals at the harbor," Captain Taylor informed Fin in another obvious attempt to provide some measure of comfort.

Fin nodded idly, his mind still drifting to the well-being of his loved ones. "I sometimes wonder if I'm the reason all of this started. If I hadn't become a diplomat for the coven, would there have been any reason for a power struggle?"

"The first witch and devil have been at odds and causing problems for ages," Hannah said with a scoff. "And how is everyone else's greed your fault?"

"Is it greed that is making the entire coven act this way?" Fin asked philosophically. "Because to me, they are trying to do what they think is best for the world. They are trying to think of their purpose as witches."

"Inciting a war does not seem like a balancing act," Captain Taylor argued gruffly.

"People have always incited wars," Fin pointed out. "And, believe me, I don't think everyone has pure motives behind this particular war. As Kasim Jelani said to me long ago, people don't start wars because they are strong."

Hannah looked dubious at this point.

Fin smiled a little. "Greed is a weakness. It means you cannot be satisfied. It's a sign that a kingdom or group is not sated in some way. Its leaders may be corrupt. There could be a famine. Or oppression… But these explanations mean something is broken."

No one said anything for a while.

"In that case… I hate how weakness leads to this many people getting hurt," Hannah grumbled.

Captain Taylor grunted in agreement.

"Me too." Fin crossed his arms and moved closer to the table again. "When this is all over, how about we invite Sirs Lewis and Andrews back to Austice and we all have a good drinking night?"

The captain and Hannah grinned in response.

"As long as that wife of yours agrees not to challenge anyone to a drinking contest again," Hannah insisted with a wary tension in her voice.

Fin chuckled. "I can't make that promise. Maybe I'll try to get Mackenzie Harris to take on the task."

"Oh right. Like you need someone setting *more* fires in your keep."

Fin squinted at the ceiling and drifted closer to the table. "Lady Mackenzie does have a small problem with arson. But with everyone there, I'm sure we could manage something."

"I bet you three silver at least one chair will be broken and two fires will be set." The captain leaned back, folding his beefy arms.

"I'll take that bet." Hannah gave a devilish smile. "I'll bet that this time they'll manage to cut down the impressive display you have on your entryway ceiling."

Fin sighed and fixed Hannah with a very flat look. "By the way, Taylor, did I ever get around to telling you who Hannah has been having nightly meetings with?"

Hannah launched herself out of her seat and grabbed Fin by his shirt with both hands, her eyes gleaming. "Did you learn nothing after seeing what I did to your son?"

Fin cleared his throat.

"You didn't know about Hannah and Mr. Howard?" Captain Taylor asked Fin, sounding genuinely surprised.

Both Hannah and Fin whirled around. "*What?*" they spluttered in unison.

The captain snorted. "I saw you and Mr. Howard stumbling out of a closet in a state nine years ago."

"Why didn't you say anything?" Hannah demanded. She released Fin and collapsed back in her chair.

Taylor shrugged. "It wasn't my business."

Hannah thrust a finger in the captain's direction while staring wildly up at Fin. "When did he become the decent one of the group? You should be ashamed, Ashowan!"

Fin grinned. "Taylor's twelve children broke him in. Annika made me stop at two. I have too much energy to be passive."

"Arsehole," Hannah muttered.

Sighing, Fin tilted his head, still smiling at his friends. "I miss Harris. He always made me seem like the lesser evil."

The trio descended into their familiar banter and camaraderie, a solace amid the cloud of darkness that hung over the kingdom. While Fin knew his worries would be waiting with gnashing teeth for him come morning, he could at least enjoy a moment of reprieve with old friends.

The physician's dark eyes squinted over tiny spectacles perched precisely halfway down his hooked nose. Eli had heard him make at least three quiet throat clearings. A bead of sweat rolled down the side of his face. His fingers delicately pinched Eli's wrist as his gaze darted back to Tam.

The nobleman's smoldering stare had in no way gentled.

The physician stole a glance at Eli. She raised her eyebrows at him. The index finger on her left hand tapped her thigh expectantly.

"If I may…" The physician gave yet another small cough. "Be so bold as to ask… But… Often the mother knows before physicians such as myself whether or not she is expecting again. You have two other children who—"

"Is she or is she not pregnant?" Tam interrupted bluntly.

Eli felt the physician jolt nervously; his fingers trembled against her wrist.

She took a deep breath, and after a silent warning look at Tam, addressed the physician herself.

"We would prefer that you, with your expertise, confirm whether or not I am."

The physician licked his lips and pointedly avoided Tam's stare. The poor man didn't know that Tam wasn't angry, just anxious—though if one didn't know him, that would not be clear. Really, Eli could tell he was barely containing his restlessness while waiting for the news. She wasn't much better, but she was hiding it more adeptly.

"W-well, my lady, your heart is beating quite hard, so I am—"

Tam made a noise that could've been heard as growl, but Eli could tell it was really a stifled groan of pain over the suspense.

The physician looked close to tears.

"Tam, if you are going to scare the physician, you can wait outside," Eli ordered irritably.

"I'll wait right here," he responded firmly.

Eli opened her mouth to tell him to stop being a donkey, but she was interrupted by the physician.

"Ah! There!"

"What?" Eli and Tam demanded at the same time.

"Just a moment." The physician was squinting at the coverlet Eli rested on as he continued holding her wrist.

Eli spared a glance at Tam and barely stopped herself from laughing. Both his hands were gripping his hair as he stared with demented eyes at the physician.

With a sigh, she addressed the man-shaped pile of nerves. "Tam, everything will be fine."

"I know that! I just want to know what—"

"My lord, please, I'm trying to focus," the physician blurted, a faint note of desperation in his voice.

Eli watched a slight twitch tweak Tam's right eye.

Oddly enough, witnessing Tam's descent into a sub-basement of madness made her feel much better about the whole experience.

"Aah." The physician leaned back on his stool, his hand falling to his lap.

Both Tam and Eli stared at the man. At the beginning of their meeting, he had looked like he was in his late fifties. At present, he could've passed for his eighties thanks to the dense tension in the room.

The man sat in silence.

"Well?" Again, both Eli and Tam said the same thing at the same moment—and with matching snappish tones.

"I'd like to check again—"

"Oh, for the love of—" Tam swung around, stalked over to the bay of windows, and seized the sill, his head dropping.

"Why do you want to check again?" Eli was barely managing her own annoyance.

"Well, I'd hate to get the both of you excited for only for me to be incorr—"

Eli's head spun. "We should be excited?"

What answer was she going to be excited about, again?

Wait. Did the physician even know the answer to *that* question?

Eli sensed Tam straighten from his place by the window. He had gone very still.

The physician reached back over and plucked up Eli's wrist again. She barely felt it as tremors of excitement or panic—she really couldn't tell which—took over.

"Breathe," the physician counseled gently.

Eli hadn't even realized she'd been holding her breath.

And just when she was relatively certain that she might start shaking the man herself, the physician sat back with a sigh and a smile.

"All done. My apologies for the delay. I can tell you are quite nervous about the news—"

"WILL YOU PLEASE JUST TELL US!" For the third time, Tam and Eli spoke in perfect unison.

The physician's open mouth closed as he gave a sheepish, apologetic upturn of the lips at Eli. He then subtly shifted a little farther away from Tam, who had moved silently closer during his second inspection.

"Congratulations, my lady, you are expecting."

Eli's jaw dropped.

A rush of emotion surged through her. Tam turned into a very pale statue.

"It is still early, but given the approximate timing of your last cycle, I would place your delivery around early spring."

"Pl… Please leave us." Eli heard the waver in her voice. Luckily, despite the stress she and Tam had just put the man through, the physician rushed out of the cabin without needing much more prompting.

When the door latched closed, Eli sought out Tam's gaze. The instant their eyes locked, Eli felt the tears come, and she realized she was smiling harder than she ever had in her life. "Holy Gods."

Tam dove for her, wrapping her in his arms as she continued to shake from the complete shock. She heard him whisper the same words into her hair. "Holy Gods."

"It doesn't even feel real!" Eli said. She allowed her cheek to rest on Tam's warm shoulder, which still smelled of peppermint and frankincense.

"It really doesn't."

"I mean…" Eli trailed off as Tam gingerly pulled away from her, though he grasped her hands and seated himself beside the bed. "I barely know you."

Tam stared blankly at her. "What a time to say that."

"But… I just met you in early spring of this year! It's been what… nearly five months since I first met you? It's too quick—and don't you dare say anything about your family's virility again."

"It *is* fast for us to have this kind of development. Are you…" A nervous expression came over Tam. "Are you alright with… this?"

Blinking, Eli lowered her eyes and took stock of her emotions.

She had expected to be angry, sad, or nervous about this outcome. Exasperated, even.

But she was dumbstruck to discover she was…

"I've never been this happy in my life. I've heard some women can go a bit mad when expecting, so maybe that's why. But… I guess I'm… excited. Really excited to just—just have a home. With you. And Luca. And Penelope. And whoever this is." She gestured vaguely around her middle. "Excited to have a life that I made. Before, you talked about your keep in Sorlia. We could read in the library as a family. We could have tea together in the garden, and I would never have to…" More tears were gathering in Eli's eyes as she spoke, but she swallowed down the brimming emotion to finish her sentiment. "I will never have to suffer alone. I'll actually have a family. A good one."

As she stared into Tam's face, she could see he was becoming quite emotional himself over her reaction.

And so she did what felt absolutely right in that moment. She cupped Tam's face in her hands and kissed him. He kissed her back readily. It started to lead to more than just a kiss, but Eli paused. "You're my family, now, Tam. We're together in this. For always."

"Thank Gods for that," Tam murmured affectionately back.

Still smiling so widely her cheeks ached, Eli couldn't help but add one final comment before she allowed them to fully enjoy their celebration.

"Maybe in the future, you ask me before you get on any more ships, hm?"

CHAPTER 10

A PRIVATE PARTY

"Did grandpa beat up the king, too?" Luca asked eagerly, his eyes wide.

"No!" Tam exclaimed, though he struggled against a laugh. "No, I specifically told you this particular story to demonstrate how you can solve problems without violence!"

"Oh…" Luca settled down on his haunches, his disappointment undisguised.

Penelope sat beside him seriously. "So? What did Finlay do?"

Tam eased back into the wooden folding chair. They had pulled it out for their story time after dinner, seated on the deck around the small round table.

"Well, the king decided that the knights should work in his kitchen. And so they had to work with the very maid they had bullied, and if they gave her any trouble… ? There would've been even worse consequences."

After watching the end of the story make its way through the children's minds, Tam rose from his seat with a stretch, his mouth stretched wide in a yawn.

"Isn't the maid in the story the one Harris said learned when to be mean?" Penelope wondered astutely.

Tam nodded with a smile, then turned and gestured to the stairs belowdecks. The pink evening sky cast the deck in a rosy glow.

Luca frowned at his father, then looked at the stairs in confusion. "Why are we going belowdecks?"

"Time for bed," Tam explained without dropping his arm.

"What?" Luca looked around frantically. "It's not even night yet!"

Tam stepped toward the stairs, looking over his shoulder. "The captain wants the crew to run some drills this evening, so we need to get out of the way. Come on. You can read in bed for a little while."

Luca's mouth twisted, and his eyes lowered with disappointment.

Guilt needled at Tam's gut, even though he knew he was ushering the kids away for a perfectly good reason. A hint of pain in Luca's eyes said he was upset about more than this new bedtime. Still, the boy got to his feet and trailed after Penelope, who strode forward without a word of complaint until she stood beside Tam.

Watching the way Luca dragged the soles of his boots over the deck, she huffed in disapproval and turned with her hands on her small hips. "Oh, come on. I'll even read with you; it isn't that bad."

Luca made a valiant effort to smile at Penelope, but he only managed a closed-lip version. He seemed unable to meet her eyes for more than a moment.

Tam forced himself to stay quiet as they descended the steps of the ship and made their way down the galley.

"Wait!" Luca whirled around, and Tam pretended not to expect this delay.

"Can't I read or—or listen to more stories in the cabin with you and Eli?" Luca implored, a spark of hope lighting his face.

Tam took his time to make it seem as though he were thinking about it. Rocking onto the balls of his feet, then back onto his heels, his hands finding his pockets. "I suppose. Eli has been quite busy today, but if we're quiet, it shouldn't be a problem."

Luca beamed. "I'll be quiet! You'll be quiet, too, won't you, Penelope?"

Penelope rolled her eyes. "I'm always quiet. You're the loud, smelly one."

"I'm not smelly!"

"Yeah, you are!"

Tam cleared his throat loudly and raised an eyebrow at Penelope.

She scowled back up at him. "He does stink."

"There are nicer ways of saying—you know what. Let's not talk about this right now. I'm sure the sailors will be coming up soon, and we don't want to get in their way." Tam set one hand on each child's shoulder and propelled them down the passageway toward their cabin.

When they arrived in front of the door, Luca immediately reached for the brass handle, making Tam catch his wrist gently, stopping him.

"I think I'd better knock to make sure Eli isn't changing." Tam smiled warmly at his son, knocked three times, paused, and then knocked another two times.

At first there was silence… the sound of scuffling…

"Come in!"

Without another word, Tam pressed the handle down and sent the door swinging wide to reveal…

His and Eli's cabin brightly lit, the table crowded with desserts, tea, and interestingly shaped packages wrapped in brown paper and tied with brightly colored ribbons.

"SURPRISE!"

"BKAAW!"

"Me-OW!"

Eli, Hamil, Bes, Captain Sun, Tam, and Penelope shouted, accompanied by the chicken duchess and Kraken, as Luca stared dumbfounded.

"What are we surprised about?" The boy looked up at his dad in confusion.

Tam balked, then answered with a chuckle. "The party, Luca. We're celebrating your birthday!"

"Oh!" Luca blinked, then stared at the table, his eyes homing in on a cake with thick white frosting topped with raspberries. "So I get to eat some of the desserts… ?"

Everyone grinned as Tam laughed quietly and Hamil strode forward.

"Of course you get to eat the desserts, young Luca!" Hamil declared. "It is a joyous celebration for you! You have grown and learned a great deal in the last year, and we should celebrate all that you have lived and what you bring to the world!"

"O-oh," Luca repeated, slowly clasping his hands in front of himself.

"Everything alright, Luca?" Tam asked, stepping into the room and closing the door.

"Um… Well, I… I've never… I don't know how to… Do I have to do anything?"

Tam's smile faded from his face, and he felt emotion prick his eyes. "All you have to do is have fun."

"I can… I can do that, then. Thank you for… For um…" The boy continued to stammer.

Tam's gaze snapped to Eli, and he could see the shared pain and anger on Luca's behalf.

There was a tense stillness in the room as Captain Sun, Hamil, and Bes looked with dark suspicion at Tam and Eli.

Penelope stomped her foot, grabbed Luca's hands, and bonked her forehead against his.

"Don't be a crybaby! Let's eat cake and see your *presents!*" she squealed jubilantly. Which was so out of character for her that it momentarily stunned everyone.

Luca snapped free from his emotional stupor. A smile drifted up his face, making his brow relax.

"Okay! Do you get presents, too?" he asked curiously.

"Nope!" Penelope answered. She shook her head, her small single braid of dark hair dangling over the side of her head flapping.

"That's not quite true," Bes interjected delicately, her eyes darting around the room. "There are usually party favors for guests."

"Oh. Well… Not for this party!" Penelope shrugged indifferently. "I know because I helped!"

"You knew?" Luca asked, wide-eyed.

Penelope grinned proudly. "Of course!"

The two children continued to chatter away as they sat at the table.

Eli, having drawn herself away from the tense stares among the other adults in the room, helped the children cut the cake the ship's cook had been able to whip up. She offered everyone slices. It was nothing short of a miracle that any raspberries had remained fresh enough to decorate the cake this far into their journey.

Meanwhile, Hamil, Bes, and Captain Sun managed to drift closer to Tam while appearing as casual as possible.

Tam tensed, his mind racing as he wondered how exactly he should explain things.

"Pardon my intrusion," Hamil began lightly. "I had heard this morning on deck that the young man there didn't really celebrate his birthday, but I find myself quite curious why he seems so..." Hamil trailed off, his expression still casual.

Captain Sun didn't contribute, but he did tilt his head in silent agreement with the Lobahlan's curiosity.

Tam cleared his throat awkwardly.

"Of course I have no business asking the details: I am merely a guest upon your ship, Lord Tamlin, but I quite like your son. And from what I've seen, you do as well, so I am... confused," Hamil added a little too hastily, which revealed his nervousness in even broaching the subject.

Tam cast a quick glance at Penelope and Luca as they happily devoured the weighty slabs of Eli had provided them.

"I did not know about Luca's existence until earlier this year, and we are most likely going to adopt Penelope as her mother has passed," Tam provided delicately.

"Aah... Oh." Hamil had started to nod along, but when he realized what exactly Tam was insinuating, his easygoing façade balked.

"Oh... OH!" Bes caught on a moment after her companion. Though she looked a little more sheepish upon the realization of Luca's origins.

"Yes. And if anyone has an issue with that, keep it to yourself," Tam kept his voice quiet, but he ensured they all could hear the hardness behind his tone.

The Lobahlans were quick to bob their heads in assent, but Captain Sun looked a bit uneasy... until he locked eyes with Tam, and whatever he saw made the seasoned Zinferan sailor flinch.

"Alright, everyone! Come on and eat this cake!" Eli called out sternly. "It would be rude for this to be put to waste."

Everyone dutifully returned their attention to the birthday party. Upon rejoining the children at the table, they discovered that Kraken and the duchess chicken had both succumbed to an early party nap right beside the cake.

"I can really have this?" Luca all but shouted in awe as he turned over the sextant in his hands.

Tam sat beside Luca, his arms crossed and his legs stretched out in a relaxed pose. "Of course. I paid Captain Sun here good coin for it."

"That means we can look at the stars together at night again!" Luca was practically bouncing in his seat.

"That's right. I had to send mine back home to Daxaria when we left Junya, so this is perfect. Especially because as we are traveling north, we're going to see constellations from a new angle," Tam supplied. Luca hugged the instrument to his chest tightly, his joy leaving him speechless.

"Tam?"

Looking over, Tam found Penelope standing at his side, holding the odd brass trinket Wixim had given him over a fortnight ago. "Where did you find that?" he asked with a raised eyebrow. He was relatively certain he had kept it stowed in a locked drawer beside the bed.

"I…"

Tam turned at Eli's voice, drawing everyone's eye to her. "I pulled it out when we were… going through things," she finished haltingly, trying to avoid referencing their search for gifts for Luca.

What they had managed to scrounge up was the sextant, a fine whittling knife Tam had purchased from one of the sailors, and a sketchbook that Jiho had kindly packed onto the ship.

However, Tam hadn't even realized they'd pulled out the prototype of Chronos, the first witch's device.

"What is it?" Penelope stared at the device curiously.

Carefully, Tam plucked up the circlet on its chain from her small palm and pressed the tiny button at the top. At least he assumed it was the top, given the delicate hinges on the bottom. As he remembered, the brass cover sprang open to reveal the glass face.

The clattering of a fork on porcelain jolted everyone's attention upward to Bes and Hamil. The Lobahlans were staring in shock at the Chronos-esque device.

"Do you know what that is?" Eli asked, straightening her shoulders and leaning back in her seat.

Bes and Hamil shared a wordless glance.

Then, in unison, they looked back at Eli and responded, "No."

The flat, dubious look Eli gave them had Hamil pointedly picking up his cup and taking a drink while Bes—who had been picking at her slice of cake prior to that moment—suddenly loaded a massive forkful of frosting into her mouth.

Tam was about to ask another question when Kraken slowly lifted his head from his nap at the same time as the chicken duchess.

Hamil and Bes froze at the eerie movement of the animals.

Kraken unfurled, then brought himself to the edge of the table, lowered his chin, and glared at Hamil.

The chicken duchess rapped a claw against the table in front of Bes, who gulped loudly.

As much as Tam wanted some more answers about the mysterious item the dragon had given them, it *was* still Luca's birthday, and it wasn't as though the Lobahlans were going anywhere for the remainder of their journey.

"How about we all go above deck—Luca, the sailors managed to tie a swing up on one of the masts, so you can give that a try."

Whirling around, his mood in no way diminished despite the temporary spell of tense silence, Luca threw his arms around Tam, instantly easing the discomfort in the cabin.

"This is the best birthday *ever!*"

CHAPTER 11

LEARNING ABOUT LOSS

Tam leaned against the ship railing in the cool night. He listened with a fond half smile as his son and Penelope giggled and shrieked while playing on the swing the sailors had carefully constructed for them.

Much to Luca's immense delight, the men had even performed a mock scrimmage. Belatedly, Tam thought it maybe wasn't helpful to his goal of persuading Luca away from viewing violence as a good thing. With nothing that could be done retroactively, however, and the knowledge that Luca was having a marvelous time for his very first birthday party, Tam decided not to worry too much.

Instead he glanced over and down at Eli. She stood at his side, wearing loose, belted tan pants, a billowing pale-blue silk shirt tucked into them, and a thicker long white coat.

She looked absolutely beautiful.

"Are you still in shock?" he asked quietly.

Eli didn't look back at him. Her brows were riddled in a pensive frown as she stared across the deck at the Lobahlans, who were chatting with Captain Sun.

"I want to know about that Chronos thing," Eli returned seriously. "I know you stowed the first witch away in your void, but that isn't going to be a permanent solution. She might already be out." Eli gripped her coat sleeves, her tone irritated and stiff.

Tam tilted his head. "Well, we still have the whistle. And Wixim said even he wasn't sure what the Chronos predecessor could do. My bet is that if it were truly useful, Aradia would have kept it."

"I'm going to make the Lobahlans tell us what it is. Harris's sword that turns you twenty years younger when you hold it was something their people crafted. The Lobahlans clearly have some understanding of imbuing weapons with magical power that no one else does," Eli reminded him, her attention never shifting away from the Lobahlans.

"How would you like to pry the information out of them?" Tam asked, only a little concerned at what her answer may be.

At last, Eli leaned back to look at him. "I have more information on the kingdoms than quite literally anyone else. I can get two young, sheltered Lobahlans to spare me a few details."

Two shrieks of excitement from the children had Eli and Tam leaning forward to make sure all was well. That confirmed, the couple resumed their conversation.

"As impressive as you are," Tam ventured carefully, "a lot of that is because you were able to work alongside the monarchy and nobility for long periods of time."

Eli straightened. "Are you saying you don't think I can find out what I want to know?"

Tam rubbed the back of his neck before answering. "I didn't say that. What I mean is that there may have to be some strategizing in how we approach them."

Eli rounded on him. Tam could tell things were about to get heated.

"I wasn't just going to charge up and ask them what was going on," Eli declared sternly.

"Didn't say you were."

"What did you think I was going to do?"

Tam dropped his hand from his neck. "Try and befriend them, and then gently broach the subject?"

"I'm not the friendly type," Eli said dismissively.

"Okay…" Tam trailed off uncertainly. "So you are planning on… ?"

"I'll make them think I'm afraid of what the device can do. I'll work myself up and catch Hamil off guard. If I can make myself cry, he'll probably tell me something about it."

Tam paused thoughtfully. That was a pretty good approach. Hamil *did* seem prone to blathering, but… he wasn't the one who had revealed the intricacies of their government.

"Do it with Bes. Not Hamil," he advised. "And whatever she says, I'll go to Hamil afterward and act angry. I'll say Bes said something to upset you about the device and pressure him to clarify."

Eli's earlier disgruntlement eased as she leaned forward conspiratorially. "Alright. I was planning on approaching them tonight."

Tam shook his head. "They will be on guard. Do it tomorrow to make it look natural."

Eli considered this. "I suppose."

Tam reclaimed his smile as he reached out and clasped her upper arms. "Besides. We need to keep enjoying Luca's birthday party."

Smiling back, albeit a little more wearily than Tam, Eli nodded.

"So are you going to answer my earlier question?" Tam asked. He wrapped his arms around her and pressed her back to his chest so that they could both face outward to watch Luca push Penelope on the swing.

He expected Eli to not remember what he was referring to, but she surprised him. "Yes. I am still shocked. I don't feel pregnant, so it's hard to think that I am."

"Hmm." Tam pondered her response. "I imagine if my mother heard you say that, she might feel a bit envious. She said her symptoms came on quickly."

"What about your sister?"

"Kat isn't someone I'd categorize as 'normal' when it comes to health," Tam replied evenly.

Eli sighed. "I still think the doctor might be wrong."

"Weren't you saying earlier that you were craving jam and toast, and were feeling unreasonably angry with me?"

"You were just being infuriating. There doesn't have to be another reason. And jam and toast is tasty. People crave things without needing a reason to."

"My da always said that cravings were indicative of a person's health."

Eli made a noncommittal noise in response.

"Shall we go see if Luca and Penelope have burned through enough energy to be able to sleep?"

Eli snorted. "They could probably stay awake until dawn at this rate."

Tam chortled along with her. "I guess it's going to be a late night. When do you want to tell them about the baby, by the way?"

"When I'm absolutely certain I'm pregnant," Eli responded swiftly.

Tam laughed. "When will that be, do you think? When you're in labor?"

Gently smacking his arm, Eli didn't bother answering his jibe.

Instead they continued to listen to the creaking wood of the deck, the children's laughter, and the soft rush of water as their ship parted the inky waves under the starry sky.

That moment of calm and happiness concluded a day they would never forget.

Sitting on a stump he had fashioned into a chair of sorts atop a grassy hill, the devil looked over the scene peacefully. The lush hills were blessed with adequate rains and days of sun. A breeze cast rippling waves through the grass that the sheep had not yet grazed upon. Small, fluffy white clouds drifted lazily across a pale-blue sky.

The smell of sweet grass and the occasional cloud of hay dust found its way to where he sat observing the slow moment of the day. Neighboring farmers strolled along their fields. Two red barns could be seen in the distance near whitewashed cottages. Only one house rose to two stories: a wooden farmhouse with a deep green roof, white walls, and finely paned glass windows. It stood out among the other humble homes.

The devil tilted his head, staring at it, then lazily allowed his attention to drift over to his own home.

It was whitewashed like many of the others, though a loft had been stacked on half of it.

He smiled.

They had just finished rethatching the roof two weeks ago, and the garden was already filled with bright-green shoots.

"There you are!"

Blinking himself free from his moment of appreciation, the devil turned around to stare up at the woman with long sandy-brown hair, dark, vibrant green eyes, and a smattering of freckles over the bridge of her nose.

His smile broadened, and he held out his hand.

She stared at it, still catching her breath from the climb up the hill, then took it and allowed him to pull her to sit on his lap.

"Jordy is here to see you," she announced. While her voice was quiet, the devil could feel the stiffness in her body.

Taking in a long inhale, the devil made no move to stand, and settled farther back into his chair. "I told Jordy I wasn't going to do any kind of work or deal like I did in the past. I promised you."

She didn't relax. "You could at least hear what he has to say."

"Mare," he started, but then he trailed off and dropped his forehead against her back. His fingers found their way around her hands and gave them a reassuring squeeze. "I'll go talk to him. You don't need to worry."

"I'm not worried!"

"Yes, you are."

"I'm not! I'm just…"

The devil lifted his head, pausing. "Disgruntled," he finished for her without masking his surprise and concern. "Why?"

"Because it isn't so bad if you still do a little bit of your old work! Not all of your deals had to do with murder, coups, or mass thefts—"

"Mare, it's a slippery slope. Besides, if I don't make any deals, my sister won't find us. It's easy for her to track me down when I'm involved in that kind of work," he argued while leaning to the side to better see her face.

"Didn't you say she's probably off in Troivack right now? Why can't you—"

The devil released Mare's hand. "What is going on?"

She stood back up and turned to face him, wrapping her arms around herself.

He rose to his feet as well. "Is it about money? We have more than enough sheep to earn all the coin we need to last through the winter, and the neighbors are all very kind and helpful. Even if we—"

"This isn't what I wanted."

The devil felt his heart drop as realization plunged him into its horrible coldness. How had he missed it before? How had he not noticed?

"We met because of your deals. We... We got to meet different kinds of people, saw new places, and drank good wine. The only people I talk to now are the elderly neighbors, and I spend most of my day doing chores. I'm bored—and you aren't facing your sister! You're hiding. And you're using me as an excuse." She flung out her arm over the landscape that only moments before, the devil had thought was even more beautiful than the Forest of the Afterlife.

"Would you prefer I become a merchant?" he asked softly, already sensing where this was going. He had thought she was different than the others.

"Maybe? I don't know..." She turned away, looking over the fields instead of at him. "You're the son of the Gods, and yet you feel like a normal man."

"So you wanted to marry me because I'm powerful?" The question didn't even bear the sharpness of accusation. It was more bored, albeit streaked with pain.

She rounded on him angrily. "No! It's just... I loved all of you. Including the part of you that made you different from other men."

He stared down at her. His heart twisted in his chest.

It had been a long time since he had felt this kind of hurt. At least thirty years. It was the pain of losing the happiness and eternal love he had been ready to carry for her.

"I see. Loved. As in, you don't still love me. You've already moved on." His eyes drifted over her head after he made his observation.

Maybe he'd try traveling to Troivack after this ended. Who knew? Maybe his vengeful sister had finally worked out a way to end his life, and he could stop enduring these horrible moments.

Mare was already taking a step away from him. Apparently, the conclusion of a marriage of seven years wasn't worth more words to her.

"Can I ask you something?" the devil called suddenly.

Amazingly, Mare turned back around.

"When was it that it stopped?"

"What?"

"Your love for me. When did you start not to love me?"

Mare briefly gripped the plain beige skirt she wore, then released it. Her face scrunched up in thought. There was a detachment in her eyes devoid of the spark and warmth that had made the devil love her. It was disturbing to see how different it made her.

He supposed that's what he got for swearing off prodding at her emotions deeper than surface level.

"I don't know. I think my love got mixed up in the admiration and thrill of it all. Your own parents—the human ones that raised you—even they treat you with reverence. You walked into a room and could command it. You and I were able to do things that no one could dream of doing. I loved that you were gentle with me, though. I loved that you found normal life with me so extraordinary. But I guess I just loved that you were the extraordinary. It's the normal I don't like. So the more normal life became, the less I loved you."

Ah.

He'd been on a pedestal.

Wanting the untouchable isn't as appealing when you've touched and had it.

How... simple.

The devil wondered if Mare realized how normal she was for that.

"I see. Well. I suppose I will leave you to file the paperwork for our divorce with the magistrate." He turned, his hands finding their way into his pockets as he stepped down the hill. Though his legs shook, he did his best to ignore it. Yet even the effort of ignoring his physical state and acknowledging the pain he felt in his heart made his body feel heavy and weary.

"Did you even love me? You seem perfectly fine." Mare sounded utterly detached.

The devil was moderately aware of the fact that tears filled his eyes. But he didn't bother feeling self-conscious about it as he looked back and smiled at his wife.

"I love you, and have loved you without being able to stop since the day you walked in and told me you needed to make a deal. You just aren't the first human to disappoint me. Though you were the first that I put all my trust in. But that's my fault. I really should have known better than to start changing my opinion."

And with that, he made his way down the hill. The beautiful scene from before remained the same, only now it had become forever tied with one of his worst days on earth.

Tam's eyes flew open. His heart ached, and tears rolled down his face.

But… there was a warm hand on his forearm. He looked down at the hand, then up into Eli's concerned face.

"Bad dream?" she asked softly.

He rubbed his face. "Yeah."

It took a moment, but eventually Tam realized Eli did not seem in any way sleepy. When he finally looked at her again, he frowned. "Did I wake you?"

"No, no, I just… I can't sleep."

"Why is that?" Tam drew himself up onto his elbows worriedly.

Eli fidgeted. "Well, it's just… I… Tam, what if…"

"What? What is it?" He leaned forward, and laid his hand over her own that still rested on him.

"What if the baby has a tail?"

Tam balked. "Pardon?"

"Or fur! What if it's covered in fur? Or has whiskers? Oh Gods… I wish I could ask Wixim about this."

Tam barely stifled the laugh.

Eli still heard it, and next thing he knew, his heart-wrenching dream was pushed to the back of his mind, as he instead found himself in a detailed discussion about whether or not his future child would be born a beast-human hybrid.

CHAPTER 12

CLOSE CONNECTIONS

"**B**ut no one would want to be friends with them!"

"You never know... We could always teach them to do it in private."

"It would also mean that they were licking themselves."

"Erm... I guess, yes."

"See? It'd be awful!"

Tam let out a long sigh before he took a delicious sip of coffee.

He and Eli were still deep in discussion on the issues that might arise if their future child was part beast the morning after Luca's birthday party. In this particular instance, they were debating whether the child would come out with fur and, therefore, cough up hairballs. While Eli had worked herself up to the point that her shoulders nearly touched her earlobes, Tam had adopted a far more relaxed air. There were a large number of troubles in their present, and he felt no need to borrow concerns from the future.

"I don't think I should turn into my familiar form until after the baby is born," Eli announced, her hands gripping her teacup a little more tightly.

"Whatever you think is best." Tam nodded agreeably.

Eli's eyes snapped to him.

Tam had been about to take another sip of coffee, but the intensity of Eli's stare made him pause.

He gazed back at her patiently.

"You think we're going to be fine," she assumed evenly.

"I do."

"That's easy for you to say," Eli scoffed. "You try thinking about birthing something with claws."

Tam recoiled.

"*See?*" Eli emphasized triumphantly.

Tam hid his laugh behind a cough before setting his cup down on the table and leaning over to grasp Eli's hands. "That does sound terrifying. And these are all valid worries…"

"You think I should focus on our other problems instead of this one?" Eli guessed knowingly.

Tam grinned.

Eli wore her periwinkle-blue Zinferan dress dotted with red flowers. Despite the two untamable cowlicks in her chin-length hair, she looked beautiful to Tam.

Dropping his eyes to their joined hands, Tam rubbed his thumb over Eli's knuckles. "You should think and worry about what you want. I can't imagine what it's like growing another person. But… upsetting yourself when there is nothing to do but hurry up and wait might be hard on you, and I want you to feel comfortable."

Eli didn't speak straightaway. Rather she looked like she was lightly gnawing on her tongue before she managed to respond with, "It's a shame you dislike being social. You're annoyingly adept at giving diplomatic answers."

Tam dropped his chin to his chest with a quiet snort.

"There is a genuine worry that fits into this line of questions," Eli ventured carefully.

Tam lifted his head, his good humor sobering in the face of her serious expression.

"If… If the child is affected by my having ancient beast blood in me, it is possible that it could change *when* I give birth. Cats give birth after only being pregnant a few weeks!"

Tam straightened.

That *was* a very valid concern.

"Wait." Tam paused. "You said you didn't manifest your beast form until you were older."

Eli blinked at his recollection of her past. "Yes, that is true."

"So wouldn't it stand to reason that if our child inherits that ability, they wouldn't have any kind of trait or transformation until they, too, were older?"

Relief seized Eli. "Gods, you're right." She closed her eyes and let out a long breath. "That does make me feel better."

Rising partially out of his seat, Tam brushed a kiss over her forehead before settling back down. "I'm worried, too. Trust me. I'm relatively certain I'm going to be having a mental breakdown when you go into labor."

The corners of Eli's lips rose. "I'd like to see that."

Tam's jaw dropped in mock offense. "Gods, you wish emotional torment on me. Just who have I agreed to spend my life with?"

Eli gave a quiet cackle as she, too, eased back in her seat. "Don't worry, you haven't married me yet. There is still plenty of time for me to scare you off."

Tam slowly crossed his arms and raised an eyebrow at Eli. "I'd marry you this instant. But we're getting my parents together to attend. As you should know by now, I do my utmost to keep my promises."

Eli tilted her head, a warm gleam in her eyes, as she allowed the hand Tam had seized to drift back around her teacup. "I do."

"You seem happy today. I like it."

Eli set her cup down on the table. "Yes, well. Aside from our persistently expanding horde of children, all we have to do today is force the Lobahlans to tell us what they know about the device Wixim gave us."

Tam rose to his feet and rounded Eli's chair to rest his hands on her shoulders. He pressed his thumbs into her and rubbed them in slow, careful circles.

"Oh." A groan of pleasure escaped Eli's mouth, which happened to have a very *un*relaxing effect on Tam, but he shoved such thoughts to the side as he continued to massage.

"When did you want us to start prying that information out of them?" Tam asked, letting his sights glide over to Luca and Penelope. They were subjecting the Lobahlans to their every whim, which included being pushed on the swing, playing card games, and the occasional bout of hide-and-seek.

"After lunch, people are usually sleepy, and so they aren't as quick. We'll do it then." Eli replied with a slight slur as she continued to enjoy Tam's work on her shoulders.

"Alright, sounds like a plan." Tam bent over and brushed a kiss along the side of Eli's neck, making a flush of goosebumps appear. He grinned and lingered near the spot.

Clearing her throat, Tam noted the way she shifted. The sails slapped in the wind, but otherwise things were quite quiet on the deck.

"You know…" she began as the tops of her ears turned red.

"Mm?" Tam kissed her neck again.

"It's not like I can get *more* pregnant."

"I like the way you think there, Taejo."

"Ugh. I'm not the emperor's adopted daughter anymore, remember?" Eli's head swiveled to stare up at Tam, who let his hands slip to her upper arms.

"And so what name should the magistrate read out during our vows?" Tam heard the huskiness in his voice. Thanks to the fact that his mind was swimming with all kinds of private activities, he didn't particularly care.

Eli licked her lips. Evidently, she was not unaffected by the mood.

"Just Elisara… or maybe Harris?"

Stunned, Tam couldn't help but eventually give another short laugh. "Oof. Mackenzie and Oscar Harris as your guardians? Harris is going to have a *field* day with my father if he gets to say they are in-laws."

Eli bristled a little, but she did so with a grin of her own. "That sounds like their problem."

"Right. Well. *I* don't exactly feel like calling you Harris, so I guess I'll keep working on finding a good nickname."

"Do we really need one? It isn't like my name is difficult to say." Eli stood with Tam's help, and the pair casually wandered closer to the stairs that would take them back down toward their cabin.

"I'd like to have one. It's a name that only you or I could use, which makes it fun."

"You want me to call you Ashowan?" Eli wondered while glancing up at Tam.

Tam winced. "Too many people call my father that."

"Lin? From your full name, Tamlin?"

Tam shot a flat look in response, then made another suggestion of his own. "Your alias in Zinfera was Ellie; what about that?"

By this time, they were halfway down the ship's passageway, and they had to slow as their eyes adjusted to the darkness. The rest of their stroll passed by quickly—though that was most likely because they both happened to be taking long, hurried steps.

"I'm not too fond of Ellie." Eli waited as Tam reached for their cabin's door handle. He followed her into the room and shut the door behind them.

"I could just call you 'wife.'"

"But I'm not your wife."

Tam prowled closer, forcing Eli to back up. She jolted when the backs of her thighs hit a table.

Tam stooped down and picked her up—making her squeak—and plunked her down on the table surface. He slowly pushed her skirts higher so he could stand closer to her.

He lowered his head, his mouth hovering over hers as he said, "You will be my wife someday, and it better be someday soon."

They were so close that when Eli's breath hitched, he heard it just fine.

"To be honest…" Eli had to pause to swallow. "I don't really care if we do or don't get marrie—"

Tam kissed her with a faint growl, cutting her off.

When he eventually stopped, he didn't fully pull away again, as he ended the discussion by saying, "Well, I damn well do care. And you better get ready, because there are a lot more things I'm going to want to do with you after the fact."

Despite the flush in Eli's cheeks and glassiness in her eyes, she still managed to respond with a faint, teasing question of her own. "Oh? Like what?"

Tam felt his expression turn roguish as his hands wandered up her sides. "You'll see. It's a surprise."

And then he was kissing her again. As a result, both of their respective patience seemed to run out as they indulged in a leisurely morning of closeness that had them remaining in their cabin until lunch.

"Really?" Luca's smile made his entire face glow.

"Yes! But don't tell them I told you!" Penelope whispered, pressing a finger to her lips.

The two children sat on the deck with a pile of their playing cards messily stacked after a game of Battle Eight. It was almost time for lunch. The Lobahlans had retreated to the round table that Tam and Eli had abandoned a while ago—for some unknown reason.

"Do you know what it is?" Luca persisted, leaning in conspiratorially as two sailors strode by.

Penelope smirked and nodded, her eyes following the men to make sure they were out of earshot.

"Ooh!" Luca giggled, absolutely thrilled as he clenched his fists and proceeded to do a funny little dance one of the sailors had shown him the night before. "Will you tell me?"

"Maybe! Maybe if you do everything I say, I will."

"Aw!" Luca's jubilant mood dropped, but then he stilled, his eyes turning pensive. "If I tell you a secret, will you tell me?"

Penelope perked up for a moment before turning skeptical. "You don't have one. You're bluffing."

"I'm not! I swear!" Luca declared earnestly.

Penelope's eyes narrowed. "Really?"

"Really!"

She scooted closer to Luca. "Alright, if you tell me, I'll tell you."

Luca grinned again and brought up his hand to whisper. "My bad dreams are getting better. I don't see sad things and scary monsters anymore!"

Penelope pulled away, annoyed. "That isn't a secret! Why would it even *be* a secret?"

Hurt, Luca frowned. "Because I don't tell people about my dreams, and I don't get to be happy with anyone else about it."

Penelope scowled. She looked like she wanted to argue more, but she had no choice but to accept such a sweet confession that made her feel reluctantly special. And so she leaned forward with a sigh, cupped her own hand around Luca's ear, and told him a tidbit of information about the future that she knew Tam and Eli would most likely want to know very, very much.

And when he heard the answer, he surged to his feet and started jumping up and down, unable to contain himself.

"YES!"

Giggling, Penelope joined him in jumping up and celebrating the secret news she had shared.

CHAPTER 13

THE DASTARDLY DAXARIANS

Nervously, Bes glanced over her shoulder to watch the Daxarian family that had saved them while they enjoyed their lunch. She and Hamil had opted to eat separately under the guise of giving the family some alone time, but really Bes was desperate to speak more privately with her friend.

"Where do you think they got it?" she whispered hastily to Hamil, who lounged at her side with his eyes closed and his face turned toward the sky.

He didn't even crack an eye, which pricked Bes's already delicate nerves.

"Who knows? They said the pirates are becoming a real problem, and we know not all of our Lobahlan ships make it back," Hamil speculated lazily.

Bes twisted her mouth as her index finger tapped the back of her other hand nervously.

"What exactly are you afraid of?" Hamil asked.

"You know magically interfering with time is against Lobahlan laws!"

"Yes. And we are not in Lobahl. They can make their own mistakes."

Bes shot him an incredulous look. "You can't be stupid enough to think that Lobahl won't be affected if they make a big enough mistake."

Realizing he was not going to continue quietly enjoying his leisurely time in the sun, Hamil pulled his feet off the chair he had been using as a footrest. He leaned an elbow on the luncheon table where their empty plates sat and stared flatly at Bes. "We have two choices. Tell them. Or don't. We've most likely already said too much, and telling them would probably mean they have a lot of questions," he pointed out with uncharacteristic seriousness.

Bes shifted in her seat to face Hamil better. "What if there is someone *in* Lobahl making that stuff?"

"You heard them! The first witch and devil are out and about! One of them probably had something to do with it. But you never know, maybe they've figured out how to make magical tools in the other kingdoms."

Bes scoffed. "Their government and kingdoms sound practically archaic. And they themselves seemed clueless. I doubt they've gotten that far."

Hamil sighed. "So what do you want to do, O righteous one?"

Bes rolled her eyes at him. "First, I want to take a closer look at that watch and find out if it even works."

"Mm-hm, and how do you think you'll be retrieving their watch… from their room… in a locked drawer?" Hamil's smile was taunting.

Scowling, Bes responded, "I figured we could sneak in or use the children as a diversion of sorts."

"And what will you tell them when *you* get caught, and these people from a *barbaric* kingdom decide to toss you overboard?"

"You're going to help me, Hamil," Bes announced with implicit warning lacing her tone. "We're in this mess because of you, and I want to know the situation with that magic tool if we are stuck on a boat with it for another week or two."

"Goddess. Do you hear yourself? We're on this boat *only* for another week or two! Why are you worrying? These ants are not coming into our home!"

Bes squirmed. "What if as soon as we get to Daxaria they do something terrible to us? What if we are imprisoned? Or they want to kill us? Or—"

"Why in the world would they want to kill us in their own kingdom when they could just as easily cut our throats and dump us overboard with no one the wiser?"

Bes clamped her mouth shut.

Hamil leaned back, a coy shine in his eyes. "You know what I think?"

"The fact that you are thinking at all is a big enough surprise."

Hamil ignored her barb. "I think you are loving the thrill of these new people and the mystery and danger. I think you desperately want to get involved. Maybe you think you can enlighten these *heathens* and become their savior. Be a hero."

Bes leaned back, incensed. "I do not!"

Hamil guffawed and turned his attention over to the Ashowan family just in time to see Luca launching a forkful of his lunch at Penelope, who shouted in protest. Lady Eli was quick to reprimand Luca, who barely smothered a mischievous grin. The one called Lord Tam reached over to Penelope with a napkin.

"I personally want to ask them a lot of questions about the Sun Queen," Hamil mused with a half grin still tugging up his mouth.

"I'm still not quite clear on whether she was always royal, or if she married into the family," Bes remarked with an eyebrow raised.

Hamil tilted his head in agreement. "True. We don't know if she was the daughter of the previous king, or if her husband was." He sighed. "See? It's a good thing we took a little detour on our seafaring adventure! Look how much we are learning! I understand about protecting our homeland, but we should be more aware of what's happening in the rest of the world."

Bes didn't object.

Another long span of time passed as they watched the family without comment, until Hamil let out a soft moan and turned to his companion. "Alright. I'll help you take a look at the watch. But only because I'm curious about it. Maybe they call it something different and so it has different functions."

Bes smiled, unable to hide her excitement as she swiveled around in her seat. "Maybe we suggest to the children we play hide-and-seek, or… or we make them show us something that they find interesting, or—"

"Don't you recall meentioning just now that it is in a drawer in Lady Eli and Lord Tam's cabin?"

"Great! So we know where they'd keep it!"

"Both those drawers had locks. Like I mentioned before," Hamil reminded.

Bes's shoulders sagged.

Seeing this, Hamil chortled. "You're so easily dissuaded. I can pick the lock. I'm just letting you know that it will delay us."

Bes perked back up, her smile lightening her entire face.

"Bok."

Hamil and Bes jumped aggressively when they realized that the strange chicken that everyone seemed to call "Duchess" had silently appeared on the table at some point during their discussion.

They jumped a second time, though slightly less clumsily, when they noticed the fluffy black cat called Kraken at their feet.

"Do you… Do you think this cat turns into that beast we saw earlier?" Bes asked in a whisper. "You know… the one that circled our ship."

The fluffy cat blinked slowly, and for whatever reason, it made Bes gulp.

"Yes, I do seem to remember *the giant winged cat*! Dawit would be salivating over that ancient beast hybrid," Hamil added offhandedly.

"Hamil! Focus! Is. This. That. Beast?" Bes didn't take her eyes off of the cat for an instant.

"I can't say. But this chicken… I don't know why, but its eyes are terrifying me right now."

"BAKA!"

Bes gave a short shriek, and Hamil made a garbled shout of alarm, even though the chicken had only moved one step closer to them.

"Everything alright?"

For the third time, Hamil and Bes yelped and reared back in surprise. Lord Tam had also appeared without them noticing his approach.

He shot them questioning looks, his sights drifting to the chicken and cat only briefly before moving back to them.

Bes pressed her hand to her chest and took a steadying breath. "Y-yes, we… we're fine."

"Tell me… Is this a… a… *pet* chicken?" Hamil ventured with a subtle tremor in his voice.

Lord Tam pressed his lips together as though trying not to laugh.

The chicken clucked quietly. How was it that it managed to sound indignant?

"No. The chicken is not a pet. But the chicken is important. Do not hurt the chicken under any circumstances."

"W-why?" Bes croaked.

The Daxarian nobleman cleared his throat and rubbed his mouth. He seemed to struggle against wanting to laugh, and Bes desperately wished she knew why.

"Well, if you hurt the chicken… War will probably be declared against Lobahl. So mind her. Watch where you step on deck."

Bes's gaze darted nervously to the hen, who fluttered her wings, making her cringe back in her seat even more.

"A-a war? Over a chicken? Are you… You're teasing us, Lord Tam." Hamil tried to smile good-naturedly, but he also pointedly avoided looking at the chicken again.

Lord Tam shook his head somberly. "Not at all. Very bad things will come about if *anything* happens to that chicken."

He turned as though meaning to walk away and let them stew on that ominous note, but Bes couldn't resist asking, "What about the cat?"

Lord Tam froze. Then, looking over his shoulder, he responded, "He's his own force of nature. I'd avoid annoying him. And maybe hide your shoes somewhere safe at night just to be sure."

Bes opened her mouth to demand an elaboration, but Lord Tam had already placed a sizable distance between them.

Silence filled the air, until Hamil slowly inclined himself over to Bes and said, "I really wish he would've taken the animals with him if he was going to be so frightening about them."

Bes didn't dare take her eyes off the chicken. "What if neither of them are that giant winged beast, and it's somewhere else on this ship?"

Hamil's jaw flexed. Then he whispered, "Let's snoop a little belowdecks when we go hunting for that watch."

Bes would've said something along the lines of *I told you so* in reference to her concerns for their safety. But she found remembering to breathe a little troublesome as she was locked in an unfortunate stare-down with the chicken that could allegedly start a war.

"Hamil, might I have a word?"

The Lobahlan turned around and did his best to cover his yawn.

"How may I help you this afternoon, Lady Eli?" He smiled pleasantly as the noblewoman approached him in the ship passageway. A post-lunch nap had been his objective.

Lady Eli did not smile back at him.

She wasn't the warmest of people, Hamil surmised.

"I… I was wondering if you might tell me a little more about that trinket that Penelope pulled out during Luca's birthday."

Hamil stiffened. "Erm. I'm sorry to say, my lady, I really don't know anything—"

"I'm scared."

The declaration was said with only a slight hitch in an otherwise level voice.

Blinking, Hamil lowered his chin slowly. "Are you… Are you scared of the chicken?"

Lady Eli's eyebrows twitched. "No. This has nothing to do with the duchess. I'm scared of what that device does. My husband acquired it in Zinfera, but we have no idea what it is, and despite my cautioning him against taking it, he did."

Hamil carefully folded his arms as he listened. Lady Eli spoke in an odd way. Though she seemed to always talk in this direct, even manner, at present it sounded like she was *trying* to inflect emotion into her tone. It reminded Hamil of some of his father's assistants or advisers.

"I see." He nodded along to make sure he seemed to be listening interestedly.

"So." A tic of annoyance flitted over her face. "I could tell that you and Bes knew what it was, and what it might do, and I would appreciate you telling me if it is dangerous."

An unnatural look overcame the lady then. Her eyes were becoming squinty, and she breathed a little heavier through the nose. Was she trying to cry? Or was she trying *not* to cry?

Either answer made Hamil want to inch backward away from her. "Erm, well, as I said, I-I really don't know anything—"

Outright irritation flattened Eli's face. "Did you ever stop and think how *you* might also be in danger from the device? If you really don't know anything about it, why are you so calm?"

She advanced on Hamil, making him throw his hands up in the air and say, "It looked harmless enough to me! What power could a tiny brass watch have?"

"A watch?" Eli stilled.

Hamil cringed.

Damnit.

"What's a watch?"

"Ah… erm… it… tells time."

"Like a sundial?" Eli pressed, making Hamil retreat until he felt the wall of the ship's passageway behind himself.

"Y-yes, but it's more specific than that. It breaks down the ascension of the sun and the moon into increments. Hours. Minutes. Seconds."

Eli tilted her head interestedly. "I have heard people say, *Give me a second,* but I'm not aware of where it comes from."

"Yes," Hamil nodded. "That is a Lobahlan phrase. Usually they mean that they need more than a second but… you know."

Eli stared blankly back at him, which indicated to Hamil she did not, in fact, know.

"So… do you… feel… better? My lady? It's just a device that tells time."

"It sounds incredibly useful. To measure something so accurately. But would it not be null and void when the days grow shorter in winter?"

"Not at all. It helps us measure how long we need to last until spring comes again by offering a constant marker to reference when the days start getting longer and shorter—though I'm told Lobahl has different season lengths and temperatures compared with other kingdoms."

"Hm. Why are you and Bes nervous about the 'watch'?" The lady wagged a finger at Hamil curiously. He suddenly had the very unpleasant memory of being interrogated by his nanny whenever he'd gotten into mischief growing up.

"We aren't nervous!" Hamil heard himself declare a little too quickly.

He watched with sinking dread as Lady Eli's eyes narrowed.

She didn't say anything, merely stared at him. But when he was not more forthcoming, she evidently decided he needed more persuading. "Need I remind you the purpose of this conversation? I want to know if this watch could be dangerous."

Hamil's heartbeat quickened. There was a predatory glint in Lady Eli's eyes that reminded Hamil of a large animal becoming irritated with its dinner. He would've taken his beloved nanny at this point.

Why are these foreigners and their pets so damn scary?

"It's just… some… people. In the past. Have made watches… magic."

"Yes, the first witch has a device that stops time by using mage crystals. Do you believe this watch can do the same?"

Hamil silently begged the Goddess for divine intervention.

Bes was going to kill him…

"Eli?"

I'm saved!

Lord Tam appeared at his wife's side.

"I'm surprised you are *here*. Having a chat… with *Hamil*."

Oh Goddess, no…

The nobleman's dark eyes swiveled curiously over to him.

"I happened across Hamil's path," Eli informed her husband tightly.

Lord Tam fixed his unwavering attention on Hamil. "And what were you two talking about?"

Hamil widened his eyes and hoped that the lady would understand that she really shouldn't relay any of the private Lobahlan information—

"He was telling me that the device we have might be dangerous, as it seems similar to the first witch's. He called it a watch. It measures time in increments, though I'm not exactly sure the breakdown of time yet. He was about to tell me if he thinks the watch can do more than just that."

Tam nodded slowly as he listened, but he did not look away from Hamil. He didn't even blink!

The Lobahlan could feel sweat building over his lip.

Lord Tam lifted his chin; his eyes became cast in shadow as a result. "How about we all go into my and Eli's cabin and have a bit of tea while we chat, hm?"

Hamil barely resisted a whimper.

He was starting to suspect he may have to part with a lot more knowledge than he had any authorization to…

And that meant that if Bes didn't kill him before they got home, then his father most certainly would.

CHAPTER 14

THE FORGOTTEN FEW

Ansar's nails dug into his palms.

His boots scraped against the gravel of Wixim's cave as he paced. "It's been a fortnight since Aradia disappeared. How has she not returned?"

The golden dragon's eyes cracked open from his spot curled up on a large rock.

Wixim sighed. He missed Harris.

"Mr. Ansar!"

Spinning around toward the call, his gaze landing on one of the Daxarian witches who had joined them, Ansar straightened in expectation.

"Our informant from the palace sent a missive saying the Daxarian queen left a few days ago to come after us," the witch relayed grimly.

Ansar's jaw worked as he tried not to lose his temper. "Have we received any word from the Coven of Wittica about sending a ship?"

"No news yet," the witch said.

Ansar looked toward Wixim, his frustration bright in his brown eyes.

The dragon stared back, bored.

"You couldn't have just eaten the queen?" Ansar asked tightly.

A low growl rumbled in the back of Wixim's throat. If the human thought it was so easy battling the burning witch, he was welcome to try it himself.

"Alright. We'll start to pack up. Wixim, you will fly us to Haeson. We'll commandeer a ship of our own and head toward Daxaria. You will come with us."

Wixim slowly lifted his long neck until he could glare down sufficiently at Ansar.

He hadn't really cared about the human who allied himself closely with Aradia. He loved her—that much was obvious—and he took good care of her. However, Wixim had little patience for delicate beings giving him attitude when they should be grateful for his help. If Aradia did not return soon, he may have to think again about joining the devil's side of their centuries-long feud.

Ansar stared back up at Wixim, unperturbed by the show of warning.

Wixim snarled, then before he could have time to react, the dragon swooped down and wrapped his mouth around Ansar.

He didn't bite, but he did lift his head up and shake the human around in his mouth before spitting him back down on his cave floor.

The Daxarian witch who had remained in the cave and seen the whole thing squeaked as Ansar let out a loud groan from the drool pool he found himself sprawled in.

Ansar coughed several times, struggling to come to all fours. When he did, and he finally managed to open his eyes, he discovered Wixim's green gaze boring into him, mere inches from his face.

Wixim huffed, sending Ansar's wet hair fluttering back.

He watched the drenched human take a fortifying breath, his shoulders slumping forward.

"Sorry."

Wixim waited.

"I'm sorry that I was rude to you. Will you please help us get to Haeson?"

Wixim tilted his head and tapped his claw.

It took the human a few moments to guess what the dragon was waiting for him to say.

Ansar looked over his shoulder at the witch, who was wringing her hands. "Leave us."

She bowed quickly and practically bolted from the cave.

Shaking his hands in an effort to dry them, Ansar stepped away from Wixim before rounding back to face him, his former brusqueness gone.

"We need reinforcements. Especially when Aradia reappears. Waiting around for her to come back means risking being caught," Ansar explained. "I don't like leaving her alone here anymore than you do. But getting her back with just who we have now—yourself included—isn't enough. Not with the Daxarian queen in the Zinferan palace and the concubine no longer of use to us."

Wixim took a moment to consider this reasoning.

While he was by no means pleased about the idea of abandoning Aradia, her companion was right.

"I recommend you come with us to Daxaria."

Wixim's head came up.

"I'm going to send another missive to the Coven of Wittica to try and get them to intercept Tamlin Ashowan. He needs to be captured and held with the boy until Aradia can get her hands on them."

Another rumble rolled out of Wixim.

Ansar paused at this. "I didn't say we should hurt them. Not unless Tamlin fights against us," he added with a bit of poison in his voice.

While Ansar was reasoning out their next steps perfectly well, Wixim knew that the human's intense hatred toward the Ashowan family was unlikely to resolve itself, even once Aradia had returned.

Wixim readjusted his position on the rock, crossing his scaly legs over one another. Regardless of how Ansar felt, he had made a serious oversight. Wixim stared at him, hoping he would realize the fact.

Ansar frowned up at Wixim, evidently not connecting the dots. "So will you come with us?" he pressed.

Sighing, Wixim dropped his head in frustration but gave a slow nod.

Ansar frowned. "Is something wrong with my plan?"

Wixim nodded again.

"The part about going to get help?"

Wixim shook his head.

"The part about you coming with us?"

Again, Wixim indicated that this was not the issue.

"About arranging the coven to capture Tamlin Ashowan?"

Wixim raised a claw and tapped his nose in confirmation.

"What about it?"

The dragon gave Ansar a flat look in response.

The human appeared equally irked by their difficulty in communicating.

In the past, Aradia had relayed Wixim's responses. Her absence was far more annoying than Wixim had imagined it could be.

"You don't think I should try to capture Tamlin Ashowan... Is it because you think he is too powerful?"

Wixim tilted his head side-to-side.

"Is it because you worry the devil will get hurt in the process?"

Wixim made the same motion with his head to indicate that this was also part of the issue, but not the main one.

With a great sigh and no small amount of shelving his dignity, Wixim lifted himself onto his hind legs and mimed the shape of a dome.

"I don't... know what that means."

"Hrr," Wixim grumbled.

Then he mimed holding a frying pan, shaking it, and tossing something in the air.

Ansar watched blankly.

Wixim tried stirring an imaginary pot.

Ansar blinked.

A quiet roar echoed out of Wixim before he cradled his arms together as though rocking a baby, then puffed his chest up.

Ansar's eyebrows shot toward his hairline.

"Tamlin Ashowan... is going to have another baby... ?"

Wixim was tempted to eat Ansar for real.

Luckily, Ansar belatedly put the pieces together. "The house witch! Tamlin's father!"

Wixim flopped back and nodded.

"You're worried what the house witch will do if he learns his son is captured. I see. Well, that would only be a real issue if the house witch was aware of his son being taken by the coven. His wife and children are at large, and thanks to both of the covens' interference with the missives to and from the monarchies, they have next to no information."

Wixim wanted to caution Ansar not to underestimate the house witch, but he doubted he'd be able to act out the intricacies of his point so that the human could understand.

The house witch had been favored by the Gods, and so any interference from him could lead to greater problems than they could manage. Even with two covens at their backs. Fate that was already woven was hard to pull free of.

"We'll leave after sundown for you to bring the first group of witches to Haeson. I will wait behind with a few others. I know it isn't likely, but I am hoping Aradia reappears before you come back for the last of us, and while the Daxarian queen is out in the forest we can simply stop by the palace and pick her up." A sad smile touched Ansar's face.

Wixim knew that despite the human's optimism, Aradia was not likely to reappear. Not that he had specific reasons, aside from the fact that he knew Tamlin was powerful.

But there was no point in trying to convey this to Aradia's companion, and so he watched the young man leave the cave.

Settling back down on his rock, Wixim slowly closed his eyes again.

While he still didn't relish in the idea of fighting with Elisara, he *was* looking forward to the chance to get a sort of revenge on the house witch's blasted cat, who had called himself an empurror.

Kraken the cat would, if Wixim had his way, learn in the near future that ancient beasts were to be respected without question.

At the very least, the little hairball would definitely think twice about swatting at his tongue.

Thomas Julian sat outside Wixim's cave, his eyes fixed on the ground as the witches gathered anxiously around the bonfire, whispering amongst themselves.

He wondered if it had occurred to them that even if Aradia returned from wherever Tamlin Ashowan had sent her, they would not win the war. The sound of heavy footsteps echoed up to the mouth of the cave, and Thomas didn't need to look to know Ansar was coming out to share the new plan with everyone.

I'm finally going home… Thomas thought somberly, his brown eyes lifting to the sky.

Ever since he had betrayed Eric Reyes, the current king of Daxaria, Thomas had been in hiding in Troivack with Penelope's parents and Ansar. It had been more than seven years since he had seen his own parents, siblings, or Uncle Likon.

But the time was drawing closer. He could feel it. The moment when his years of living in fear, of being discovered as a hidden ally of Daxaria's monarchy, would finally come to an end. He had made the decision to hide with the first witch's people when they approached him for information during his time working as Eric Reyes's assistant. When Ansar had originally approached him, he had wanted to report the occurrence to the then-prince, but then…

He had thought of his Uncle Likon — of how he had taught Thomas to gather information, to wait patiently for the right opportunity to bring down villains. Something in him had known. Known this was his fate.

I just hope I get the chance to be of use before the Ashowans save the world again.

A low, throaty sound drew Thomas's attention as Wixim poked his head out of the cave. The dragon was staring at him, which startled Thomas. He hadn't noticed the ancient beast's arrival. He was used to blending into the background and being unnoticed. There was an air of wisdom around the ancient beast that made Thomas Julian internally squirm, no matter how much he tried to ignore it.

Wixim held Likon's gaze, a most unnerving air of knowingness around him, but then the dragon turned and continued to make his way out of the cave without so much as another blink.

Thomas let out a shaky breath.
Soon. Soon it would be over, and one way or another, he would finally be able to exist in peace.

"A bit of a wider footing… There you are!" Captain Taylor cajoled.

A sweeping arch of a wooden sword through the air was met with an encouraging whoop from the sidelines.

It was a beautiful summer day, and Antony was receiving some rare attention from the captain of Daxaria's military to work on his sword training. The boy smiled for the first time in what felt like weeks.

Before she'd left, the queen had taken on the task of educating her sons in swordsmanship, but since she had been in Zinfera, their studies had fallen to the wayside.

Antony reset his feet, intending to repeat the move he had just executed, when a knight rushed forward.

"Pardon me, Captain Taylor, but His Majesty and Lady Mackenzie are requesting your presence."

"Ah. Excuse me, Your Highness."

"We only just started!" Antony called dejectedly, the tip of his wooden sword falling to the dirt.

Captain Taylor smiled apologetically. "It may only take a moment. Mind continuing to practice what I just showed you?"

Antony's lips pressed together.

He battled against complaining. He'd been told time and time again that things were very busy for his father's council, and with his mother away, things were especially tough.

So he didn't say anything.

Even though his throat tightened.

The captain was already striding out of the training ring, leaving Antony alone with his training dummies as the knights around him worked on their own. He stared down at the ground. What was the point in learning swordsmanship? It wasn't like they were going to let him be king, anyway. Even if he wanted to become the captain one day, wouldn't Daxarian citizens have a problem with that as well as it was a position of power over humans?

It was all confusing, and it made him angry.

The pleasant breeze that had been weaving its way over the ring strengthened, and the wispy clouds above started to thicken. Antony could feel tears starting to burn his eyes. He didn't understand what was going on, and the grown-ups didn't like answering his questions.

Maybe he should just run away. It wasn't like he was that important anymore, anyway. His own father barely had time for him or his brothers aside from bedtime. During the day, the only people they really got to talk to were their teachers. Grandpa tried to see them at breakfast, but he was worried about Grandma…

And Uncle Tam was gone.

The temperature in the ring continued to lower as the clouds above let out an ominous rumble.

A few of the knights near Antony turned their sights to the sky in confusion. But then one of them glanced at the prince.

"Your Highness? Are you…"

"I'm fine!" Antony snapped.

A crack of thunder that sounded like it shattered the sky rang out, making the earth tremble.

The men all took a step back, and Antony felt more wretched than ever.

Barely swallowing past the lump in his throat, he turned on his heel and hurried over to the exit to the training ring, his ears burning.

He'd run away.

He'd hide. Then he wouldn't get upset and make it rain anymore.

Maybe he'd come back once his ma was home.

"Hey, Antony!"

He'd just set foot on the bottom step of the castle when he heard Charlie's voice. Looking over his shoulder, he saw both Charlie and Asher bolting toward him, coming from the direction of the kitchens. "Hey," he said glumly when his brothers skidded to a halt.

"We were going into the forest to play dragon and knights! Want to come?" Asher asked brightly.

"We heard thunder, though, so maybe we can play in the greenhouse!" Charlie suggested, turning his grin to his oldest brother.

Antony's grip on the handle of his wooden sword tightened. He debated not telling his brothers his plan, but… something Uncle Tam had told him ages ago sprang to his mind.

Your brothers are your first friends. Hang on to them as best you can. Listen to them and make sure they listen to you.

"Hey… Charlie? Asher?"

"Yeah?" Both Charlie and Asher tilted their heads in an identical manner as they answered in unison.

"I'm gonna run away. Want to come?"

Charlie and Asher paused in surprise.

Antony felt his heart slam against his chest. They were going to tell on him. He just knew it! Then he'd have to hear a lecture from his grandpa and father about—

"Sure! You pack our clothes, Asher gets the food, and I'll go make up a story to tell Grandpa Norman about why we'll miss dinner!" Charlie plotted seamlessly.

All at once, relief and gratitude swelled in Antony's chest.

He struggled not to cry as a comforting warmth seized him. "I'll… I'll also steal some maps so that we… so we know where to go."

"How about Sorlia? It's the most fun!" Asher crowed delightedly.

Charlie grinned. "And if the grown-ups catch us, we can just say we were moving before them to help! We're supposed to go there anyway, right?"

Antony couldn't help but smile back at his brother. "Right." He then looked to Asher. "Don't just steal cookies for this, okay? We need meat and bread. Cheese! Maybe apples."

Asher's mouth pursed in displeasure and vexation. "But *some* cookies, right?"

"Some," Antony agreed with a nod.

Then Antony put his hand on Asher's shoulder. Charlie put his hand on Antony's, and Asher put his on Charlie's.

It was their secret way of agreeing on a plan before breaking up to see it through.

The three boys nodded to one another, and then, without another word, they all marched off to complete their tasks, not once doubting that this was a spectacular plan.

CHAPTER 15

DEVIL IN THE DETAILS

T am drummed his fingers once over the surface of the table in his and Eli's cabin.

Hamil gulped.

Eli's stare bored into his face.

"Look, I-I really shouldn't be telling you anything! It's bad enough that I've already shared this information!"

"You called this—" Tam held up the brass device from its chain, making it swing like a pendulum. Hamil's eyes tracked the movement nervously. "—a watch. Why? Why a watch?"

"Because we… We watch the time. It is how we organize appointments. Our lives. Jobs. Even our doctors use it for—"

"Doctors?" Eli interrupted interestedly.

Hamil clamped his mouth shut.

Tam and Eli shared a look.

"Is this dangerous?" Tam leaned forward, holding out the device toward Hamil, who gave a subtle flinch. He didn't respond.

Neither Tam nor Eli spoke. Merely studied him with unclear emotions.

The ship deck rocked beneath them more noticeably than it had that morning. Thus far the voyage had been filled with mostly sunny days and the occasional drizzle, but the captain had predicted that they were due for a storm or two.

"We were told this could not do anything. But given the circumstances under which we received it, it isn't out of the question to assume that something *could* be done with it," Tam said quietly. "Daxaria and Zinfera are at war with their covens and the first witch, Hamil. We need every advantage."

"*You're* a witch!" Hamil burst out before he was able to stop himself.

Tam arched an eyebrow. "I am. But I am brother to the queen of Daxaria, and the methods the covens are using to separate themselves from the Daxarian and Zinferan monarchies are not acceptable. They've aligned themselves with the first witch, who has cost a great many people their lives, and more."

Hamil relaxed. "The first witch has her reasons. Your sister has killed countless people herself. Who the villain is depends on which side you stand on." He shrugged.

Both Eli and Tam stilled. "So in the war, you would side with the first witch."

Hamil grimaced. "I didn't say that. I'm just saying there isn't an easy good-versus-evil scenario in most wars."

Tam's lip twitched. He jerked his hand again, sending the watch swinging, making Hamil jolt backward.

"What. Does. This. *Do?*"

"You yourself said the first witch has one that stops time!"

"That isn't what this one does, or she wouldn't have had another built," Tam argued.

"Then I don't know!"

"*Then look at it!*"

Hamil cringed away.

Regardless, Tam seized Hamil's hand and pressed the watch into his palm.

Hamil yelped an objection, but when nothing happened, he stopped. Then, carefully peeling one eye open, he looked at the watch in his hand.

When he was certain it wasn't about to explode sometime during his next breath, he tilted his head in curiosity. Bringing it up closer to his face, he squinted at its back, then pressed the button to make the brass cover spring open.

"Hm." He held the device up to his ear. "What're the odds you have something that can unscrew the back?"

"There aren't screws on the back. Only on the hinges," Eli reminded him.

Intrigued, his former panic forgotten, Hamil started fiddling with the top button. He twisted it a few times. Paused. Then lifted the watch to his ear to try again. "Huh."

Lowering it once again, he unscrewed the top button until he could pull the long pin out. Then he laid it delicately onto the table and removed the glass covering the numbers and notches.

He stared at the bare face of the watch thoughtfully for a moment before pinching the tiny nub that the two spindles on the watch were attached to. He twisted until that, too, popped off.

Carefully, he turned over the watch in his palm, and the face came out. Hamil set that on the table beside the pin. All that remained in his hand was the watch's brass shell and a thin layer of gears.

And below the gears… was an empty groove. As though something was missing from that spot.

Hamil let out a large breath of relief. His free hand coming to his chest.

"Well?" Eli asked expectantly.

The Lobahlan gave a small start. He had forgotten he wasn't alone. "This watch can't do anything magical. It doesn't have a crystal."

"A crystal?" Tam straightened in his seat.

Hamil looked at him sardonically. "Yes. Please tell me the other kingdoms at the very least have crystals."

"The mages do. I mentioned them before," Eli supplied, narrowing her eyes at the perceived condescension.

"Aah… mages?" Hamil was unsure what she was referencing. "Wait! No! Mages! Yes! That's what engineers were called ages ago!" He chuckled. "We call them engineers in Lobahl. They power the crystals to help the city run. Things like hot water, air control for the summer months, water purifying, toilets, and—" Hamil stopped himself, clearing his throat.

Tam and Eli looked at each other. Again, whatever they were thinking or trying to convey to each other was unclear to Hamil.

"If this watch had a crystal, would it stop time?"

Hamil stared at them flatly. "Weren't *you* the ones who just said that if it worked that way, the first witch would've used it?"

"So she would've known it needed a crystal to work." Tam lowered his gaze to the table.

"Why did you keep holding it up to your ear?" Eli wondered, her even stare not wandering from the Lobahlan.

"Watches tick. They make a regular, measured noise as the cogs work."

Her eyes gleamed with interest.

Tam chuckled as he looked at Eli. "You really want to be even more organized with your time, don't you?"

She blushed tellingly, and Hamil found he couldn't help but smile a little at the genuine affection between the couple. Maybe they weren't as terrifying as he thought they were. Maybe they really were just scared and had stumbled upon—

"Where did you say you got this again… ?" Hamil prodded.

Eli's and Tam's stony expressions returned in an instant. They didn't reply.

Hamil leaned forward and didn't disguise his indignation. "I've shared a lot with you! Why can't you just tell me that? I'm just worried that someone is illegally making things that can stop time!"

As Tam leaned back into his seat, he moved his hands into his pockets.

"A dragon gave it to us. Along with a sword that turns the wielder younger by twenty years, and a whistle."

"Oh." Hamil nodded slowly, then paused. "Which dragon?"

Neither Tam nor Eli masked their surprise.

"What do you mean, *which* dragon?" Eli's voice jumped an octave.

"I mean… odds are I haven't heard of them. No one really wants to go to the mountains and count how many we have spilling out, but you never know. One with a device is probably one of the ones that—What?" Hamil balked at their gaping mouths. "What did I say?"

"There are *multiple* dragons in Lobahl?" Tam spluttered.

Hamil opened and closed his mouth.

Damnit.

He hated to admit that his father had been right. It really was important that people who ventured out into the world be trained on how *not* to share literally all of their secrets.

"W-well. I… I assume so. No one really goes near the mountains. Like I said. There's nothing but the desert north of the city, and then the Romethio Ocean past the mountains, so it isn't as though someone is going to get a head count."

Neither Tam nor Eli looked like they bought that for an instant.

"Tell us about the dragons and we'll tell you which one gave this to us." Tam's gaze had turned to steel again.

Hamil eyed the door. He could just try to leave.

"That won't go well."

His head snapped around to stare at Tam with wide eyes. A pulse of fear shot through him, prompting a fresh swath of sweat to form on his brow.

"Tell me," Tam ordered quietly.

"O-or what?"

Tam looked over his shoulder at Eli, who appeared a little wary. Was Hamil imagining it, or had Tam just winked at her?

"Or we'll tell Kraken to sleep in your cabin and take extra-special care of you."

Hamil scowled. "He's a cat. I think you just made up all those things earlier on deck to use him against me."

An unnerving smile lifted Tam's mouth. "Believe what you want. Just don't make me talk to the chicken."

Hamil stood without hiding his indignation. "Honestly. This is the thanks I get? I come in here, give you answers to your questions—"

"We had to pry them out of you. This was potentially a dangerous device, and you weren't going to give us any kind of warning even after we saved you." Tam rose to his feet, his towering height making Hamil take a single step toward the door.

"There are *children* aboard this ship," Eli added sternly as she, too, came to her feet.

"W-we just assumed that you both knew you were tampering with things you shouldn't! It's bad manners to shove your nose in someone else's business!"

The couple drew closer to Hamil as he continued taking every inch he could toward the door.

"Don't you want to know which dragon gave this *watch* to us?" Tam asked while picking up the brass cover and its affixed cogs in his hand.

"Not that badly I don't!" Hamil swung around and desperately seized the door handle, only for Tam's large hand to appear in front of him, holding it closed.

Hamil shrank against its surface. He turned to see Tam staring down at him with an unnervingly calm expression. The Daxarian really hadn't seemed that large before…

"Would you feel better if my wife ordered us some tea and it was just you and me having a chat?"

Hamil opened and closed his mouth. He remained pressed against the door. "I-I am the son of the Judge of Lobahl. I know you do not understand what that means, but I am—"

"Hamil…" Tam leaned down, and Hamil couldn't help but develop a mild case of trembling in both of his knees. "I've pissed off an immortal daughter of the Gods. The rank of a person doesn't scare me that much these days."

Steeling himself, Hamil tried again. "Even if hurting me means war with Lobahl?"

"No one knows you and Bes are here, Hamil." Tam's voice was a whisper.

"So you'll kill me if I don't tell you what you need?"

"I never said that. I merely warned you not to make me tell the chicken."

"Why do you smell so good?" Hamil uttered distractedly.

Tam's face turned blank as he fell into what Hamil could only assume was a puzzled silence.

Hamil clamped his lips shut. He hadn't meant for that thought to slip out. But he was alarmingly drawn to the scent of mint and frankincense. It made it difficult to focus on the ominous atmosphere the Daxarian nobleman was expertly constructing.

Clearing his throat awkwardly, the Lobahlan tried to reclaim his earlier righteous indignation. "What you're suggesting, Lord Tam, is that I won't be going back home to tell people what you've done!"

Overcoming his earlier bafflement, Tam laughed softly. "Because I'm willing to bet you're going to get a lot more caught up in what's happening with the two kingdoms than you realize. And as a result, a mild… *warning…* is most likely going to slip your mind."

"I doubt it," Hamil ground out.

Tam smiled, making Hamil frown. "Hamil, there are two things you should know. The first? Daxarians also share the belief that some encounters are by the hair of the Goddess."

At the mention of his homeland's belief that people were tied together by a hair of the Goddess herself to weave fate, Hamil's countenance softened ever so slightly.

"And the second thing?" Hamil asked, trying to maintain the façade of confidence.

"You're already doomed by association."

"What? What does *that* mean?" Hamil demanded, his composure already destroyed.

Instead of a verbal response, Hamil watched with shock and dread as the Daxarian's eyes filled with blackness that grew from the center of his pupils to cover even the whites of his eyes.

In the shadows of the cabin, Hamil had thought it was a trick of the light… but then he noticed the silvery dark wisps emanating from Tam. As menacing shadows wavered from his body, what little dim daylight the Daxarian nobleman hadn't blocked out with his body winked out.

Hamil froze.

"It means—" A trickle of playfulness came through Tam's tone that Hamil didn't care for one bit. "—that you, Hamil, son of the Judge of Lobahl, happen to owe the devil a favor."

CHAPTER 16

ADDITIONAL ACCOMPLICES

Crickets sang in the darkness, and a nip in the air suggested that the summer would soon begin to wane. Only one other sound settled over the castle of Austice: quick, light footsteps that could have been mistaken for an animal skittering across the flagstones of the courtyard.

"Oof!"

"Ssh!"

Charlie and Antony turned in unison toward Asher, whose toe had caught on one of the stones, nearly sending him face-first into the ground.

"It's not my fault!" Asher said in a strained tone.

"Come on," Antony said gently, reaching back to grasp his brother's hand.

The boys reached the covered walkway and proceeded down the hallway they knew all too well. It was a risky stretch of the castle regardless of the depth of the night. If any of the serving staff happened to be milling about, they would instantly notice the three princes.

The corridor that led to the servants' dining hall and the kitchens was pitch black, but Antony halted when he heard the telltale sounds of regimented steps.

"Darn," he murmured, sinking back.

"What is it?" Charlie whispered.

"Guards."

"We could leave out a window," Asher suggested helpfully.

"Yeah. Good idea." Antony's eyes darted over to the servants' dining hall. "It'll be easier to find a window down another hall."

And so the boys retreated. When they once again approached the covered walkway, a shadowy figure appeared. The boys gasped in unison.

"There you are," a familiar voice said with a sigh. "I thought you'd already left."

Antony squinted against the shadows. "Ass?"

The thirteen-year-old Aster Fuks, son of Earl Les Fuks and grandson to the infamous Dick Fuks, stepped back into the moonlight, revealing his grinning face. "The one and only!"

"What're you doing here?" Antony demanded after a quick glance over his shoulder to ensure the knights weren't patrolling closer.

"I saw you packing earlier and figured you might be doing something like this."

"And?" Antony asked sharply. "Are you here to stop us?"

Ass snorted, then held out a backpack in front of himself. "I'm here to go with you. You three need someone a bit older to help out."

Antony frowned. "Why would you come with us?"

Ass sighed and slipped his backpack onto his shoulders. "All kinds of reasons. One: I'm supposed to help the princes. That's the role of a good vassal!" Ass turned slowly and started walking down the covered walkway, Antony falling into step at his side with Charlie and Asher behind him. "Two: This seems like fun. Everyone is so serious lately, and it's annoying."

Antony listened and weighed the validity of the older boy's words.

Those reasons did sound like something Ass would think.

"Do you even know where we want to go?" Antony changed topics as they approached a door he'd never entered. Without a moment's hesitation, Aster pushed it open to reveal a room stacked with chairs and tables... and at the back, a tall window.

The older boy strode forward, opened the glass, and gestured toward Antony to climb through while Asher and Charlie closed the door. "I created a diversion in the rose maze, so we should be fine to head south. Were you thinking of going to Xava?"

"Sorlia," Antony supplied, inching toward the window. "What kind of distraction did you use?"

Ass smirked again. He hadn't quite grown into his long front teeth yet, and his dark-green eyes glinted mischievously. "I might have given my grandfather a glass of wine."

"Is that safe?" Antony asked with a frown.

"Didn't you set your uncle on fire during the coronation?" Ass retorted glibly.

Antony cleared his throat before saying, "He asked us to!"

"And my grandpa is always asking for a glass of wine! The physician says it's fine if he has a glass once in a while!"

"Then why was it a good distraction?" Antony demanded next.

"Because it's the full moon."

By this time, Charlie and Asher had joined them by the window and were already clambering out.

Antony waited for clarification on Ass's response.

Sighing, the adolescent finally added, "My grandpa thinks the full moon is the best time to dance naked."

Antony decided he didn't want any more details and jumped out the window. Ass followed. The four boys then set off at a jog toward the King's Forest.

"So..." Ass easily kept up with the princes. "Where in Sorlia do you plan on staying?"

Antony balked. He hadn't thought that far ahead. He'd really only been thinking about escaping the castle unnoticed.

"Right. So I'm sure your family owns property in Sorlia, but if you don't know where it is, I know my father has a place on the water we can go to," Ass announced confidently.

"Okay. That sounds good," Antony agreed while also trying to not make it obvious that he was out of breath.

After reaching the first row of trees, they all slowed down to better watch their footing.

"His Majesty is a decent hunter, and he has the best of the best serving him. How do you plan to avoid getting caught?" Ass continued briskly.

"We'll travel as far as possible tonight, then I'll cover our tracks."

Ass glanced at him in the darkness with a raised eyebrow. "How are you going to cover your tracks?"

Antony arched an eyebrow back, and gave a slow smile.

Thunder rumbled above.

Ass's attention snapped up toward the sky—it had been clear moments before—but then his face split into a beaming smile as he realized Antony was causing it. "Brilliant. The rain should wash away our trail. Alright. Let's go, Your Highness. West is that way."

With a nod, Antony turned to the shadowy woods, though he hesitated when a swaying pine bough drifted ominously out of the dark. Suddenly, no fewer than a thousand fireflies shot toward the boys in a bright, glowing cloud.

Antony recoiled until Asher stepped forward. "Can you help us see?"

Dumbfounded, everyone watched as the fireflies broke off into two groups. One lined the air above, and the other framed a neat path on the ground below that stretched off into the distance.

"Your Highnesses… I'm sorry we all didn't hang out much sooner," Ass managed faintly.

Asher looked over his shoulder at Antony, who grinned back at his little brother proudly.

"Let's go." Charlie plundered on ahead.

Letting out a long breath and ignoring his pounding heart, Antony followed with Asher at his side and Ass behind.

So far, their escape was off to a fantastic start, and with someone a little older along to help, their journey would undoubtedly be a smooth one.

Rain thrummed against the window of Bes's cabin. She lay on her bed, her thoughts adrift among worries for her future.

Her father would probably lock her in her room and put bars on her window after all this. He'd definitely never let her get married or get a job. All because she'd gotten restless. Curious. And Hamil, her childhood friend whom her father had reluctantly allowed to remain near her, had goaded her into going on an adventure.

Closing her eyes, Bes took in a deep breath.

This had all gotten out of hand. First they'd shot past Troivack—too far from Lobahl—and now they were stuck on this ship with Daxarians, who were in a tornado of calamity and magic. As much as the story intrigued Bes, she didn't want to be an active character in it.

We just need to figure out where and what that winged beast is, and whether or not that watch is what I think it is. Then at least we'll know what's going on.

A flurry of knocks jolted Bes from her musings. Sitting upright, she eyed the cabin door warily. Maybe she'd just pretend to be asleep. She didn't think it would be a good idea to go investigating the beast or the watch when the Daxarian family was belowdecks.

However, the pounding grew more and more insistent. Bes sighed. Only one person would unleash such a barrage on her door. So she opened it, intending to give Hamil an earful for being so loud. But she didn't get the chance—Hamil rushed in and shut the door firmly behind himself. He reeked of sweat, and he looked unwell.

"We're in serious trouble."

Coming from Hamil, this declaration made Bes nauseated with panic. "What? Why?"

"That… That nobleman. Tamlin. He isn't… He isn't what he seems," Hamil explained in a furious whisper. "He's the devil!"

Bes stared at Hamil, then slowly lowered herself to sit on the edge of her bed. "Hamil, what do you mean?"

"*I mean he's the actual devil!* Son of the Goddess! Twin of Aradia, the first witch! He is the Beast Sympathizer! The Enlightened Prophet! The Cursed Liberator! *Shall I go on?*"

Bes snorted. "He's not the devil, Hamil. Be serious."

Hamil dropped to his knees in front of her and grabbed her hands. "Bes, I am not jesting. This is too serious to be jesting. I saw his eyes fill with blackness. I saw the darkness with my own eyes. *He called himself the devil.*"

Bes paused as she studied Hamil's face. After giving his sincere tone a little more weight, she replied, "He's a witch. Not the devil. It's possible he is one of the chosen witches who don't have a straightforward elemental power."

"Why don't you think he's the devil? Do you really not trust me?" Hamil implored.

Bes gave him a rueful smile. "I trust you more than I should, but… It's a gut instinct. You know I'm never wrong about that."

Hamil's eyes narrowed. "What I've seen means less than your 'gut instinct'?"

Bes shrugged. "For now it does."

Settling back on his haunches, Hamil crossed his arms. "I guess I won't tell you what I learned about the watch, seeing as you don't trust me."

Bes straightened. "What? You saw it? What is it?"

"No, no! You clearly think I'm a liar or an idiot, so I don't have to tell you anything!"

Bes pursed her mouth.

Then, in a blur of movement, she snatched Hamil's ear and dug her thumbnail in.

"OW! DAMNIT, WOMAN!" Hamil roared.

"Dummy! We are in this mess because of you! You owe me for the rest of your life! What. Did. You. Learn?" She released Hamil. Then, fixing him with an imperial stare, she sat back and crossed her legs and arms.

Rubbing the side of his head, Hamil scowled up at her. "The watch needs a crystal. Until it has one, it can't do anything. It can't even tell time."

Bes let out a sigh of relief. "Thank the Goddess for that. Did you learn anything about the ancient beast hybrid?"

"I didn't. But I think there is a lot more to that chicken than they are letting on," Hamil grumbled.

Bes stared at Hamil's expression and noted the genuine annoyance and anger in his eyes.

"Alright. I'm sorry that I hurt you, and that I don't believe you about the devil. I just… I need to see it with my own eyes. You know that's always how I am," she consoled.

Hamil wriggled his shoulders. "I'm right about him being the devil."

Bes reached out and gently grasped Hamil's chin before turning his head to make sure she hadn't accidentally made him bleed. "I guess I'll just have to wait and find out for myself."

Rolling his eyes, Hamil allowed Bes to inspect his head.

Then, apparently acquiescing that he maybe did owe her, just a little, for the heaps of trouble they found themselves in, he added, "I… *might* have mentioned to the Daxarians that Lobahl has a lot of dragons."

Bes's grip on his chin tightened. "What?"

"I didn't tell them anything else! But they said they got the watch from a dragon! So I accidentally mentioned that—"

"Hamil!" Bes dropped her hand, her eyes wide. "If you tell them too much, they'll imprison you for the rest of your life back home!"

The young man hung his head. "I know. But the jamar can try getting threatened by the devil and see how they fare! Though weirdly enough, the devil kept saying the chicken was worse…"

"Oh, for the love of— I've had it with all this talk about the chicken!" Bes snapped. "And that cat! They are glorified pets and that's that! Now, once we are in Daxaria, we have to write to our fathers, and Hamil, Goddess help you, we're going to have to lie. But until then: Keep. Your mouth. Shut!"

Hamil scooted away from Bes sheepishly, making her tense. "Well, here's the thing…" He rose to his feet and inched toward the door, making Bes stand up with rising panic.

"Hamil… Hamil, what did you do?"

"Bes… Bes, listen to me, Lord Tam really is the devil! A-and we owe him for saving us, so I… I might have… said we'd help him figure out what the watch can do… because it might do something other than stop time."

"*Hamil!*"

"I'll see you at dinner!"

Before Bes could lunge at him again, her friend had bolted from the room and slammed the door shut behind himself.

Letting out a shout of frustration, Bes dropped her face to her hands.

Goddess… Maybe they would've been better off getting killed by the pirates.

CHAPTER 17

COERCION WITH A CAUSE

Smoothing the brilliant-red silk of her skirt, Bes held her shoulders back. She lifted her chin and took deep, steadying breaths.

As the occasional splatter of rain broke free of the sky, Tam watched her from his discreet corner, fighting back a smile.

"Why are you looking at her like that?" Eli asked pointedly at his side.

Tam turned a wry look down at Eli. "Because I can tell Hamil told her about our conversation and she's coming to confront us. She's trying to bolster her confidence."

Eli's brows twitched. She looked over at the Lobahlan woman, whose gaze swept over the sailors. "But why did you smile?"

Tam barely stifled a snort. "Eli… are you jealous?"

She growled in response.

Tam moved his grin back to Bes and waited until the young woman noticed that she was being stared at and gave a small jolt.

"Eli… I smiled because I'm anticipating her coming over here and telling us something useful. I was also thinking how naive she and Hamil seem despite only being eight or so years younger than me."

His sights never left Bes as she made her way over to them, but Tam still heard Eli's grumble of annoyance.

He glanced at her again, his smile turning cheeky. "Do I need to take you back to our cabin and show you that you have my complete attention?"

Her cheeks flamed. "Lusting after someone is—"

"Are you seriously saying I don't love you now?" Tam rounded on her so quickly he startled her into silence.

It took Eli a moment to collect herself. "You left Luca's mother when she was pregnant, how can I—"

"Oh, we are most definitely talking about this later," Tam murmured seriously as Bes reached them.

"Pardon me, Lord Tamlin, Lady Eli." The Lobahlan woman smiled congenially.

Eli made a threatening noise in the back of her throat.

Tam felt a tiny bit flattered—especially as he knew much of Eli's sudden insecurity didn't run particularly deep. He wondered if it had to do with the pregnancy-related mood fluctuations she had described.

"Bes. It's good to see you. Hopefully the storm this morning didn't frighten you."

The Lobahlan woman nodded vaguely. "What are you and your wife doing up on deck, Lord Tam?"

"Oh, just getting a breath of fresh air and checking to see if the kids can come up to play," Tam returned evenly.

"I see, I see…" Bes trailed off awkwardly. "Lord Tam, yesterday, Hamil came to see me after you and Lady Eli spoke with him. He seemed rather… alarmed."

"Did he now?" Tam feigned innocence.

Bes blinked at him; her eyes seemed to twitch with suspicion. "Yes. Might I inquire what your magic is, Lord Tam? He seemed rather misguided in his interpretation of your power."

Tam arched an eyebrow and looked to the sky. "Odd. I didn't really use my abilities around Hamil yesterday. What did he say he saw?"

Bes opened and closed her mouth before glancing at Eli. That was a mistake. Eli looked like she was about to pounce on her. Tam tried to catch Eli's eye and wordlessly remind her they didn't *want* to terrify the Lobahlans, but she didn't spare him any attention.

"Oh, he was saying something silly about you being the devil," Bes announced lightly.

A slow smile moved up Tam's face. "Did he now?"

Bes hesitated. "Well… yes. Yes, he did. I assured him it was most likely your magic that made him see things and that it was a misunderstanding."

"Hm. Eli?" He looked down at his side. "Did I tell Hamil I was a witch, or did I say he owed me a favor and that I was the devil?"

"That he owed you a favor and that you are the devil."

"Right. I thought so, too." Tam turned back to Bes, who had gone rigid.

"You can't be the devil," she said with a breathy laugh of disbelief. A shiftiness in her eyes betrayed her nervousness.

"And why is that?" Eli bit out.

Bes recoiled ever so slightly. "Th-the devil… Uh. He has never been happy. He walks a lonely—"

"I think we're sailing right now. No walking required," Tam interrupted good-naturedly as he drew himself up to his full height. The Lobahlan woman didn't look like she'd be able to form a response anytime soon, so Tam clarified. "Bes, Hamil wasn't being dramatic or making things up. Everything he told you is more than likely true. We will be arriving in Daxarian waters over the next few days, and I'm going to be honest, there may be a lot of dangerous people waiting to intercept us. Part of the reason I told Hamil what I did was so that you both could mentally prepare. I also did it to let you know that you both might be in danger now that you've traveled with us. I can try reaching out to some of my contacts in Rollom to find you a place to stay or connect you with the magistrate, but even so there might be some who want to question you two."

Bes shrank back, her fragile confidence cracking.

Tam held up his hands. "I'm not trying to put you in danger. But you should know what's going on."

"And you should be as forthcoming as possible about the watch," Eli added coolly. "There is enough going on without throwing in a magical device that could be unstable."

"Hamil already told you it needs a crystal!" Bes pinched her lips shut again after her outburst and took a step backward.

Sighing, Tam uncrossed his arms and stuffed his hands in his pockets. "We'll talk about the watch later. But for now, Bes, I'd like to know how you want to proceed."

The young woman's eyes darted between Tam and Eli. Her throat bobbed.

It was at this moment Tam found that he was rather glad that Eli had changed their plan and instead targeted Hamil to interrogate. He felt bad enough making the young woman this fearful already… and they hadn't even reached Daxaria yet.

Henrietta shivered.

She was there. She didn't even need to look to know. The sickening flush through her stomach told her.

"Bok."

Henrietta whimpered. Tightening her shut eyes, she hollered out, "Y-you're only making me think that I'm right for turning you into a chicken in the first place!"

"I think her ruffled feathers might be a little justified."

Henrietta's eyes snapped open.

She hadn't even heard the arrival of Tamlin Ashowan.

But there he was, staring at her through the cell bars, the pale daylight from outside illuminating his face just enough for her to make out his handsome features.

"Buka."

"I can't speak chicken, but I imagine you didn't like the pun?" Tam asked his mother lazily.

"Bok."

"S-she said you're just like your father," Henrietta managed.

Tam's gaze softened, and despite herself, Henrietta felt her heart skip a beat.

"So you can understand her?" he asked.

"I can… though I kind of wish I couldn't," Henrietta said weakly as she pressed herself against the damp planks at the back of her cell.

"Henrietta… regardless of who wins this war, you assaulted my mother with magic. When she was already injured. And was not attacking you."

"She is not a helpless victim!" Henrietta exploded, pointing at the chicken, whose beady eyes would forever haunt her dreams. "The things she's said! The things she has described doing…"

Tam cast a very flat look down at his mother. "Did you really have to go that far?"

"Buka!"

"She says, 'You try being a chicken,'" Henrietta relayed with a croak.

"Look." Tam dropped his head for a moment. "We will be docking in Daxaria in two days. I've no doubt the Coven of Wittica is going to attack us before or after. I do not want my mother defenseless in her chicken form when that happens."

Henrietta swallowed. "I won't change her back."

"So if she accidentally dies, you will be fine with that?"

Henrietta fell silent, and her gut roiled.

This had gotten beyond out of hand.

She had always loved her ability. She used to have the best time playing with her brothers and sisters, turning them into chickens and racing one another… How had it become a weapon?

"I don't want anyone to get hurt," she whispered.

"Is that why you haven't turned anyone else into a chicken? Or is it that you have to touch people to change them?"

"I-I can only turn at most three witches into chickens. It's harder if they're more powerful," she admitted weakly. "I only turned the duchess because Mr. Ansar told me to. If I changed you, I-I was fairly certain your familiar would eat me, and I don't know if it'd even stick with your type of magic."

"While I appreciate not being a part of the poultry family, my side of the conflict with the covens and monarchies is not the one instigating violence."

Henrietta flushed. "This was all supposed to be a—a discussion! A peaceful parting from the monarchy."

"That might have been what they told you it would be. Or maybe it's true for some of the coven elders who agreed to the rebellion, but that has not been how either coven has handled this." Tam crouched until he was closer to Henrietta's eye level. "Henrietta, please turn my mother back into herself. We will release you once we are on Daxarian shores and you can choose what you would like to do from there."

"If you let me go, she'll hunt me down." Henrietta nodded toward the duchess.

This time the nobleman didn't spare his mother a glance. "I won't let her. Henrietta, turn her back before something happens. If you don't, then I'm afraid we won't be able to let you go."

"I-I would just be a deadweight to you! You can't just take me… with… you…" Understanding flooded Henrietta, and with it came tears. "Oh. You'd kill me."

Tam shook his head, holding her gaze. "I wouldn't do that. I'd tie you up somewhere and have you remain imprisoned, yes, but I'm not going to have you killed."

"Why not? You've killed other people before!"

"I have, but they were maliciously trying to attack or imprison me or my loved ones. You… have turned my mother into a chicken. While not the best first impression to make with my family, I'm relatively confident we can look back at this and laugh. A lot. Assuming she gets turned back, and nothing serious happens to her as a result."

Henrietta wasn't convinced. She shifted, her eyes lowering to the floor. Her head was beginning to throb.

Tam waved his hand, drawing her attention back to him. "I have to ask… What is it exactly that has made the first witch so convincing to all of you? What did the Daxarian monarchy not do to support the Coven of Wittica?"

Henrietta shifted on her spot on the ground. "Lord Tamlin, you know that witches are supposed to help maintain balance in the world, right?"

"Of course."

"But… that isn't what we do anymore, is it?" she asked hesitantly.

Tam paused, then slowly seated himself on the ground. "It isn't?"

"Look at your own father," Henrietta continued, her voice steadying. "He should be in a kitchen, cooking food and making a home for people to find rest in. To feel safe in. He is supposed to represent a simple way of life. A balance in a home. He could teach so many people what that looks and feels like;

instead, he's been shoved into the role of a political adviser. He's been tasked with the safety of all Daxaria! Pushing the interpretation of his magic to mean all Daxaria is his home…" Henrietta trailed off. "Your father isn't meant to be a soldier. He is meant to be salvation. But since he has become a diplomat, he can't fulfill his calling."

Tam listened seriously. "Isn't what he does with his magic his choice?"

"Can you honestly say that he is happiest acting as a duke? Attending council meetings? When *is* he happiest? Where is his magic thriving?"

The truth of her words wedged a very rough weight into Tam's chest.

His father had always hated politics. Had always slogged through his work at the behest of his wife…

He felt Henrietta watch him steal a glance at his mother.

Compared with earlier, the chicken didn't look frightening. Rather, there was a bit of a sad droop in her head.

"I grant you, your sister seems perfectly fit to be a soldier. A warrior. But I don't know that she should be queen." At this, Tam opened his mouth, but Henrietta continued, "I don't mean that she isn't a good person, or that she doesn't want to protect Daxaria, but… even from my brief interaction with the queen, she doesn't seem like the type to patiently make decisions. Her power seems to lie in motion and physically heroic tasks."

"There is next to no one who is an absolutely perfect fit to be a king or queen, or in any position of power," Tam argued softly.

"No… But witches are here to do specific things. We have great power for a reason: to do great good with it. But we can't do our best with our power if we are shoehorned into roles that don't fit us." Henrietta paused, a smile subtly pulling at her lips. "I actually met your father once when I was a child. He came to the coven school in Xava. I remember thinking he seemed so tired and stern, until he started making us all lunch outside. I'll never forget that day. We all went for a picnic, and he made our lemonade glasses chase us. Kraken was with him… We all got to pet him, and he even played hide-and-seek with us."

Tam watched the way Henrietta's eyes softened and warmed at the memory.

"I think, Lord Tam, that witches should have an organization that supports them to best explore their powers, and that will help us decide the best way to use the magic the Goddess has gifted us. I think the monarchy should stay human, and that the covens should work closely with them. The majority of the world doesn't understand witches. It'd be nice if witches didn't force themselves into a role because they had no other options."

When she finished speaking, Tam didn't say anything for a while.

Henrietta stole a glance at the duchess, but the chicken wasn't looking at her. She had turned quite still.

"Can I ask… is turning people into chickens really the best power to have in a war?"

The question was a little teasing, and despite the situation, Henrietta couldn't help but smile. "No one knows exactly what I'm supposed to do with this. I do think I'd like to get back to my papa's farm one day."

"I hope you return home one day, too," Tam said softly.

Henrietta nodded in acknowledgment.

Silently, Tam found he couldn't deny the valid points she had made regarding his father's magic and where his powers were best suited. Nor could he bring himself to entirely disagree with her reasoning.

However, these points brought forth a different question for him. What exactly was his own peculiar magic meant to do?

CHAPTER 18

A DIRECT DEFENSE

"G o fish."

"Do you have any… nines?"

"Go fish."

Bes narrowed her eyes suspiciously at Hamil. "Oh really?"

Her friend looked up from his dwindling hand of cards innocently. "Would I lie?"

Luca and Penelope giggled.

"Yes. Yes, you would. Because you always cheat at cards. I just thought you would be on better behavior with the impressionable audience we have," Bes sniped.

Luca looked at Bes curiously. "What's *impressionable* mean?"

"It means you're prone to copy what you see," Hamil answered before Bes could. "For example, you might try to smile at a pretty girl the same way I do to make her blush for fun."

Luca wrinkled his nose. "Why would I do that?"

Penelope loudly sighed. "Can we please keep playing the game?"

Hamil lowered his cards and leaned an elbow on the small table where they played. "You need more fun, Miss Penelope! Enjoy yourself and the day a little more! Otherwise, what's the point of life?"

"Not everything in life is fun," Penelope responded drily while moving some of her own cards around in her hand.

"Well, what do you like to do for fun?" Bes interjected interestedly with a kind smile.

Penelope looked at the Lobahlan woman disapprovingly, making Bes shrink back in both surprise and awe. The look would have made any strict grandmother proud.

"You like playing hide-and-seek with me!" Luca reminded brightly.

"Only because you're actually quiet during that game."

"Don't be mean," Luca said with a frown.

Penelope paused and met his eyes, then with her mouth twisting to the side, she quietly responded, "Sorry."

"Do you like reading?" Bes pressed again, her tone still gentle.

The little girl gave a noncommittal shrug.

"Drawing?" Hamil prodded.

Penelope crossed her slim arms over her chest. "Who cares what I like?"

"We do. We're asking about it because we care." Bes settled her cards in her lap patiently.

The girl narrowed her eyes suspiciously. "Mm-hm."

"I kind of want to know." Luca faced Penelope squarely. "You always play what I want to play, but you don't say what you want to do."

A pink flush appeared in Penelope's cheeks. "I'll tell you later."

"You don't want to tell *us?*" Hamil asked with mock offense.

Penelope shot him a withering stare. "I barely know you."

"We have spent days playing together! You know us quite well!" he argued sincerely.

"People who are desperate for me to trust them aren't usually good people."

The maturity of Penelope's response succeeded in stunning Bes and Hamil into silence.

"Can we keep playing?" Luca swiveled in his seat so that he could once again rest his elbows on the table.

"I just wanted to know what I did to make Ms. Penelope feel so wary of me," Hamil bristled.

Luca's gaze snapped up, and the sudden blankness in his face was entirely out of character. "She doesn't want to talk about it. Let's play the game."

Startled, Hamil neither moved nor spoke until Luca dropped his attention back to his cards. "Goddess, Luca. You reminded me of your father just then."

Luca didn't respond.

Hamil sighed and, cocking a disapproving eyebrow, glanced back at his cards. "I guess at least you didn't threaten me…"

This time, both Penelope's and Luca's gazes rose up to fixate eerily on the Lobahlan.

"Why was my dad threatening you?" Luca slowly placed his cards on the table, the seriousness on his face alarming in more ways than one.

Hamil's eyes rounded. Moments ago, they had been sweet as pie, but now they looked like they were about to punch him in the groin and steal his coin without a second thought.

"What… is wrong with this family?" he whispered to Bes.

She regarded the children thoughtfully. She didn't feel as disturbed by them as Hamil did. "I think this family is frightened, and they've only had themselves to count on. Though I don't know why they are so afraid." She paused. "Especially with that winged beast belowdecks keeping them safe."

"Wha—" Luca started to say in response, his brow furrowed, but Penelope cut him off.

"Our family isn't your business."

Hamil chuckled. "I hate to tell you this, tuts, but your father has been hinting that we might be stuck together for a while yet."

The children shared a look, then turned back to the Lobahlans.

"We'll see," Penelope responded evenly.

Bes shifted uncomfortably in her seat. The children were surprisingly sharp. She would've thought they'd be overly eager to talk about the winged beast on their ship. Which then made another thought occur to her.

"I admit, I'm curious about the large flying cat. Lobahl doesn't have many hybrids of ancient beasts."

"Hy… brid?" Luca sounded out slowly.

Hamil's pointed look at Bes's profile went ignored. She already knew she was going out on a limb revealing this much.

"Ancient beasts sometimes have babies with one another, or even humans, and it makes different animals."

The way Luca's face lit up completely eradicated the ominous shadow that had settled over him moments before. "I know how babies are made! And my dad told me all about imps and sirins!"

There was a beat when both Hamil and Bes struggled not to laugh. "Right, right… So if, say, a sirin and a dragon have a baby, they may have something like a phoenix. Though, again, it's rare. I've never seen a cat with wings before," Bes elaborated while doing an impressive job—in her opinion—at subduing her smile.

"That's because a dragon didn't make Kasha," Luca blurted indignantly.

"Kasha?" Hamil tilted his head interestedly.

"Hey!" Penelope yanked on Luca's sleeve, her finger pressing into her lips. "Ssh!"

"Oh!" Luca pressed his lips together. When he turned back at the Lobahlans, he scowled.

Hamil held up his hands, and Bes gave a nervous laugh. "Sorry. I was just explaining why I was curious about the flying cat. The one I think you just called Kasha."

"Hmph." Penelope set her cards down on the table. "I don't know that I like you two anymore."

"You liked us at one point?" Hamil asked with a teasing grin.

Penelope glared at him, then turned to Luca. "Let's go play somewhere else."

Visibly disappointed, Luca nodded and jumped down onto the deck.

The day was warm, and the sun was out. Off in the distance, everyone was able to glimpse the shadowed outline of Daxaria. As a result, the sailors seemed to be particularly busy that day organizing themselves for their time ashore.

The two children had only just reached each other's sides when a thrumming rush of air made everyone turn. Two women and a man flew in the air just above the ship's rail, and a fishing vessel off in the distance rushed toward them.

One of the women, whose wild black hair was threaded with white, curled a finger toward Luca.

Hamil launched himself from his seat, grabbing Luca right before a rush of air wiped his feet out from under him, making him come down hard on the deck. The move would have easily swept Luca over to her.

"ELI!" Penelope shrieked.

Bes was rushing toward the little girl as the three witches descended onto the ship's deck.

The male witch opened his palm, and a whip of water flew up from the sea behind them and launched forward. Hamil curled himself around Luca. Bes, having reached Penelope, wrapped her arms around her protectively, her back to the witches.

However, the water rope didn't hit its mark. A massive black cat landed between the children and the witches and let out an echoing roar. The witches backed up a single step.

The sight of the beast didn't deter the witches for long. As the water witch summoned three more tendrils of water, the two other witches flexed their hands. One began to float, and the other summoned a fireball…

Only they were interrupted again.

First by a smaller fluffy black cat launching himself at the fire witch's ankles and making her yelp.

And second, by a bellowing cry: "FIRE!" followed by a thunderous boom and the sound of splintering wood. The witches—save for the fire witch, who was losing her struggle against Kraken and was already in the process of falling on her arse—turned and found that the handy fishing boat that had expediently joined them had a new, rather large hole in its hull, stopping it in its place.

Before they could react to this strange new development, the boisterous shout of Captain Sun echoed overhead.

"EVERYONE! I BELIEVE THIS IS A PERFECT TIME TO FORMALLY INTRODUCE THE CANNONS!"

"Well, that explains it," Tam managed between gasping laughs.

"I mean, I know I'm not the most powerful witch, but at least it did something!" Henrietta wheezed.

"I thought it was just some new detail about the kraken we didn't know about!" Tam clutched his stomach as his abdomen ached. "A feathered tentacle… I should've worked it out sooner that it was you who'd done that."

Henrietta wiped away a tear from her eyes as she still continued to laugh. "It's the only reason I got away!" Her good-humored expression dwindled.

She had been one of the few survivors of the sea monster attack when she'd been with the Coven of Wittica weeks earlier. Without needing to ask, Tam could guess that this was the reason for her somber expression. He'd visited the chicken witch often since their initial conversation about the coven's philosophy behind the rebellion, and Tam had learned that Henrietta was a good person who cared a great deal about others and the world. Sadly, they would soon land in Daxaria, and then things would get really messy; Tam wasn't sure what would happen with Henrietta.

He sat with his back on the opposite side of Henrietta's cell, his arms braced on top of his knees. His mother had wandered off at some point during their lengthy conversation. Judging from the dimming light outside the small port window, he could tell dinnertime was nearing.

"I'll change your mother back once we reach Daxaria," Henrietta's soft voice called over the brief span of quiet.

Tam smiled at her, his fingers fluttering against his palm. "Thank you. I'm guessing you're only going to do that after we dock so she won't have time to torment you?"

"I… *never* would've imagined the wife of the house witch would be so scary," she said with a shudder.

Tam chuckled again, his eyes searching the young woman's tired face. "Even scary people need to have someone that cares about them."

Henrietta nodded slowly. "I wish we could be friends, Lord Tam. I don't get along with most people. Even if they're witches."

"I'm seriously judging the people you've had the misfortune of putting up with. You're hilarious."

Henrietta beamed, but the twinkling smile didn't last as her eyes lowered. "You're making me really hate this war."

"You didn't before?" Tam asked wryly.

Henrietta rolled her eyes. "I already told you it's more violent than I thought it'd be."

Tam raised his eyebrows, causing her to make a noise of irritation that reminded him of his sister.

He was just about to say something along the lines of how he had left his children unattended for long enough when a shout rose from above deck with the sound of splintering wood. Simultaneously, a terrifying image came into his mind.

Three witches had come aboard. And they were dangerous.

He instinctively knew that this was one of the first times Kasha had utilized their connection as witch and familiar, and she was sharing this image, trying to tell him to get the hell above deck.

As he leapt to his feet nimbly, his mother darted by with impressive speed, clucking.

Tam briefly touched the knives at his back to make sure they were still securely fastened. He was about to bolt above deck to find out what was happening when Henrietta once again called out, "Is it the coven, do you think?"

"Probably. We're only a day or two away from Daxaria," he responded grimly, already in motion.

Henrietta nodded. Another thud sounded above them. It seemed violence had once again found them. Tam felt his gut roil.

It wasn't quite the homecoming he had been dreaming of having, but it wasn't exactly surprising. He only hoped that at the very least he'd be able to set foot back on familiar land before he suffered any other great problem.

CHAPTER 19

FLYING THE COOP

After the brief distraction of a giant hole blowing through their escape vessel, the witches rounded swiftly back on Kasha.

Behind her, Bes and Hamil ushered the children away. The crew, with cutlasses clutched in hand, cautiously approached the intruders while Kasha swung her great paws at them. She nearly got the best of the water witch. He threw himself against the railing in an effort to dodge her alarmingly large claws. His brown curls flopped against his forehead as he staggered, regaining his balance. However, he did not take this barrage of attacks lightly. With a curling lip, he drew five tendrils out of the water. They whooshed forward, snaking around Eli. The water witch clenched his hand into a fist, and the rope streams tightened, effectively binding Eli down to the deck. If she hadn't braced her paws, she might even have slammed against the planks.

"Get the boy!" the water witch barked at his companions.

The fire witch was still struggling against Kraken on the ground, however, and the air witch was doing her best to carefully step around him.

The water witch continued staring down at Kasha, his eyes narrowing as she struggled against her restraints. "You're nothing but a big cat, Lady Elisara. Do not feel guilty when we take the boy. There is only so much one—"

"BAKAAAA!"

The warrior screech of a chicken broke through the man's monologue, right before a flurry of wings, beak, and claws descended upon him. Scratching, pecking, and wing beating sent him stumbling backward.

"What… ARGH… the hell… is—" He at last seized the chicken by the neck. "Got you!"

However, this alarming attack had distracted the water witch from the much larger animal with the impressive teeth. He had no time to react as the shadow appeared over him and Kasha's great jaw closed around his head. With a subtle flex of her jaw, the water witch went limp. The chicken fell from his hand right before Kasha tossed his body over the edge.

She snarled and huffed at the body as though saying, *Good riddance.*

Rounding over to the fire witch, who was working to free herself from her own feline assailant, Kasha had lifted a paw to knock that witch overboard as well when a child's yelp sounded behind her.

Swinging her head around, Eli spotted the air witch snatching up Luca. Hamil lay unconscious on the deck. Bes screamed at the witch, her arms still around Penelope.

Eli's legs flexed. She would not let the witch get away with Luca, but before she could move, Tam appeared in a rush of black-and-silver aura.

His knife cozied up to the woman's throat, his other arm wrapping around her body, pinning her own arms to her sides and forcing her to drop Luca.

The boy scrambled over to Hamil, grabbing his shoulder and shaking him.

That was all Kasha had time to notice before she heard the meaningful thud of a heeled boot getting purchase on the deck.

Heat gathered in the air over Kasha's shoulder; her fur rose, prompting her to instinctively back away. A stream of fire blasted past the front of her face. Several of the Zinferan crew members scattered with shouts of alarm. Tam yelled. He then disappeared and reappeared in front of the fire witch, with the air witch's wrists still firmly in his grasp. He unceremoniously delivered a chest-height kick to the fire witch, sending her into the sea.

Another boom from below wafted up to Eli, followed by a stinging, smoky scent.

The air witch struggled against Tam, fruitlessly, it seemed. That is until Eli noticed that Tam suddenly looked as though he wasn't able to breathe. Tam responded instantly. The void appeared, and in the woman went.

By the time the void closed around her shrieking face, Tam collapsed on the ground, gasping for air.

Kasha shifted back to her human form.

Crouching beside Tam, Eli rested a hand on his back. "Are you alright?"

Coughing, he managed to nod.

"Holy… Gods… You're… How… *What…* ?"

Eli looked over her shoulder at Hamil. He was sitting up, gaping at her as Bes knelt beside him. She was staring in just as much awe at Eli.

"Are you hurt, Hamil?" Eli called back, ignoring the shock on the Lobahlans' faces.

Neither Hamil nor Bes seemed to be able to answer, so Eli shifted her attention to Luca and Penelope. They were standing back warily near the crew members who had been forced away from the fight when the fire witch had joined the commotion. They looked at Eli uncertainly, then at Tam, who was taking ragged breaths on the deck.

Letting out a long sigh, Eli held out her hand to the children.

Luca took a nervous step forward…

Then two more witches dropped down on the deck: a man who had to be another air witch, given that they were flying, and… Louise Riddel.

The Daxarian coven leader stared down her nose at Tam and Eli.

The air witch turned toward the children.

"Don't you take another step," Eli snarled.

Tam's head came up, and when he registered what was happening, his eyes filled with blackness.

Louise Riddel frowned, but she didn't falter.

She merely raised her hand, halting the air witch in place. She stepped over to Tam and Eli as the two rose to their feet. Eli's attention homed in on the air witch in case he tried to sweep away Luca or Penelope in a gust of air.

Another resounding bang sounded, followed by yet another crunching sound that made everyone turn to find that the fishing vessel was barely above water. Five other heads bobbed just over the waves of the Alcide Sea. The witches that had been aboard the sinking boat.

Eli and Tam's eyes swiveled back to the coven leader, who did not bother masking her ire.

"Captain! I don't think we need any more help from the cannons!" Tam hollered without taking his eyes off Louise Riddel.

Captain Sun was oddly quiet, but Eli didn't hear any additional explosions from the new weapon Jiho Ryu had designed. In the back of her mind, she had to confess that the cannons seemed to be a rather effective weapon to have aboard a ship.

"Lord Tamlin." Louise regarded Tam. He straightened his shoulders, but his eyes did not return to normal as he beheld her.

Eli wondered if he was doing that on purpose.

"You will get off this ship, and if you try to come after my son again, I will not react reasonably," Tam informed her stonily.

The coven leader rolled her eyes. "He is not your son, he is the devil."

"Haven't you heard?" Tam's voice came out a whisper, but there was something strange about it…

Eli tried not to show her surprise when his voice echoed and warbled unnaturally around them all. At times it sounded like he was a breath away from her ear, and yet she could hear his words repeating and fluttering around everyone else on the ship.

Louise Riddel stiffened. Eli guessed she was struggling to appear indifferent.

"I have heard some say that you are the devil, but you will not fool me, Lord Tamlin. I know it is impossible for you to—"

Darkness swallowed the world.

Eli was unable to stop herself from jolting. Tam had somehow managed to bring not only himself into the void, but also everyone who had been on the boat near them—including some of the crew, Hamil, Bes, Penelope, Luca, and the other air witch.

How had he done that? He hadn't even been touching any of them! He'd never been able to do anything like this before.

Luca and Penelope took advantage of everyone's moment of confusion and fear, bolting straight for Tam and Eli.

Grabbing their hands, Eli found that their presence helped steady her once again.

"You can believe what you want," Tam said, the reverberation in his voice only more powerful in the void. "And I can leave you here to decide whatever that may be."

The coven leader's breath hitched, but she held her ground. "You are not the devil."

Tam shrugged. "It doesn't really matter what you think. I hope you enjoy your time here in the void."

Eli glanced nervously at the crew members, who were looking more than a little concerned that they, too, might be left in the vast darkness. She hated that she couldn't outright ask Tam in that moment about what he was doing.

When the world outside the void snapped back into view, things were more than a little problematic. During the time when the crew had been in the void, the sudden shortage of sailors had left it impossible to maneuver the large vessel, which had slammed into the partially sunken fishing boat and damaged their own hull.

"Lord Tamlin! Is everything alright?" Captain Sun was descending the steps from the stern.

Eli glanced over and found that the sailors had indeed returned to the deck, as had Hamil and Bes. The poor Lobahlan woman had already launched herself toward the railing to be sick, though it was a bit tough to reach across the tilting deck. Their ship was listing as it took on water.

"Dad?"

Luca's worried tone drew Eli's attention back to Tam, who was swaying on his feet.

Moving that many people in and out of the void without touching them must have taken too high a toll.

Releasing both Penelope and Luca's hands, Eli slipped her shoulder under Tam's right arm in time for his left knee to buckle.

"Captain Sun, can we make it to shore?" Eli asked as the captain reached them.

The Zinferan was eyeing Tam nervously, but after quickly wetting his lips, he managed to answer. "We might make it to the southern isles, but with the ship as it is, we cannot maneuver the rocks closer to Rollom."

Eli nodded grimly. "Very well. Is there anything we can do to help repair the boat?"

"No, no. The two of you have already— Oop!" Captain Sun ducked and caught Tam's other arm, holding him upright just as his other knee gave out.

Tam leaned drunkenly to the right.

"Dad? Dad, are you okay?" Luca moved in front of his father, fear bright in his eyes.

"He just needs to rest, Luca, alright?" Eli tried to sound gentle, but Tam was actually quite heavy, and her words came out more a grunt. The captain jerked his chin, ushering over a crewman who'd seemed in a stupor after the trip to the void. The sailor moved to help.

The two men continued to assist Tam down the stairs belowdecks, and Eli was about to follow them, but a rush of water hitting the deck made her slowly turn back around.

The witches that had been in the water...

Five of them appeared.

One lifted a hand, summoning up ten tentacles of water. The fire witch, drenched from when Tam had thrown her overboard, burst into flames. Then, once the blaze had dried her, she gathered two balls of fire in her hands. Two of the other witches threw down fistfuls of dirt, and in the blink of an eye vines grew up out of them, flailing about in the air. Suspicious green smoke poured out of the last witch's mouth.

Eli pressed the children down the stairs behind her.

Damnit. I don't know that I can take on five of them. She didn't want to keep turning into Kasha. It was risky enough doing it once without knowing what it would do to the baby.

Regardless of her sinking suspicion that she was not going to win the fight, Eli stalked forward, her hands clenched into fists.

Some of the witches smiled coldly at her, some merely looked serious. Even if she told them she was a familiar, and according to Kraken, hurting her would break some divine law, they looked like they could suppress her without harm quite easily.

Letting out a long breath, Eli braced herself to shift…

When the witch with green smoke coming from her mouth spun rapidly in the air and vanished.

Instead, where she had been standing perched a black-feathered chicken.

Eli blinked, baffled.

The singing waver of steel snapped her attention back up from the chicken in time to see the fire witch fall to the ground with a knife in her neck. Shortly thereafter, the blade was followed by an arrow launching itself into the water witch. Another knife sailed through the vines into one earth witch's chest, followed by another arrow to the other one's eye.

All before anyone could catch a proper glimpse of their assailant.

Eli turned, slowly.

Standing a little to her right, with a compound crossbow resting on her shoulder and an almost bored expression, was the duchess.

As a human.

With Henrietta the chicken witch at her side.

Annika Ashowan stared down dispassionately at the witches littering the deck. "I think I'm a bit rusty. One of them is still alive."

"Of course one is still alive! She's a chicken!" Henrietta squeaked, flinching away from the sight of their fallen adversaries.

Annika Ashowan sighed. "The earth witch also still breathes. But we can leave her alive if you like. It'll be my thank-you for helping."

Henrietta glared.

"Your grace?" Eli could hear the faintness in her own voice.

Annika's attention slid over smoothly to her, and a warm smile touched her face. "Sorry that I was a bit late. Henrietta needed to be persuaded."

A gentle brush of fur around Eli's ankles startled her. Looking down, she found that it was only Kraken staring up at her.

Then she remembered that the children had been right behind her. They should not have witnessed the violence their grandmother had just doled out! Eli sought them out, and instantly a whoosh of breath left her when she realized Luca and Eli stood farther down the steps behind Annika and Henrietta. From their vantage point, they couldn't have seen anything.

"Are you feeling alright?" Annika asked with a note of concern.

Eli swallowed.

Actually, she felt a little dizzy…

"I'll be fine, I'll just go check on Tam."

Annika's eyebrows twitched. "Tell you what. How about you take my arm and we both go see him, hm?"

Eli was starting to feel a headache coming on. Which was the only reason she didn't grumble at the duchess's obvious attempt at placating her like a child.

Instead, she accepted the woman's arm and carefully descended the rest of the steps.

By the time she reached the bottom, Luca was already darting ahead down the passage—presumably to open the cabin door for her—surprisingly, it was Penelope who grasped Eli's free hand.

As she walked, her body feeling a troubling mix of too light and too heavy at the same time, Eli did remember to be thankful for the fact that at least they wouldn't have to worry about Kraken eating the duchess should they be a little bit late feeding him his breakfast.

CHAPTER 20

CATAPULTING INTO CATASTROPHE

Eli watched the duchess regard the cabin she and Tam shared with an appraising eye.

Captain Sun and the sailor who'd helped carry Tam to bed had left, saying they would go retrieve the physician—Hamil was most likely being tended to first, as he had withstood a head injury. Henrietta had been placed in the care of the captain while the two women waited to see if Tam would wake up once more.

"It's interesting," Annika said, still peering at their surroundings.

"What is?" Eli busied her hands with brushing Tam's hair out of his closed eyes.

"As a chicken, I could see more colors."

Eli paused, then turned to the duchess, who had yet to look in her direction. "How curious."

"Quite." The duchess sidled over to the round table that was covered with drawings and notes from the children as they worked on their homework.

"I can tell this one is Penelope's." Annika smiled at the tidy handwriting, the neat lines of addition and subtraction. "And this, Luca's." The paper beside

Penelope's had lots of answers crossed out, followed by a doodle of a cat and chicken. The duchess laughed softly.

Eli said nothing.

At last, Annika turned around to lock eyes with her. "So. You and my son are courting?"

Eli wasn't entirely successful hiding her grimace. "Kind of."

The duchess arched an eyebrow, and sweat flushed up Eli's back.

"Do you plan on getting married?"

"Most likely."

"Then why not say you are courting? Or betrothed?"

Eli almost whimpered. "We've been busy."

The duchess nodded as her sights drifted over to Tam, who appeared to be sleeping quite peacefully throughout this discreet interrogation.

Godsdamnit, Tam. Of course you're asleep for this.

Clearing her throat, Eli decided a change of topic would be best. "Once we land in Daxaria, do you think it will be safe to send a message to the duke?"

Annika's gaze flitted back to Eli. "I'll get in touch with my contacts at the brothels, but a bird would most likely be intercepted given the state of the covens and kingdoms. I don't even think we should go to my estate in Rollom. It'd be too easy for the coven to find us there." She paused. "Can you please enlighten me on what exactly my son's magic is?"

Eli had opened her mouth to ask where she thought they should go next, but was forced to close it and adjust her next words. "That is best answered by Tam."

Annika studied Eli, her emotions unclear before she folded her arms and walked toward the bay of windows. "You know… We've always wondered what about his magic terrified him so much. Fin and I… we'd stay up late into the night trying to deduce what it could be. They say a witch's power is evident to some degree in their personality. Tam was always observant, and he preferred to stay hidden. We wondered if he saw death's carriage driver. Or if he saw something in people that no one else could." The duchess continued peering out over the sea as the deck beneath her boots slanted, a sure sign they were continuing to take on water. She showed no hint of distress. "We've been worried about Tam for more than two decades."

Swallowing, Eli forced herself not to fidget.

Annika rounded back to the bed. "I won't make you tell me. Though this"—she gestured at the bed vaguely—"is unwise if you don't wish to marry."

Eli couldn't hide her twitch.

The duchess smiled. "I'll stop now. I hear the physician."

Eli turned and found that, sure enough, the heavy, clomping footsteps of the man were echoing down.

"I'm guessing that Tam has taxed himself a little too much with his magic. In your familiar form, do you think you'd be able to transport everyone to safety?"

Oh, Gods. How can I explain I'm hesitant to shift unless it is an emergency because of the baby? Her stomach clenched.

The Goddess chose to smile on Eli as the cabin door swung open and the physician stumbled in.

"Lady Elisara! I heard there was a skirmish! I was told your husband fainted, but that it was you who stood against the witches! In your condition, you shouldn't—"

Eli leapt to her feet so hastily that the man stopped talking.

The Goddess, on occasion, had a cruel sense of humor.

Her wild eyes locked on the man, who blinked in astonishment at her reaction.

"Condition?"

The duchess's comment drew the man's eyes upward. "Why, I… Lady Elisara, is this a witch?" the physician asked in a panicked whisper. The man had never laid eyes on the duchess in her human form before.

Eli seized the front of his tunic and flung him toward Tam. "Lord Tamlin is the one who needs your assistance. I am perfectly healthy. And normal. I shall leave you to treat him in peace. Excuse me, I should check on the children."

She fled.

Hurrying down the passageway, her mind instantly tried to reason out the safest place to retreat from the duchess.

The Goddess must have felt badly for revealing Eli's news before she wanted to, as Luca and Penelope charged up to her, providing the perfect distraction.

"Is Dad really okay?" Luca burst out as, he skidded to a halt in front of her.

Before Eli could answer him, Penelope joined his side. "Is the boat really sinking?"

"Yes, and yes. Tam is going to rest, and then we are going to try to land in Rollom. Are you two alright?"

"Yeah!" Luca crowed with a bounce.

"I didn't like the-the void," Penelope announced, shooting a questioning look to Luca as though to confirm she was referring to the black eternal space correctly. While Tam had taken her there once before, she had had her eyes closed.

He nodded and twisted his mouth sympathetically.

Eli reached out and gently cupped both of their faces. "I'm sorry you had to go there. We'll try to avoid you having to return in the future. Now we should most likely start packing."

Luca bobbed his head in agreement, and Penelope's eyes lowered to her toes.

Eli's hands fell from their faces. "What's wrong?"

The little girl's eyes darted around Eli.

She guessed it had something to do with the duchess quietly drifting forward.

"It's just… I finished it this morning."

Eli's eyebrows rose. "Ah. I'm sorry. I'm sure she'll still enjoy it."

"She doesn't need it anymore, and I don't want to give it to the new chicken. She was a bad lady." Penelope's lips quivered.

Pushing past her surprise, Eli knelt down. It was rare for Penelope to show her vulnerability. The stress of the day most likely had worn her out more than she realized.

Annika joined them. "What about the new chicken?"

Penelope hastily wiped at her face. "It's nothing!"

Eli gently clasped her hands in her own. "You can tell the duchess. It's alright."

The little girl's chin was practically pressed into her chest when she said, "I made you a hat. Not… Not you now. When you were a chicken."

"You made the duchess a hat?" Luca interrupted interestedly.

As though saying the words aloud disintegrated the last of her control, Penelope broke out in a sob.

Eli gently rubbed Penelope's arms.

"Oh dear." Annika knelt down beside Eli. "Penelope, I would love to see this hat. And you know, I think I'll ask Henrietta to change me back into a chicken now and then. It was so handy getting to talk to Kraken, I think it'd be great fun to do again. So I can absolutely use that hat in the future."

"Re-really?" Penelope sniffled, her red eyes lifting to the duchess.

"Really." Annika smiled, a telling shine in her eyes. "It means the world to me that you made that. Thank you, Penelope."

The renewed wave of tears from the little girl had Annika pulling her into her own arms, hugging her and comforting her the best she could.

Luca reached over and tugged on Eli's sleeve. "Can I get a hug?"

Smiling, Eli pulled him into an embrace and felt the tension in her body from the fight earlier melt away.

"Eli, will the baby be able to turn into a cat, too?"

Eli's heart clogged her throat.

"You dummy! I said it was a secret!" Penelope exploded, whirling out of the duchess's hold.

"Oh, right! Sorry! I was just asking!" Luca flushed guiltily. "Sorry, Eli! I'm sorry! I didn't mean to tell!" Tears of his own started to mount.

Eli couldn't speak even if she tried with all her might. So she decided not to overthink it and pulled Luca into a tight embrace.

She didn't need to look over her shoulder to know the duchess's eyes were boring holes into the back of her skull.

If the Goddess could make up her mind whether or not she likes me, I'd be grateful.

"I go down for a nap, and next thing I know the boat's sinking and my mother's not a chicken."

Everyone's heads snapped round to see Tam slowly trudging up the passageway, his face pale. The physician hurried past him and even managed to scoot around the children in an obvious effort to flee the Ashowan family. It seemed they really had not made the best of impressions on him.

"Is everyone okay?" Tam asked while his gaze rover over the children. He frowned with evident concern at both Penelope and Luca's tearstained faces.

When he looked up, Eli watched him register the way his mother was gaping at her.

Tam shot Eli a questioning look.

She gulped, and from that alone, she could tell he understood exactly what had just come to light.

Annika's head turned with all the smoothness of a rusty hinge, her eyes flashing up at her son.

He gave a guilty smile while nervously slipping his hands into his pockets. "Ah… So… Would anyone like a cup of tea?"

Aradia opened her eyes blearily and flinched.

She was surrounded by a sea of colors that hurt to look at. She raised a hand to her head, which was already starting to ache. She was lying on a hardwood floor. The smell of incense wafted over her…

Distant shouts echoed farther away from her. She tried to force herself to sit up, but the movement made her dizzy.

"Aradia, first witch, daughter of the Gods. You are under arrest for treason against Zinfera and Daxaria."

Aradia managed a half smile, though she still pressed her fingers into her eyes. "Hi, Kat. It's been a while."

"I wouldn't have minded if it were longer," the Daxarian queen retorted acidly.

Cracking open an eye, Aradia peered up at the redhead, who was flanked by two Zinferan soldiers. "Come now. We never did have a proper night of drinking during our time in Troivack."

"Yeah. Because you arranged a rebellion and war that kept me busy."

"It's important to keep busy. Have hobbies. They make us women so much more interesting." Aradia forced herself to sit up. "Have you ever met a woman without hobbies? She's either barely surviving or boring as dust."

Aradia leaned back on her hands as she continued to adjust her senses to being back in the real world. Had she shifted forms again?

Ah.

Yes.

She now was a young redheaded woman, judging from the lock of hair over her shoulder.

She must have died of starvation or dehydration in the void and regenerated. At least her old clothes still fit this new body. Death must have helped her leave the void. Or Tamlin Ashowan had exerted too much power and she slipped out when he was weak. At present, she was back where she had been standing in the Zinferan palace before Tam had forced her into the prison of nothing.

Rough hands seized Aradia under her arms and hoisted her up. She yawned.

The Daxarian queen stepped forward as though intending to search her. If she did, that would be a problem. Aradia's vials of water from the Goddess's Pool, which would help her wield magic once more, were still stowed within the inner pocket of her coat.

The first witch made a show of appearing as tired and weak as possible. "Before I get locked up for eternity, and so on, mind telling me how your brother came to be the devil?"

Kat froze. "He's not the devil."

Aradia allowed a smug smile to tug at her mouth. "He said he was. He wields darkness and fear, from what I can see. I just don't know how the devil managed to put himself in the Ashowan household for so long. Did he simply kill off the real Tamlin Ashowan?"

Kat slapped her.

Aradia had expected she'd do as much, and so she reached up to touch her face and didn't lower her hand instantly. If she moved casually, she could grab the bottle and down its contents without being stopped.

"My brother is not the devil. He has been by my side since the day I was born. Your own brother is somewhere off in the world. I don't know where."

"Oh, so you are absolutely certain that the child is his own, too?" Aradia asked lazily.

Kat's eyes narrowed, then she looked at the guards.

Now!

Aradia's free hand snatched the bottle inside her coat. She flicked out the cork with her thumb and downed its contents in one gulp.

She saw Kat's sword spark with red, but it was no use.

Pure magical power surged through Aradia's veins once more.

The ground shattered as an earth spike shot upward, knocking back everyone but Aradia as she grasped its pointed peak.

She knew Kat would recover quickly and come after her, so Aradia directed a few fireballs at the surrounding palace walls right before she blasted open the ceiling with a powerful burst of air.

The instant she saw the blue sky, she smiled and allowed her body to go weightless.

By her next breath, she was flying through the air, and the palace shrank beneath her.

Sighing in pleasure, Aradia stretched as her body soared toward the harbor. She would have to thank Tamlin Ashowan the next time she saw him; he really had given her the gift of the best rest of her entire life. A true rest.

And now?

She felt perfectly ready to get back to work.

CHAPTER 21

DEPARTURE FOR DAXARIA

"Your Majesty, you cannot leave!"

"Really? Because it sounds to me like all of your problems just flew back to my own kingdom!" Kat didn't slow as she descended the Zinferan palace steps with her personal guard, Broghan Miller, at her side.

A small cluster of Zinferan nobles trailed after her.

"Your Majesty, they could return!"

"Then I'll come back. But I'm relatively certain they are heading back to Daxaria to continue being a problem," Kat argued as she touched down on the main floor of the palace and looked over her shoulder toward the doors.

Late-afternoon sun poured in.

It had been a busy few days.

First, she had traveled in the alleged direction of the golden dragon's cave. But four days before they reached the dragon's lair, they watched him fly overhead heading toward Haeson.

After a rushed return to the capital, they had learned that the dragon and the remaining coven members had stolen a ship and set sail. Presumably northwest toward Daxaria. Of course, during Katarina's meeting with the emperor, as she tried to tell him she needed to get home, the first witch had reappeared in the same spot where she had been pushed into Tam's void.

By the time Kat had bolted there, Aradia had just begun to stir, but the damn wench had had a trick up her sleeve.

Stalking toward the doors, Kat felt her heart quicken at the thought of the dragon and the first witch arriving in Daxaria without her being able to warn Eric or her da about it.

Gods, they may even run into Tam and Eli on their way.

Kat was halfway down the hall, the Zinferan nobility murmuring at her back, when Jiho Ryu stepped out in front of her. Her father's old friend gave an apologetic smile.

Kat halted and eyed the man warily. "Jiho."

He bowed. "Your Majesty."

Jiho's eldest son, Bong, joined his father's side and bowed to the Daxarian queen.

Kat casually rested her hand on her sword hilt. "Come to see me off?"

Wincing, Jiho drifted closer. "I wish I could simply bid you farewell, but unfortunately… things are a bit more complicated."

Kat tapped her toe impatiently.

"You see, Lady Elisara made a deal of sorts with a nobleman named Lord Kim. She even signed a document."

Bong produced a scroll.

Kat's stare lingered on the face of her father's friend before she snatched the paper. Unfurling it, she shot her eyes across the page.

She snorted once she'd reached the end. "The emperor has a competent concubine to name as an heir to the throne. I provided her name. Daxaria *and* Elisara have no more business here. The emperor, or this Lord Kim, cannot claim that there is a state of emergency where Elisara would need to take the throne. Besides, she has done more than enough by helping get rid of Soo Hebin." She thrust the document back at Jiho.

"Her Highness Deoh Rin, whom you recommended to be named as heir, does not have enough support to hold the throne without challenge. Things are already tumultuous as is, and I worry not only for her safety but for Zinfera's stability as well," Jiho pressed.

Kat lifted her chin. "Elisara doesn't have any support, either. Not here in Zinfera. In fact, she hasn't even been here for the better part of a decade. She has not lived among these people. She has so little claim over this position that it's bloody confusing why the emperor is so damn set on it. And Zinfera was already unstable thanks to Soo Hebin. So with all due respect, Jiho, you can toss that contract into a manure pile for all it's worth. Good day." Kat resumed her brisk march down the hall.

"Your Majesty," Jiho called out again.

"I'll tell my father you said hello!" Kat proceeded out of the palace into the glorious sunshine without giving Jiho another chance to try to convince her to stay. Broghan hurried his steps so that he wasn't as far behind her.

"Will everything really be alright if you just leave?" Broghan asked.

Kat scoffed. "What's the emperor going to do, declare war? With no coven, his military power divided, and his farming communities disrupted thanks to Soo Hebin?"

"A war can unite a kingdom again," Broghan reminded uneasily.

Kat gave her Troivackian-born bodyguard a sidelong glance. "Even if he wants a war, it will take him time to organize one, and with the mess Soo Hebin made, he has to select an heir and start the process of getting them situated to take over. He doesn't have time to do more. He's dying."

Broghan stiffened. "Oh. I thought that because he had woken up, he was going to recover."

Kat shook her head before climbing into her carriage with Broghan following afterward. "Don't repeat that detail."

Broghan grunted as he sat down. "While you're sharing secrets, could you tell me everything you did shut up in your room since we arrived? You told me to make myself scarce when we got here."

Kat shrugged. "I just didn't want you getting involved in anything illegal I wanted to do."

Broghan scowled. "Most people use their personal guards to do the illegal things *for* them."

"You sound really ungrateful, you know that?" Kat leaned her head against her fist, her elbow propped on the open windowsill as the carriage lurched into motion. "Did you make sure Princess Kezia and Sir Cas were sent home safely?"

The knight nodded. "They set sail early this morning without issue."

"Good. Hopefully by the time they reach Troivack, we can send a missive updating them on what is happening." Kat's attention moved toward the window. "It's really annoying being cut off from talking to everyone. I don't like how unaware we all are of what's going on elsewhere."

"How do you think the Troivackian queen will react to the news that the devil is back?"

At this question, Kat tensed.

Her stomach churned as she remembered Aradia's words from two days earlier. Her claim that Tam was the devil echoed out in Kat's head.

What did the idiot go and do? She ran her tongue over the peaks of her molars. *Is he trying to protect Luca? That seems the most likely…*

"Queen Alina is a logical person. She will wait until she hears the details of what is happening," Kat eventually reasoned aloud.

"Do we want Troivack to wait, though? Wouldn't it be better if they sent military help, if the fight is going to take place in Daxaria?"

Settling back into the sun-warmed cushions of the carriage seat, Kat gave a partial grimace. "Yes and no. I'd like to think settling everything in negotiations is still possible. We just need to cut off the head of the beast to make it possible."

"You think cutting off the head of the first witch will wrap things up?"

"Worth a shot. And if we can't kill her by beheading, we can imprison her again."

"She was imprisoned before and somehow still managed to influence the coven to start this whole rebellion," Broghan reminded her.

"Yeah, but I'm hoping that things haven't progressed as planned. If we take the mastermind away during the chaos, they might be more willing to settle this without bringing outright violence."

"I have to admit, I didn't think *you'd* be such an advocate for nonviolent confrontations."

"I did a lot of damage to the Zinferan army," Kat said grimly. "I helped bury enough of them. It was a good reminder that conflict isn't something to be taken lightly."

"Between burning down part of the palace and decimating a good unit or two of the emperor's army, I'm shocked you weren't locked up at any point."

"I was locked up to begin with when I first was here. The emperor doesn't really have a leg to stand on. Especially when he's banking on me placating the Troivackian monarchy so they don't take exception to Kezia being injured."

Broghan stared at the queen in silence for a long while. "It kills you to be this politically responsible, doesn't it?"

Kat's lip curled. "I get to wear pants. I'm counting whatever wins I get, being in this whole queen role."

The knight smirked in response. They'd known each other since they were students of the esteemed Troivackian military leader Gregory Faucher. Back then it would have been impossible to imagine Katarina showing any kind of restraint in aggravating situations.

Kat changed the topic, folding her arms and slumping back comfortably in her seat. "Are you excited to get home to Daxaria?"

Broghan nodded slowly. It had taken him some time to adjust to living in Daxaria, far from his family and friends in Troivack.

"How is it going with that girl you mentioned… Gina, or something?"

"Jen," Broghan corrected. "And that has resolved already. Actually, I'm… I may be getting into an arranged marriage."

Kat blinked. "Last I heard no one from Troivack wanted to marry you given that you brought shame to your family for, you know, trying to kill me."

As students, they'd had a very interesting time getting to know each other.

"This woman is… in a similar situation as myself. She… fell out of grace."

Kat nodded along, her mind starting to turn away from the conversation given Broghan's reluctance to say more. But then what he said pricked a back recess of her mind. A woman who had fallen out of favor… She had a sudden hunch.

"Broghan? This woman… She wouldn't happen to have any relation to the deceased Sebastian Icarus, would she?"

Broghan avoided her eyes.

"Broghan… Are you… telling me that you are going to marry Selene Icarus? The woman who said my marriage to Eric wasn't going to last? The one who publicly insinuated I was a whore? And who was, in general, a massive pain in the arse? I mean, don't get me wrong, she was absolutely fun to torment, but it'd feel like I was being a tyrant if I did the same stuff now as a queen and if she were your wife."

He scratched his long black beard, still refusing to look at her.

Kat barely stifled a groan. "Is she any less… her?"

Broghan cleared his throat. "She continued to train with the sword after you left. I hear she's even bested a knight or two in sparring."

"So she's deadly *and* annoying."

Broghan let out a long breath. "I was hoping you might find a position for her in the military here."

Kat's eyebrows shot upward as the carriage jostled around them. "The conservative, traditional Broghan Miller wants his future wife to have a position in the military?"

He flushed. "I think it'd help her stay out of trouble."

Grinning, Kat continued to stare at her personal guard as he squirmed under her attention. "You've grown up a lot, Broghan. I mean that as a compliment."

"Why does it feel like you're taunting me?"

"Bah. You know I'm not that evil."

"I don't believe I do."

Kat cackled. "Alright. I'll find a position for the soon-to-be Mrs. Miller. Maybe I'll post her at the docks. You might not like working in close quarters with your spouse."

"Speaking from experience?" Broghan probed.

Kat stuck her tongue out. "Eric and I manage just fine with the pack of nobility surrounding us. So, when are these happy nuptials due?"

Broghan settled into his seat a little more easily. "It depends on this war. There had been talks about the end of summer."

"Mm." Kat's mouth twisted thoughtfully. "I guess we will see. Out of curiosity, do you think Selene spent a lot of time around her father's keep in the year before she came to court?"

"I don't believe so. Otherwise, she would have been jailed or executed along with her father."

"Good. It'd be a bad dynamic if she had tormented Elisara while she was a slave in the duke's house."

Broghan paled.

"You'd forgotten about that, hadn't you?"

He nodded.

"Right. Well, here's hoping that wasn't the case! Because I have no doubt that if they'd crossed paths, things would not have been pleasant. I was the daughter of a duke, and Selene still tried to bully me."

Broghan's discomfort turned pained as he gaped at Kat.

The Daxarian queen reached over and gave a reassuring pat to his knee.

"Maybe be extra nice to my brother's wife when you see her, hm? I watched her slap a woman into the ground—and that wasn't even when she was a giant cat with wings."

The rest of the carriage ride to the docks was silent.

Kat would never admit it, but she actually was looking forward to seeing Lady Selene again. Mostly because it'd be nice to have a woman to train with, but also because, on occasion, it was refreshing to have someone who not only was mean to her, but to whom she could be mean back.

It was good news that helped the Daxarian queen distract herself from the fact that she knew she was leaving Zinfera on horrible terms, and a war was waiting for her back home.

Sighing quietly, she hoped that Tam was at the very least able to reach Austice without any trouble, and they could start planning a proper reception for the first witch and her fancy lizard.

CHAPTER 22

A MOTHER'S MACHINATIONS

"If asked whether you or Kat would have multiple children outside of marriage, I would not have guessed it'd be you!"

Tam's mouth flattened. "Please let me tell Kat you said that."

Annika's nostrils flared. "No!"

With a sigh, Tam decided to try and defend himself a little. "Mum, Penelope isn't mine by blood—"

"Two out of three is more than enough!"

Tam cleared his throat. "I didn't even know Rosaline was pregnant. If I had, you know I would've done whatever I could."

"I don't know that I can believe that! Eli says you two aren't betrothed! Yet here you are sharing a room, with a new little one on the way."

Tam wrestled down an emotional response to his mother's sharp words, though his tone was still clipped when he spoke. "I want to marry her. She's the one who wants more time. Should I strong-arm her into wedding me to add to my sins?"

Annika opened her mouth furiously, then clamped it back shut. Her dark eyes flitted to the bank of windows in Tam's cabin. The deck beneath their feet was noticeably sloped, but the ship still dragged itself toward Daxaria.

"Mum. You of all people know these things just happen."

Her attention returned to him, her eyebrow raised. "You listen to me, Tamlin. If it weren't for the fact that I suspect Luca is the devil, I would be significantly angrier about you leaving him."

Tam felt as though he'd been doused with ice water.

"He's not the devil."

The duchess slowly folded her arms over her chest. "On that note. I've been hearing that you keep announcing that you yourself are the devil. I know better. And I can take an educated guess on why you're doing it."

Tam felt his insides turn to steel as he straightened his shoulders and stared down at his mother.

She gazed back up at him, unbothered. It seemed as though she was going to continue to lecture her son, but then… her formidable expression eased, and instead weariness and concern replaced it.

"Tam, I'm scared of you taking on that fate."

Caught completely off guard by his mother's vulnerability, Tam briefly wondered if this was just her manipulating him to see her point.

"It's the best way to protect my family."

"When did I stop being your family?"

"Don't do that." Tam frowned angrily.

Annika didn't falter at his reaction. "Do what? Tam, something will happen to you if you continue on this road. Do you really think that you will come away from this unscathed? And do you really think your parents, your sister, and your nephews won't be affected by that?"

"You all don't need me like they do. Eli, Luca, Penelope… the new baby… Don't you get that this is mine? My responsibility, and mine to protect?" Tam insisted passionately.

Annika studied her son.

Tam braced himself.

"You've wanted something of your own for a long time. Your own space, your own life… I'm not blind, Tam. And I know you left Daxaria saying as much."

The duchess paused as she let out a long breath. "Everything is just… fast. You've taken on a lot, and you've done it in a matter of months. And you're right. You do have a responsibility to Eli and the children. Which is another reason why you need to exercise caution when announcing that you are the devil."

A flicker of the foreboding sensation that Tam had buried deep in his heart made its way into his throat. His vivid dreams flashed briefly into his mind.

Part of him wanted to crumble in front of his mother. His strong, brilliant mother, who always seemed like she could bend the world into a sailor's knot if she damn well chose.

But he had decided this fate for himself.

He already had an inkling what might happen, but he also suspected what the consequences for Luca might be if Tam didn't do this.

Slipping his hands into his pockets, Tam pressed a smile onto his face. "You seem even angrier with me than you did with Kat when she eloped with the prince. At least, with what I was told. You know. When you all left me in charge—"

"—Of running the two noble houses. Yes, yes. I'm starting to side with your sister in the belief that you need to let that go," Annika said curtly. "It's been your constant jibe for nearly eight years."

"That experience aged me ten years. I'll stop complaining about it when the decade's up."

Annika stifled a grumbling laugh before returning to her somber countenance. "Tam. While you might have started a family on your own, that doesn't change the fact that you can still count on the people you came from for help. Just like you would do anything for your own children, your father and I would do anything for you."

Tam nodded. "I know. Can you… Can you trust that I'm doing what I think is best?"

"I've always trusted that. I just think I can help you find an improved solution."

Tam tentatively chewed on his tongue.

He knew a lot of people met their downfalls by not asking for help.

Hell, Harris had lectured him about it. His father had lectured him about it…

"How else can I protect Luca from the first witch coming after him? I can't put that fate on another innocent person." His heart beat a little faster in his chest.

Tam tried to remind himself that he was not weaker for asking his mother's insight, but he still felt the burr of discomfort in his chest.

If she was surprised by his acceptance of her offer of help and advice, she didn't show it. Nor did she act smug about it.

"We can't. That's the short answer. What we *can* do is focus on a way to send the first witch back to the Forest of the Afterlife without the devil being a part of it. She managed to open a gateway before. So what if this time we open it for her?"

"There had to be an equal exchange. She was going to bring over more ancient beasts in exchange for the devil last time," Tam reminded. "Though I have no idea how she's planning on taking the devil back with her this time."

Annika's fingers fluttered against her arm. "We should talk to Kraken about what would be an equal exchange. We don't really want something coming through from their side."

"What would come through if both the devil and the first witch returned, I wonder… Or maybe if they both go back, there is no price," Tam mused distractedly.

"I suspect the Coven of Wittica knows far more about this than they've let on," Annika lamented.

Tam stilled. "Do you think they'd have records of it on the Isle of Wittica?"

Annika gaped at Tam blankly before a slow smile rose in her face. "My dear, are you suggesting that we perhaps discreetly tour the coven's island?"

Tam grinned back at his mother.

He knew the mere notion of this thrilled her.

"It's probably a little more vacant than it normally is, with so many of their members either in Zinfera or out looking for me."

"And it *is* a grave matter regarding a pending war…"

"You've wanted to do this for years, haven't you?" Tam asked lightly.

Annika looked like a child who'd been gifted a bucket full of sweets. "They would never let me join your father when he'd go submit his reports and reviews!"

Tam laughed. "Alright. Should we break into the coven's archives before or after going to see Da?"

Annika bristled—most likely at the idea of prolonging her separation from her beloved husband.

"It's practically on the way to Austice. We'd just pop over, and then be on our way! It'd take three days at most!"

Tam chortled. "I'll go tell Eli. I've noticed she's better at making plans in advance, whereas I'm usually better at improvising when unpredictable problems crop up."

Annika turned with her son to head toward the cabin exit. Before they reached the door, she grasped his arm. "Why won't Eli marry you?"

"She likes to torture me."

The duchess fixed her son with a dry stare.

When he realized his mother was not going to accept that answer, he dropped his head and continued, "I think she likes and needs to exercise her freedom to choose how her life goes. And I'm not going to pressure her or make her feel bad for that—so don't you go trying to change her mind."

Annika's hand fell away, and she bowed her head. "I understand now. You have my word."

Tam bobbed his head in appreciation and was about to continue out of the cabin when his mother spoke up.

"I'm excited to finally have a granddaughter to dress up. I already have some colors in mind for Penelope once things calm down. Ooh. I wonder if she'd let me put her in matching clothes with the whole family."

"I'm noticing that you assume the rest of us would be onboard with this plan of yours."

"After all I've done for all of you, a portrait with coordinated outfits is the least you could give me," Annika declared boldly.

Tam opened the door for his mother. "You are not honestly trying to make us dress up to match *and* sit for a portrait the entire time. Kat's boys haven't gotten a portrait done since Asher was a baby, because they won't sit still."

"I'm sure between myself, you, Eli, and Penelope, we can manage something."

"Why is it that neither Kat or Eric, you know, their parents, are expected to wrangle the monsters?" Tam asked indignantly.

"Because their solution is to let their children run around outside to help them deal with their abundance of energy, but if they are already in the outfits I have in mind, that won't be possible."

Tam groaned.

"Do you think Luca will be the kind to tear about?" Annika wondered while glancing over her shoulder at her son as he closed the door behind himself.

"Depends. I don't know if he'll shy away from Kat's monsters or become the long-lost fourth Ashowan hellion."

Annika's brows furrowed thoughtfully.

"Before you start plotting how to educate him before he meets his cousins, you should probably know Eli and I are already a little bit concerned at how much of our… *illicit* lifestyle he has been privy to as of late," Tam finished delicately.

Annika slowly rounded back on her son.

He pressed his lips together in a facsimile of a smile.

His mother's next word carried an edge. "What?"

"I just mean he might be a little too… *comfortable* with stealing, setting fires, and occasionally punching men in their groins. Though it's usually only bad men with the latter."

Annika stared at Tam blankly.

"In my defense," he continued. "It's not exactly like we've been in ideal child-rearing environments and situations, though Eli got him a tutor for a while in Junya!"

The duchess's lips puckered tightly before she managed to say, "I'm aware that you have been in some tough spots on this trip—and you still need to inform me of the details surrounding your magic—but from here on out, I will help keep Luca from getting any terrible ideas."

Tam wondered if he should point out that, given how influential Harris had been on Luca the past few weeks, she'd have her work cut out for her, but he didn't really want to test her tenuous calm.

So the mother and son continued making their way back up onto the main deck to rejoin everyone else. Just before they mounted the stairs, Tam once again turned to Annika. "How did you convince Henrietta to change you back?"

The duchess lightly touched her neck just behind her ear. "The coven was attacking. It was an emergency."

"That doesn't answer…" Tam trailed off as his mother proceeded up the steps. He sighed. She was the same as ever.

But that wasn't a bad thing, and besides. Who knew? Maybe she could find a way for them all to have a happy ending. Even if they were successful breaking into the archives on the Isle of Wittica, Tam's hopes about finding a better solution to the devil dilemma were as high as his expectation that Luca wouldn't punch another man in the balls.

That was to say, not high at all.

With nothing left to do but go up and soothe Eli's anxieties, Tam set to climbing the stairs.

All in all, similar to what his sister had described, their mother had responded quite reasonably to the news that he had fathered a child... again. Allegedly. Out of wedlock. Which left him wondering if perhaps his father would be the dramatic one.

CHAPTER 23

READY TO DROWN IN DRINK

Jiho Ryu sat with his hands clasped in his lap. The Zinferan emperor's index finger tapping the round table in his chamber.

The last maid filed out, closing the door behind her.

"Tell me your thoughts, Jiho. I've practically heard them screaming at me the past few weeks," the emperor ordered roughly. He eyed the decanter of wine on the table between them longingly. He wasn't supposed to drink any more according to his physicians, and it had been rather upsetting to hear.

Jiho smiled, then lifted his gaze to the ruler. "I'm sorry, Your Excellency. I will try harder to think more quietly."

"Don't get clever with me," the emperor warned, though a gentleness in his tone indicated he wasn't all that bothered.

Jiho chuckled softly, his right foot bouncing a little. "I don't understand your fixation with Elisara," he began delicately. "I know she is intelligent, and that she has a very interesting ability. However, she has no support from her birth family and has been alienated not only among the nobility, but throughout the entire kingdom, as a result of Soo Hebin's rumors. To name her as an heir... I am sorry to say, I agree with the Daxarian queen. It does not make sense. Your

Excellency, if you had another five years to turn the tides in her favor, we could manage something. But when you have less than a year…"

The Zinferan ruler eyed Jiho calmly. "You know me better than most, Jiho. Why do you think I want her?"

Jiho grimaced before answering. "Because your mother adopted her and had great expectations of her. And because your mother was able to do the impossible and rise in power, you expect Elisara will do the same. But she is not your mother. She does not want to be here in Zinfera. She wants to be with her new family, and I do not mean to offend you, Your Excellency, but becoming an enemy of the Ashowans is in no one's best interest."

"We will see if the Ashowan family holds on to their power after they deal with whatever is happening on their shores," the emperor pointed out, tilting his head casually. "What do you make of the concubine Her Majesty Katarina Reyes recommended? Deoh Rin?"

Jiho leaned forward in his seat. "I see why the queen and her mother believed she would be a good option. She is levelheaded and does not let greed get the best of her. She does have some power behind her—her brother is a noble. Rank five. He owns most of the shipping vessels in the small towns between Haeson and Gondol. He has two sons. Her cousin is a noblewoman, a widow in Bani who was married to a rank six. Deoh Rin has maintained the most men-at-arms under her and has not given a single one to Soo Hebin's army."

The emperor's eyebrows rose. "That is quite reasonable. Can Deoh Rin withstand the chaos of Zinfera?"

Jiho let out a long breath. "If we start making amends with Daxaria, they will help. And if they can't, they will speak to Troivack on our behalf."

"I believe matters between us and Daxaria are fine as they are. The new queen burned down part of my palace and slaughtered a number of my men. If there weren't so much confusion right now pertaining to Soo Hebin's treason, the people would be screaming for a war of revenge."

Jiho nodded somberly. "I've already done what I can to spread the word that Soo Hebin was attempting to hold the queen and her mother hostage, and that she aided the first witch in escaping Troivack."

The emperor tilted his hand. "It will take time."

Silence settled between the two men for a time. The warm sunshine of the day gleamed against the polished floorboards, and distant chimes rang in the breeze outside.

"Should I let your advisers know you wish to call a meeting to name an heir?"

The emperor hesitated. His eyes turned thoughtful as he settled back into his chair. "Not yet. I want to personally interview no less than five candidates. I'd prefer if it were some of my older children that have survived here in the palace."

"Your Excellency, we could try to track down some of your other offspring that Soo Hebin sold," Jiho suggested a little too quickly.

The emperor's gaze flitted up to him. "I will assign a small unit of men to investigate. I fear most of my resources will be spent reorganizing the military and nobles." He paused to cough. "Tell me, are there any who remain loyal to Soo Hebin?"

Jiho cleared his throat. "After Lord Yangban's recent… outbursts, and his wife taking over his affairs, things have been quite unstable for her followers. Particularly with the death of Captain Woo suppressing the common people. Her followers are not only lacking the ability to intimidate due to the key leaders being disposed of, but they are disorganized."

The emperor gaped. Then, with a brief closing of his eyes, he lifted his wrinkled hand to touch his brow. "And of course, I've already been told the Ashowan family is responsible for Captain Woo's demise."

Jiho's eyes trailed along the beautifully painted ceiling. "I was not present for any of these events, so I cannot say with complete certainty—"

The emperor sighed. "Assemble the advisers. I shall inform them about the five candidate slots, as well as the search for my lost offspring."

"I… would like to raise one small possible problem," Jiho ventured. "Be wary about the nobles who may simply place their own children in front of Your Excellency claiming to be of your blood. Especially with the younger children, this could be done with the purpose of status climbing."

"I can simply say that none of the offspring that are found can be considered as a candidate. I will, of course, consider them. But the nobles won't need to know. That can be kept between us." The emperor cast an affectionate smile at Jiho, who inclined himself politely in response.

"Then I'd best leave and see to putting these exciting events into motion." Rising from his seat, Jiho clasped his hands in front of himself and bowed once more.

"Did you…" The emperor cleared his throat, raising his chin proudly. "Did you miss me, Jiho?"

Lifting his eyes to the old monarch, Jiho smiled with his mouth closed. "I did."

The emperor snorted. "Liar."

Jiho stared at the emperor for a long while until he looked back at him. "No one is like you, Your Excellency, and it is good you are awake."

Another long spell of wordless communication passed between the two men.

Eventually, the emperor nodded, his face touched with age spots and creased with understanding. Pain weighed down his shoulders as he waved away Jiho. Taking his cue, Jiho rose, bowed wordlessly, and departed.

Alone, the monarch stared out the window.

In a way, he wished he had never woken up. It was one thing to fall into a dreamless sleep. It was another to prepare the world so your absence would be easier for the ones you cared about most.

Shivering on the slick dock, Tam, his family, Hamil, Bes, and Henrietta waited. The old Daxarian sailor limped over to them, clutching a lantern.

Despite the fact that the sun had not yet set, the rains had come again, and heavy mists rolled off the water.

"If you'll come with me, we can arrange for you all to stay at the inn," the sailor explained without bothering to lift his face to them. His short, well-kept white beard was easy to see in the dim light.

Their ship hadn't even been able to make it to the docks of Rollom.

Captain Sun, though an experienced captain and sailor, had never learned how to navigate the rocky shoals that surrounded the southern isles of Daxaria. And so they'd had to send for help from the nearest island.

The Isle of Quildon.

"Out of curiosity, whatever happened to the old cottage the Ashowan family used to live in?" Tam asked before thinking better of it.

He had heard the stories of his father's youth there on that very island, but he himself had never visited. So despite the fact they were trying not to reveal their identities, he thought it worth the risk.

The old fisherman gave a long, world-weary sigh. "We had to make it a shrine. Too many people kept coming by wanting to see it. No one could ever live there in peace. It's a waste of a good cottage, but at least it's good for our people. It's why an island this small even has an inn. Everyone wants to see where the Daxarian hero grew up."

When no one asked a follow-up question, the fisherman waved them all forward. "This way. Mind your footing. The rains have made this path slick with the mud."

Tam looked down at Luca, who was sniffling, then at Penelope, whose trembling lower lip was tinged with blue.

Bending down, he scooped both children up in his arms with a grunt and continued forward after the man.

The four sailors who had joined them on land picked up the three trunks they'd packed. Behind them on the dock, Captain Sun spoke with another sailor about requesting aid from the Rollom harbormaster in the morning.

Tam cast a glance back at Eli. She nodded, confirming that she felt alright to climb as Annika laced their arms together.

Hamil offered his arm to Bes and Henrietta, and both accepted gratefully.

By the time they reached the top, night had fully descended over the group, and Tam had to put the children down, his muscles screaming at him. Before he could try to roll out the ache in them, Penelope and Luca each seized his hands. They moved closer to his sides as he continued onward.

Fortunately, the whitewashed inn was only a short way off the path up ahead. The windows glowed, and four chimneys puffed out thick smoke.

Clambering up the wooden steps onto the porch, Tam threw open the door without bothering to read the front sign. He ushered everyone in, including the sailors carting up their trunks. As he stepped inside, a wall of heat hit Tam's face that almost hurt when it met his frozen skin.

"I heard we have some shipwrecked guests!" A woman's voice drew the drenched group's attention over toward a roughly constructed counter. She had thick, curly honey-blond hair, thin lips, and kind green eyes; she appeared to be in her early forties. She strode over to them. "My name's Johanna. You tell me what you need, and I'll do what I can to help."

Tam swept his gaze over the rest of the room to see that the small tavern part of the inn was mostly empty, save for three men wearing black wool coats and sitting in front of the stone fireplace with pints in their hands.

They all had black beards and pale skin.

They looked part Troivackian.

Like Tam.

They eyed him with interest, but Tam pretended not to notice.

"Apologies for the imposition," Eli said. "My husband and I can share a room with the children. The three women can be in a room together, while I believe the young man over there"—she gestured toward Hamil—"can share a room with the captain and his first mate, if that sounds agreeable to everyone?"

Annika bowed her head in assent, and Tam glanced over to Bes and Hamil, who managed to nod despite their chattering teeth.

"That should work. I only have one other room, though the barn is watertight, so the rest of your crew can rest there. If that is not amenable, I do know some of the families on the island are open to housing a few folk here and there for some coin."

"That should be fine, thank you, ma'am." One of the Zinferan sailors inclined himself politely.

Johanna smiled in appreciation. "Well." She plunked her hands on her hips. "I'll go send my daughter up to start making the beds, and in the meantime, how about I serve you all some stew and ale?"

To Tam, it sounded heavenly, but his mother spoke before he could say as much. "I don't suppose you have any Troivackian moonshine on hand, do you?"

At this question, the three men in front of the fire fully turned in their seats and beheld Annika.

"Finally," one of them called out, a slow smile climbing his face, revealing blinding white teeth. "Guests with taste! I happen to have a bottle or two stowed behind that counter that I'd be happy to share for the right price."

Annika gave a half smile of appreciation. "Tell you what. I'll pay you coin, but if I manage to outdrink any of you, I get half of what I paid back."

The men chortled.

Tam stared at his mother's profile flatly, and Eli looked at Tam in concern.

"You have yourself a deal, ma'am," the Troivackian who had made the offer retorted.

Annika beamed. "Wonderful." The duchess made her way over to the men while everyone save for Tam and the children—who had no idea what was happening—watched anxiously.

"Tam, I understand it has been a long day, but your mother might make herself ill," Eli whispered.

Tam turned his dry expression down to her. "Eli… do you remember how much moonshine you had to order and pick up when you worked at our keep in Austice?"

She frowned and nodded slowly.

"My mother is the one who drinks eighty percent of that order."

"*In a year?*" Eli exclaimed in shock.

"In a season."

Eli turned her bulging gaze toward the duchess's back. "Tam, is she well?"

Tam sighed. "She's about to be. Don't worry, we'll go check on her in a bit. First, I think we'd better find some blankets for the kids."

While Eli's feet may have started moving toward the counter, where Tam was already heading with the kids at his side, her attention remained glued at the table where the duchess was in the process of removing her cloak and sitting gracefully down beside one of the men.

Seeing this and chuckling a little to himself, Tam found he was curious how Eli would react when she saw his mother's true passion.

Drinking games.

CHAPTER 24

THE GIFT OF GOSSIP

Tam sipped his ale while slumped against the tavern wall. He had straddled the wooden bench to give his back a place to rest as he watched the scene before him unfold.

The three Troivackian men had rosy cheeks and were laughing bawdily as they spoke in the old Troivackian tongue among themselves.

Tam watched his mother as she lightly tapped the corner of her mouth with a napkin.

The stew that had been served for dinner had been a fish stew. So his mother, who disliked seafood—much like Luca—had only consumed bread and cheese for her dinner. Throughout, she imbibed the moonshine she loved so dearly.

Tam didn't bother weighing in on the situation. He knew better.

"Alright," one of the fishermen, named Levi, started. "We've been having a nice warm-up for this little wager of yours, ma'am. But it's getting late. I think we should move this along." He waved to Johanna, who shot him a disapproving glance before reluctantly carrying over a tray full of small, crudely made shot glasses.

As she lined up three shots in front of each man, she lowered her voice and addressed Annika. "Ma'am, I do not think this is wise."

"Oh, come now, Johanna! This fine woman here is the one who staked the wager!" a fisherman named Ezra interjected while grinning at Annika.

Tam barely resisted a snort of laughter.

"I do have one concern," Annika announced, her eyes drifting up to Johanna, who was already starting to smile in understanding. The duchess gestured to the three shot glasses that Levi was in the process of filling with the clear moonshine. "I thought this was supposed to be a challenge?"

Levi halted as his two companions gaped at Annika in momentary shock before breaking out in laughter.

Johanna sighed pityingly.

"Well, Johanna? You heard the woman! Think you have a few more glasses to spare?" Levi asked with a grin.

"I have twelve more, but that's it," she returned tightly.

"Four glasses more for each of us. That sounds perfect, thank you." Annika gave a kind smile.

Johanna looked to Tam. She seemed to be expecting him to step in and stop the madness.

He shrugged in response. He'd probably go to bed soon. Eli and the children were most likely already fast asleep.

Sighing, Johanna retrieved the last of the shot glasses and returned. She added the glasses into the existing lines, and Levi continued topping them up. Once he was done, he set down the mostly empty bottle and plucked up his first glass.

"To Quildon! May she continue to hold our homes!" The group clinked glasses, downed their shots, and plunked them down on the table before grasping the next one.

The men grinned at Annika, who smiled politely back.

The third fisherman, James, was too impatient to wait longer for his next drink, and so he bellowed, "To the sea! May she continue to favor our boats and share her abundance!"

Again, the liquor was tossed down.

The men paused before grasping their third glasses, eyeing Annika with barely concealed excitement. They must have been expecting her to keel over or at least sway in her seat.

Instead, they were greeted with a merry twinkle in her eye.

As the men around her hesitated, the duchess raised her glass. "To Daxaria. With the finest fields, the finest folk, and the finest fates."

The men lifted their glasses, uncertainty touching their faces.

The third glass went down.

By the fourth, they seemed to regain their former confidence—most likely assuming Annika would simply pass out rather than give any warning sign.

By the sixth, their confusion and wariness were mounting.

Tam eyed their pallor. He hesitated before finishing his ale. Normally at least one man would be looking ready to lose his dinner, but all three men looked perfectly fine.

Tam's eyebrows rose. He wondered if his mother might *possibly* be in over her head.

She didn't spare a glance or bat an eye as the seventh shot went down.

"I must confess"—Levi's words were a little wetter as he slurred—"you're more Troivackian than I realized."

Annika lifted one shoulder demurely. "I enjoy a glass now and then."

Tam coughed.

This made his mother finally look at him. She quirked her eyebrows in silent challenge.

"Why doesn't your son join us?" Ezra asked, still clutching his shot glass.

"Oh, he needs to arrange our passage back to Daxaria tomorrow morning. Best to do so with a clear head," Annika said lightly.

Tam set his tankard on the table. "Out of curiosity, my mother and I were talking about how we saw some boats being magically propelled on our journey. It seemed odd."

A discreet lowering of Annika's eyes told Tam she was pleased with him for thinking to raise the matter in the present company.

Levi snorted. "Right? The entire kingdom seems like it's lost its mind. First there's all the rumors about the dragon in Zinfera, then the news of the first witch escaping… Now the princes are missing and the military is scouring the kingdom."

Tam felt his stomach plummet. "What?"

"You've all been gone long, hey?" Ezra tripped over his words as he swept his glassy gaze over Tam. "The queen went to Zinfera, an' the three princes took off. At least that's what they're saying on the mainland. I'm thinking that something don't smell right about any of this."

James snorted. "Like what? The queen being held for ransom in Zinfera an' the princes going into hiding? What don't smell right 'bout that?"

Tam's eyes cut to his mother. She was sitting so rigidly, she looked as though one flinch would make her snap.

"I dunno," Ezra countered. "Maybe the first witch is already here and Zinfera is stopping the queen from coming home. The Wittica Coven probably went to save the queen, an' the king stashed away the princes."

"You dumbarse," Levi scoffed. "Why would the king send out the army to look for the princes if he knew where they were?"

"Does anyone have any idea which direction they might have been going?" Annika's sharp voice drew all attention back to her.

They must have forgotten that she was there.

"Not really. Some think they're hidin' with the coven. But I heard from a maid at the Duke Cowan estate…" Levi dropped his voice, "the king is on the outs with the coven."

Tam's mind raced. The boys were missing… Could the first witch have taken them?

"I thought Duke Ashowan could find his family if they were in danger?" Tam forced his voice to sound easygoing.

"Well, that's the other strange thing about this, innit?" Ezra twirled his salt-and-pepper beard between his fingers, clearly enjoying his captivated audience. "That's what makes me think that somethin' else is going on."

Annika's finger tapped the table. "Gentlemen, if you'll excuse me, I'd like a word with my son."

"Ah-ah!" Levi burst out with a triumphant grin. "No running off now! That would not be fair, ma'am, a deal's a deal."

Annika rose from her seat, unbothered, then plucked up the moonshine bottle and downed the rest of its contents in three large gulps. She placed the empty bottle on the table and pulled her cloak back on. "Ask Johanna to bring the other bottle so you can catch up. That was an additional three drinks."

What she had just consumed was significantly more than three drinks.

The formerly boisterous air around the table dissipated and was replaced with shock as Tam rose from his seat and rounded the table to join his mother's side.

The pair then stepped back out into the cold, wet night, moving with both purpose and complete silence.

"I think the boys ran away," Tam said as soon as they had found a discreet wood shelter to have their discussion.

"Perhaps… But why?" Annika pressed worriedly.

Tam folded his arms against the biting wind that whipped past his shoulder, which didn't fit within the protection of the wood shelter. "All it would take is one of them to get the idea and the other two would follow. It could've been for any number of reasons. It could be because Kat's away. You know Eric doesn't do well when she's gone."

"Yes, but your father and the former king are there. They would be helping."

"Mum, they don't know anything that is going on. We've lost communication for weeks in Kat's case, and months in mine. Da and Eric are probably losing their minds. You heard from Kat that they attempted to ransom her. She also told me that Da saw you get hurt. With the ransom, they would also know that the Coven of Wittica is looking for a war. Da might not be at the castle if he went to Wittica to investigate."

Annika tilted her head thoughtfully. "It *is* strange that your father isn't able to find them. It would mean they aren't afraid."

"Exactly."

"But how in the world have they managed to avoid the soldiers? Antony's only just turned seven!"

Tam grimaced. "I don't know."

The duchess stared out over the cold, blue mists. "Where would they go, do you think? If they have run away, and even people on this remote island know about it, then the coven would hear about it, too, and they could snatch them up."

Tam pondered this silently. "Call it a hunch… but my bet would be Sorlia."

"Why?"

"Because Xava would be too easy for Da and Eric to get to, Rollom too far. And to get to Sorlia, they'd be able to travel in the woods for the first few days of their journey, which would give them lots of places to hide."

Annika considered this. "Still… this doesn't make sense."

"We don't even know how long they've been missing," Tam pointed out. "Eric and Da would've looked for them on their own with a small search party for the first day. Maybe even two. And I doubt that the men inside the tavern here know the actual timeline."

Annika jerked her chin down grimly. "When we reach the mainland, I'll contact the brothels and send riders out to every other establishment we own to ask them to keep an eye and ear out, as well as multiple people on horseback to the castle in Austice."

"You should go with one of them." Tam's voice was quiet.

Annika's brows twitched. "Oh?"

"Go tell Da everything. I'll go to the coven and try to get the information on how to send the first witch home. In Xava, I'll check for a message from you to see if the boys have been found yet. If not, I'll go straight to Sorlia from Xava."

The duchess stared at her son for a long while. The only light source was a lone torch they had borrowed from the front of the inn that gave off the occasional hiss as spatters of rain assaulted its glow.

"I understand why you are suggesting this. We need someone to communicate and find out what exactly is happening with the king, and you think you are the best person to go to the coven because you, too, are a witch."

Tam nodded slowly.

"Do you think Eli should go with you or come with me?" Annika asked tightly.

Tam let out a breath that appeared as a cloud of vapor. "I'll ask her. It is hard to say where she will be safest. I can help protect her, but if she and the children are with me, I'll have to defend multiple people in the event of a fight."

"Given that there is a hunt for Luca, that still might be the better option."

The conversation lapsed as both mother and son turned over this new plan in their minds.

"Tam?"

He looked down at his mother's face.

Her cheeks were pink from the cold and drink, but there was an intensity in her eyes as she prepared her next question.

"What is your magic?"

Tam gave a slow, weary smile. "Ether."

Annika's lips tightened curiously.

Sighing, Tam allowed the void to rush forward, consuming him. He then stepped through his void and back from the darkness to appear behind his mother. He heard the tail end of a gasp leaving her mouth. He tapped her on the shoulder and found her sharp elbow driving back into his gut.

Tipsy or not, the duchess could always defend herself.

Annika whirled back around, her eyes wide. "What was that?"

Coughing, Tam managed to straighten himself, though he didn't doubt that he would find a rather nasty bruise in the morning. "Ether. I have a void I can move into, and I can travel to different places. I move through matter. I exist in the void, between things, and among things. I can go to places I see or know very well. The farthest I've been able to travel without seeing the place has been a few leagues."

Tam could hear his mother's sharp intake of breath. He reached up and rubbed his neck as he waited for the deluge of questions she would undoubtedly have.

Surprisingly, all she managed was, "I always said you seemed to be off in a world of your own."

Tam blinked. Then a genuine laugh escaped him. When he was done, he rested his hand on his mother's back and gave her a gentle push. "Come on. Let's get back. You have a drinking game to wrap up, and I'm going to bed. We'll finish this plan in the morning."

CHAPTER 25

THE FAULT OF THE FALLEN FATHER

Kraken swatted Henrietta's knee.

She regarded him with a raised eyebrow.

The emperor had been brought in by the sailors last night in the protection of a watertight trunk.

Kraken bopped her knee again.

"Again, I can only speak to chickens," she repeated. "And we left that witch I had turned during the attack with the Zinferan crew. I could turn the duchess into one for a bit again if you'd like?"

Kraken gave a quiet huff of annoyance.

Henrietta sighed in equal exasperation as she finished pinning her braid in a crown around her head. "You'll probably have to wait until we all reach the mainland, Empurror. I'm sorry."

Evidently pleased that the chicken witch had at the very least addressed him properly, Kraken rubbed his face against her skirts and rounded back over to the window of the room.

A knock at the door made Henrietta rise. She straightened the small vest she had buttoned over her faded rose-colored dress.

Opening the door, she found the Zinferan princess, Elisara, peering at her in that unnervingly direct way of hers. "Grab your things. We'll be leaving before lunch."

Henrietta slowly nodded.

Elisara turned, her expression smooth and uncrackable. Her tan pants and light-blue tunic complemented her skin, making her complexion glow. Her straight black hair was freshly washed and tucked behind her ears, and for once she didn't have a child at her side. It made Henrietta realize how frosty a woman she normally was.

"Excuse me?" Henrietta ventured.

Elisara swung back around.

Henrietta almost backed up a step, but instead she clasped her hands in front of herself. "Kraken keeps trying to talk to me."

The princess waited.

"If you could try speaking to him in your beast form, that might be best. I'm not sure that the duchess would much appreciate being a chicken again," Henrietta finished with a nervous laugh.

Elisara stared blankly at her, then dropped her gaze to Kraken, who appeared in the doorway. "We'll figure out a way to talk soon. There is some news, and we need you."

Kraken blinked and trotted down the hall to her side.

"Uh, right. Right…" Looking over her shoulder at the room, Henrietta belatedly remembered that until a day ago she'd been a prisoner, and therefore she had no belongings to leave behind.

Scurrying after the princess, Henrietta touched down onto the tavern floor. She spotted Eli seating herself down in front of a plate of eggs and thick slices of brown bread that made Henrietta's mouth water.

"I'll get your plate in a moment, dear."

Henrietta nearly jumped out of her skin when the tavern keeper brushed by her on her way to Bes, Hamil, and the duchess—who looked like she was asleep atop the table—all eating their own breakfasts in a quiet corner on their own.

In the pale light of the cloudy day, Henrietta took in the tavern. The previous night, she had been too exhausted to have a proper look. It was sparse, and its whitewashed walls were bare save for a crude painting of a lone tree and a span of green grass in a wooden frame. The benches and four tables were made of the same wood as the floor. They were heavy but well crafted, built to take a beating. The fireplace was already lit, and it helped heat the air, which should have been much warmer, given that it was summertime. Despite this, a chill still kissed her nose.

The stern voice of the Zinferan princess called Henrietta's attention back to her. "Henrietta."

"Ah, yes." She quickly rounded the table and seated herself across from her. "Where are the children?"

"Penelope and Luca are washing dishes to see who is faster at it," Elisara explained.

Henrietta balked. "Er… That's… helpful of them."

"Hardly. It was the only way they would stop fighting about it."

"Oh, now, I disagree." Johanna reappeared with a steaming plate heaped with food that she set in front of Henrietta. "They are being marvelously helpful, in my opinion! Your children are absolute delights, ma'am." The innkeeper beamed.

A startlingly bashful smile instantly bounced to Elisara's face as she blushed. "Thank you."

With a wink, the innkeeper turned and disappeared back through the round door propped open in the back left corner—presumably it led to the kitchen.

"How can I be of help… ?" Henrietta asked, nervously plucking up her cutlery.

Elisara busied herself taking a generous, crunchy bite out of her toast. Her eyes fluttered closed as she openly savored the food, with its vivacious raspberry jam.

Henrietta felt her nerves settle a little more around the woman, and so she, too, tucked into her meal without hurrying the conversation.

"Have you ever been to the Isle of Wittica?" Eli questioned crisply.

Henrietta bobbed her head as she loaded her fork with the sunny scrambled eggs. "A bunch of times."

"Good. Do you think you could draw the access points to both the island and the building layouts? Tam has been there himself, but only twice."

Henrietta paused, taking another bite, her fork slowly lowering as it dawned on her just why such a request would be made. "I… I wouldn't recommend trying to do what I think you're trying to do."

Elisara raised an eyebrow, unbothered. "Oh, if I go or Kraken does, the witches that are most likely guarding the isle won't attack us."

"Why not?"

A mystifying look rose on the woman's face. "Because we could make it well known I am a familiar, and they already know Kraken belongs to Lord Finlay. And as you should know, it breaks the divine law."

Henrietta blanched.

The princess plucked up her second piece of toast and took her time enjoying another bite before explaining.

"And if they try to subdue us without harm, we'll just have to pick a fight"

Tam stared at the cottage as the wind whipped at his clothes relentlessly.

Dried flowers were tied to the shutters and along the fence at his back, left by people coming by to glimpse the humble beginning of Finlay Ashowan.

And humble it most definitely was.

The entire cottage could have fit in the dining room of their keep in Austice.

Tam eyed the ghostly remains of what would have been the garden, off to the right side of the house. He could see a rake and hoe on the ground, rusting. Those had most likely been left behind by one of the people who had attempted to live there.

His heart thrumming, Tam approached the front door of the cottage. He clasped the handle and pushed the chipped door open. It wailed and stuttered but granted him entry.

Stepping into the dark room, Tam was greeted with a faceful of cobwebs. He briefly reeled back to swipe at his eyes.

With the webs cleared, he stared around the room. He spotted the old cooking table covered in half-melted candles. Evidently others had come inside and stayed awhile. Behind the table, the stone-and-plaster fireplace sat cold.

The door to the tiny room to Tam's left had fallen off one of its hinges and lay uselessly amid the dust and debris. The broken spindles of a forgotten rocking chair caught his attention.

So this is where Da came from.

A tightening sensation bloomed in Tam's chest.

"Dad?"

Tam jumped at the sound of Luca's voice. He whirled around and saw his own son staring up at him curiously from the cottage doorway.

"Luca! Is everything alright?" Tam breathed after regaining his composure.

Luca peered around the room before entering. He closed the door behind himself with great effort; a strong gust of wind tried to buffet it back.

Tam watched, amused by his son's efforts, then noticed that his pants were starting to look a few inches too short. Had he really grown that much already?

Once the door was successfully closed, Luca dusted off his hands. "Everything's fine, but Grandma wanted me to tell you that the boat to take us to Rollom will be here soon."

"Right... A boat..." Tam hesitated.

Gods help us. Hopefully we don't find out we're having twins, or I'm swearing off ever getting on another boat for the rest of my life.

"What is this place?" Luca continued to the cooking table before his eyes jumped up to a far corner of the room. He suddenly frowned.

"Your grandfather used to live here when he was growing up," Tam explained, pulling himself free from his spiraling thoughts.

Luca's attention didn't shift from the corner, his face motionless.

"Is something wrong?" Tam ventured, drawing closer.

"Bad things happened here."

Tam froze. "What?"

Luca blinked rapidly, his face flinching. "They were so sad... And scared..."

Swallowing with difficulty, Tam touched Luca's shoulder. "They had good years later. Did you hear about Finlay Ashowan's father from someone?"

Tears spilled from Luca's eyes as he shook his head adamantly while backing away from the corner.

"No. I can... I can feel it."

Tam dropped down to his knees as he gently grasped his son's shoulders. "Luca, look at me. It's alright. No one is sad or scared here right now."

Tam had just lied.

The idea of Luca sensing that place's long-ago emotions was alarming in more ways than one. Most importantly, sensing emotions in any capacity was a power of the devil's. Was it starting to manifest in Luca?

"D-Dad, can we… Can we please leave?"

Tam tried to give an encouraging smile but failed, so he simply nodded and stood back up while making sure to grasp Luca's hand. Once they were back outside in the fresh air, Luca's troubled mood seemed to ease a little, but not fully. Tam struggled with whether to tell Luca more about the cottage and why he might feel what he did. Would it maybe help him feel less upset?

With a long exhale, he began. "Your grandfather, Fin, was scared of his own father. Fin's father, Aidan Helmer, was not a good man. He would hurt his wife and son. He was someone who believed that because of the kind of witch he was, he was better than humans and mutated witches, and therefore he could treat those who weren't equal to him badly."

Luca squeezed Tam's hand. "Kind of like…" He paused, tears coming back to his eyes. "Kind of like how people look down on bastards?"

Tam's worry turned to horror. His hands trembled as he reached up and brushed back Luca's hair, which fluttered in the wind. "Your great-grandfather and the people who say those kinds of things? They're wrong. No one in this world is born beneath someone else. A person's life is not worth less just because of how they entered their world. The Goddess doesn't spurn a common man for being common. A human for not being a witch. Or a child like you who… who should have had his dad this whole time." Tam felt his own tears rise as his voice cracked. "Never. *Never* think you are less than anyone, Luca. Or that you don't deserve kindness or good things."

"But I…" Luca struggled to form words as a sob choked itself from his throat. "I'm broken. I wasn't born right."

"There is no right way to be born, Luca. Not as a person. We all just live the best we can, but everyone—*everyone*—deserves to be raised with love and not be looked down upon. Do you understand?"

"I feel wrong things, though! I know bad things! Things people don't want other people to know, and I don't… I don't mean to! I'm evil! I shouldn't know those things! Even th-the Goddess! Th-they say she would never give another person power over minds or feelings, but I can feel things other people feel—"

Tam enveloped Luca in a hug. "You can't help what you just know, Luca. It doesn't mean you aren't a good person. Just because someone smells something bad, it doesn't mean they are responsible for the smell itself. You haven't used how other people feel to hurt them, have you?"

He could feel Luca shake his head against his shoulder.

"See?" Tam's voice was a whisper. "That's my boy. I'm proud of you, Luca. You've always been a good boy. And I love you no matter what. That will never change. I promise. You are not evil. You've *never* been evil."

Luca's sobs overtook him, rendering him incapable of speaking.

Tam's own tears spilled over as he held his son, refusing to let him go until he was ready.

He couldn't make up for the years of pain Luca had endured in this life or the others, but he hoped Luca understood that he no longer had to be alone. He wasn't anything more to Tam than his child, and as his father, Tam would move worlds for his son.

CHAPTER 26

REVISITING THE ROSEY GLASS

Aradia stood with her hands clasped behind her back at the top of the tallest tower of the Coven of Wittica's keep. She tiled her face upward toward the sun; the icy wind pierced through her thick wool coat, but she couldn't have cared less.

"P-pardon me, Your Magnificence," an earth witch called to Aradia, the woman's chattering teeth nearly drowning out her words. "We believe we have spotted the ship that Lord Tamlin boarded with the devil."

Aradia took another deep breath of refreshing, cold air. Then she opened her eyes and rounded back to the tower roof entrance, where the earth witch stood with the door open.

Once she'd stepped back into the dark stairwell that smelled of damp stone, Aradia grasped a nearby lit torch and proceeded down. "Where were they spotted?"

"They managed to make it to the Isle of Quildon, and presumably they are already in Rollum."

The first witch continued down the winding staircase.

"Their ship sustained damage—we believe from the confrontation with Louise and the others."

Aradia nodded to herself as she listened to the witch named Bea. "Alright. And do we have any witches there that can intercept them or watch them from afar?"

· "We do, but the citizens are becoming… wary of us. Word is quickly spreading that things have become tense between the covens and the crown."

"Ah." Aradia touched down on the top floor of the tower. Its stone walls were barely visible beneath the luscious plants that climbed the walls and ceiling. The windows remained firmly shut against the howling wind but allowed the sunshine to fill the hall. Aradia deposited her torch in a nearby holder and continued walking. "Any news on Ansar's ship?"

"He is still more than a week away."

Aradia rounded the curve of the wall, her eyes drifting to a particularly bulbous thicket of fresh raspberries. She reached out to pluck a handful of the juicy berries. After enjoying the fruit, she continued to the next staircase.

"Have the witches in Xava locate Tamlin Ashowan and his family. They are not to approach them. Just keep an eye on them. I will be assembling the ancient beasts shortly, but first I plan on paying the Daxarian king a visit."

"Yes, Your Magnificence."

"Tamlin and his mother will most likely be going to one of the brothels that they own for assistance, but I doubt they will wait there for long."

Aradia touched down onto the next level where, instead of inner walls leading to rooms, stone railings with intricately carved spindles opened to the middle of the tower to reveal a waterfall pouring down the remaining stories into a fresh pool on the ground. The first witch paused and watched the small clusters of witches around the pool at the bottom as they read or practiced their magic.

"Bea?"

"Yes, Your Magnificence?"

"Gather who remains of the coven council on the island. We will go over the plan. While I'm not opposed to a battle, I believe our victory can be achieved through negotiations and a bit of quickness."

"When are you hoping to take the devil from Lord Tamlin again?"

"Once I've gotten the king to agree to separate the coven from his rule. By that time, Wixim will be here and can help ensure that he upholds the agreement even when I've returned to the Forest of the Afterlife. There is no point placing another target on our back before then."

Aradia could feel Bea's eyes fixate on her profile.

"What?"

"Where were you… exactly?" she asked slowly. "In Zinfera, when you couldn't be found."

Aradia arched an eyebrow and turned to face her. "I was in a space that Tamlin Ashowan's magic has access to. A void of nothing."

Bea, a woman in her thirties, shrank back at this answer. "How did you escape?"

A fond half smile lifted Aradia's mouth as her eyes drifted to the stone floor. "An old friend helped me."

"Should Lord Tamlin do that to us, is there any way for one of us to find our way out?"

Aradia paused, then somberly replied. "No. Not unless he lets you out."

Bea gulped.

Aradia resumed walking toward the next set of stairs. "I'll ask the ancient beasts to be on standby in the event we aren't able to avoid a direct fight."

Blinking herself free of her thoughts, Bea bowed her head once more. "Yes, Your Magnificence."

Aradia's heart fluttered in her chest. Her time in the void had shown her just how wonderful a true rest from the world would be. And she could hardly wait to, at long last, be free of her earthly responsibilities. Once she managed to help the witches of Daxaria start following their true path, there was little more to do aside from die with her brother.

"Are you sure you want to do this?" Eli asked from Tam's side.

He didn't move his sights from the building in front of him. "Yes."

The couple stood outside a Rollom tavern with a pretty arched roof and a window box overflowing with delicate white flowers. A bustling street lay between them and the rounded door, which was made of pale wood and adorned with a circular window.

The wooden sign hanging above the crowds of the day read The Rosey Glass.

Tam let out a long breath. "Even though Wixim told us the truth about Luca, I need to know more. I need to know what exactly happened." He looked at Eli, who wasn't quick enough hiding her subtle grimace. "You don't have to come inside if you don't want to."

She tensed, then slowly folded her arms. "Luca is my responsibility now as well. I would also like to hear what this Rosaline woman has to say."

A humorless smile found its way up Tam's face. "Are you agitated because of how she treated Luca?"

Eli frowned. "Of course I am. He is the kindest child I've ever met, and everything I've heard about his time with her was subpar at best."

Tam tilted his head. "Well, we'll hear what she has to say, though we'd better be quick. As capable as my mother is, I don't like leaving the kids by themselves."

"Agreed."

The couple shared a final look of understanding and strode across the street.

Upon entering the tavern, Tam found himself hit with a wave of memories. The last time he'd been there was when he and Rosaline had ended their courtship.

It was still the same warm, welcoming place. The bar in the center of the small room was made of the same light-colored maple wood as the door, floors, tables, and benches. Lanterns, unlit in the daytime, hung upon every post. Colored tiles that Tam knew Rosaline had hand-painted hung around the walls and pillars.

The tavern wasn't overly busy, since it was the odd time between lunch and dinner. However, one large, brutish-looking fellow was leaning over the bar toward a woman…

A short woman with honey-blond curls and captivating dark-blue eyes. She stood with a tankard in hand as she dried it with an old towel.

"—I already told you once, Keseph, go home. Liam won't be happy to hear you've been scaring off customers."

Tam tensed.

Her voice was clear and calm, but her posture was rigid.

"An' I said after one more! For the road! Issa hot day out there! C'mon Rosie. Rooosie," the drunk named Keseph rumbled as he reached out to grab her chin.

Rosaline's eyes flashed as she darted back a step.

"Oy!" Keseph hollered belligerently. He tried to snatch one of the bottles from behind the bar while his other hand shot out to make another grab at Rosaline.

Tam didn't think. He crushed his boot heel into the back of Keseph's knees, seized his hair as he started to fall to the floor, and smashed his forehead off the bar.

Keseph crumpled to the ground, unconscious.

Tam's heart thundered in his chest as he placed his hands in his pockets. He felt how still Eli was at his side. He should've exercised more control.

Rosaline's face snapped up.

She stared right at Tam…

And didn't react.

Tam waited.

And waited.

Then it dawned on him… she didn't recognize him. He almost blushed. It *had* been eight years since they'd seen each other.

"Hi," Tam greeted awkwardly while taking a step toward the bar.

Rosaline backed up another step, her brows twitching in confusion.

A strong hand grabbed Tam's bicep. "Hey. Get the hell out of my sister's—"

Tam had barely turned to see Liam's face when Eli drove her elbow into his throat. He dropped to the ground with a gasping choke.

"Liam!" Rosaline cried out, tossing the tankard in her hands down on the counter with a clatter as she darted out from behind the bar. "Both of you, get out!" she shouted upon reaching her brother's side.

Tam spared Eli a quick look, to convey his surprise.

She gave a single-shoulder shrug.

Turning back to Rosaline, Tam slowly crouched beside Liam, putting himself at eye level with her.

"Let's try this again. Hi, Rosaline. It's been a little while. I used to tell you my name was Joe Voll, and I believe you gave birth to my son eight years ago."

Rosaline went deathly pale, and even Liam stopped trying to gasp for breath on the ground as he turned his purpling face to gape up at Tam.

Tam kept his attention fixed on Rosaline. "Do you think we could go somewhere to talk in private?"

Rosaline clasped a cup of cold water in her trembling hands. She had tied up her hair into a messy pile atop her head as the three of them sat in the office on the second floor. The small room had a cluttered desk, two short couches with faded floral upholstery, and a low table between them beside a window overlooking the street.

Liam had begrudgingly left them alone for their chat, which really was for the best. He'd glared daggers at Eli, and Tam in turn had to stare the man down.

Rosaline's younger brother was more or less the same as Tam remembered.

"I… I can't believe it's you," Rosaline began quietly. Her tired eyes rose nervously. "You're just so different."

Tam didn't comment on that observation.

"How is… How is the boy?" she asked stiffly.

Tam struggled to ignore the thorny vine of anger that seized his heart. "He's good."

Eli must have sensed that Tam was having a hard time starting the conversation, because she took matters into her own hands. "You briefly explained in your letter why you never named him, but regardless of what your brother's opinion was, it is more than a little peculiar that you didn't."

Rosaline's eyes fluttered over to Eli. Seemingly coming out of her daze, she put her cup on the table. "I'm sorry, who are you again?"

Eli arched an unimpressed eyebrow but didn't introduce herself.

"Rosaline. It is very strange you didn't name him, and furthermore… hurtful. I was surprised to hear how Luca lived before he found me."

"Luca," Rosaline whispered.

Tam hesitated, then nodded. "Yes. I named him Luca."

Rosaline swallowed and slumped back into the couch. She seemed… relieved.

"What happened after I last saw you?" Tam pressed.

Rosaline's hands gripped her peach-colored skirts. "I… It… It was a little while after you left that I found out about the boy, and I didn't have your real name—as I said in my letter—"

"Rosaline." Tam paused, then leaned forward. "I need the whole truth. I know almost everything I should know about Luca, but... his past with you doesn't make complete sense."

Rosaline's eyes darted to Eli.

Eli stared back coolly.

"I just didn't want to be a mother. You remember that. You knew I didn't want—"

"You could have chosen not to finish the pregnancy when you learned about it. But really, what we are asking," Eli interjected sharply, "is whether you are lying about giving birth to Luca. Or if someone gave him to you and ordered you to lie about how he came into your life."

Rosaline shot to her feet, her cheeks flushing. "*Who the hell are you?*"

"Rosaline," Tam called out gently. His dark eyes locked with hers, holding her in place. "I know Luca isn't like most people. I need to know how that happened. Was there an ancient beast that came and gave you the child?"

Her breath audibly stopped.

"If so, you are not in trouble, and I'm not going to do anything about it. I will happily leave here and never bother you again. I won't send Luca back to you. But I really do need to know what happened."

Rosaline took a steadying breath, then crossed her arms over her chest as she stared at Tam. "Gods... You used to be so quiet, and not nearly so arrogant."

Tam felt his face harden. "Rosaline. You realize you're not answering any questions."

"I don't owe you any answers. There's the door." She jerked her chin toward the exit.

"Rosaline, people are in danger because his history is unclear. I just need to know how Luca came to be."

"Let's see. There was red wine, and you had just gotten back from some sort of brawl. We went into my private room where—"

"I'm giving you until the count of five," Eli cut in sharply.

Tam's head snapped around at the same time Rosaline dropped her arms back to her sides.

Eli stood. "Someone is trying to kill Luca. This isn't the time for whatever past hurt you've harbored. Stop being a child and answer the damn questions, or does the safety of your eight-year-old son mean nothing to you?" There was a flash of a gold glint in Eli's eyes that was so quick, Tam wondered if he'd imagined it.

Rosaline's face reddened. "He's *evil!* Are you seriously saying I should have treated him as if he were norm—"

"Careful." Tam rose from his own seat. "Rosaline. If you truly believe that he is dangerous, then you really do need to tell me everything, and if you still refuse to explain, I am afraid I can't keep this matter quiet."

Rosaline glared up at Tam. "And what the hell does that mean, *my lord?*"

"It is starting to sound like you genuinely believed that Luca could have been capable of doing something horrible. Therefore, it would need to be investigated just who you were trying to hurt."

Silence rang loudly in the air.

"And he's not evil," Eli added gruffly.

Rosaline turned her withering stare at Eli, her contempt undisguised. "Fine. You want the truth? The absolute bloody truth? And once I give it, you'll go away and stay away?"

"I promise," Tam affirmed steadily.

Rosaline clenched her teeth as though she still was fighting the urge to kick them out. But eventually, she gestured back to the couches. "Fine. Sit. I don't want to have to ever talk about this again."

CHAPTER 27

BAD BLOOD

A *little more than eight years ago…*

Rosaline braced her hands on the counter, her head dropping to her chest as she battled back the bile that burned the back of her throat. Despite the chill of the wintry air that blustered into her tavern as the door opened and closed, sweat beaded along her hairline.

"This food poisoning is really getting the best of you, hey?" Liam's worried voice sounded out beside her as he placed an empty crate back under the counter at her feet. He had just returned from delivering their empty bottles to the distillery to get them refilled.

"Gods… Was it the tuna stew we had last month?" Rosaline managed between deep breaths.

A cup of water was placed in front of her.

She gulped it down thankfully, only for her stomach to roil in retaliation for being disturbed.

"Liam! Another ale! And Rosie, mind getting us more—oh, hey now. That food poisoning has to be finished with you!" Daryl, one of their regular customers, called out in surprise.

"I tell you, I'm tempted to see a physician." Rosalie pushed herself to stand back straight. "This bloody sickness has me exhausted and I have a business to run."

Liam grimaced as he eyed his sister sympathetically. "I've been telling you to go for a month."

"Ugh." Rosalie attempted to take a smaller sip of water. "I'll step out back for a breath. I probably just overdid it with the winter solstice stress is all. I'll give it another week to see if it wraps up."

Liam sighed and shook his head at her, but she wasn't in the mood for his quips.

Smiling at her customers as she passed them on her way to the back of the tavern, she grabbed her thick pink shawl from the back hook—it'd been a gift from her last paramour—and exited into the snowy street.

Tilting her face up to the inky sky that was sending down thick, wet flakes, she let out a heavy breath and relished the quiet.

Sidling over to a nearby stack of pallets that the ale delivery man would take next time he showed up, she sat down with a moan. Her lower back was throbbing.

Gods... I know I don't bleed often, but this course feels like it is going to be a nightmare.

A funny sensation seized her then. It was like her mind had brushed past a very obvious thing.

She stilled.

She cast her thoughts back to the last time she saw her former paramour. The young man with long black hair who hid in corners. He was quiet. Smoked cigars. He had had a soft, low, smooth voice that Rosaline had loved to listen to. The way he'd talk about books he'd read, or about the stars, it always lulled her into a state of relaxation. She'd lay her head down on the table in front of her after the tavern had closed, and she'd simply listen to him talk. More than once, she had fallen asleep there, and he had gallantly woken her and offered to carry her to bed.

He was younger than her, but he was attractive. Sweet. Unassuming. A nice dalliance.

They'd ended as things did when they acknowledged they were simply too different for it to continue in any more meaningful way. He was most likely from some kind of influential family, given the quality of clothes he had always worn, and Rosaline had no interest in getting tangled up in power struggles.

At present, she swallowed as panic and suspicion rose.

That can't be it. I can't be pregnant. I was told it would be highly unlikely to happen. I gave up on that idea ages ago.

But that funny inkling had sunk its teeth into her mind. So the very next morning, she forced herself to roll out of bed far earlier than she wanted to and made her way down the road to the physician's home where local patients were tended to.

The physician was a woman, which at first made Rosaline feel a lot better, but after a series of questions and tests, she informed Rosaline that without a doubt, she was indeed pregnant.

Rosaline's ears rang. It felt like all the blood in her body had drained out of her.

The physician kept talking, saying something about taking care of herself, then something about options if she needed help…

Rosaline had risen, thanked the woman, and left. She'd returned to work and finished the evening in a daze.

Her brother had asked where she'd gone earlier. She had lied and said something to the effect of talking to a vendor about a better price for eggs.

By the time the dinner rush had slowed down, Liam had shooed her off to bed again, claiming she looked ready to drop.

It was there in her bed, lying across the quilt her mother had left her when she'd died, that she'd stared up at the ceiling and finally willed her brain to come back to life.

I should probably try to tell him. *He doesn't live in Rollom, but he says he runs messages to different brothels. I could probably go to the brothel and tell them he has an unpaid tab here, and they'd let him know. He'd get the message and come…*

But then what?

Another voice, one more harsh but reasonable, echoed in her head. *You don't want this. You were disappointed at first when you thought you couldn't have children, but then you found your dream of owning the tavern. And here you are! You did it! You'll probably lose customers if they think you are wanton. Just deal with this now, and nothing will change.*

Rosaline sat up, a little uneasy, but settled on her decision. It really was the most logical one to make.

The next morning, she got up early once again and asked the physician for the herbs to end her pregnancy.

She'd been told to return in three days; they would be ready then.

With that complete, Rosaline was starting to feel marginally better. Nothing was going to change. Everything was taken care of.

Then she'd entered the tavern that was not open yet, and *he* was there.

A black-haired man with the most disturbing eyes she'd ever seen. They were an aqua blue that would have been exquisitely beautiful were it not for the three pupils that spun slowly around in each eye.

Her throat felt dry.

The hair on her arms rose up.

This man was dangerous.

"I'm sorry, sir," she said, already wondering if she should start screaming, "but the tavern isn't open yet."

The man tilted his head, his eyes roving over her body.

Rosaline backed up a step.

"It is as I thought. Good. This is easier." He nodded to himself, seeming satisfied.

"Sir, my brother is upstairs. I would hate to have to get him involved in—" The world spun. In a whirl of water and snow Rosaline was rendered speechless as her tavern vanished. After this alarming magical display, she doubled over and vomited on snowy ground.

"Apologies for the sudden travel. However, this is a delicate matter."

Rosaline stumbled, and a large, strong hand grasped her elbow as she tried to make sense of her surroundings once more.

She was standing on a cliff's edge. Before her lay the inky, frothing tempest that was the Alcide Sea; the cloudy sky above her spanned endlessly off toward the horizon.

"You are carrying an Ashowan child?"

Jolted from her shocked observations, Rosaline backed away from the creature she now knew without a doubt was not human.

He sighed. "We were worried we'd have to do this with the Ashowan daughter, so this is exceptional news. I must confess I was starting to doubt if my tampering was enough to make this successful, but it looks like I've finally had some good fortune."

"What do you want?" Rosaline continued backing away from the creature. Now that he wasn't seated, she discovered he was incredibly tall. At least seven feet.

The creature pulled out a vial filled with what looked like ash. "I want you to bake this and eat it. Oh. And add a few drops of blood, too."

Rosaline felt like she would be sick again. "No! Why would I—"

"You have a brother you care for, yes? The one back at your tavern?" The creature raised his eyebrows expectantly.

Rosaline felt tears well up in her eyes as they moved to the vial in his hand. This was a threat. But why? Why her? "What does that do?"

"This will be the advantage my master needs. We have never tried it before, and we only have one other vial left. There isn't much time, either."

"No! Enough cryptic *shit*!" Rosaline shrieked, as she trembled. "What is it? What does it do? What does it matter if I'm pregnant or not?"

The creature stared at her, the three pupils in each of his eyes turning slowly. "Do you really want to know?"

He glided closer, moving at such a liquid speed she didn't have a chance to back away again.

"These are the ashes the devil can be reborn from. My master has suffered for eons, and his sister has disposed of his allies one by one through the years. Even I cannot protect myself from her for long. So I am ensuring he will be placed in the safest vessel possible. The safest bloodline available. We have never tried this, as I said. My master did not believe it a just thing to do, but desperate times make rules of stone crumble under its grind."

"That… That will make my baby the devil?"

"It will. Only it will also be perfectly human. A human of the Ashowan bloodline. As well as the devil. He will be unlike anything he has been before, and in turn, this may change his fate."

"I don't want this. I won't do it," Rosaline whispered, her throat tightening. "I didn't even want this baby to begin with."

The creature sighed. "You will be compensated, and I do not expect you to keep the child for long once it is born. Just be sure not to name him if you wish him gone from your life later. Naming a creature creates a connection of fate between you. I would also recommend waiting some time before sending him off to the Ashowan family so that suspicions are lowered. Perhaps seven years?"

"You keep saying the child would be of the Ashowan bloodline…"

The creature pressed the vial into her hand. Rosaline tried to yank herself free from his grasp, but his hold turned to iron.

"That young man you bedded and who has fathered your unborn is the Ashowan heir."

"*No!*" Rosaline shouted, once again struggling against the creature. "He's Joe! Just Joe!"

"Believe what you want, but you will consume this vial of ash, or I will destroy your life. And if you try to get rid of that child, you will wish for death. Understood?"

Tears were overflowing Rosaline's eyes.

Why? Why did this have to happen to her? What had she done that was so wrong?

"Nothing you say will change this." The creature's three pupils spun faster, and Rosaline realized with surging dread that she was utterly helpless against this thing.

But there was one thing she could control. And it was the lone thread of control that she grasped with all her might.

I… Can never love this child. And damn the Goddess for giving me such a horrible fate.

Present day…

Tam felt sick.

He reached up and rubbed his mouth, feeling the tremor in his fingers.

Even Eli was silent.

Rosaline stared at the table in front of her. "I've hated you for a long, long time, Lord Tamlin."

Tam couldn't bring himself to speak.

"That… That boy. I owe *nothing* to him." Her voice rasped. "I did not want him. I didn't want any of what happened. And now that I've told you, I'll probably find some other horrible thing coming after me, won't I? Now that you know what he is. Now that you know that child should be locked away, or—"

"Stop… please," Tam whispered brokenly. He dragged his hands over his face before forcing himself to speak again. "Rosaline, I am… I am so sorry for what you went through. That you were doing all of this alone. Under duress. That you were threatened to… to have Luca. If you need anything, the Ashowans will provide it."

"I don't want anything from you," Rosaline informed him quietly; his horrified reaction to her trauma seemed to gentle her a fraction.

"I wasn't finished," Tam said calmly. "Please don't ever repeat this story to anyone ever again. Luca isn't the devil. He isn't evil. The imp was wrong—that was the creature that made you do this, an imp." Rosaline tensed, but Tam continued. "He… Our son… He's just a child. You never have to see him again. You never have to do anything for him again. But he has no fault in this. I'm the one you should keep hating. The enemies of my family did this to you, but that isn't Luca's fault. So please don't… Don't talk about him like that."

Rosaline's breathing quickened as her eyes grew red. "What about his dreams, hm? His nightmares? He dreamed of those beasts. Beasts like the one that came and made me bake those damn ashes into bread and eat it."

"He would have heard stories of ancient beasts. Children have nightmares," Tam explained gently.

"No. No, I… I know children. I've seen children. He is not a normal child. He isn't right. The way he just knows what kind of person someone is at a glance…" Rosaline shook her head.

Tam's hands gripped into fists that he forced himself to release. "Rosaline, that's because of something else."

"Liar." She choked on the word. "I birthed him. I raised him. I may not like him, but I know him. And I know what he is."

Tam was finding it hard to control his emotions. "Rosaline. I'm the one like that. He's… He's just like me when I was a kid."

Rosaline stared at him. Anger and pain practically pulsated from her. "I've not told people what that boy is before, and I'm not about to start screaming it in the streets now. I'm free of him. At last. Believe or say what you want, but I don't want to see you or him ever again."

Tam couldn't say anything more to that.

So he stood, his entire body numb. Eli joined him.

They descended the stairs, leaving behind Rosaline in her office, and headed toward the door. The luncheon patrons chattered jovially around them, a jarring brightness against the dark cloud that clung to Tam as he wove around tables.

"Dad?"

Tam stopped. His eyes ripped up from the floor to see Luca standing in the doorway of the tavern with Penelope at his side.

His heart was still stinging sharply from everything he had learned.

Luca shouldn't be here. He shouldn't have to see the people who hated him.

Eli moved first. She swooped down and grabbed Luca, hoisting him onto her hip as she hurried out the door. "Don't look back, Luca," Tam heard her whisper urgently. "Just hang on to me, alright? Don't ever look back here."

Tam raised his shaking hand to once again rub his mouth as he continued toward the door with heavy steps.

Penelope grabbed his dangling arm, and then she slipped her hand into his.

This small gesture made Tam look down and see her concerned brown eyes as she peered up at him. She had changed so much since they'd found her. Her face had softened. Even her eyes seemed to have widened as she glared less, and their shade of brown seemed warmer.

Tam stooped down and picked Penelope up as they continued down the street.

"Luca said we were near where his mother lived," Penelope explained with a hint of nervousness. "He was just going to show me the tavern quickly. Grandma is standing over there to watch us."

Tam looked with a start to see that his mother was indeed on the other side of the road. There was a knowing gleam in her eyes as she studied Tam's face.

He held her gaze, then looked at Eli who had reached the duchess's side once she, too, had spotted her. He saw in Eli's expression complete understanding of all he was feeling and thinking. He wasn't sure if that made him feel better or worse.

Then Eli turned to look at Luca in her arms, and surprising them all, she leaned over and blew a raspberry on his cheek, resulting in him shrieking in surprise and giggling.

The playful move made Tam blink. He stopped a short way from his family as Eli set Luca back on the ground.

Then she did the unthinkable by gently cupping Luca's face, forcing him to look at her, and saying, "I am the luckiest mother in the world, having a son like you." The barest hint of tears shone in her eyes, but they quickly vanished by the time she looked at Tam and Penelope. "And I am beyond grateful, Penelope, that you are our family now, too."

The little girl wriggled in Tam's arms. "You haven't officially adopted me yet… But… it will be good when you do. Someone has to take care of all of you."

Tam managed a small smile. "Well, I know my mother, for one, will appreciate that very much."

Penelope smiled shyly in response.

Clearing her throat, Annika stepped forward. "Alright, everyone. Let's have lunch, and then I'd best be off to see the king."

Tam bobbed his head and continued walking away from The Rosey Glass with Eli at his side. He doubted he would ever be able to forgive himself for being a part in Rosaline's suffering. He had no idea how to come to terms with the fact that he was still grateful beyond words not only to have Luca, but also to know he had been right.

Luca was his. His own flesh and blood… He just also happened to be the devil.

But really, who didn't have a little devil of their own?

CHAPTER 28

A SNOOPY SEER

Hamil glowered at the broken watch on the table before him. He crossed his arms stubbornly across his middle. His right knee bounced as he sat in the cellar of the brothel where he and the ragtag group from the boat had been staying while they sorted things out.

Tamlin Ashowan had instructed Hamil to see if there was anything of interest about the watch.

Hamil gently prodded a molar with the tip of his tongue in the dim lighting.

The room he sat in smelled damp and musty, but the rows and rows of wine and ale barrels suggested he might be able to enjoy the local variety at some point in the near future.

During the first week of their time on the mainland, the Ashowans had insisted they all stay sharp and not venture outside in order to avoid drawing attention. So the opportunity to sample some refreshments had been as dry as the Lobahlan desert.

Halfway through the second week, Tamlin, Eli, the children, and the duchess—whom Hamil thought was rather charming—had ventured off. Since their return, it had been a quiet remainder of the week, but Hamil and Bes had been promised a good meal and wine before they all parted ways.

Drawing himself back to the present, Hamil sighed, leaning his forearms against the edge of the table and eyeing the brass gears that gleamed in the torchlight. Honestly, nothing seemed all that strange about the watch. The only sign that this particular device was supposed to tamper with time was the compartment for the crystal.

"Do you even know how to put that back together?"

Hamil launched away from the table with a yelp of shock, only to find that Penelope had crept up silently near his right shoulder.

The little girl wore a lovely lilac-colored dress made of light chiffon, and her long, dark hair was partially pulled back. The duchess had ensured the child had had an impressive wardrobe in a short amount of time; she seemed to take great joy in styling Penelope's hair every morning.

"Erm—yes. Yes! I think I— Yes, I remember how it goes back." Hamil cleared his throat. "I'm just trying to see if I missed anything."

Penelope tilted her head at the pieces on the table and took a quiet step forward. "And?"

Hamil barely stopped himself from laughing. The expectant, serious tone in the little girl's voice sounded like that of a woman twenty years older.

"I can't see anything."

"Have you still not tried to put a crystal in?" she asked patiently.

Hamil cracked a half smile. "Ah. I do not believe putting in a crystal is a good idea. You see, if this watch does what I think it can, then it would do something that could be very bad for a lot of people. Not to mention it is quite difficult to get a crystal. I'm told the mages here in Daxaria guard them carefully."

Penelope's dark-brown eyes studied his face, her hands clasped behind her back as she leaned over even more closely to the table's surface and squinted. "If you already know what it does, why take it apart?"

Hamil cleared his throat again, a guilty flush climbing up his neck to warm his cheeks. Why was no one watching this child?

"Well, we aren't *exactly* sure we know what it does. But we *probably* know."

Penelope straightened with a disappointed downturn in her mouth that almost looked as though she were trying to imitate Lady Eli. "So you should put the crystal in to figure it out."

"No. Remember how I said it could be very bad for a lot of people?"

"How?"

Hamil pressed his lips into a thin line and weighed his next words carefully. "It's hard to say."

The little girl made an irritated sound with her tongue that prompted Hamil to stand. "Shouldn't you be back upstairs with Luca, Miss Penelope?"

Penelope didn't budge from her spot beside the table. "If you had a crystal, could we try putting it into the watch?"

Hamil drew his shoulders straight as he stared skeptically at the child. "Why?"

Penelope's eyes darted away as she shrugged innocently. "Would people die if the crystal was put in?" she ventured on without answering the previous question.

Hamil took his time answering. There was no way she had a crystal, right? Then again, hadn't this family surprised him at every turn?

"I don't believe they would die."

An excited glint sparked in the child's dark eyes. "Then why don't we just check?" Penelope pulled one of her hands from behind her back and held up…

A crystal.

On a chain.

Like the one the engineers would wear back home in Lobahl.

Hamil swallowed. "Where did you get that?"

His mind raced. They were in a brothel… Was it possible that she had stolen it from one of the customers? Or had she taken it from one of the sailors? Or the captain of the ship? Or from someone back on the Isle of Quildon?

"Let's try it." Penelope turned her eager face to the watch pieces.

Hamil moved to grab the crystal from her hand, but despite her attention being elsewhere, she was still paying enough attention to him that her hand snaked away from his grasp and into a discreet pocket in her dress.

"If you're too chicken to do it, I'll just try it myself sometime," Penelope announced matter-of-factly.

"Miss Penelope. Your family is oddly afraid of chickens, so I rather think being too chicken is a compliment. And just so you know—" Hamil bent down to be eye level with the child. "—this watch will never be left unattended and should not be taken lightly. It could do something like stop time, and you might get stuck in a world where no one can move but yourself. Or you could accidentally move something. Like a vase. Then a maid might trip over the vase, bruising her shin, and so she is late serving wine to her master, and this makes him angry, so he punishes her. Then her husband is angry that she has been treated so poorly, so he comes and tries to confront the master, only he gets himself killed." He took a breath. "Do you see what I mean now?"

Penelope's expression didn't budge. Instead, she said, "You didn't even notice me walk up behind you in an empty room. I can steal that watch really easily."

Hamil made an irritated noise in the back of his throat before grasping Penelope's shoulders and turning her back toward the cellar stairs. "I am bringing you to your mother, and I am telling her you stole a crystal from somewhere, and that you are going to try to tamper with something that could put you in danger."

Penelope whirled back around on him, wrenching herself from his grasp. "We're already all in danger! Can't you tell? And—And something about that watch is really important! I heard Tam and Eli talking about it! So we should know what it does, and we can figure that out! Tam said you were supposed to, and now we can!"

Hamil was about to give another speech on how the watch was dangerous, but Penelope was marching back over to the table.

She frowned at the pieces and then started to pick them up and fit them together. Only she was doing a terrible job. She could damage the gears with the force she was exerting; Hamil had to lunge for the pieces in her hands in an effort to save them.

"Enough! You might hurt yourself!"

Penelope's emptied hands curled into fists. "Put it back together and let's try the crystal. Or... Or else!"

Hamil's shoulders drooped, his longing for that promised divine cup of wine deepening. "Or else what?"

Penelope's eyes narrowed. "I'll say you hurt me."

Hamil blinked. "But I haven't."

The child then shocked him beyond reason by slapping herself across the face.

"Good Goddess!" Hamil snatched her arm to stop her from doing such an alarming thing again.

"I'll say you hit me," Penelope informed Hamil in low tones, her cheek already a bright pink.

Hamil nearly whimpered. "Tell the truth. This is an organized crime family, isn't it? Your father calls himself the devil, your mother is a giant hybrid beast, and your brother… He generally seems lovely. But he got really intense that one time!"

Penelope's mouth pursed. "Just put it together!"

"You know, I'd heard the occasional rumor about your family. About how wholesome you all were." Hamil lowered Penelope's arm but didn't let go. "Now I'm even questioning if the Sun Queen is as impressive as rumors say, or if she just has a bad temper and a good sense of where to stand for optimal lighting."

"Are we doing this or not?" Penelope insisted, her voice nearly a whine.

Hamil lifted his gaze to stare blindly ahead of himself. "I don't ever want children."

Turning back to his worktable, he briefly recalled how once upon a time he had enjoyed Penelope's company, and how frivolous those early days aboard the ship had been…

"What are you waiting for?"

Hamil plopped himself down in his chair before grumbling to himself, "Father always did say the real world would surprise me."

Penelope frowned. "What are you? A baby? The world is awful. Now hurry up!"

Hamil reeled back. "You're a beloved family member of one of the most influential families in multiple kingdoms. You of all people shouldn't be saying that kind of thing."

The little girl's lips quivered.

She looked away.

Hamil turned back to the table. He knew it wasn't the kindest thing to say with him being aware of her birth parents having died… But she *was* blackmailing him.

"I'm sorry I was mean. I don't need to be mean to you. Thank you for finishing the watch," she croaked. "I sometimes forget to be nice."

Blinking, Hamil turned back to see Penelope's face tilted toward the ground as she twisted awkwardly back and forth.

It took a moment, but eventually Hamil remembered he was technically the older one, and so he shouldn't hold a grudge against an eight or nine-year-old. So he returned his attention to the watch. "Why do you even want this watch fixed so badly?"

"I think more bad stuff is going to happen and… and this might help us."

Hamil carefully refitted the gears back together. "And why's that?"

"Reasons."

Shooting a dubious look over his shoulder, Hamil didn't press that particular topic. "I do need to know where you got that crystal."

Penelope fidgeted a little. "It's fine. The person I… I took it from they—they won't be… *too* mad."

Hamil narrowed his eyes but resumed reassembling the watch.

Penelope drifted toward his elbow but didn't say another word as she watched him work. At one point, Hamil glanced out of the corner of his eye at her and noted the way her brows knit together in interest.

He continued his work until at last the watch was whole once more in his hand, then he popped open the back and stared at the empty compartment. His heartbeat fluttered.

"Give me the crystal."

"I'll do it." Penelope's voice was quiet.

When Hamil turned around in his seat, he fixed her with the most serious look he could muster. "No. This is dangerous, remember, and—"

She snatched it out of his hands and bolted across the room.

"EY!"

Hamil rushed over to where Penelope had managed to wedge herself between two ale barrels. He tried to follow after her, but the size difference proved detrimental. This meant he had no choice but to watch as she pulled the crystal out of her pocket, pressed it into the back compartment, and, with shaking hands, turned it back around.

Sweat trickled down Hamil's forehead as he waited for something to go horribly wrong.

But nothing happened.

He let out a breath of relief.

That is, until Penelope reached up and twisted the pin at the top. She stumbled backward until she thumped against the wall.

"Penelope! Get back here! Now! You need to—"

Hamil's words were cut off as Penelope lifted her eyes, and he discovered they were filled with pure white light.

"Wh—"

A swell of light gathered over the glass watch face, then formed an orb and drifted upward. Two more followed shortly after.

Hamil's entire body tingled with a sense of power he had never encountered before.

The orbs of light proceeded to shoot out in separate directions, but all stopped when they had reached equal distance from Penelope. Then they stretched wide and tall.

Hamil gaped, at a complete loss for words, when images slowly appeared within the orbs.

In one orb, Penelope sat curled up in a cage in what looked like a ship's cabin.

Hamil barely managed to tear his eyes away from it, but he forced himself to look at the next image to find the duchess sitting in a sun-filled window with Penelope in front of her as she spoke with a warm smile while she pinned Penelope's hair back. It looked like a scene that could have taken place earlier that day. On shaking legs, he stepped back from the barrels.

Then the third image was of Penelope, Luca, two red-haired boys, and a blond boy standing on a grassy slope at night. Each of them screamed soundlessly. Luca suddenly bolted away from the line of children, though the image moved slowly.

Hamil's eyes widened as the scene pulled away from the line of children and revealed a battle—one filled with knights, witches, and ancient beasts. Four figures were gathered away from the battle, all facing something Hamil could not see...

His heart felt as though it had ceased beating as he witnessed the dark, terrifying vision; then the scenes flickered and were replaced with white light. The lightened shapes collapsed back into orbs and whizzed back to the watch still held in Penelope's hand.

And just as quickly as it had happened, the watch ceased to look special in any kind of way.

Hamil tried to swallow away the uncomfortable feeling in his throat, but it remained parched with awe.

A soft rustling snapped his attention back to Penelope, who had sunk to her knees.

There were no words that could come to Hamil as he tried to form some semblance of a logical explanation for what had happened.

Regardless, he crouched. "Penelope... Please come out now."

The child nodded; she was visibly trembling. She stowed the watch, with its crystal, in the pocket of her dress and crawled out from between the barrels.

"Are you alright?" Hamil asked gently.

She remained slumped on the ground for a moment. But when she lifted her face, she revealed a flood of tears pouring from her eyes. She let loose a heartrending sob, and the words: "I w-want Tam and Eli! *Dad!*"

Hamil was caught between wanting to get her parents and staying with her to make sure she didn't do anything else dangerous.

A cloud of black-and-silver vapor whooshed out from behind Hamil, and by the time he had blinked, there stood Tamlin Ashowan, the wisps of magic already dissipating.

Tam dropped to his knees and gathered Penelope into his arms as she cried. He gently laid his hand over the back of her head, making soothing shushes as he managed to stand back up with the child in his arms.

When he turned back around to lock eyes with Hamil, the expression on Tamlin Ashowan's face had the Lobahlan feeling a mite faint.

"What the hell happened?" Tam growled.

Hamil felt his own unsteady hand come up to rest atop his head. "Uh. I don't... know. But I think Penelope might have a better idea than she lets on."

Tam did not look in any way placated by this answer.

And Hamil had the disappointing premonition that he wasn't going to be enjoying a glass of wine anytime soon.

CHAPTER 29

ARADIA'S ARRANGEMENT

Giving a single nod, King Eric Reyes barely managed to hold on to his temper.

The news that Captain Taylor had just delivered had not been what he'd been hoping for.

The elite knights combing the woods and countryside had not been able to find any trace of his sons or Aster Fuks. In the beginning, there had been signs the boys had been headed toward Sorlia, but their trail had suddenly gone cold. Fin was on his way back to the castle after having contacted some of the businesses in which his wife invested in Sorlia to have them watch out for the group of child runaways. He had also alerted both the small staff that cared for their Sorlia estate and the staff caring for Lord Les Fuks's keep to send word should the boys appear on their doorsteps.

Eric raked a hand through his hair as the captain of Daxaria's military stared at him sympathetically.

"Lord Fin says he still hasn't had any visions to indicate that the princes are afraid," Captain Taylor reminded him carefully.

"I know," Eric bit back. He was well aware how brash he sounded. "But if something does go wrong, it can go wrong quickly. With the coven no longer at our disposal—with the coven as an *enemy*—you know as well as I do it's only a matter of time."

The military man pressed his mouth in a thin line, making his salt-and-pepper beard bristle.

Eric cursed and placed a hand in his pocket as he turned away. "There hasn't been any update from Kat or her mother. In fact, even the Zinferan merchant ships haven't come as they were supposed to, and we have no idea why. Has the first witch already taken over Zinfera? Is the Coven of Giong running things?"

The captain looked in the same direction as the king, out through the open arches that overlooked the courtyard. Eric stared blindly at the bright, sunny day that did nothing to lift his spirits. An unease permeated every nook and crevice without discrimination.

"Ah! Captain Taylor!"

The king glanced back over his shoulder in time to see Hannah, his head of housekeeping, approaching with a tray ladened with two slices of peach pie, a teapot, two cups, a container of sugar, and a dainty pitcher of milk. The entire tea set was painted with blueberries. While it wasn't what the king's food would normally be served on, Eric always enjoyed the fun dishes Hannah discreetly added to the castle's stores.

"Pardon me, Your Majesty." Hannah gave as much of a curtsy as she could manage with the fare in her hands. "I thought you two would be in the council room a little while longer."

Eric glanced at Captain Taylor, who visibly tried not to show his thoughts. But Eric already knew the military man was going to sit and enjoy that slice of pie, since he had only just returned from leading the search for the princes in the area north of Xava that morning.

Sighing, Eric put extra effort into gentling his demeanor for Hannah's sake as he turned and gestured toward the council room door. "You two should enjoy the tea and pie. I need to try contacting Rollom again."

Captain Taylor was just starting to bow in assent when his eyes abruptly cut to something over Eric's shoulder.

Eric whirled around, silently blaming his lack of sleep for his dulled senses. Otherwise, he would have noticed sooner that someone was approaching.

Then he registered what he was staring at.

There was a young woman with strawberry-blond hair and round, clear blue eyes flanked by two towering beings…

Imps.

Eric almost reached for his belt, but he hadn't clipped a sword on that morning.

"Aradia," he called, squaring himself as the woman, clad entirely in black, approached him.

She arched an eyebrow and quirked her mouth in amusement. "I see my new appearance does not fool you, Your Majesty."

Eric heard the creak of leather behind him, and he knew that Captain Taylor was reaching for his sword. The king held out his hand, stopping the movement.

"What are you doing here?" His heart thundered and his mind buzzed. What did this mean? How did the first witch get all the way to the castle without him hearing a word? Was Kat safe?

If she hurt Kat, I'll kill that bitch myself, even if it costs me my life.

"I'm here to have a conversation, Your Majesty." Aradia smiled coldly, as though sensing his thoughts.

"Where's Kat?" Eric asked, his head slowly tilting over his right shoulder as he ignored the threatening looks the two imps were giving him.

The first witch gestured toward the door of the council room. "We can discuss Her Majesty's safety in—"

Faster than Captain Taylor could react, Eric pulled the knife from the man's belt without a glance back and leveled its tip at Aradia's eye. "There won't be a discussion unless you tell me directly if my wife is safe."

The two imps drifted forward, but Eric didn't flinch.

Aradia held up her hand, stopping them.

"As I was saying before you interrupted me, once we discuss the more pressing matter of two covens declaring war on Daxaria and Zinfera and their demands, I'd be more than happy to share with you Her Majesty's whereabouts."

Gruesome thoughts filled Eric's head as he continued staring down the first witch. "There will be no discussion of terms if this is a threat to her safety. This will be a war."

Regardless of the knife leveled at her face, Aradia rolled her eyes. "Forsake the lives of thousands of innocents all for your wife. What a king you are."

"You might not know this, because it's been a while." Eric's hand wrapped around the neck of Aradia's black tunic and yanked toward him. The knife drew even closer to her eye…

The two imps hissed like boiling kettles, but again, Aradia raised a hand, keeping them still.

"My wife is the actual hero. I'm the sick fuckup who will burn this world to the ground if anyone hurts her."

Aradia blinked at his rush of breath but otherwise seemed unfazed. "For how boisterous and devil-may-care your wife is, I would have thought you'd have mellowed a little."

Eric allowed the tip of his dagger to move closer to the first witch's eye. "Where is she?"

"Last I saw her she was perfectly fine." Aradia sighed. "I can't tell you where exactly she is right now, as I have no idea. Can we get on to more official matters?"

Eric's grip loosened fractionally as he registered the lack of deceit in Aradia's face. Though he knew she was an exceptional liar, he trusted his gut, which told him he would have felt something.

"Is the duchess safe?"

Aradia didn't mask her irritation. "I haven't a clue. Now, if you do not release me and agree to this conversation that I came to have *in peace*, I will be forced to make this day a rather bloody one."

Eric wished he could simply throw her into a dungeon and declare the whole mess sorted and done with. However, it wasn't just the first witch he had to deal with; there were the imps and the covens, too.

So with no small amount of hatred over his lack of power in the situation, Eric slowly released her and gestured to the council room.

Straightening her tunic and leather corset, which had gone askew, the first witch stalked into the room with the imps following behind her.

Eric watched her go, then turned to the captain. "Wait out here."

Captain Taylor frowned. "Your Majesty, I should be there for your protection—"

"You can't protect me against those imps. There is no point in both of us risking our lives," Eric interrupted, his tone firm.

"There has to be something we can do!" Hannah insisted. The head of housekeeping looked between the king and captain, her brows furrowed and her eyes bright with panic.

Eric set his calmest stare on her. "No, Hannah. There isn't. Fin won't be back for a little while, and we have no witches in the castle. The stone golem loyal to Pina is out at sea. The first witch knows this. It's probably why she's here. If she's being honest about this being a peaceful talk, then maybe this won't end with bloodshed."

Hannah glanced at the captain. "I have a bad feeling about this."

Captain Taylor met her eyes before turning back to Eric. "As do I. Be careful, Your Majesty. I'll be just outside here."

Eric nodded, then moved into the council room and closed the door behind himself.

If Aradia found it strange that Eric was having the conversation without anyone else present, she didn't show it.

Eric seated himself at the head of the table, as he always did for council meetings. His stomach was leaden as he stared at the first witch. A strange foreboding filled the air, despite Aradia's insistence that this would be a peaceful talk. He didn't like it one bit.

"Your Majesty, I'll get to the point. Witches are too different from humans. They should have a government of their own to keep them organized."

"They already have that. In the covens," Eric reminded her curtly.

Aradia sighed. "They need their own leader. One who actually understands what it means to be a witch. Even your own council thinks witches are too different to be named a king."

Eric didn't bother asking how Aradia knew about the incredibly private matter of succession for Daxaria. He already had guessed that the coven leader Louise Riddel had been fully immersed in this betrayal.

"That's because we the people have only just started to adjust to the idea of witches being a fixed part of our society. We understand that big changes must be made slowly. Finlay Ashowan has made great strides in this matter."

"Speaking of the house witch…" Aradia settled back into her chair while crossing her arms and legs. "There is talk of his son, Tamlin, not inheriting the dukedom."

"Because the dukedom was granted in light of Lord Finlay's contributions as a diplomat. With Lord Tamlin presumably not taking on the role, what reason is there for the title to stay the same? But I don't see how this is relevant to what your original ransom request proposed." Eric's words rang with disdain.

Aradia's foot bobbed in the air. "The point is that your kingdom is struggling to offer witches any stability, yet you continue to make decisions about the role of witches in society without comprehending their true purpose and abilities. That is why either a temple or an independent state should be granted to the covens. Or a disbursement of power with witches having their own representatives like Lobahl where political matters are much more evenly distributed."

"Separating witches from humankind would inspire a great divide in the people again."

"Some separation is expected. And that is not a bad thing. In recent years, you and your father have worked to bring about harmony between the two groups. You've done it by humanizing witches in the eyes of the common people and by elevating witches with significant power and showing that their abilities are there to serve the humans." She paused, her expression neither hostile nor eager. "The longer you try to push that narrative, the bigger the collapse will be when the truth comes out."

Eric frowned. "Witches *are* people. They have the means of controlling the elements, but they feel love and hate; they eat and sleep. They marry humans. Have family with humans."

"How many humans do you know who can't allow themselves to get angry or they'll burn their house down?"

"Two. I don't know if you've ever had the pleasure of meeting Lord Oscar Harris or his wife, Lady Mackenzie. And that's just on my council," Eric retorted flatly.

Aradia balked but recovered after a moment's thought. "Alright. What about a prince who misses his mother and can't stop causing a torrential downpour that nearly destroys the farmers' crops for an entire city?"

Anger flared in Eric's chest, but he battled it back just enough to silently concede… she had a point there.

"You are thinking of how to minimize the world's awareness of witches, and as a result, you keep trying to put them in boxes that do not fit them. Your son Antony? He has weather magic, which is phenomenal and powerful. What if instead of worrying that he'll drown your city, there was a place he could go, fully supported by others of his kind? He could learn to safely master his powers without fear of hurting someone else."

Whichever way Eric had thought the discussion was going to go, it wasn't this. "Then the organized witches would be convened under one government, but who would hold them accountable if they started attacking humans? Common people would be powerless."

"The fact that they were hunted to near extinction here in Daxaria decades ago shows that is not the case. Furthermore, that is not a witch's purpose. Again, this is something that you human rulers have not grasped." Aradia uncrossed her limbs and leaned her elbow on the council table. "Witches exist with a holy purpose. They are here to help humans find balance with nature. I think you and your father have managed as well as you can, but we can make this world even better, Your Majesty. We can make a place for witches like your son to master their craft. A land they can call their own. And if they choose to live on Daxarian or Zinferan, or Troivackian land, then they can register with those kingdoms. You would have full awareness of who is coming and going, as would we."

Eric listened and drummed his fingers on the table. "I see the merits of your argument. However, years ago, you supported a man by the name of Aidan Helmer. Aidan Helmer didn't dream of a utopia for witches. He wanted power, and he even went the extra mile of being a disgusting human being by believing there was a hierarchy to witches based on their power."

Aradia's eyes lowered, and a brief weariness took over her features. "I lost a friend because of that temporary allegiance." She lifted her somber gaze to Eric. "Aidan Helmer was a means to an end. I was stuck in Troivack decades ago, when women were not treated kindly. Additionally, if I had tried to rise in power or implement the changes I'm proposing, my brother would have quashed them."

Eric openly expressed his doubt over her words.

"I do not believe that there is a hierarchy to witches and their powers. And you are more than welcome to ensure this as this new land is developed," Aradia assured calmly.

"You led a rebellion that slaughtered thousands of people in order to bring ancient beasts from the Forest of the Afterlife for you to command."

"To suppress my brother," the first witch snapped before she closed her eyes and took a steadying breath. "Your Majesty. I have *always*, and at great detriment to myself, worked to bring about peace between humans and witches. It was my brother who did everything he could to destroy that. I was desperate in Troivack. The devil… he has bested me for far too long. Once I succeed here? Once I've helped set up a safe place for these kingdoms for my kind? I will happily leave."

"If what you're saying is true, why didn't you try to align with us sooner? If you're really as well intentioned as you say—"

"There needed to be enough momentum from the covens. Witches needed to understand what I was trying to do, and I needed enough support. I also needed a strong enough defense to stop my brother from interfering." Aradia suddenly looked the millennium or so that she had lived; she once again slumped back in her seat. "Your Majesty. You've had your own struggles with ruling and battling against the weight of representing your people. You've struggled to protect those you care about—"

"Mostly from you and your brother," Eric reminded.

Aradia shot him an imperial warning look before continuing. "I've been trying to protect all of humanity and witches since I was put here. I've endured things that broke me. But now, at long last, I have organized with the covens. I have enough power behind me, and all that is left is to reach an agreement with yourself, and the Zinferan emperor, and to get ahold of my brother. He and I will go home, and this will all be over."

The king remained silent as he turned over her story in his mind.

In a way, it lined up with what they knew.

She still had committed heinous crimes. Crimes that if Eric thought too much about them, he would slip into a storm of all-consuming rage. However, he also knew that he himself had done abhorrent things in desperate times. He couldn't imagine the sins he'd rack up if he had endless lives, and what the first witch was suggesting was the dissolution of the chaos and suffering.

"If we reject this proposal, will you go to war with us?"

An enigmatic half smile climbed Aradia's face. "I've already swayed enough people, and I can tell that you are seeing my point. So if you reject it, I won't declare war, but it may find its way to you regardless."

Eric didn't like her overconfidence, but he also knew she wasn't exactly wrong. Even so, he had to confirm. "To reiterate. If we reject this, you yourself will not declare war or bring in the ancient beasts."

Aradia's expression shuttered. Then she straightened up in her seat. "I will only declare war and involve the ancient beasts if you choose to protect the devil. So, Your Majesty. Do we have an understanding?"

CHAPTER 30

THE DUCHESS'S DEPARTURE

Tam watched his mother's profile as she stared thoughtfully at the opposite wall.

She had been scheduled to leave for Austice after lunch, but the incident with Penelope and Hamil had paused her plans.

Penelope had settled down with a warm cup of milk tea clasped in her hands, while Luca sat beside her and gently stroked her hair. The fact that she allowed him to do this showed the extent of her distress.

Hamil stood in the doorway to the small, cozy sitting room they had gathered in, located at the back of the brothel, and gnawed on his thumbnail.

"So three images. Past, present, future, like what we've read about, and what Penelope has said she sees when she holds someone's hand," Tam began slowly from his seat on the fuchsia couch across from Penelope.

Part of his hesitancy was because his mother had had a... somewhat strong reaction to learning that Tam had indeed fathered an illegitimate child, and that Rosaline had been forced to suffer because of him. A shoe may or may not have been wielded with more deadliness than a seasoned soldier with a sword. Though she had stopped when she realized the distressed state he was already in.

"It sounds like that is the case, but, Penelope, is it possible that those images were your own future? Have you ever been able to see your future?" Annika gently posed the question from the armchair between the two couches as Penelope sniffled into her cup.

"I have… dreams… But it's hard to tell what are predictions and what are just my mind," she replied thickly.

"How can this be…?" Hamil whispered before dropping his hand from his mouth and making a slow circle on the spot. "How can you all be so… much? A seer, a devil, a hybrid ancient beast… All that's missing is the first witch and we have some kind of, of a reckoning!"

"Don't forget the dragon," Tam couldn't help but prod at Hamil with a weak note of good humor.

Hamil shot him a look that made clear he did not appreciate it.

Smiling guiltily, Tam turned back to his mother, his elbows still braced on his knees.

Eli had not yet returned from her outing. She had gone out earlier with the madam of the brothel to arrange for their few belongings to be sent to the Ashowan keep in Austice, and for transportation for the rest of them. Tam had no doubt she would help give Penelope a better sense of security in that moment.

"Alright, Penelope, why don't you go back to your room and rest, hm?" Annika suggested with a kind smile.

The little girl gave another sniffle, then nodded. Sliding off the chest she had seated herself on, she set down her teacup and, with her head lowered, exited the room.

"Luca," Tam called softly. "How about you go finish your math homework?"

"Aw!"

Tam shot his son a firm look that had the boy grimacing, but he slowly followed his sister out of the room with heavy footsteps.

Once the adults were alone, Tam turned to Hamil. "Have you ever heard about something like this before?"

Hamil shook his head. "Seers are incredibly rare, and after a few bad incidents with the other watches that had been used to stop time, experimentation was banned."

"This doesn't change anything," Annika announced suddenly.

Both of the men looked at the duchess in confusion.

"We aren't going to make Penelope do anything with it again. We should destroy it and that will be the end of it." Her somber eyes cut from Hamil to Tam.

Hamil let out a long sigh of relief. "Thank you, your grace. That is absolutely the wisest thing to do. I must say, I've been saying something similar for—"

"I disagree. I think we have to let Penelope decide what to do with it." Tam's interruption was followed by stunned silence. He met his mother's gaze head-on. "As Hamil says, seers are rare, and the fact that the watch might only be used by Penelope suggests that, somehow, it was meant to be hers. Maybe not *now*, given the fright she just had, but eventually, she may wish to use it to help her understand or utilize her own abilities. I say that we keep it safe for her, and if she decides she wants to destroy it when she is an adult, she can, but... that's my opinion."

Annika pursed her lips.

Hamil spoke up first. "Lord Tamlin, this isn't—"

"You yourself said that seers are rare even in Lobahl. The watch supposedly can't be used by anyone else. So what's the harm?"

"Because we don't know that it can't do other things! Furthermore, what if Penelope shouldn't have that kind of powerful item?" Hamil exclaimed while moving farther into the room.

"Is everything alright in here?" Bes and Eli appeared in the doorway to the sitting room. The Lobahlan woman stared at Hamil as though he were growing a tail, and Eli shot a questioning look in Tam's direction.

"Why is Hamil being serious? What's happened?" Bes asked, pointing at her friend and fixing the duchess with a worried look.

Annika rose from her seat. "We discovered what the watch does. Hamil will share the details with you. For now, I'm afraid that regardless of today's discovery, I'd better start my journey back to Austice. I'll stop in Sorlia to ensure the brothels are aware they should be watching for the princes, and see if I can dig up any information on their last known whereabouts. Bes, Hamil, please give my regards to Duke Cowan. He will host you and keep you safe until a vessel is available to take you back to Lobahl. He is a good friend of our family and will ensure no one knows that you are here."

Hamil's jaw clamped shut as he visibly struggled to give up his argument from earlier.

"Tam, Eli, you two come with me while I prepare my horse."

The duchess didn't wait for any arguments as she lifted her chin and briskly strode out of the room. Hamil and Bes shared another long look, but Tam knew they would only discuss everything once they were alone, and they were not likely to share their thoughts with anyone else.

At last, with her final saddlebag buckled onto her chestnut mare, Annika looked at Tam and Eli, who stood waiting in the middle of the stables.

"Tam, I'm going to take the watch with me. I think you are right that it seems fated to belong to Penelope, but right now, we cannot afford for it to be stolen or broken, given what you two are going to set out to do."

Tam agreed, procured the watch from his pocket, and handed it over to his mother, who slipped the chain over her head and tucked it under her tunic.

"Do you two have any ideas on how you are breaking into the Coven of Wittica's records?"

Tam nodded.

"Good. If any problems come up and you think you will be delayed longer than a month, I want you to return to Austice. The family needs to be united right now while we sort this out. Not having any means of communicating has been too much of a problem."

Again, Tam nodded.

In the hazy glow of the sunshine that poured in through the open barn doors and illuminated the clouds of hay dust, Annika openly studied her son. Then, folding her gloved hands in front of herself, she stepped forward.

"Protect my grandson and granddaughter. I believe in you and love you. Be safe. Once you arrive in Xava, be sure to alert our businesses there if your father hasn't already." A short but meaningful farewell. Tam could see the warmth in her eyes, conveying to him that regardless of recent events, she did not think less of him.

The duchess then turned to Eli. "You. Take care of yourself and my next grandchild. I know you are a sensible woman, and I already trust your judgment a great deal. I know Kraken annoys you, but do listen to him. As much as I am loath to admit it, he has been right more times than I care to count. Even when his opinions and suggestions seem outrageous. And yes. Yes, I agree that he can be *very* vexing."

Eli inclined herself respectfully in response.

"Also. I understand that you want to carefully consider marrying my son before any sort of official betrothal…"

What? No! No, no, no! Tam widened his eyes, in an attempt to wordlessly communicate that she needed to stop. Talking. *Now.*

Annika Ashowan, predictably—much to Tam's chagrin—ignored her son and continued on to say, "I just want you to know that I think you would make an exemplary addition to the family, if that is what you choose."

Tam calmed down fractionally.

"But if you prefer to remain single, you will also have my support. As much as I adore our family, I'm not oblivious to the fact that we are…" Annika trailed off as she peered at the barn's beams thoughtfully. "Busy? Complicated?"

"Nosy and intrusive, more like," Tam muttered.

Annika's eyes narrowed on her son, but when she spoke again, she still addressed Eli. "And don't worry about the child. We will support the two of you in every possible way in either scenario."

Eli remained bowed as she responded. "I trust in the Ashowan duchy's reasonable handling of such an outcome."

Tam rounded on her. "You really know how to inspire confidence in our relationship."

Eli straightened and raised an eyebrow at him. "I was simply expressing my appreciation of the duchess's generous sentiments. Why are you so insecure?"

Tam stared at her flatly. "I can't tell if you are seriously asking me that."

Surprisingly, after a beat of silence, a slow smile rose on Eli's face.

Tam folded his arms.

"My apologies," Eli said while barely stifling a chuckle. "I don't mean to continuously torture you like you think I do. I just don't know what other woman says she loves someone, raises his offspring he had with another woman, carries his next child, travels with him to other continents, shares his bed—"

"Where are you going with this?" Tam cut in loudly.

Eli sighed then laughed. "My point is, you know I'm not someone who is going to spout ballads about loving you. However, my actions should make my sincerity clear enough."

Tam pressed a hand to his chest. "And yet you haven't purchased a ring for my finger. Is this all I am to you? Someone who, in your words, is too handsome? Someone to bring you fine tea leaves and jam biscuits? Your human shield?"

A polite cough interrupted the couple, snapping their attention back to Annika, who didn't mask her amusement. "Need I remind you both that we are in a rush?"

Eli blushed, and Tam grinned before he turned back toward his mother. "Sorry. I'll see you in a month at most."

Annika bobbed her head right before Tam leaned down and kissed her cheek.

When he'd finished, the duchess grasped the reins of her horse and began to lead the mare out of the stable, though she paused in front of Eli. She cast an appraising eye over the younger woman's body and gave what sounded like an agitated huff. "You say you are two months into your pregnancy?"

Caught off guard by the nature of the question, Tam frowned while Eli blinked rapidly. "Yes."

Annika's mouth twisted. "And you haven't had any morning sickness? No sore back? Sore feet? Headaches?"

"No, I haven't." Eli shot a questioning look at Tam. "I believe I've put on a small amount of weight, but it's negligible."

"And we did confirm that she was pregnant with the brothel physician," Tam added, wondering if his mother was doubting Eli's condition.

"Yes, yes, I know that. I just…" Annika paused as she turned to her horse and mounted it gracefully. "I had a horrible time being pregnant. Your sister, Tam, as you know, also had a terrible time being pregnant. I think I'm jealous and annoyed." She sounded mildly surprised.

"I'm… sorry?" Eli did not hide her confusion over how to respond.

The duchess merely gave another long, beleaguered breath. "I'm happy for you, Eli, that you don't have those symptoms. It just makes me wonder two things."

Tam and Eli glanced briefly at each other before looking back up at the duchess.

"The first is why women have such varied experiences. The second"—the duchess gave a half smile—"is if this is indicative that you are carrying a witch, and whether or not this has something to do with their magic."

Eli shrugged. "No one but the Goddess can answer the first question, and regardless of the answer to the second, it changes nothing."

Annika tilted her head. "True. But it's fun to wonder."

Then with a wink, the duchess squeezed her horse's sides and set off through the barn doors, leaving Tam and Eli behind to prepare for their own departure to Xava where they would go on to infiltrate the Isle of Wittica.

CHAPTER 31

THE GLOOM OF GUILT

By the evening of Annika Ashowan's departure, it was time for both Hamil and Bes to leave Tam and Eli's company.

Having solved the mystery of the watch, Tam had followed through on his promise. He arranged for the Lobahlans to spend the rest of their time in Daxaria with Duke Cowan, where they would wait for their ship home. Duke Cowan was a trusted friend of the Duke Oscar Harris, who had become acquainted with the Ashowan family over the years.

Hamil had avoided Tam for the remainder of the day following the incident with Penelope, until the time had finally come to bid farewell. The pair stood near the brothel's stables; as he approached, Tam noted the way Hamil subtly placed himself in front of Bes.

He barely resisted a wince. He couldn't really fault the man for not feeling amicable or trusting toward him.

"Hamil, Bes, I hope you enjoy your time with Duke Cowan," Tam called with a light, airy tone.

Hamil's grim expression didn't budge. "Thank you."

Tam stopped a respectable distance away from the pair. "I know you two aren't going to think of me fondly, but I do hope you know how much I appreciated your assistance."

A small jerk of Hamil's head was all Tam got in response.

"Right." Tam stowed his hands in his pockets and bounced onto the balls of his feet as he peered down the quiet side street in the waning daylight. The sky flushed with pale blues and purples, and two bright stars poked their heads through the colorful visage to herald the coming night. The cool breeze brought with it the scent of grilling meat, and muffled sounds of laughter came from the various establishments nearby.

"You don't need to wait with us," Hamil informed Tam, his voice tight.

"Better that I do for safety's sake. Duke Cowan has a witch that can help guard you two, but I'm going to be cautious until you're in his care."

Hamil's eyes narrowed. "You do realize we are more afraid of you than whatever alleged war is taking place, right?"

Tam felt his cheeks warm as he cleared his throat. "I *am* sorry about everything. Under different circumstances, I think we all could've gotten along well."

"I'm not holding my breath," Hamil muttered.

Tam felt his cheeks warm at that, and so he cast his mind about for a change in topic. "It's starting to get chilly at night, hm? Already seems like autumn is getting closer."

Leaning forward from her protected position behind Hamil, Bes shyly joined the conversation. "I have always wondered what autumn in Daxaria would be like."

A little relieved that Bes didn't completely hate him, Tam smiled. "The colors are wonderful, and the harvests are celebrated with all sorts of great festivals. If you ever get the chance, I recommend visiting Sorlia or Xava. Given that they have the largest farming communities, they have the best—"

"I take it that is our escort?" Hamil interrupted loudly. His eyes were homed in on the wooden carriage, varnished and gleaming, rocking its way closer to where they stood. It was a style of carriage often used by merchants; Duke Cowan had astutely provided a discreet way to transport the Lobahlans.

"It should be. I'll confirm with the driver and witch before you two board." Tam moved forward and waved at the driver who, upon reaching the trio, pulled the horses to a stop.

The carriage door opened. Out stepped a man with short, black curly hair and dark skin, wearing a fine deep-blue coat. As soon as Tam locked eyes with him, the man broke out into a smile.

"Urick!" Tam didn't hide his surprise. "I didn't know you were working for Duke Cowan! Last I heard, you were the head of one of the coven schools!"

The older man was another friend of the Ashowan family, and son of the mysterious yet famous royal botanist of the Austice castle. "Well, the schools are temporarily closed, and with everything being so uncertain, I thought I'd lend my talents to the Cowan duchy. Glad to see you're alright, Lord Tam! I heard you'd been missing for a while."

Tam chuckled. "Something like that. Anyway, this is Hamil and Bes. They ran into a bit of trouble with some pirates, so we brought them with us back to Daxaria, but they need to get home." Turning back to the aforementioned pair, Tam was mildly taken aback by the utter shock on both Hamil's and Bes's faces.

"You're Lobahlan!" Bes sputtered in awe.

Urick grinned. "I am Daxarian, but my father and aunt are Lobahlan. It is lovely to meet you both."

Bes and Hamil looked at each other in amazement, then back at Urick.

Hamil spoke first. "What is your father's last name?"

Urick opened the carriage door for the duo, still grinning. "Jelani."

Surprised, Bes's hand came up, as she thumped Hamil's chest with the back of her knuckles. "Jelani! You mean your father is *Kasim* Jelani? He is the one who designed and grew half of Judge Mago's gardens in Lobahl! There are public gardens and parks that he and his family—"

Hamil's hand came up and clamped over Bes's mouth. "It is *lovely* to meet you! Shall we talk more in the carriage?"

Laughing, Urick nodded and helped them with their luggage. Tam then informed Urick that the other members of the Lobahlan crew were staying elsewhere in the city. He would send the list of establishments that housed them, so they could all reunite when the time came for their employers to set sail.

With the Lobahlans safely stowed in the carriage, Tam gestured with his head for Urick to step away from the vehicle.

Once out of earshot of the driver and the carriage occupants, Tam spoke quietly. "What news have you heard about the covens and the kingdom?"

Urick grimaced. "Things are tense. A lot of witches have gone into hiding already. Mostly because the general public is starting to get wary, thanks to the confusion."

"Would you say the majority of the witches are involved in the rebellion? Half?" Tam already feared the answer.

Urick's gaze wandered away as his mouth pressed together thoughtfully. "I was certainly startled when the news came out, but I have a friend or two who did come to me and tell me they had been privy to the coven's plans. So it is hard to gauge how many are aware of what is going on. The coven leaders are saying they want a state of their own. A place where witches can live, where the coven rules and acts as its own government without reporting to the crown."

Tam nodded somberly. "I've heard about it. Allegedly they've been pushing this agenda into the schools for years. I'm glad to hear you weren't a part of it."

Urick let out a long breath. "A lot of people are becoming desperate and afraid. Some of the witches are scared they will start being hunted again; others are getting angry that the coven is doing this. Then there are the ones who believe in this movement and what it stands for. I'd say the witches in Rollom and Sorlia tend to be more satisfied with the way things are, while the ones in Xava and the small towns have been more heavily swayed."

"I'm guessing that the witches in Austice are more of the mind that things should stay as they are, because of my father and sister's influence?"

Urick hesitated, and Tam could tell that he was once again not going to hear good news.

"They are incredibly divided in Austice. I'm told that because of how often the coven leaders visited the city for council meetings, they took every opportunity to reiterate their agenda in the schools and with their allies."

Tam stared at Urick. It was evident there was a little more to it than he was saying… so he raised a quizzical eyebrow and waited.

The ice witch made a noise of disapproval, then revealed the reason for his reticence in saying more. "Prince Antony… when he affected the weather in Austice and the farmers nearly lost the majority of their crops for the year… he upset a great deal of people."

"He's a child!" Tam exclaimed before he could stop himself.

"I know. I know he's a boy, but that kind of ability? It's already making people nervous. Which in turn, I imagine, has placed a lot of stress on the king. While it made sense at the time for the queen to attend to matters in Zinfera, it seems to me that things are teetering quite dangerously toward civil unrest. Her Majesty needs to come home and help show the people that they don't need to be wary of witches, and that she can help curb Prince Antony's magic when he can't control it."

Tam had the very unpleasant premonition that there wasn't much chance things would resolve as tidily as they'd hoped with the first witch's removal. If the entire kingdom was yet again at odds over witches, then they were all in for a very tough few years.

Weariness seeped into Tam's body.

He just wanted everything to be finished so he could go home with his family.

Urick attempted to console Tam's obvious stress. "I'm sorry I didn't have better news for you."

Tam tried to smile for Urick's benefit.

The ice witch clapped a hand on Tam's shoulder. "Things will work out. Your father is most likely going to whip up some magical solution that will make us all wonder why we bothered getting so serious in the first place. I like the new haircut, by the way! And I didn't know you trained. You look good! I'm sure everyone back in Austice will be happy to see you back home."

This time, when Tam felt the urge to openly recoil, he managed to keep it from his face.

"Thank you for taking care of the Lobahlans. I'm sorry to say I didn't make the best impression."

Urick chuckled. "Did you ignore them and read the entire time?"

Tam shifted his feet awkwardly. "Not exactly."

Turning to the carriage, Urick issued a wave over his shoulder. "Oh, Tam. You probably didn't offend them as badly as you think."

"I don't think a lot of people respond well to threats to their well-being."

Urick laughed again as he climbed into the carriage.

Tam reached up and rubbed the back of his neck. Evidently, the man thought he'd been jesting...

Well, given the way Hamil and Bes had reacted to him, Tam doubted they would keep their experiences with him to themselves.

Sighing, he turned and headed back to the brothel. "I might be getting a new reputation sooner rather than later. To think I left Daxaria wishing it would change. Didn't think it'd get worse…"

His right shoulder pressed into the doorframe, Tam stood in the hall of the attic quarters they'd been given by the brothel owner. He stared at Penelope and Luca, fast asleep in the same bed, their hands clasped over the blankets.

Eli's whispering footsteps came to a halt at his side.

"You'll wake them," she murmured.

Tam smiled gently without taking his eyes off the children. "I know. I'm going. I was just checking on them." He reached over and quietly closed the door, moving out into the hall. "Luca is growing like a weed. We need to get him clothes that are a little bigger once we get to Xava." He shook his head in awe as he and Eli proceeded toward the end of the hall. The door there led to their shared room, which was draped with several swaths of colorful fabric. The faint musk of incense clung to the air.

"Penelope, too. She probably would appreciate a pair of pants as we keep traveling and moving," Eli added as Tam opened their door and gestured her through.

Once Tam had closed the door behind himself, he nodded belatedly, his eyes trailing the floor.

"Are you alright?"

His gaze snapped up to Eli, who had seated herself on the bed and was staring at him with her head tilted.

Blinking himself back to the present, Tam smiled. "I have you all to myself now. Why wouldn't I be alright?" He stepped over to Eli, cradled her neck, and kissed her meaningfully.

When he eventually pulled away, he saw the heat in her cheeks and heard her quick inhalation.

However, she leaned back, her dazed eyes once again becoming focused. "I mean, are you alright after what happened with Rosaline? We haven't really had a chance to talk about it."

Tam's hand fell away from Eli's neck as he straightened. He lowered himself down to sit on the edge of the bed beside his beloved and grasped her hand. "I... don't know."

Eli's mouth twisted. "There wasn't much you could do."

"I know... I guess I just wish I had checked in with her at least once."

A rueful smile found its way onto Eli's face. "While I would agree, I do see what you mean about her not seeming to be the type to appreciate that kind of gesture."

Tam bobbed his head in acknowledgment, but once again his mind drifted to less-than-pleasant thoughts.

"She could've found a way to contact you. She even said so. You thought you were being respectful."

"She still suffered because of me. Because my family has some kind of fate with the Gods and the devil, she got tied up into it. She had to go through something no one should. Ever."

Out of the corner of his eye, Tam could see Eli turning to face his profile. "That is not your fault."

"Feels like it is. I think I need to teach Luca about the value of abstinence if he starts looking at girls."

"You're still glad you had him, though."

Perhaps Eli had meant to say the words as a question, but really, the volume and firmness behind them hinted to Tam that she perhaps had some of her own anxieties tied to the whole ordeal.

Lying back onto the bed, Tam tugged Eli down to lay on his chest. Taking in a deep breath, he only let it out after closing his eyes. "That's where my guilt comes in. I'm just so happy he's mine. Happy that I have him. Rosaline had to suffer, and I... I can't say I regret it." Tam struggled to swallow past the stone lump that had formed in his throat.

Eli squeezed his hand. "There isn't a right answer to how someone could handle this or how to feel about it."

"Sadly, I'm aware," Tam chuckled bitterly. "You want to know the other thing I'm terrified of? One day..." He opened his eyes. He didn't bother battling the tears that rose up. "One day Luca is going to ask about his birth mother. And I... I don't know what I'll tell him."

Tam could feel Eli lifting her face to him, but he couldn't look at her. Couldn't allow himself to find any sort of solace in her eyes.

"You'll tell him his mother was brave, and that she did the best she could. But when she wasn't able to be strong anymore, the Gods sent me to him. He's mine, too, Tam. You made it so."

At this, Tam relented and met Eli's gaze. The calm determination and tenderness that greeted him felt even more powerful than he had anticipated.

Left with no other option, he hauled her up to himself so that they could be face-to-face.

This meant that he could easily press a kiss to her forehead before murmuring, "That sounds perfect. Let's say exactly that."

Tam proceeded to hug her to himself, silently thanking the Gods for her existence.

Despite her face already growing slack with sleep, Eli still managed to say, "An abstinence talk isn't a bad idea, though. I don't exactly want to be a grandmother in ten years."

Unable to help himself, Tam burst out laughing. "Sure. We can talk to him about that, too."

CHAPTER 32

HENPECKED

"So the fishing vessel will drop anchor here. I'll row us as close as the rocks will let us get. Then I'll take us through the void to the top of the island." Tam pointed at the map spread out on the table in front of himself, Henrietta, Eli, and Kraken. "From there, Henrietta, you say there may be a patrol?"

The chicken witch nodded. "There could even be an air patrol that sees us from afar."

Tam's eyes narrowed on the map thoughtfully. "The problem is that I don't know exactly how far the distance limits are for my magic, and during this venture is not the best time to figure it out. And if I try to experiment beforehand, I could accidentally drain my magic."

It had been three weeks since they'd bid farewell to the duchess, Hamil, and Bes. Since then, they'd traveled to Xava and taken up residence in a brothel madam's personal property while she stayed in her quarters in the brothel. Tam had gone to let his family businesses know about the princes, but discovered his father had beat him to it. This told him that it had been a few weeks since his nephews had first gone missing.

The brothel madam's cottage was surprisingly small and sweet, with whitewashed walls, periwinkle-blue-painted window frames and doors, and thriving flower boxes matching the color. The view from its back lawn was spectacular, as it was positioned on a quiet cliffside street overlooking the Alcide Sea.

At present, Luca and Penelope were playing out in the yard with a leather ball they had found in one of the baskets the madam had in her home. It was possible she had once had children of her own.

Eli placed her hands on her hips, and her next words were said in careful tones. "We were already banking on revealing Kraken and myself in the event we got caught, so…"

Tam lifted his gaze. He had a sneaking suspicion what she was about to suggest, and he already didn't like it.

Eli locked eyes with him. "Let's just land right at their front doors and force our way in."

"No." Tam hadn't even waited a full breath before dismissing the suggestion. "They won't know you are my familiar and may attack before you land. We don't know exactly how people are punished for harming a familiar, but I doubt it's immediate, and furthermore you aren't taking that risk. They attacked you on the ship without asking any questions, and there is no reason this venture will be any different."

Eli scowled, but she didn't appear to disagree with his reasoning.

"Kraken, any thoughts?" Tam asked.

The familiar stared at the map, blinked once, then leapt up with a chirp and sat down.

Everyone waited, then watched as he raised a paw and gently tapped at the base of the Isle of Wittica where the dock was.

"There is a witch there logging arrivals. If we fight our way up, they can just block the stairs, and then we'll have wasted our energy," Tam explained.

Kraken tapped again, then looked into Tam's eyes and mewed.

There was something they weren't seeing.

Tam squinted at the map.

As the moments dragged on and he couldn't discern whatever it was Kraken was trying to show, he stood back straight with a sigh. "Henrietta, is there anything else about the dock that could help us?"

The chicken witch twisted her mouth as she locked eyes with Kraken. "Er—Lord Tam, there is one way to figure out what he's saying. As you know, I can only talk to the people whom I've turned into chickens, but your mother was able to converse with Kraken in that state. So I… um… I could turn you into a chicken and you could talk to him yourself."

A long, drawn-out nasally breath sounded from Eli as her lips quivered, but the upper half of her face remained still.

Tam allowed a dry smile to rise. "Wouldn't I be a rooster?"

"N-no… I… uh… can't turn men into roosters just… justchickens." She murmured the words so quickly they slurred together as her cheeks burned.

Tam dropped his chin to his chest with a weary chuckle as Kraken meowed boldly. Presumably he was in favor of this new plan.

"Alright. That'll be fine. You can turn me back immediately after though, right?"

Henrietta paused, opened her mouth, then closed it again with a wince.

Tam folded his arms. "How long do I have to be a chicken before I can be turned back?"

The chicken witch dusted imaginary dust off her skirt, avoiding his gaze. "By dinner I should be fine to turn you back. Possibly sooner. Turning witches into chickens is harder than turning humans into chickens. Especially if they're powerful—and, my lord, you are definitely powerful."

Tam watched Henrietta's bashful expression carefully. "Are you *sure* that it will only be a little while then?"

"I think so, but I really can't know for certain," Henrietta rushed to say, her cheeks pinkening.

Tam turned to Eli. They were still technically being hunted by the coven. If there happened to be a surprise attack, and Tam was a chicken, things could be tricky.

Eli met his stare head-on. "I think if Kraken knows something useful, it's worth you being a chicken for a little while."

With the final opinion in, Tam sighed, then stepped back from the table and held his arms straight out. "Alright. Feather me up."

Another snort sounded from Eli as Henrietta rose from her seat with a pained smile and lifted her hand. "Don't worry, Lord Tam, it… it *shouldn't* hurt."

"What do you mean *shouldn't—*"

Tam felt his insides compress and suck in on themselves. A roaring wind that felt like his eardrums had burst overcame him. It was horrible!

And then…

It was done.

Quick, but unpleasant.

Tam blinked. *Huh. Mum was right. The colors* are *different as a chicken.*

"GODSDAMN FINALLY!"

Tam let out a shriek as he tried to stumble back, but his buttocks bumped against the table leg as Kraken leapt down and prowled in front of him.

"YOU! YOU RECKLESS, UNGRATEFUL KITTEN!"

Tam could do nothing but gape. Kraken had such a low voice compared with the squeaks and chirps he emitted when Tam was in his human form.

"*I have wanted to show you my back paw for weeks now, boy,*" Kraken growled.

"W-what?"

"*You think you're going to die. You think you are destined to die in place of the devil. I know the way your idiotic mind works. Your father was the same. Wanting to die for the greater cause. Well, I can say to you what I couldn't to him. PULL YOUR HEAD OUT OF YOUR ARSE!*" Kraken's voice boomed. Tam dazedly wondered if it sounded like a yowl to Eli and Henrietta.

Tam's chicken legs gave out from underneath him. How had Kraken known what he'd suspected? Sure, he had mentioned his sense about the darkness coming for him, how he suspected he had always meant to take on the moniker of the devil, and how he'd asked the familiar to watch over his family… Okay. Yes. It did sound obvious.

Kraken loomed closer. "*You will not be dying. Not until you reek of age and babble about fat great-grandchildren. You dare to accept a fate for yourself that would devastate my witch?*" A black paw draped itself over the back of Tam's neck as he lowered his mouth to Tam's head. "*Think again.*"

Tam cleared his throat. "*What was it you were trying to tell us about the island?*"

"*I've raised you since you were in change cloths. Try to die before I say so and I will stalk you in the afterlife.*"

"*Kraken. We're on a time limit.*"

The paw that clubbed the back of Tam's head wasn't a surprise, but Tam still winced at the claws.

"We aren't through talking about this, kitten." Kraken's paw plunked back down on the floor as he turned back to the table and, with a wriggle of his backside and a slight scrape of his nails on the floorboards, he leapt back up onto the table. *"Get your feathered ass up here."*

Tam gradually pushed himself back to standing, though his entire body felt awkward. He tried extending his wings, but one of them whacked the chair on his left, which sent him bobbing forward.

He looked up at Henrietta, who had without a doubt been listening to his one-sided answers to Kraken the entire time. *"Mind putting me on the table?"*

She smiled congenially and did as he requested. Once he was back staring at the map at Kraken's side, Tam was about to repeat his question to the cat when Eli burst out with a squawk.

Tam jumped. She had her hand shielding her face as she laughed. He had never heard her laugh this hard.

Maybe I should let Henrietta turn me into a chicken more often.

Kraken let out an impatient rumble.

Eventually Eli managed to settle herself down, though when she made eye contact with Tam, she yet again lost control.

Tam turned to Henrietta. *"Do I have funny feathers or something?"*

Henrietta smiled politely, though there was a twinkle in her eyes. "No, my lord, you just are…" She visibly struggled for the words. "Normally tall? A bit intense? Ominous?"

Tam was caught between embarrassment and confusion. *"Me? Intense? It's just the situation! I'm the mellow one of my family!"*

Henrietta was unable to stop the laugh that escaped her mouth. "My lord… forgive my saying this, but that doesn't say much."

Tam grumbled.

"You were the one saying we were on a time limit," Kraken reminded Tam curtly.

"Right. Sorry. What is it you wanted to tell us?" Tam strutted closer to where Kraken sat as in his peripheral vision, Eli gradually calmed down.

"Every fortress has secret tunnels and routes for the owners to escape. Find the tunnels. There is only one exit point on this island."

Tam balked in the face of such an astute point.

He repeated it to Henrietta, who relayed it to Eli.

Eli's eyes widened as she whirled on Henrietta. "Do you know where those tunnels are?"

The chicken witch shook her head. "That is above my status as a coven member."

"I can sniff them out," Kraken huffed confidently.

"It'd still be hard to approach the dock without drawing an attack," Tam reminded.

Kraken peered over his shoulder at Henrietta. *"Does the coven know the chicken witch is in our care?"*

"Probably."

"But they wouldn't know she is aiding us, would they?" Kraken persisted.

Tam paused, then tried to lower his voice. He had no idea if it worked or if chicken sounds stayed at the same volume for Henrietta. *"Kraken… She can still turn on us."*

Kraken came to his feet and meandered over to where Henrietta stood, listening, her expression tense. *"You can tell this witch that should she betray a familiar that trusts her, she can expect a very gruesome consequence."*

Tam turned to face Kraken's back. *"I'd like to hear more about this alleged holy law at some point, Kraken."*

The familiar didn't say anything, merely gave a purring laugh as he slinked off the table and flopped over in a sunspot just behind Eli.

It was then Tam discovered that chickens couldn't sigh. He gave up on expressing his exasperation as a chicken when Kraken wasn't even listening, instead explaining the new plan to Henrietta. He tripped over delivering Kraken's threat, and watched her flush with no small amount of guilt.

"I won't betray you. I… I still believe a separate place for witches is what we should be aiming for, but I agree that the way the covens are trying to achieve it is wrong." Henrietta's words wavered, but her conviction was steady.

Tam thought he bowed his head in appreciation, but the movement was a lot quicker than he intended, and he wound up pecking the table.

He was secretly glad he couldn't blush in this form.

He did his best not-a-real-chicken walk over to Eli, whose mouth was quivering again, and tilted his head.

Eli pressed her lips together helplessly. "Hrmmm."

There was no way she knew that he was spiritually grinning ear-to-ear. So he decided to give his dear one a bit of amusement and, as loudly as he could, screeched. "BKAAAAAA!"

Eli was on the floor in hysterics instantly.

Tam looked over at Henrietta, who was staring at him with an oddly tender expression.

Sidling over to Tam as his beloved continued to gasp on the floor, the chicken witch leaned down and whispered, "I've never seen someone become so warm because of their loved one." She nodded at Eli who was still struggling to breathe through her hysterics.

Tam felt his heart swell with pride.

Eli was a frosty woman, but to know he could bring out such fun in her? Gods… He'd get turned into a chicken every day of his life if that's what it took.

CHAPTER 33

A BUMPED-UP BETROTHAL

Tam swept his hand through his wet hair in an attempt to keep his black locks out of his eyes. His hair was now long enough that he needed to tie half of it back. It was just before the dining hour, and he had been returned to his human self. Though he had insisted on a bath afterward to chase away the odd prickling sensation in his skin from the experience.

He reached for the clean tunic he had set out atop the battered pine dresser and tugged on the garment gratefully. A cool breeze sailed through the small open window to his and Eli's room. As he tucked his tunic into the top of his pants, Tam heard the bedroom door opening and closing. He looked over his shoulder, though he already knew who it would be.

Eli casually stepped into the room, her right hand coming up to cradle her lower back. She watched Tam with a cool mask of observation in place.

Her hand placement drew Tam's eyes downward. He paused. Blinked. Then slowly straightened.

"You already have a bump. When did that happen? That seems early."

Eli's calm demeanor dissipated as her cheeks flared a delicate pink. "I'm just bloated! It happens! Besides, the physician said around three months it wasn't uncommon to show a little, and it really isn't that noticeable. These pants were tight to begin with, and I'm not moving around much, *and* you keep feeding me. Most people wouldn't think anything about it, I just—"

Tam smiled and took two quick steps to wrap his arms around Eli, quieting her string of defenses. "I'm just surprised. And if I'm being honest? Excited. I hadn't noticed it this morning. I know it won't be apparent to anyone else, but… well… obviously, we know differently."

He was lying just a little.

The curve of her middle was actually quite telling. The physician had said every woman experienced pregnancy differently. According to what Tam was seeing, while Eli did not have many negative symptoms, evidently she did show early. Tam silently appreciated Eli for remembering to confirm that they were not in fact expecting twins.

"It feels like this happened over the course of a day," she mumbled into his shoulder.

Tam brought his focus back to the present. "How do you feel about it?"

Eli sighed. "Awkward."

Tam chuckled. "Does it make you feel better to know I'll be a chicken again tomorrow?"

She paused. "A little."

Laughing again, Tam leaned away from Eli. He kept his arms locked around her as he peered down yet again at the evidence of their next child.

"So, feel like making an honest man out of me once we get back to Austice?"

Eli's lips pressed together, but there was a playful twinkle in her eye that revealed she didn't mind his teasing. "I don't know… I'm not sure I'm ready to be tied down."

"Are you planning on leaving me as soon as you have our third child?" Tam feigned a look of hurt.

She gave a pensive twist of her mouth. "I do still have to become a magistrate, and I'm told infants cry a lot."

Tightening his hold, Tam whirled Eli over to the bed. He backed her into the footboard to force her to lie down so he might climb atop her, making her laugh.

"If I have to, I'll hire three wet nurses so you can study without issue." The tip of his nose was less than an inch from hers.

She sighed with a smile. "I guess that would help."

"Is that a yes then? You'll marry me?"

Eli wriggled beneath him, but Tam lowered his greater size over her until he felt the bump against his own stomach. It was hard not to let on how giddy that sensation made him.

She laughed a little more. "You're too impatient, *my lord.*"

Tam emitted a faint growl, which ignited an entirely different kind of shine in Eli's eyes.

However, after a quiet moment, she spoke. "I… I'm not saying no… And I'm not saying yes," she began slowly. "You see, it will be more complicated to get married than you think. With my departure from the imperial family, I'll have to file paperwork if I want to be a part of Lord Harris's family. That would take a while. Not to mention Daxaria will already be busy handling the fallout from the coven. So—"

Tam did not bother hiding his pleading expression. "A betrothal isn't as complicated. I'm not asking you to marry me tomorrow—though I would—but can we say we are *getting* married?"

Eli didn't answer straightaway as her eyes moved to the ceiling.

Seeing this, Tam's eyebrows twitched. He slowly eased off her to sit on the edge of the bed. "Is there something that is bothering you, or that you're worried about when it comes to us getting engaged?"

Eli joined him at the edge of the bed.

Tam braced his elbows on his knees and loosely clasped his hands while he waited for an answer.

She fidgeted, and her previously happy expression dwindled.

Tam's gut twisted unpleasantly.

"I've just seen things go wrong. I've seen the best of people and places change and trap a person. I'm scared that something will happen and that I will once again be stuck and powerless."

As much as it pained him to admit, Tam had of course heard his own fair share of horrible stories where a once-loving partner changed into something awful. Someone abusive, or complacent…

"I know that no matter who gets married, it's a risk. The sanest and best-tempered of people can become vile. You can be a princess in allegedly one of the safest places in three kingdoms and still get kidnapped. And in my experience, when you bet on a more influential person or place, you risk more going wrong. Tam, you are a member of one of the most powerful families—arguably—in the world. I can't..." Eli trailed off and licked her lips before continuing. "I can't get trapped again. I don't have the strength to survive it again. As much as I believe you are a good person from a good family, I know how wrong this could go. I've lived through great things falling apart, and I can't do it again."

Tam felt an unpleasant mix of nausea for Eli's past traumas and pain.

He understood what she was saying and why.

It didn't make it easier to hear.

"Is there anything I can do that would make you feel more secure about moving forward?" Tam asked, his voice soft.

Eli gave him an apologetic smile. "I don't know that there is. You've been perfect. I know I'm… I know I'm hurting you even though you joke about it a lot, and I'm sorry."

Tam reached over and grasped Eli's hands, which had fidgeted through the conversation. "Thank you for talking to me about it. If there is something I can do to help you feel more comfortable, please let me know."

Tears rose up in Eli's dark eyes and shone in the pale light. "You've already done everything possible. You don't throw that we're having a baby in my face. You don't point out how the baby would be looked down on by some people. You don't try to tell me that our familiar bond means our souls are compatible… I expected all of that, and you wouldn't be wrong for saying it."

Tam leaned over to gently kiss the top of her head. "I don't need to say it, because you're smart. Obviously, you would have thought about those points, and you would've already figured out what you think about them."

Eli sniffled.

Tam didn't bother commenting on the fact that the uncharacteristic emotion was most likely due to pregnancy. He'd made that mistake only once. He'd received the silent treatment for the better part of a day before he had plied Eli with jam cookies, her greatest craving as of late. She hadn't been wrong when she'd complained that he kept trying to feed her. Feeding her seemed to make her happier. So Tam kept doing it, and he would keep doing it until the physician or Eli told him to knock it off.

"What kind of wedding would we have?" Eli's question caught Tam off guard.

He grinned as his eyes drifted thoughtfully to the floor. "A small one. Obviously Luca and Penelope would be there, along with my parents, Lord Harris and his wife if you wanted, my nephews, Kraken, Pina… That sounds good to me."

"What about Bong and Jeong?" Eli frowned. "And why didn't you list your sister?"

"I wasn't invited to her wedding. Seems fair." Tam shrugged while giving Eli a boyish smile. As immature as the sentiment was, they knew he would invite Kat regardless of what he said.

"Don't you have any other friends?" Eli prodded next.

Tam arched an eyebrow. "And here I mistakenly thought you would've wanted a quiet wedding."

Eli snorted. "I don't want to offend anyone. You *are* a future viscount and duke."

"Oy. You know as well as I do that I probably won't become a duke. Especially not with everything going on with the covens."

"Oh, right."

"Besides. If you recall, I had alienated myself rather efficiently before you came along."

Eli tilted her head back and forth as she wordlessly acquiesced to his point.

Tam lowered his hand from Eli's neck to rub soothing circles along her back.

The cottage was quiet aside from the sound of gulls crying in the distance outside. The cool breeze and warm sun made for a rather pleasant, sleepy atmosphere.

"A small but proper wedding… Is that even possible given I'm…" Eli looked down at her middle as she trailed off.

Tam raised his eyebrows and pressed his lips together. "Erm. What is a 'proper' wedding in your mind? Because I'll be honest with you, the fact that my illegitimate son will be attending might thwart that objective."

At this reminder, Eli's stressed expression eased away, and she suddenly looked confident and bright. "You're absolutely right. Why would we want a proper wedding if it meant Luca couldn't attend?"

Tam grinned. "So… You're saying we are betrothed, or you are just talking hypothetically?"

Eli's expression flattened as she angled herself on the bed to face Tam's profile directly. "Fine. You can call me your betrothed. But I don't want a wedding date set."

Tam's face felt like it had been ignited with joy.

Seeing his reaction, Eli blushed. "Gods… Why your mother was ever worried about you remaining single, I'll never know. Don't worry, Tam. One day you'll make a beautiful groom."

He tossed his head back dramatically. "Thanks. I'll grow my hair out for the occasion."

At his silliness, Eli succumbed to another laugh. "Gods. I love you. You are clingier than I would've thought, but I love you."

His smile changing to a smirk, Tam pressed a very loud kiss into Eli's cheek. "And you're stuck with me."

"Not yet I'm not," Eli muttered through her own smile.

Tam ignored this and instead focused on kissing Eli on the lips, to stop her from making any attempt to take back her agreement. It was another small step for their relationship, but a giant one for Eli. Despite the fact Tam was supposed to break into the sacred buildings on the Isle of Wittica the very next day, he couldn't help but bask in the moment. It felt nothing short of divine.

Eli halted their kissing. "Oh, one thing about the wedding."

Tam would've agreed to get married with his face painted like a beaver's if it just meant he could keep kissing her.

"Harold the donkey is banned from the ceremony. He can join the reception."

Tam managed to steal another kiss before responding. "But he'd make the prettiest flower mule in all the land."

Eli tried to object between his advances and laughing, but didn't quite succeed, and so they basked in the moment without allowing anything else to detract from it.

CHAPTER 34

A CONNIVING COVEN

"The elders are not expecting you." The gruff witch manning the lone dock at the base of the Isle of Wittica scowled down at Henrietta. The sloshing waves beneath the dock nearly swallowed the small fishing boat Henrietta had arrived in. It bobbed in the water next to a larger vessel that dwarfed it.

Tam strutted around the man's feet, once again in chicken form.

Henrietta wrung her hands together. "I just escaped from the Ashowans, and I want to report back so that I have permission to return home."

The dock witch stiffened when he heard the mention of the famous family. His blue eyes widened, and he even tried to stand marginally taller, though the pronounced hunch on his back stopped the action from doing much.

"How'd you escape *them?*" he asked suspiciously.

Henrietta gave a weak smile. "I was with the duchess, and she wanted to return to Austice quickly. She was trying to place me in the care of her allies when I managed to run away."

The man stared at her for a long moment before his thin lips curled upward in a cruel smile. "Well, aren't you lucky. You see—oop!"

Kraken slinked forward from under Henrietta's skirts and wove around the man's legs. Taking her cue, Henrietta shoved the witch off the dock into the water.

She bolted to the open iron door at the end of the dock, with Tam and Kraken close on her heels.

She barely managed to slam it shut before she heard a bellow of rage behind her, and the telling splash of water being pulled from the Alcide Sea. A thundering wave slammed into the door from the outside controlled by the dock witch.

While Henrietta panted, sweat already dripping down the side of her face, Tam inspected the narrow tunnel they found themselves in.

"We have to hurry. There are witches stationed halfway up the stairs. That witch outside will raise the alarm, and they'll come running," she whispered.

Kraken was already prowling the cave they found themselves in.

Tam noted the staircase to his left that was carved out of the cliff and appreciated that there was some light. High above them, at the top of the stairs, a round glass ceiling braced against the cloudy sky, illuminating the tower of rock with pale light.

"I've been here before, and this particular corner always smelled interesting," Kraken called from the back of the stairs on the ground.

Tam hustled over to his side. He peered at the rocky corner, but nothing was obvious. There wasn't a door cut out, or a hatch. Just the regular grooves and pocked face of a normal cave.

Kraken pawed the ground and grumbled, right in time for another deafening crash of water against the outside of the door.

"I don't think we have much longer!" Henrietta's panic was audible.

Kraken kept sniffing as Tam moved back along the stairs trying to spot something that would hint at a tunnel.

Then it dawned on him. *"An earth witch could move the rocks if they managed to create a hole in part of it that wasn't load bearing. Kraken. Can you pinpoint where the tunnel would be on the other side of the door?"*

His father's familiar's eyes gleamed in the dim light as they turned to him. *"Yes. Straight ahead from where I'm standing. How can we move the rocks?"*

Tam turned to look at Henrietta, who was stumbling over to them. The poor young woman was trembling.

"Henrietta, do you know if I can still use my magic as a chicken?"

"I d-don't know. No one has tried before," she admitted.

Shouts echoed down from higher up the staircase, sending Tam rushing back over to the corner.

He closed his eyes and inwardly cheered when he discovered he could still feel his magic brewing in his being, albeit significantly weaker.

He'd never tried to go somewhere he couldn't see before, but if he was quick, he could attempt to feel his way through the stone while in his void and come back to get Kraken and Henrietta.

And so that is what he did.

He fell back into the void and felt through his senses the rocks, the moisture, the mollusks that dotted the stones. Then he felt the heaviness of rock disappear.

Without time to properly assess how wise it was to do so, Tam snapped out of the void and nearly bokked in relief when he found himself standing in a darkened tunnel.

There was no time to celebrate. He shifted back into the void, through the rocks and back beside Henrietta and Kraken.

"Both of you. Touch me. There is a tunnel."

Kraken draped his fluffy tail around Tam's neck while Henrietta dropped to a crouch and laid her hand on his back.

The sound of boots clattering down the steps above them grew louder, and so Tam yanked the three of them into the void as quickly as possible. He shuffled forward in the void, ensuring Henrietta and Kraken were still touching him, then once again moved them out and into the tunnel.

Henrietta let out a choking breath filled with relief, while Kraken gave a huff.

"I-I can't see anything." The chicken witch sounded close to tears.

"Follow the sound of my voice. I'm close to Kraken," Tam said, already positioning himself in front of the chicken witch and behind Kraken, who naturally took the lead.

Amazingly, whatever chaos was happening in the staircase and cave they'd just left behind could not be heard in the tunnel. The rock was too thick.

"This way," Kraken beckoned as he trotted ahead.

Tam followed, listening for Henrietta's hesitant steps behind him.

The tunnel, it turned out, did not have stairs of its own as it rose through the tower of stone, but rather continued to slope steeply upward.

They had to stop and rest three times for Henrietta, who struggled to keep up, but at long last they reached a dead end.

Kraken sniffed the air, then padded closer to the wall and pressed his ear against its surface.

"It sounds as though this is the meeting room. There are people in there."

Tam swore softly. He'd wanted to get in and get out faster than this.

"You sure you know where the archive is?"

Kraken gave a huff of annoyance. *"It has the best nap spots on the island. Of course I know where it is."*

The familiar's tail had been swishing back and forth, but just as Tam was about to ask a question about how far exactly the archive was from the council room, Kraken went perfectly still.

Then he jolted back with a chirp.

"What?" Tam asked, already dreading what new complication had presented itself.

A low, purring chuckle resonated from Kraken. *"Don't worry, kitten. Things will be fine. Let's turn back. There is another exit a short way back. It isn't as close to the archive as this point, but it is going to be empty, or at least less guarded."*

Tam clucked in irritation but relayed Kraken's message to Henrietta. The poor chicken witch barely stifled a moan.

Regardless of their feelings about this change of plan, Henrietta and Tam followed Kraken once more. Tam couldn't help but wonder just what had Kraken heard that had made him react that way. He almost seemed in a better mood… and that raised all kinds of alarm bells in Tam's mind.

Finlay Ashowan thrummed his fingers against the large, round mahogany table where he sat in the presence of the Coven of Wittica council members.

The elders looked haggard.

The glowing blue resin in the middle of the table cast their faces in an almost deathly blue pallor.

"I'm not here to speak with the first witch," Fin informed them all coolly. "I'm here because I know my grandsons and young Lord Aster Fuks are here. I saw the view through my grandson Charlie's eyes."

Two out of the five coven members shifted in their seats.

"Either you just found the princes and were going to write my son-in-law a letter telling him as much, *or*"—Fin's tone became bladed—"you were going to hold them hostage as a negotiating point for the first witch's scheme. And *that* would mean that the coven is now using *children* as war pawns, which would be the end of the amicable relationship the coven has with Daxaria. No negotiations. No discussions. No warnings. This will be a war."

Only two of the coven members could maintain a cool, composed face as Fin glowered dangerously at them all.

A balding man with a long face, sagging jowls, and a ring of black hair around his head spoke up. "The princes are not here." His light-green eyes glinted in the pale light of the room.

Fin leaned back in his chair and leveled the earth witch with his stare. "You don't want to lie to me right now, Racine."

The older man's expression thundered. While he may have only been ten years Fin's senior, he looked nearly double that.

"Your grace, you came to this island under a white flag. To declare war would be—"

Fin slammed his hand down on the table. *"The abduction of children for your games is the matter at hand, Racine."*

"I already told you," Racine rasped. "They aren't here."

Fin felt icy wrath seeping through his veins. "Then show me the dungeon."

It seemed to Fin that the council members were collectively holding their breaths.

Racine slowly rose from his seat and, with a sweep of his arm, gestured to the door. "By all means."

Fin was on his feet in an instant, and was already turning toward the exit when he saw the boulder coming for the side of his head.

He dodged it just in time, but not before a blast of air shot him back against one of the bookshelves along the wall, sending books raining down onto the floor. Gasping, he fell to the ground. He managed to catch himself just before his face smacked into the stones beneath him.

He laughed darkly.

When he lifted his face, he saw the five coven members on their feet. A fire witch was already holding two balls of fire at the ready, and a water witch was drawing the liquid from her goblet and fashioning a ball of water in her hand.

Slowly, Fin pushed himself to his feet, wincing against the broken ribs that were already mending in his chest, thanks to his curse.

"I guess this is where our partnership ends." He slipped his navy coat from his shoulders.

None of the coven members said anything.

Fin's attention was drawn to the air witch, who was reaching into his own pocket. She withdrew a vial of powder. And Fin didn't need to ask what it was.

Witch's Brew.

The drug that would addle his wits and power.

He let out a shuddering breath and felt his eyes fill with white light as his magic hummed to life.

The coven members flinched.

"You see… I was already able to confirm that my grandsons were here. Because the instant I stepped on this island, my power came back. It was a big risk coming here, but you all may recall what I did back during the war with Troivack. I made a house rule. I have my magic wherever my family is."

The air witch moved to uncork the vial, but Fin lifted his hand and flicked his wrist. As he did, a shield exploded out from the middle of the council table, sending the council members flying back into the walls.

The fire and water witches were knocked unconscious.

That left the two air witches and Racine still standing. The air witches had been able to cushion their falls with bursts of wind, while vines surged from Racine's pockets, cradling him before he could hit the wall.

"Sit back down," Fin growled to the remaining three. "Or I will make a new house rule for all of Daxaria. Something along the lines of how any witch that has been a part of kidnapping children loses their magic forever."

All three witches paled.

"Let's try this again." Fin strode back toward the table, blue lightning starting to crackle around him as he walked. "Where are my grandsons, and did you hurt them? If you lie again, I will not hesitate to do what I need to."

Three bolts of lightning shot the ground in front of the three remaining witches.

Fin glowered darkly at them. There wasn't a trace of kindness or mercy to be found anywhere in his face. "Am I clear?" His head swiveled over to Racine, whose vines were still twitching, as though the witch commanding them wasn't entirely convinced to stand down. "Or do you want to know what a house witch does when someone hurts a child in their home?"

CHAPTER 35

THE UBIQUITOUS UNCLE

The Isle of Wittica from afar was an impressive grouping of towers. Some were rounded at the top, others pointed. Some had peaked windows, others circular. Some tower walls were covered in climbing vines, others bare stone. Given each tower's uniqueness, it was hard for one to make a strong impression. However, one did still manage to stand out: the thickest, square tower, which sat in the center of the island. Light beamed in from a circular window on its face beneath its pointed roof, and a waterfall poured from a cavernous hole in its core, flowing into a pool on one of the stone balconies.

Against the sky and Alcide Sea, it was a stunning image.

Though many of the island's structures were impressive, Tam and Henrietta learned that they meant something that did not impress them: hills and stairs.

Even if he were in his human form, Tam doubted he would have been able to follow Kraken's brisk pace without growing weary and out of breath.

Finding the next tunnel exit had been the easy part.

The three of them had appeared in a vast, round room, with a staircase made of white marble that touched the wall on each side. It had appeared to be an entryway... one that was remarkably empty.

"Shouldn't there be guards, or a patrol… ?" Tam glanced around nervously.

Kraken purred. *"They're a little busy right now."*

"What do you mean? What's going on?"

The feline merely trotted toward the stairs. *"It's a surprise. Come along, kitten. We don't have all day."*

"This isn't the time for surprises, Kraken!" Tam bolted after the cat, his trepidation tripling as he followed the fluffy haunches.

Kraken still didn't elaborate; he merely guided Tam and Henrietta up the stairs, then took a left. After moving down a narrow hall with beautiful, whirling golden patterns in its floor, he took a right into another narrower staircase. They climbed up another two stories, then exited into a hall that looked similar to the one they had left, but a frantic rush of voices could be heard on the opposite end.

Tam paused as he heard the words. "I don't want to fight him!"

"He won't kill anyone! We just need to tire him out!"

"Kitten!" Kraken barked. *"Keep moving!"*

Tam wished he had the muscles to frown.

Henrietta panted quietly behind him. Glancing back, Tam noticed that the chicken witch was half slumped against the wall, her hands on her knees.

As much as he wanted to let the poor woman rest for a moment, something felt off.

"Come on," he encouraged quietly as he hopped up the stairs after Kraken.

Henrietta gave a beleaguered nod and continued to trudge onward.

By the time they had finished climbing the stairs and exited the hall, even Kraken gave a long huff out before sweeping his head to the left. *"This way. It's just past the waterfall. The door on the left."*

To get to said door, Tam realized that the walls disappeared and the floor merely acted as a slick bridge over the waterfall itself.

Tam took a tentative step forward and listened. He couldn't hear anything over the roar of the waterfall, so he bolted across the open chasm, splashing through puddles as he went.

Henrietta's steps were close behind him.

She hastily opened the door that was, thankfully, unlocked.

Slipping inside, Tam balked at the sight that greeted him.

There was a large stained-glass window, more colorful and beautiful than any he had ever seen before. It depicted a large tree with four trunks, and intricate roots that webbed down through the glass. One of its higher branches was aflame; leaves artfully blew around another. Fine, gleaming water droplets that almost looked like they were moving covered the leaves of one branch, and lastly, white blooming flowers filled a final branch.

Above the image, a banner of pale yellow bore the phrase: nature is all.

Then at the bottom of the image were the words: without it we are nothing.

An intense prickling sensation coursed through Tam as he stared at the window.

"You are on your own in here, kitten." Kraken's voice broke through Tam's whirling thoughts, making him blink.

"Right. Henrietta?" Tam swung around to see Henrietta's own gaze fixed reverently at the image. *"We need to learn how to banish the first witch. Any idea where to start looking?"*

The chicken witch visibly struggled to move her attention, but when she finally did, she swallowed and nodded. "There is a history section. I've heard the other coven members mention it."

Henrietta shuffled around the room, her eyes drifting over the signs as she peered down the aisles and aisles of books.

Meanwhile, the longer Tam waited, the more he ruffled his feathers.

The silence and lack of witches they'd encountered was bothering him more and more. They should have had to dodge a patrol or even just someone casually going about their day…

It didn't help that the smell of lightning lingered in the air.

"Found it!" Henrietta called from the far back left of the library.

Doing his best to keep focused on the task at hand, Tam bobbed his way over to where Henrietta stood.

A long row of shelves greeted him, all of which were filled with thick tomes in leather bindings—though some looked like they might crumble at the slightest touch.

"Perfect. We need books about the Forest of the Afterlife, and about the first witch. Pull out any texts you think are relevant. We'll take them with us."

Henrietta's hands gripped into fists as her eyes scanned the shelves.

Who knew how long they'd have? Still, worrying about it would just waste time they could have spent looking.

Having come to this same revelation, Henrietta plunged into the history texts while Kraken sat at the end of the aisle, his ears twitching, and his sights fixed on the doors.

The trio darted out of the archive as soon as they'd found three promising tomes. It hadn't taken them long, but they hadn't been able to be thorough in their search. Tam hoped that the books weren't useless.

As they ran back down the corridor they had originally come from, they reached the walkway over the waterfall. From there, Tam could see that the sky outside had darkened with thick storm clouds. Thunder cracked in the distance.

They were halfway across the walkway over the waterfall when a loud shriek sounded.

Tam's heart lurched, and he froze in his tracks. Then Kraken's head swung around, and he bolted back the way they had come as quickly as his legs would carry him, moving past the door to the archive. *"CHANGE OF PLANS!"*

Tam didn't even get the chance to ask what in the world was happening as Henrietta followed Kraken in a sprint while clutching the satchel of books to her chest. Tam kept up as much as his two scrawny legs would let him.

Just before the end of the hall, Kraken attempted to stop and turn left. But his fluff worked against him, making his back paws slide as he scrambled clumsily down a different narrow staircase. This allowed Tam and Henrietta to catch up.

The three of them raced down the stairs, though Kraken darted out of the tower on the next floor. Tam still didn't get the chance to ask what was happening before Kraken shot out the doorway and then entered another doorway directly beside the stairwell… that led to more stairs.

At this point, Tam was becoming dizzy, not just from the winding staircases, but also from the island's confusing layout.

As they descended the new set of stairs, it almost seemed as though they were crossing into an entirely different structure. One that was less winding. The halls, doors, and windows were squarer, made of coral-colored marble.

Kraken didn't falter for an instant. He barreled to the right, down another set of stairs that appeared to lead outside, then stopped.

With a rush of clucks, Tam skidded to a halt beside the familiar.

"*What is going on?*" Tam managed, vaguely aware that Henrietta had hung back out of sight.

A low growl rumbled in Kraken's throat. "*Look.*"

Turning, Tam was doused with icy horror.

In the middle of the stone balcony stood a young boy.

A boy with red hair.

He wore a blue blindfold as a man with shoulder-length black hair crouched down in front of him, whispering something to him that made him flinch.

"*Antony.*" Tam choked on his nephew's name. Then a flutter of movements out of the corner of his eye drew his attention over to where he found his other two nephews by the balcony railing, along with… Lord Aster Fuks.

The thirteen-year-old's hands were tied, his mouth covered in a gag. Tam felt what little magic he still possessed as a chicken gathering in his chest. The need for violence thrummed in his being.

Charlie and Asher weren't bound or gagged. They sat on a stone bench on either side of a woman with curled chestnut hair, their hands folded in their laps, their small faces lined and pale.

Tam turned back to the doorway, where Henrietta peeked around, her expression distraught. Her breaths came quicker and quicker…

"*Henrietta. Turn me back. Now.*"

"But… I don't know how we'll… How we will be able to leave I can't turn you back after—"

"NOW!" Tam knew he had essentially just released a chicken shriek.

He felt the stares of the witches on the balcony swivel to the back of his neck.

Henrietta was trembling, tears already glistening in her eyes, but she held out her hand. Tam felt the unpleasant sensation of exploding from his skin, and the ripping out of feathers. But when it was finished, he stood as himself once more.

But that wasn't all. He'd had time to prepare before he left for the island, and so he wore light armor and a sword across his back.

"UNCLE TAM!" Tam heard Asher shriek.

"KRAKEN!" Charlie shouted next.

Antony whipped around, his blindfold stopping him from seeing his uncle, but the witch behind him clamped his hands on Antony's shoulders and started whispering.

Tam drew his sword. "YOU!" he bellowed.

The witch holding Antony didn't stop speaking to Antony.

Tam's heart pounded, and his ire razed his voice of reason. He felt everything around him pointedly. He could taste the salty air, he could feel the stinging wind on his cheeks…

When the witch didn't release Antony, Tam shot through the void and out.

Seizing the witch's throat, Tam backed him up to the railing of the balcony. Tam knew blackness filled his eyes, and he was glad for it. The witch squirming in his grasp took a moment to register this detail, but when he did, Tam watched his terror paralyze him.

"D-devil—"

"Godsdamn right." Tam shoved him off the edge of the balcony and rounded back to the boys.

The woman who had been sitting beside Asher and Charlie was on her feet.

Tam heard the vines before he saw them. They had snaked up from below the balcony, waved in the air, and dived for him. He shifted through the void and reappeared in front of the woman. She shrieked, but Tam didn't have a chance to toss her into the void.

She disappeared all on her own.

A chicken clucked near Tam's feet.

He looked up at the stairs to see Henrietta with both hands raised. Apparently the earth witch had been less powerful, and therefore easier to transform.

Tam gave Henrietta a nod of appreciation.

She jerked her chin down in response.

Tam felt the darkness clear from his eyes as he turned to gaze down at Charlie and Asher. The boys flinched.

"Boys," he rasped. "I'm sorry if I scared you just now. Are you… Are you alright? What has—"

"MMMRmm ifh hrm urf orl."

Aster Fuks danced in front of Tam and gestured toward the gag in his mouth.

Immediately sheathing his sword, Tam reached for the knot at the back of the gag, but when he discovered it was too tight to remove, he was forced to cut it loose with his dagger.

"Gods! Thank you, Lord Tam! It has been very annoying not being able to talk." The thirteen-year-old clapped Tam's arm good-naturedly as though they were old friends.

Tam turned toward Antony, who was already clawing at his own blindfold. Once he'd pulled it down and laid eyes on his uncle, his face broke out into a joyful smile.

"Uncle Tam!" Antony bolted to him, throwing his arms around his uncle's waist. "I'm learning to control my magic!" he cried out excitedly.

Tam paused and slowly looked over at Aster, then Charlie and Asher.

Sensing his confusion, Aster cleared his throat and stepped forward. "We're captives, but the coven said it would be a sin not to help Antony better control his abilities."

"Have they hurt you?" Tam directed the question at Charlie and Asher.

Asher shook his head.

Charlie curled in on himself, and Tam's former wrath burned in his chest once more.

Aster leaned in. "Erm… to us non-witches, they weren't overly friendly."

It took everything Tam had not to go on a warpath in that moment. Instead, he forced his expression to remain neutral. "Asher? You have magic?"

"Bugs," he sniffled in response.

Tam's lips twitched. "Your mother is going to love that."

Patting Aster's shoulder, Tam returned his attention to Charlie, kneeling in front of him. "Hey, monster," he said gently while reaching out to tap Charlie's shin.

"They said they didn't hurt him!" Antony called from behind Tam.

Tam felt his gut clench as he heard the outrage in his nephew's voice.

"Charlie… what did they do?" Tam wasn't sure he was ready for the answer.

His nephew avoided his gaze, his golden eyes fixed on the ground, filling with tears.

Fear wormed its way through Tam's anger. "Hey… Hey monster, you don't have to tell me right away, okay? I promise you're safe now, alright? We're going to get you home and—"

Antony shoved past Tam and threw his arms around his brother. "I'm sorry! They… They said you and Asher were just watching because you wanted to! I would've hit them with lightning if I'd known! I'm sorry!" he wailed.

Tam rubbed his mouth as he watched all three of his nephews succumb to tears.

He pushed himself back to his feet and turned back to Aster, who was folding his discarded blindfold. At least *he* seemed to be in good spirits. Tam lowered his voice. "What *exactly* did they do?"

Aster cleared his throat and leaned away as the three princes continued crying together. "Prince Charlie and I were put in the same room. They didn't feed us well, and mostly just said unpleasant things. Of course it's all bollocks what they said, but His Highness took it personally. Being separated from Asher and Antony made it worse."

As awful as even that was, Tam was relieved it wasn't anything more gruesome.

A boom followed by the sound of shattering stones sounded behind Tam, making him look over his shoulder in time to see…

He turned fully around in complete awe. "Wixim?"

The golden dragon's lips curled back, revealing his pristine white fangs.

Tam stepped forward as he heard the sharp intakes of breath behind him from his nephews. However, before he could say anything else to the dragon, an explosion from above snapped both Tam's and Wixim's attention upward.

A dome of blue lightning bubbled out of the top of the very tower their balcony was connected to.

Tam gaped. Then a smile of disbelief tugged his mouth upward before he looked over his shoulder at his nephews, who were scrambling back from the dust raining down on them.

"It's okay, boys," Tam called over the new sounds of fighting that echoed loudly around the island. "It looks like your grandpa is here to lend me a hand."

CHAPTER 36

A FATHER'S FRIGHT

Wixim's wings flared out, and his golden eyes homed on the lightning dome atop the tower.

"Wixim!" Tam hollered, approaching the golden dragon warily. "We have a bit of a situation."

The dragon seemed annoyed and didn't appear interested in listening to Tam what with the display of powerful magic above them; however, Kraken chose that moment to saunter over.

Rearing back on his hind legs, Wixim let out a snarl.

Kraken chirped.

While Tam didn't technically know what Kraken said, from personal experience, he assumed it was probably a winning combination of insulting and threatening.

Tam wanted to continue to watch the exchange between the dragon and the familiar, but he couldn't help but become distracted by the clamor of fighting high above, where his father seemed to be battling the coven of Wittica members. With a wince, he wondered if he should attempt to travel through the void to the top of the tower. The problem was that he wasn't entirely certain he could move through his father's shield. He might just bounce right off and fall, which would be a waste of power.

"Uncle Tam?"

Antony's hesitant voice broke through Tam's thoughts.

He turned back to the children. Asher stood at Antony's side; behind them, Charlie clasped Aster's hand. Meanwhile, the witch that Henrietta had transformed into a pretty white hen was hopping up the stairs toward her, clucking loudly.

"Can we go home now?" Antony asked, his face somber.

Tam smiled. "Of course you can. With your grandfather here, I don't even have to be creative about getting us off the island. I'm relatively certain it's your grandpa's ship at the dock. Though I might have to help him wrap things up with—"

Wixim let out a screeching roar that pierced the air and made Tam jolt, his hand snapping up toward the hilt of his sword on instinct. Because of this, he noted the flutter of a black coat out of the corner of his eye.

The witch he'd thrown off the balcony had returned. With friends.

It would seem he was an air witch.

Three other witches were now a part of the excitement, one of whom had her hair literally aflame and her eyes aglow.

"Boys, stay behind me," Tam ordered while rounding on the new attackers.

He debated taking his nephews and Aster into the void, but moving all of them would most likely drain more of his power than he could risk with this fight.

So he once again reached for his sword, and it was a very good thing he did. The instant he gripped the leather handle, he was forced to draw it in a blur as a thin, nearly imperceptible missile launched itself at his face. He was barely able to block it with the flat of his blade; it bounced off the steel with a sharp *ping*.

Tam didn't have a chance to see what exactly he'd just blocked, because hundreds of small spikes just like the first one floated out of a brunette woman's hair and shot at him in a cloud.

He couldn't dodge all the needle-like missiles, and he couldn't move into his void because the boys were behind him. So he turned his back and took the attack there.

Luckily, his light armor prevented him from feeling anything.

"WATCH OUT!" Antony screamed.

Tam barely had time to register the fact that the fire witch was launching a streak of blue flames in his direction. He and the boys hit the ground, but the intensity of the flames sent heat wavering in a haze through the air.

There was no time to recover from this attack, however, because Tam's body suddenly became light… Much lighter than it should've been.

He was floating. And he realized he was drifting up toward the cloud of flames that had gathered in the air above him. After quickly looking over his shoulder to see that the boys hadn't been affected—he was impressed to see that Aster Fuks had his arms around the younger children protectively—Tam pushed himself into the void.

When he reappeared behind the line of witches, he crouched so they wouldn't see him immediately. He dragged his palm across the trouser cuffs belonging to the black-haired air witch, as well as the dress hems of the fire witch and the witch capable of creating missiles. With a push of magical power, he sent them all into the void.

As Tam stood up, he watched the witch whom he thought had made him float. She spun around, seeming to realize that her allies had disappeared.

"What did you do to them?" she spluttered, backing up a step.

"I didn't hurt them, and I can bring them back, but there are children present. We aren't going to continue this fight here today."

The witch glanced over her shoulder at the boys, who were still in a protective huddle. Tam watched her pause as, just beyond his nephews, Kraken and Wixim still appeared to be in a heated discussion.

Kraken was in the middle of swiping at Wixim's snout.

Regardless of this, when she turned back to Tam, he could see the distrust in her eyes. "You're the devil. I'm not trusting anything you say."

He pointed at his nephews and Aster and didn't hide his sarcasm. "You don't trust that there are children? You can't see them standing right there?" She pressed her lips together. "What is happening with the house witch?"

The witch scowled at him. "That is none of your concern. Leave."

"I'd love to. But I was hoping to get a ride back to the mainland with him."

She held up her hand. "I said leave."

Tam rubbed his eye wearily. "Do you want to disappear like your coven members? No? Good. If I were to guess, I'd say the house witch is here because his grandsons are here." Judging by the way the witch was speaking to him, Tam presumed that she hadn't a clue who he was in relation to Finlay Ashowan.

The witch didn't say anything, but Tam felt himself once again go weightless. So with a sigh and a flick of his wrist, he sent her into the void with the others.

He fell back to the ground heavily. Rolling his shoulders in an attempt to get used to his weight fluctuations, he made his way back to his nephews and Aster.

"Alright boys, things should be safe here. I'll have to go up and see what your grandfather is—" Tam's words were cut off when he noticed the blue lightning overhead turning white.

His father was reaching the end of his magical stores.

Panic gripped Tam, sharpening his senses in an instant.

"Kraken! Henrietta!" he barked. "Watch the boys."

Wixim's great head swung around, his eyes narrowed.

Sensing that the dragon's wrath could prove to be an issue if he chose to follow him up the tower, Tam spared a moment to ensure that did not happen. "Wixim, if my da uses up all his magic, he'll make a curse here on this island. I'm just going to get him and the boys, then leave. For the safety of the children, will you agree to let us go?"

Kraken meowed, and he must have said something irritating because Wixim snapped his teeth at him. But when he looked back at Tam, he gave a slow nod of his head.

Tam returned the gesture in appreciation, then he set his sights at the top of the dome. If he could vanish overhead, there might be a chance he could access the interior of the shield by moving through his void. He'd just need to be able to see where to reappear while falling.

"I thought Uncle Tam didn't have magic?"

Asher's question was the last thing Tam heard before he allowed himself to be swept up into the void, and then back out, falling over the dome of lightning that had turned entirely white.

As he fell through the air above the Isle of Wittica, he only had the span of a breath to determine where he should reappear. So, without being able to assess just how many witches his father was fighting against, Tam focused on a clear spot on the stones through the shield and returned to the void, hoping that this idea would work. The cost of failure would be too high.

Fin knew he wouldn't be able to hold on for much longer.

He knew his shield was white.

But he also knew *exactly* what he would be cursing all of Daxaria and Troivack with.

If he was going to die, then he was going to make it damn well worth it.

None of the witches trapped inside his shield could use their abilities, and if they attempted to approach him, a streak of lightning would deter them.

He wished he could've seen Annika again.

Or his children.

Or grandchildren.

He had known he couldn't keep fighting so many powerful witches for long. It wasn't in his nature. Though he had at least hoped he'd be able to locate his grandchildren during the altercation. Fin closed his eyes as sweat rolled down his spine, and he gritted his teeth as he heard the shouts of concern from the five witches around him when they realized the color of his shield had changed.

Most of the council members he had first met with continued to battle him, though many more had come to run interference. Fin had blasted a good number of them off the island and into the Alcide Sea. He knew his magic would stop them from hurting themselves upon landing, and there would undoubtedly be an air or water witch to help the others return.

"You can stop now, Da. I'd rather I didn't have to carry you out of here."

Fin's eyes snapped open, and the shock of seeing his son resulted in his shield dissolving in an instant.

Wait.

How had Tam gotten inside?

Exhaustion hit Fin's body at the sudden disconnect from the curse he had been slowly weaving, but he forced himself to stay upright. He gaped at his son, whom he hadn't seen in months. Tam was changed. Completely. Fin could see it in his eyes, in his posture… he was stunned.

Tam stood tall, a sword in hand. His black hair had grown to his shoulders, but he wore it half tied back. His dark eyes, which used to dart away from others and wide spaces, surveyed the witches around them atop the tower coolly.

"My father and I will be leaving this island with my nephews, my friends, and Lord Aster Fuks. No one is going to stop us. Your dragon has agreed to this, and my father's familiar is on this island."

Two of the coven members whispered frantically to each other.

Fin watched Tam's gaze snap to them and was taken aback by the darkness in his son's face.

"Where is the door to the stairs?"

"They aren't just going to let us leave, Tam," Fin began while drawing himself free from his stupor. "They made that perfectly clear."

Tam raised an eyebrow in Fin's direction, and Fin found himself resisting the urge to frown. Just what the hell had happened to Tam while he'd been in Zinfera?

"Well, they can try to stop us, but that would make for a pretty empty island."

Fin paused. What was Tam implying?

Oddly enough, the coven members seemed to know *exactly* what Tam meant, as the majority turned to Racine with their hands in the air. Racine approached Tam, his countenance grim.

Fin shoved his hands in his pockets as he tried not to show how out of breath he was. Every moment he forced himself to stay awake was a battle.

"Lord Tam, we will happily allow you all to leave, but in exchange we want Louise Riddel and the other witches who went missing weeks ago returned to us."

Fin rounded on Tam in alarm.

"My informing you that we were leaving was not a negotiation. It was a warning." Tam's voice was hard as granite. "Louise Riddel attacked my ship with my children aboard, as well as several other innocent—"

"I'm sorry, your what?" Fin cut in, the fight completely eradicated from his mind.

Tam closed his mouth and darted a tense glance at his father out of the corner of his eye. "We can talk about that later."

"You said children. Plural. As in more than one," Fin persisted.

"Da, just… One…" Tam fumbled for words, made an aggravated noise, then returned his attention to the coven members. "We're leaving, and that's all there is to it."

Fin was gathering up another breath to start rattling off a thousand more questions when the largest feline creature he had ever seen dropped from the sky at Tam's side. It had wings. It issued a roaring snarl at the coven members.

"Tam!" Fin started forward, his hand outstretched in preparation to draw upon whatever power he could to protect Tam from the beast, consequences be damned, when Tam put his hand on the animal's shoulder.

Fin dropped his arm. He then received another shock as he watched the creature shudder and shift… into Eli.

Or at least Fin thought it was Eli. Tam was blocking the smaller woman from view as he addressed the coven once more.

Fin couldn't quite make out whatever was being said. The sounds around him started to turn fuzzy, and the wind that gusted against his face threatened to blow him over. He blinked, and when he opened his eyes again, Tam was at his side and had his arm thrown over his shoulder.

"Let's get back to Xava, Da," Tam murmured.

Despite the smothering blackness of sleep creeping into his vision, Fin still managed to say, "You… and I… are having a *very* long talk when I wake up."

CHAPTER 37

CHILDISH CHATS

Tam sat beside Eli in the carriage that was trundling its way toward Austice. The air was damp and thick with the promise of rain. After boarding the boat back to Xava from the Isle of Wittica, Finlay Ashowan had remained unconscious and had not stirred the entire day.

Luckily, the duke had already prepared a carriage for himself, the princes, and Aster back on shore once the ship had landed.

One of the knights close with the Ashowan family—Sir Lewis—had met the battered group on the docks of Xava and kindly assisted Tam with his father and the princes. Henrietta had opted to ride with the knight. As it turned out, Henrietta's family farm was on the land neighboring Sir Lewis's, and she had a great deal of questions about the crops for the year.

Tam had then sent them all off ahead with Kraken curled up on his witch's lap. Meanwhile, Tam had gone back to the cottage to find Luca and Penelope in a hidden crawl space under the cottage.

The four of them had departed immediately.

They couldn't risk the witches following them, though unlike in Zinfera, they could at least travel by the main roads, as the knights stationed along the roads would help them rather than attack. In the quiet, Tam raised an issue that was troubling him.

"I thought you were worried about turning into Kasha."

"I sensed your pain, and I saw the princes through your eyes…" Eli replied quietly.

Penelope was asleep with her head resting on Eli's lap, while Luca had also fallen asleep, but with his face splattered across the carriage window on Tam's right. Tam pointedly ignored the smear of drool, while also admiring his son's ability to sleep in such an awkward position.

"It was dangerous," Tam continued, his eyes still stuck on Luca. "I understand why you were worried, but in the future please stay with Luca and Penelope."

Eli's expression frosted over. "Is that an order?"

A trickle of sweat gathered and dripped down Tam's back in the span of a breath, moving as though it, too, feared for its existence.

He chose his next words with the same caution one might exercise while covered in lamp oil and lighting a cigar. "Well… What do you think we should do in the future?"

The silence that followed was weighty.

"I should've just gone and introduced myself as a familiar," she retorted.

"What if they had hurt you before you could say anything?"

She was quiet.

Tam wasn't foolish enough to think it was because she accepted his suggestion.

Eli tilted her head. "Remember when we had that fight outside of Wixim's cave about how I told you the rules for engaging in battle, and you were upset that I didn't approach it as a discussion?"

"Yes… Yes, I do."

She raised an eyebrow at him.

He cleared his throat. "You're right. I'm sorry that I'm not making this a discussion. I was worried about Penelope and Luca being left alone, and you getting hurt while pregnant—also that you were forcing yourself to join the fight when you have been anxious about turning into Kasha. What do you think we should do in the future?"

Eli's sights drifted over to the scenery rushing by the carriage window. "I will try to avoid getting involved as much as possible while I'm pregnant, but we should try and arrange for Penelope and Luca to have a safe place to hide in case of an emergency."

Tam nodded slowly. "At my family's keep in Austice, there are a number of secret rooms and passages."

At this, Eli raised a quizzical brow and moved her attention back to Tam. Luckily, she appeared to have let go of her earlier grievance against him. "That reminds me. Your family owns a multitude of brothels, has aliases, and a slew of underworld connections, judging from the fear and reverence those madams treat you with. I've come to the opinion that your family is not nearly as wholesome as you portray yourselves to the general public."

Tam grimaced. "That's… not entirely inaccurate. My mother… she has been a… a well-informed person for her entire life. And the information she gathers and the deals she makes have made her rather valuable to the crown of Daxaria. I started helping with her work a few years ago."

"She's a spy for the king," Eli surmised bluntly.

Tam's gaze darted to the children then back at her. He gave her a tight smile to convey that she wasn't wrong, but to maybe not be quite so open in her thoughts with their charges present.

Eli continued to stare at Tam. He could see the thoughts whirring behind her eyes.

Wanting to change the topic as quickly as possible, Tam's attention fell to Penelope. She looked sweet… nothing like the sharp-tongued child who was too smart for her own good.

"We still need to have a talk with Penelope about stealing my mage crystal for the watch," he began.

Eli looked down at the child in her lap and gently stroked her hair. "I know. She was just so frightened by it, and she did it weeks ago."

Tam tilted his head in acknowledgment. Anytime they had attempted to broach the future battlefield Penelope had seen, she would turn rigid and begin breathing rapidly.

"I don't know if I told you this, but after she and Hamil saw those visions, she actually called me Dad," Tam recalled, a smile rising up his face.

Eli blinked, her expression tensing. "Oh."

Perplexed over her reaction, Tam stared at her with a subtle frown. Until it dawned on him what her reaction was revealing.

"Are you jealous?"

His betrothed bristled.

Tam barely stifled a laugh as she avoided meeting his gaze. "Alright, I won't tease you too much."

"Good."

Tam turned to look out Luca's window. The first streaks of rain pattered against the glass, blurring the lush fields now tipped with gold as autumn neared.

"Hopefully the witches won't attack us on the road," Eli said abruptly.

"I doubt they will. They seemed to be spread quite thin." Tam resisted the urge to clear his throat, but Eli still worked out the reason for his slight discomfort.

"Is it because you keep putting witches in the void?"

"Erm… It might be. I mean, some coven members could still be in Zinfera."

Eli lifted her eyebrows dubiously but didn't comment any further. In fact, neither one said much else until the carriage pulled to a halt at an inn, which was around the time Penelope and Luca stirred from their sleep.

Without a word, Tam and Eli shared a knowing look. The children would not be tired for a long time after such a lengthy nap. Tam wondered about getting them to play a long game of tag…

Stepping out onto the soggy grass, Tam took his time having a leisurely stretch. The air had cooled and the humidity eased, making the world smell fresh. The gray clouds above dimmed what little daylight remained. At least for the time being, Tam could still see their surroundings clearly enough.

If they got up early and only stopped for a change of horses, they could be back in Austice in a day. Tam was antsy to get home as quickly as possible, motivated by the idea of being surrounded by people who could help protect Luca and the thought of a proper bath in his own tub.

Squinting toward the inn, with its multiple chimneys puffing smoke and the persistent froth of voices from a crowd inside enjoying their meals, Tam looked forward to getting a good dinner for everyone. He rounded back to the open carriage to hand Eli out, then Penelope, and lastly Luca before shutting the door and calling a thanks to the driver.

It was starting to feel as though the chaos was at long last coming to an end, and Tam was more than ready to wrap up the first witch's nonsense and get on living with his family. With any luck, Penelope's vision would be wrong, and life would soon be simpler.

"UNCLE TAM! UNCLE TAM!"

The cacophony of pounding fists on the door made Tam raise his head from his pillows. Likewise, Eli, Penelope, and Luca, the room's other occupants, stirred. The princes, Fin, and the physician had settled in before their arrival, so there hadn't been enough rooms for everyone to have their own.

Everyone gaped dumbly at the door as the cloak of sleep failed to fall off them.

Only Tam was quick to launch himself to his feet to see what was wrong, and upon throwing open the door, he discovered his three nephews outside dressed and waiting. Before he could even ask if something was the matter, all three princes paraded themselves into the room…

And behind them stumbled in Finlay Ashowan. The duke was pale and visibly weary but awake.

Tam opened and closed his mouth, then rubbed the back of his neck. His father wouldn't have known about Eli, Luca, or Penelope being in the room, and the boys hadn't had a proper introduction to anyone, either.

Moving his hands to his pockets, Tam did his best to stay calm. "Is everything alright? We all are… uh…"

"I'm decent."

Eli's voice made Fin jump. His head whipped around. The house witch blinked, then his gaze fell to Eli's round middle, where she had just cinched a robe closed. He blanched.

Tam worried his father was about to faint. "Right. So… There are some things we need to talk about—"

"Who's that?" Asher pointed at Luca's face.

Luca had risen from his pallet on the floor and was grasping his hands together nervously as his eyes darted to Tam. Penelope—who was sporting some impressive bedhead—stomped over from her own bedding to Luca's side and glared down at Asher.

Antony pointed at Penelope, though he at least didn't shove his hand close to her face. "And who's that?"

"Um. You see, I… I had kind of wanted to have a discussion with your grandfather alone first."

"He looks like you, Uncle Tam." Charlie had hung back by the door, but his attention hovered on Luca's face.

Tam quickly took in the state of the middle prince. Charlie's eyes were shadowed, and the way he hunched his shoulders told Tam that it would take a long time for the mental trauma of what he'd gone through would fade.

"It's rude to point."

Penelope's cool tone pulled Tam free of his worries for his nephew, especially once he turned and noted how she had crossed her arms over her chest. She stared down Antony, who frowned in response.

"Well, it's rude not to introduce yourself," Antony fired back.

"Kids." Tam raised his voice, drawing everyone's attention to him. "Let's try this again. This here"—he gestured toward Luca—"is my son. I didn't know about him for the past few years, but he will be living with me, and he is your cousin. His name is Luca."

"*What?*" Antony burst out.

"*Wow!*" Asher shouted, hopping excitedly.

Charlie managed to give Luca a shy smile. "Hi."

Fin reached out and gripped the corner of the dresser beside the door.

"And this is Penelope. Eli and I are adopting her, but she is actually a distant cousin of yours whom we found in Zinfera." Tam shot his father an apologetic smile before he murmured, "She is Caroline Levin's daughter. She and her husband sadly died."

Fin swallowed.

Meanwhile, the boys stared blankly at Penelope, who lifted her chin in the air as though daring them to say anything.

"And Eli is actually a girl?" Asher asked, referencing their first, albeit rushed, introduction shortly after they had boarded their boat leaving the Isle of Wittica. A physician had whisked the boys away to ensure they were not injured shortly after they had boarded, which meant a longer discussion among them all hadn't been possible.

"She is," Tam confirmed with a chuckle. "But she is also my betrothed and your future aunt."

"Oh Gods."

This utterance came from Eli, making Tam turn to her in confusion.

She blushed and, looking incredibly sheepish, went on to say, "I forgot that meant I'd be their aunt."

Tam lowered his voice. "Can't back out now."

"No ring on the finger, no guarantee, Ashowan," she reminded him with a slight growl.

Tam laughed again then returned his attention to his nephews. "You can each ask me one question. Then I think your grandfather and I should have a private talk."

All three boys raised their hands into the air.

Tam nodded. "Charlie."

"Is Eli Luca's mom?"

"She did not give birth to him, but she will be his mother by law. Antony?"

"How old are they?"

Tam chuckled. Luca had asked Penelope the same kind of question when they first met.

"Penelope is the older, around nine, and Luca just turned eight. Asher?"

"Um… Grandma always says, says that I shouldn't ask this kind of question. But—uh—Eli looks round. I mean not really, but kind of—"

Tam spared his nephew—and Eli, in fairness—from the question he was clearly trying to formulate. "Eli and I are having a baby, yes. She's due in the spring."

A dry cough dragged Tam's attention back to his father, whose mouth hung open.

Tam felt his cheeks burn.

"Alright. Tam, why don't you and your father go into the princes' room for your chat. That way I can get dressed behind the screen here," Eli suggested delicately.

She, too, was avoiding looking at Fin.

Tam bobbed his head in assent and gestured to the still-open door. "Shall we?"

His father reached up and idly scratched his forehead while clearing his throat. "Yeah. Yes. I would *very* much like a long private talk with you."

The duke ambled out of the room ahead of Tam, allowing him to share a nervous smile with Eli before following his father. He paused in the doorway and addressed the children over his shoulder. "All of you… play nice."

Luca leaned over to peer around Antony and shot Tam a wide-eyed stare that screamed *Please don't leave me like this.*

Tam tried to mouth *You'll be okay,* but it was unclear whether Luca understood him. Guilt-ridden, Tam closed the door and took his leave.

If only Luca knew how I'd much rather hang back with him and the monsters… Depending on my da's reaction, I might be meeting Death a little sooner than I thought.

CHAPTER 38

HEADING HOME

Following his father inside, Tam quietly closed the door to the inn room. His heart raced in his chest. His throat already felt dry, prompting him to swallow. His hands, which were stowed in his pockets, clenched into fists.

Finlay Ashowan was hobbling over to a tall dresser that sat beside the lone window of the room. The decor was cozy, with warm wooden furniture and dark wood floors, but it was cramped. The plush bed with its deep-red comforter was already made, its pillows fluffed. The three cots the princes must have slept on were in a similar state.

A slight creak drew Tam's gaze up to at last meet his father's bright-blue eyes, which were studying him. Fin leaned against the dresser, his expression unreadable.

Tam felt anxiety burble in his belly. He expected some kind of talk about responsibility. About thinking things through. About being careful about his actions… Maybe even about how disappointed his father was…

"Tam… What the fuck?"

Tam balked. His father rarely swore so colorfully. The flat note in his father's voice was so frank that it almost made him laugh. "I know it's a lot. It all kind of… happened. I kept my promise and didn't get married without you there, if that makes you feel any better."

Fin's eyes went wide as his exasperation visibly got the best of him. "*No, it does not!*"

Tam cleared his throat again and looked at the floor.

"Do you know that people think this boy you're traveling with is the devil? Have you even considered that he might be the devil?" Fin asked directly.

"Well, yes… and no."

"What do you mean, yes and no?"

Tam took his right hand out of his pocket to rub the back of his neck. "I had a… a person. A woman I was seeing years ago."

"Sweet antlers. Are you serious?" Fin's volume rose.

Cheeks burning, Tam nodded, but before his father could go on a tirade (that Tam had already received from his mother), he explained to the man the details of Luca's existence. In the stunned silence that followed, he went on to explain Penelope's appearance.

To his credit, Fin listened through it all without interrupting or making any comment.

However, when Tam described the conditions in which they had found Penelope—caged aboard a pirate ship—as well as how she'd grown up on the run with the first witch's minions, Fin's expression grew thunderous. Still, he did not stop Tam, who talked about how they'd dealt with the concubine Soo Hebin, the corruption of the covens, meeting Wixim, and the issue of the Zinferan emperor wanting Eli to be the next empress.

At that point, Fin gestured for them to sit at the small round table.

Pausing his stories, Tam joined his father and seated himself. Once settled, he resumed talking. He mentioned the Lobahlans, learning what the watch was, and Penelope's visions, and then he concluded the entire narrative with the fact that they now were in possession of texts about the first witch and the Forest of the Afterlife that hopefully could tell them how to defeat the first witch once and for all.

Fin let out a long, long breath.

Tam waited. His palms were alarmingly sweaty, and so he took his time to wipe them on his trousers.

"Alright. So we need to send the first witch back to the Forest of the Afterlife if we are going to keep Luca safe, and most likely we are going to need to annex the coven and send them off somewhere as they wish." Fin leaned back and folded his arms.

Tam nodded slowly. "I think we should be able to avoid an all-out battle if we can all be calm and reasonable. The only wild card being Aradia. She wants her brother to go with her to the afterlife."

Fin grimaced.

"I could just keep putting her in the void," Tam suggested, though he didn't mask his dubiousness over that being a good option.

"Your mother risked sending a brief letter from Sorlia during her search for the boys. She told me that word has come that Aradia has already gotten out, so at best that is a temporary solution," Fin replied with equal doubt. "Is it possible we could trick her into giving up? Or maybe she will accept leaving on her own."

Tam shrugged. "I don't know. First, we need to figure out how to send her away by herself. And Aradia might have some kind of trick up her sleeve like she did back in Troivack when you all last fought her."

Fin tilted his head in acknowledgment. "I suppose we'd better get ready to head to Austice. The sooner we get back, and the sooner everyone is on the same page, the better. Losing communication with everyone has been a massive problem. I'm hoping your mother has returned from Sorlia by now as well"

Tam nodded and rose to a stand.

"Tam?"

He looked down at his father, who stared up at him wearing a half smile.

"I'm proud of you."

Tam's jaw dropped. Then he closed his mouth and cleared his throat. "Despite my accidental incident with Luca's mother?"

Fin's expression turned grim. "Yes. I'm sorry she had to go through that, and rest assured, we will protect her and her business from afar, but… I think you did your best to make the right decisions. And hey. I have more grandkids! I'm not complaining about that!"

Tam felt a knot he hadn't realized had been locking his muscles for weeks unravel, and he was suddenly overcome with emotion.

Fin waved his hand, unaware of his son's state. "Besides. At this point it's practically family tradition to have surprise pregnancies."

Tam burst out with a laugh. "Yeah. I've already had some kind of talk with Luca…"

Fin's smile returned as he stood as well. The house witch's coloring was already improving as the morning sunshine filled the room.

"Ah. By the way…" Fin started, making Tam pause his walk to the door. "In… In the interest of honesty, your mother immediately knew that Eli was a woman when we met her as your assistant. She may have also suspected from that first meeting that something would transpire between you two."

Tam felt his face fall flat. "Are you serious?"

Fin shrugged apologetically. "You know your mother. And she was desperate for a granddaughter."

Tam grumbled. Of bloody course his mother had had a plan for his romantic life. "Anything else I should know?" He didn't bother hiding his irritation.

Fin clapped a hand on his son's shoulder. "Yeah. The mother of your next child is craving jam cookies. I recommend you see about getting those to her quickly. I'll stock up the kitchen in Austice for her once we get back."

Tam gave a groan mixed with a laugh as his father flexed one of the odd little skills his magic bestowed upon him: the ability to tell what food someone was craving, and what food their body needed. This even included the cravings of an unborn child.

Well. At least the talk had gone a lot better than planned—though Tam would most definitely be addressing his mother's meddling in the very near future.

Aradia stepped over the broken chair and gazed about the room.

"It was probably for the best that you weren't here for the house witch's meeting," Ansar called from behind her.

She nodded while moving along the border of the round table in the center of the coven's council room, then seated herself in the only chair that wasn't damaged or turned over.

Aradia eyed the mess around her disapprovingly. "So. The duke got his grandsons back, and we have confirmation that Tamlin Ashowan and Elisara are here once more."

Ansar pushed some toppled books aside with the toe of his boot before standing across from Aradia. "Yes. And the house witch's familiar, Kraken, has returned with them."

Aradia tilted her head thoughtfully.

"Before he let you out of the void, did Death's Carriage Driver offer you any insight on whether or not Tamlin Ashowan truly is the devil, as he claims to be?"

Aradia gave a dry chuckle. "Death is not fond of direct responses."

Ansar's eyes trailed along the wall. "We can always try the ritual with both of them present. They'd both die, but it would guarantee our success."

"It isn't a bad idea." Aradia leaned back in her seat. "Getting them both in the same spot, however, will be more than a little difficult. Especially once they're home with all their resources and support."

"Difficult but not impossible," Ansar corrected. "We can always lay a trap or ambush them while they travel. We know where they are, the house witch will be weak, and their attention will be divided, because they also need to protect the princes."

Aradia's eyebrows rose. "Reasonable. But the attack would require a large number of witches, and we are missing a great many of them. Tamlin Ashowan is powerful—luckily, he doesn't seem to realize just *how* powerful—and if the eldest prince, Antony, is able to control his magic in any meaningful way, things could get very messy."

"They won't be able to all travel in the same carriage," Ansar continued. "We can send scouts ahead of time. Odds are Tamlin and the boy will be traveling in the same carriage. We grab them, set up for the ritual nearby, and finish it all before the house witch or anyone else can do anything. Wixim can keep Kraken occupied should he present a threat. Everything works out."

Aradia paused. "You do realize once this ritual is performed, I will be gone, correct?"

Ansar gave a laugh and leaned on the table in front of himself. "What you will be is healed. You can go home and heal yourself, and when you're better, you can come back."

"To you?"

Ansar's good-humored expression dwindled. "Yes. To me."

"And what if it is not my intention to come back to you?" she pressed next.

She watched the pain blend with his confidence and awaited his answer, not at all prepared for the surprising statement that followed.

"Then I guess I'll have to practice my ability to seduce you. That way I will be prepared to die and see you once more in the Forest of the Afterlife."

A laugh burst out from Aradia. He had caught her a little off guard. "Is that so?"

Ansar smiled handsomely. "Oh, it is. I'm going to make you fall so head over heels in love with me that you'll never want to leave my side."

"You're being quite forward." Aradia knew her tone was flirtatious. Normally she wouldn't indulge Ansar quite so much, but she had to admit, his assuredness was a little charming.

"I'll beg the Gods for their blessing to dine with you if I have to. I'll gather the fluffiest animals that roam the Forest of the Afterlife and put them in a single spot just so you can pet them whenever you want."

Aradia felt her cheeks warm.

It'd been a long while since she'd felt that.

Perhaps the time in the void had changed her a little more than she'd wanted to admit. Getting to rest—*truly* rest—had left her calmer than she'd felt in years.

"Do you think we might be able to spend a bit of time together if I do those things?" Ansar's eyes twinkled.

Licking her lips, Aradia leaned forward slowly in her chair. "We can spend time as friends whenever you like."

He raised an eyebrow at her, and Aradia couldn't stop her smile from widening.

"I want to court you as more than a friend. As more than an ally. I've been perfectly clear about that."

"You've suggested it before, but, Ansar, I will most likely be serving time in the Grove of Sorrows for my own offenses. After your death, you will have long forgotten about me in the afterlife by the time I am released." It was a little disheartening to point out the reality of Aradia's situation, but she didn't want Ansar to suffer. Not because of her.

Despite her rebuttal, the mortal man showed no pain over her words. Rather, he pushed back off the table and said, "Then I guess it'll be up to you to track me down and remind me."

Aradia was about to open her mouth to discourage him further when Ansar added, "You're worth waiting for, Aradia. I have no interest in your power. I simply want to spend eternity with you in a garden having tea, and hearing you tell me about the universe."

Aradia couldn't think of anything to say; she could feel the heat in her cheeks all the way up to her eyes.

Ansar's smile deepened as he watched her reaction.

He rounded the table and approached her side. He then knelt and grasped one of her hands before planting a gentle kiss on her knuckles. "Come on. Let's go kill the devil and get you home."

Thomas felt his heart pounding. Could he go as one of the people that would intercept the carriage? Would that seem suspicious? Gods… What if one of the princes got hurt? Or Penelope? What if something happened to one of the Ashowans? Was this the moment? Was it time?

Pushing himself away from the wall where he had leaned to casually eavesdrop on Aradia and Ansar, Thomas started making his way down the hall. He wouldn't be able to send a message to warn the Daxarian king or the Ashowans with the covens combining their efforts to disrupt communication.

Wracking his mind on what he could possibly do, he realized the only thing that he really could do, was get as close to the events as possible, and wait for the best moment to help.

He let out a long breath.

Hopefully Penelope stayed safe. As smart and brave as she was, he didn't want her to suffer anymore. With his steps turning purposeful, Thomas Julian descended the next staircase he came to. The end was near, and he would do everything in his power to protect his kingdom. No matter what.

CHAPTER 39

DEATH'S DOOR

Tam rubbed his hands together against the chill.

While the trees and grasses were still green, the bite in the air told him there weren't many warm days left. Soon the leaves would change and frost would whisk itself over the grounds and rooftops in the night.

The carriage rocked its way down the dirt road toward the south of the king's forest, which would take them directly to the castle in Austice. Penelope and Luca were tucked under a cozy fur blanket, and Eli tugged on a pair of leather gloves that Tam could smell from his seat across from her.

"Just think, everyone. Soon we'll all be in my family's keep. We can rest. Bathe properly. Eat proper meals, at proper times…" Tam sighed in anticipation, a blissful smile finding him.

"It will take time for all of us to adjust," Eli reminded everyone. She shared a knowing look with Penelope, who was in a particularly prickly mood.

"As long as *those* three don't live with us I'll be fine," Penelope muttered, her arms folded across her chest.

She hadn't been fond of her new cousins.

"They seem fine…" Luca interjected warily. "Charlie was nice."

Penelope paused. "Alright. Yes. He seemed fine."

Tam felt a twinge of disappointment that their first meeting hadn't gone as well as he'd hoped. "Antony and Asher are great, too. Just give them a chance. They've been having a rough time."

Luca nodded while Penelope pursed her lips. She was visibly holding back a scathing retort.

Tam exchanged a look with Eli, then decided to move on to a safer subject.

"You know, we should probably discuss baby names."

At this, both Luca and Penelope perked up.

Surprisingly, Eli didn't object as she leaned back into the carriage seat and rested her hand on her middle. "Hm. That *is* a good idea. Especially if we don't agree on any at first. We'll need time to find a compromise."

Tam crossed his arms and cast his eyes to the red roof of the carriage as he pondered this.

"What about something after the stars?" Luca asked.

Tam paused, a thoughtful half smile coming up before he checked Eli's reaction.

She seemed open but uncertain. "Oh? Like what?"

"What about… What about Nova?" Luca shot a hopeful look at Eli, then Tam.

Eli's eyebrows had come up as she considered this. "Nova… I like it."

Tam reached over and ruffled Luca's hair. "So do I. Any boy name ideas? Penelope? Any thoughts?"

Penelope opened her mouth, but Luca spoke first.

"It's a girl so you don't need… one…"

Penelope's mouth slammed shut, but only briefly before she shouted, "I TOLD YOU NOT TO TELL THEM!"

Shock washed over Tam as he realized that Penelope must have seen their future child. He looked at Eli who, from her stunned reaction, must have come to the same conclusion.

After a quick clearing of her throat, and several rapid blinks, Eli managed to stammer out, "O-oh."

Tam reached up and covered his mouth as his face buckled under the smile he wore.

"A girl," Eli repeated dazedly as she looked at him. "I see."

Penelope sighed loudly. "I'm never telling you anything again."

Luca blushed. "Sorry. I just… I got excited because they like the name."

Tam opened his mouth to console his son and to tell Penelope to be kinder about the slip-up, but then the carriage came to a halt.

Tensing, Tam waited to hear shouts of alarm, or for the driver to come back and explain what was happening.

There was only silence.

"All of you wait here. I'll see what's going on." Tam opened the door on his left and stepped down onto the road, glancing behind the carriage, then in front.

He didn't see anything, but his senses prickled.

An eerie quiet permeated the woods, which should have been teeming with birdsong and the rustling of underbrush from critters.

The carriage transporting his nephews and father was out of sight, as were Sir Lewis and Henrietta, both on horseback.

Approaching the driver's bench of the carriage with his hand on the hilt of his dagger behind his back, Tam kept his senses honed to any slight movements around himself.

He reached the front of the carriage and found that instead of the driver, there sat a young woman. Her legs were extended and crossed at the ankles, and she was clad in brown leather pants, wearing a white shirt and black corset. Her hands were clasped over her belly.

She had strawberry-blond hair and blue eyes; despite her facial structure being different from when he'd last seen her, Tam instinctively knew who it was.

Aradia.

She smiled at him. "Hello again."

Tam reached for his power instantly.

"Do anything like last time, and the archers in the trees will shoot everyone in the carriage. We see them all. The seer girl. The boy. Your pregnant sweetheart."

Tam felt a cold terror flush through him.

"Here is what we are going to do," Aradia began casually, rising to her feet and placing her hands on her hips. "You and I are going to take a stroll into the woods. We're going to perform a little ritual. If you really are the devil, as you claim you are, then you and I are heading off to the Forest of the Afterlife together, and this can all end."

Tam's hand didn't move from the dagger. "Why would I leave my family with a swarm of archers around them?"

"Either you come with me or I shoot them." She jumped down from the carriage. "I understand it's hard not having the upper hand in this negotiation, but that's how things are. Now. Let's go."

She took three steps forward, looking perfectly at ease.

Tam's heart fluttered in his chest. "I don't get to say goodbye?"

Aradia turned a wry look to him. "No. Obviously you'd try something. Come on. I've waited centuries for this."

On legs that already had started to shake, Tam followed the first witch.

Shuffling behind her slowly, he sent a frantic, silent prayer up to the Gods that somehow Eli and the children would stay safe; that even if this really was the end for him, they would be fine.

He just couldn't believe that moments before, he had been incomparably excited to hear he and Eli were having a daughter, and Luca had picked out a beautiful name…

"Now is around the time when you tell me that the little boy is the devil, and you have just been covering for him because you're a good-hearted person who believes in protecting a child."

Aradia's voice snapped Tam from his thoughts. She had stopped walking ahead of him and waited for him to join her side.

Right.

If he didn't play the part until the end, she wasn't going to leave Luca alone.

He needed to pull it together.

Tam forced a cold smile. "And make you look foolish? Why would I do that?"

Her eyes narrowed as she studied Tam with open suspicion. "You know that if this doesn't work, I'm just bringing that child over here and doing it again, right? I can't die unless you really are my brother. I'll just regenerate a new body."

Tam paused. It was risky asking questions, but should she ask why his memory was spotty, he already had the perfect excuse. "How will you be doing this?"

Aradia's expression turned unreadable, then she continued walking.

Tam instantly kicked himself.

"Knife to heart? Stomach? Throat?"

"You choose."

"Mm." Tam scrunched up his face as he thought about it. "A short, deep cut on the throat a little below the ear should do it. It'll be quicker. What about you?"

Aradia raised an eyebrow at him. Whether or not she was buying that he was the devil was still uncertain.

"We'll see. Most likely something similar."

For a while they continued stepping over fallen logs and branches, moving farther away from the road as the carriage shrank silently in the distance.

"I must admit, you are accepting defeat quite easily," Aradia said breezily while casting another sidelong glance at Tam, who was sweating profusely underneath the black woolen coat he wore.

"Defeat? Please. I'll torment you in the Forest of the Afterlife just fine."

Gods… How could he protect Luca? The first witch was going to watch him bleed to death, figure out he wasn't her true brother, and drag Luca out. Eli would fight whoever tried to take him and would get hurt! If only he knew where the archers were hiding… As much as he wanted to, if he shoved Aradia into the void and bolt back could signal them before he could figure it out.

"There."

Tam stared at the circle of twelve-foot-tall, five-foot-wide stones before him. They blended in with the thick trees surrounding them and were spread out far enough that he hadn't even noticed them.

In the center of the circle was a lone wooden table with a dagger.

A random recollection came to Tam in the moment of panic that ensued.

"Why the stone circle? You didn't need one in Troivack the last time you tried to finish me off."

Aradia looked at him with genuine confusion.

Aha. She *hadn't* believed that he was the devil before, but the reference to their last dramatic confrontation made her doubt that judgment. He kept his cool mask in place as he waited for her answer.

None came, however. Instead, she gestured him through the stones.

"Stand across from me there." She pointed to the other side of the table she now stood at.

Tam obeyed, swallowing with difficulty.

As soon as she touched him, he would take her into the void.

He could try it right away from a distance, like he had when the coven had attacked the ship, but… there was an air about her that seemed different from last time. He didn't want to risk messing it up.

"That void power of yours is interesting. I'm also curious how you managed to become the Ashowan heir," Aradia speculated aloud casually while plucking up the dagger from the table.

Ah, now to deliver his crafted reason to persuade her. When he had first claimed to be the devil to Aradia back in Zinfera, he had dwelled for several nights on how he could explain it. The answers had come in thanks to Rosaline's story.

"I had one of my imps bring Tamlin Ashowan to the brink of death, and then had my ashes fed to him. The Ashowan heir already had the handy void ability when I took over. Though I confess, my memory is a little patchy. I got the idea from you and your Witch's Brew. The way you could manipulate the timing of their deaths and entrance to the afterlife with the drug as an exchange for ancient beasts."

Aradia's eyebrows shot up. "You agreed that you'd never do something like that! The complications it could have on your soul and the body's original—"

"You were willing to kill me as an infant as soon as I was reborn somewhere. I don't think you have any grounds to judge my actions. Besides, technically the Ashowans are descendants of your lineage, right? It makes sense that his body would be more receptive," Tam cut in while doing his best to look superior.

Aradia's mouth closed, and anger sparked in her eyes. "Gods. I don't know that you'll ever get out of the Grove of Sorrows. No wonder your power is close to that of a God."

Tam let out a long breath. "Well, I told you what I did. Now you tell me how you got out of that void."

Her expression shifting at the change of topic, Aradia wound up issuing a grin.. "Our old friend Death."

It was Tam's turn to be surprised, but after a moment of allowing the information to sink in, he recalled that Death would of course know the children of his fellow Gods.

"Now take that dagger and stab yourself however you choose. I'd like to say it's been an honor, brother, but we both know this has been a never-ending nightmare ever since the moment we came here."

Tam gestured at the dagger rather than taking it from her hand. "Ladies first."

"What? Too chicken?"

"I speak from experience: Chickens are quite intimidating." Tam moved his hands to his pockets. "But seriously. As you said, you can go first. If you're wrong, you'll just regenerate, won't you?"

The first witch scoffed. "I'm sure you think you have some sort of plan. What? Going to toss me back in the void? I suppose I *should* enlighten you on these stones, since you seem to have forgotten because of your supposed incomplete memory."

Tam felt his stomach drop straight into the deepest dregs of dread. She'd already anticipated his plan. He had started to think that if he crept up quietly enough to the carriage and remained hidden, he could try pulling Eli and the children into the void with him from afar before the archers spotted him.

"These stones come from the Forest of the Afterlife. These stone rings stand in specific places all over the world that our parents had set up for us to travel through to the Forest of the Afterlife—you know, before you decided to stop helping humans." Aradia flipped the blade in her hand once before she continued her story. "However, to ensure no witch could tamper with the stones, anyone who crosses their perimeter has their magic nullified. Meaning you only have your devil abilities right now, and—oh dear. Oh no. Thanks to the curse, I don't feel fear. You're trapped. Now. Will you die with dignity? Or will I do it for you?"

To Tam, the world suddenly became terribly beautiful and terribly sad all at once, as the realization that there didn't seem to be any way out settled over him.

It took every ounce of self-control in him not to reveal his defeated grief as he swallowed.

He wished he could've told his family he loved them one last time.

CHAPTER 40

A WISTFUL WIN

Eli frowned as she watched Tam walk away with the redheaded woman. It wasn't Katarina. The woman was shorter and had wider hips than the Daxarian queen, and her hair's red shade was too light.

Her instincts prickled.

The first witch.

Eli's hand gripped into a fist as she set her jaw.

If Tam was going with her willingly, it was because she was threatening him. Most likely using Eli and the children.

Eli's eyes swept around the brush of the forest.

There were no ditches in this segment of the road, so no one could be hiding near the ground, which left the trees.

She moved her gaze upward. The foliage was thick, but a dark patch had her narrowing her eyes.

After a moment of staring, she confirmed it was a cloak.

She slowly slid farther down the bench and leaned over Penelope to look out their window, her senses sharpened.

She was relatively certain she saw a boot toe on one branch, but she couldn't see another archer.

"What's going on?" Luca asked, his wariness tinged with fear.

Eli remained quiet as she thought about how best to handle the situation. It was obvious that if she tried to leave the carriage, they would shoot at her and the children. She released her fist and thrummed her fingers against her leg impatiently. If the first witch thought Tam was the devil, odds were she was about to try to kill him.

A seed of anxiety sprouted in Eli's belly.

"Mom?" Luca asked again, successfully pulling her from her thoughts.

Eli blinked herself back to the present and fixed Luca with her best calm stare. "There are dangerous men surrounding the carriage, and I'm trying to figure out how we can deal with them without getting any of us hurt."

Luca's eyes went wide as he looked at Penelope in a panic.

"Where's Tam?" the little girl asked, a frown drawing down her own features.

"He went off into the woods with the first witch, and I want to go get him and make sure he is safe," Eli explained evenly. "But I'm quite certain if we try to leave they will shoot... at... us...." An idea occurred to Eli.

A stupid one.

A desperate one.

But... she had a bad feeling about whatever was happening with Tam.

"Luca, Penelope... I'm going to try something," Eli began slowly. "But first, I'm going to close the carriage curtains. After that, you two are going to get onto the carriage floor. If you hear me say run, I want you to leave out my door here on my right, and scream. I also need your coats."

The children nodded, fear bright in their eyes.

"No matter what happens," Eli continued while forcing her voice to remain steady, "I want you two to stay calm. Remember, Penelope, you saw us have this baby, right?"

Penelope went still.

Eli's throat thickened.

The little girl's lips quivered. "I didn't see Tam when I saw the baby. The last part of Tam's future I saw was… was when he found out about the baby."

"But it was his future you were looking into when you saw that it was a girl, right?"

Penelope's lips quivered. "N-no. I saw it was a girl when I held your hand on the boat coming back to Daxaria."

Shoving down her terror, which was starting to spiral out of her control, Eli reached out and gently clasped Penelope's shoulder. "Everything will be alright."

The little girl had tears in her eyes, but she pressed her lips together stubbornly and removed her coat to hand to Eli.

Luca did the same, his face pale, then asked, "What are you going to do?"

Eli did her best to be discreet about taking a steadying breath as she moved over to the opposite bench.

"There are at least two archers in the trees. I think there is only one on my side of the carriage. There is a chance they have a crossbow that is able to fire three times in a row. If that is the case, I want to force him to reload before I get out, so I'm going to shield myself with the door and throw the coats."

"They might not shoot if they see the coats!" Luca exclaimed, his breaths coming out rapidly.

"They might not," Eli agreed. "But if they don't, that will tell us they haven't been told to shoot us on sight."

Penelope audibly gulped.

Eli rested her hand atop the little girl's head. "I'm sorry to scare you, but you need to understand how serious this is. Now, Luca, pull down the curtains and huddle as close to the middle as you can."

Trembling, the children obeyed.

Eli shifted over to the bench Tam had been sitting on mere moments earlier. The black velvet was still warm from him.

Feeling this sparked anger in her. They had only wanted to live in peace, and some higher power thought they could sweep in and take him from her?

She lowered the curtains on her side of the carriage and tucked her feet up, ready to spring out and transform when the time was right. She balled Luca's jacket up in her hand as she grasped the carriage handle and pushed the door open.

She waited for an arrow to hit the door. Her nerves were humming.

Nothing happened.

She drew back her arm, about to toss the coat, when a shout sounded out from the trees.

"You take one step from that carriage and we shoot."

Luca's and Penelope's panicked breath rose in volume.

Her grip on the coat tightened as she shouted back. "It's illegal to hurt a familiar."

She might have heard a sigh, but it might have just been the wind.

She threw the coat.

Nothing happened.

Mentally she cursed.

She leaned forward, sending a prayer to the Gods, then launched out of the carriage, her familiar form bursting free.

The scent of the men in the trees flooded into her mind. There weren't two; there were three. She felt a stinging, throbbing pain in her wing that was tucked to her side, but otherwise her body remained fine. She wasted no time.

She leapt into the tree to her left where she smelled the man nearest her; the other two archers were on Luca and Penelope's side of the carriage.

Eli easily loped up the tree, its boughs bending under her weight. She reached the archer in the span of two breaths, narrowly dodging another arrow he fired, and returned the sentiment by clamping her jaw down around his neck. His weapon fell uselessly to the ground.

Two other arrows were shot at her. Eli felt one graze her back, but she didn't have time to worry about it. She launched herself out of the tree, intending to soar over the carriage and latch onto the next tree infested with an archer, but she was too large, and too easy a target, and perhaps too panicked about the baby…

The next arrow grazed the side of her neck, and she plummeted atop the carriage, then rolled off onto the ground. She shuddered back into her human form, bringing herself up to her knees.

She hadn't been hurt like that in her beast form before.

With shaking hands she reached up to touch the side of her neck and discovered that her fingers came away red and sticky.

She heard the men clambering down their trees.

The children!

Eli turned to look into the open carriage door and saw Penelope and Luca trying to stifle their sobs as they stared at her.

A great shadow streaked over Eli, snapping her attention upward, even though it made her back twinge. She had another wound, but she had no time to think about that.

She caught the glint of gold over the trees…

Wixim.

Time stopped as a sudden, very calm thought claimed her.

Numbly, Eli reached with her stained fingers for the chain around her neck, and withdrew an item Wixim had given her long ago, and hoped there wasn't any fine print to what he'd said…

She blew the whistle.

She heard the men murmuring on the other side of the carriage.

"Kids, get out here *now!*" Eli shouted, her hand coming to her middle, wondering if she had already done irreparable damage to her unborn.

Luca and Penelope sobbed as they fled the carriage to her extended arm. No sooner had they done this than a gust of wind hit Eli's face. This miraculously cleared the haze of panic as she looked up at the dragon, right as the last two archers came from around the carriage and stared in confusion at the dragon's appearance.

Eli didn't bother looking at them as she met Wixim's green eyes.

She knew exactly what needed to be said. She straightened her shoulders. "These men have hurt a familiar. They have broken the divine law."

A low growl rolled in Wixim's throat, and the two archers paused, their expressions turning stony.

"You said before you would join our side if this law was broken, and I am asking you to hold up your end of the deal, or Gods help you, I will curse you. I may not be a true witch, but I will find a way."

Wixim stared at her for a long moment.

There was a rumble of thunder overhead, and a strong wind sent the temperature even lower as goose bumps scattered over Eli's arms.

Wixim swung his great head toward the archers, who each took a step back.

"No. I'll deal with them, go save Tam. He's in the woods with the first witch."

The look Wixim gave Eli suggested he was impressed.

He then turned, scrunched up his back, and shot into the woods on foot, his body moving over the ground and into the distance as though it were fluid.

Eli pressed the children behind herself, her hand on her middle.

The men lifted their crossbows, but there was the flicker of uncertainty in their eyes.

Eli surged forward, her beast exploding out once more, and with one great swipe of her paw, she sent the two men crashing into the body of the carriage.

Shifting back into her human form, Eli's knees buckled as her head spun.

She didn't know if her wounds were more serious than she had initially realized or if the adrenaline she had been feeling before was simply wearing off. She slumped against the carriage with the men at her feet and tried to focus on breathing, but her mouth felt terribly, distractingly dry.

There was a clatter on the ground. Eli cracked her eye open, then had to close it again. Her vision was already darkening.

"NO!"

She heard Luca shout. Only he sounded different than usual. He sounded angry…

Eli forced her eyes open and tried to reach out her hand to catch him as she heard his footfalls nearing, but that was when she realized what had him upset. One of the men had his crossbow held up in trembling arms as he aimed at her.

Luca was beside her, and the look on his face was foreign. He stared down at the man, his face morphed with fury and disgust.

"I said no." Luca's voice was quiet when he spoke again, and that's when Eli realized that waves of dark wisps were emanating from his body. The man on the ground cowered and gave a horrified cry before wetting himself and falling unconscious.

Eli gently rested her hand on Luca's shoulder, only for him to flinch away from her. She saw tears in his eyes as he stared up at her. It was as though he were waiting for her to be livid, or frightened.

"Thank you for helping me, Luca," Eli said softly. "I'm sorry you had to do that."

Luca sniffled, his previous ire forgotten in an instant as tears overflowed his eyes. "I don't like… I didn't want to… I'm sorry!"

Eli held out her arm and gestured him into her arms.

He looked as though he doubted that he deserved to be held, but then his legs gave way and he threw his arms around Eli. She held him close despite the rising pain in her body, then looked over at Penelope, who watched them looking frightened and stunned.

"Penelope?" Eli managed a weak smile. "Come here. I want to see that you're safe."

The little girl's movements were stiff, but when she reached Eli's side, she threw her arms around her and Luca.

At first, Luca flinched at the feel of Penelope's embrace, but when he realized that she, too, was joining the hug, he adjusted his arm so that he was hugging her back.

"You saved me, and you saved the baby, Luca. Thank you. And I promise, you won't ever have to do that again if you don't want to."

Luca said nothing, and it was at that moment that another bellow of thunder shook the sky, which was followed by the crash of rain.

Eli looked upward, the cold droplets sending her into shivers immediately. "Let's get in the carriage, everyone. Luca, make sure to grab your coat."

While the three of them piled back into the vehicle, Eli couldn't help but worry whether Wixim would reach Tam in time.

It was starting to become difficult to keep herself awake. Pain throbbed in her back and neck, and she was feeling rather dizzy. Before she let herself fall unconscious, Eli rested a hand on her abdomen and sent one final prayer to the Goddess: a desperate plea that she and Tam hadn't been allowed happiness only for it to be taken away.

CHAPTER 41

A FATE-FUELED FORFEIT

Tam gripped the handle of the knife Aradia presented to him. He was struggling to remain as calm and cool as he imagined the devil would be. A rumble of thunder sounded above them, right before the rush of rain hitting the treetops echoed around them.

"I'm surprised you don't want to do the honors yourself," he said while inspecting the fine engravings in the blade.

Aradia's eyes turned cold as her patience visibly dwindled. "Get on with it or—"

Her words were cut off as the sounds of a roar and of crushed underbrush echoed loudly throughout the forest.

Both Tam and Aradia turned. Tam frowned as he registered the flash of gold moving toward them. Wixim was here? Had he attacked Eli and the children?

Aradia's head snapped back around. "Stop delaying. Get on with it."

Tam didn't move. He needed to know what the dragon was doing.

"If I send up the signal, those archers will shoot your family."

Tam's attention snapped back to Aradia, who was lifting a whistle from underneath her shirt.

Interestingly, it reminded Tam of the one Wixim had given Eli months ago.

The moment of hesitation, however, was all the time it took for the golden dragon to reach the stone circle.

Wixim took a graceful leap over the stones, landing firmly inside them, snatched Tam in his claws, and bounded away again.

"WIXIM! WHAT ARE YOU DOING?" Aradia roared.

Tam's world was spinning as the dragon unceremoniously dragged him away from his death.

His sight eventually turned right-side up when Wixim tossed him on his back. Needing no further instruction, Tam grasped one of the dragon's raised vertebrae and hung on as he took to the sky. Tam had to clamp his legs tightly to avoid sliding off.

The rain slashed at Tam's face. It felt like chunks of hail rather than just water as they climbed up over the treetops, only for Wixim to then swerve. Tam would've liked to have seen where they were heading, but between the wind and rain assaulting him, it took everything he had just to stay astride.

Luckily, they were not airborne for long. Even with his eyes closed, Tam could sense that they were nearing the ground.

When the dragon gently landed, Tam opened his eyes to see his breath clouding in the air. His hair clung to his head, making him shiver.

It was then he noticed the carriage and the bodies on the ground.

Blind terror seizing him, Tam dismounted and bolted for the carriage. Thunder and lightning fractured the world above him. Rather than feel relief at looking inside the vehicle, shock numbed his body as he took in Eli's gray complexion, the side of her face and neck smeared with blood.

"DAD!" Both Luca and Penelope burst out of the carriage, wrapping their arms around Tam frantically.

"What happened?" he rasped, his gaze not leaving Eli's face.

A flicker of feeling came back into his being when Eli managed to partially open her eyes.

"Mom fought off the archers!" Luca explained as both he and Penelope released Tam and stepped back.

Tam climbed into the carriage and touched Eli's cheek, gently angling her head so he could see the side of her neck.

The wound would definitely scar.

"She has another one on her back," Penelope informed Tam seriously.

Tam's breath hitched.

He was about to ask Eli if she could lean forward so he could take a look at that wound when his ears caught the sound of horses galloping closer. The way he was feeling in that moment, he was relatively certain he was about to kill whoever it was. That is, until he heard the call.

"TAM! TAM, ARE YOU ALRIGHT?"

Tam cast one last fretful look at Eli, and then pulled free from the carriage. "We were attacked! Eli's hurt!"

The house witch was on a horse, and behind him on his own steed rode Sir Lewis.

"Where are the boys?" Tam demanded when he realized he didn't see the carriage.

"Captain Taylor is waiting for us up ahead to escort us all home! He's with them!"

"The first witch is in the woods! Wixim—"

Tam looked behind himself, and only then realized the golden dragon was nowhere to be found.

He didn't have time to worry about that, though, or to question why Wixim had suddenly aided them.

Eli needed to get help. Immediately.

Tam looked back at his father. "Eli's hurt. I can drive the carriage back to the castle; can you stay with her?"

Fin was already dismounting his horse. "Of course. That works out, as it looks like your own horses were cut loose. You and Sir Lewis get them hitched up, and I'll get in the back."

With a short nod, Tam set to work as his father's friend stepped off his own horse and joined him in reattaching the animals to the carriage.

The rain continued to drench them to the bone, but Tam didn't notice anymore. His thoughts barely connected as fear rocked his very soul.

Being afraid wasn't going to help Eli, though, so as time inched along, he allowed himself to slip into an empty place in his mind as his hands worked steadily.

They would get home, and they would heal her and make sure the baby was alright.

They had to.

"Wixim! What the hell are you doing?" Aradia demanded, her hand grasping the dagger tightening.

The golden dragon had returned moments after stealing Tamlin Ashowan away from her. At least the Ashowan heir had dropped the ceremonial knife when he'd been grabbed. However, as Wixim sat across from her at the table in the downpour, she noted the distance in his eyes, and the sad acceptance in the shape of his brow bone.

"Those who fought for you hurt a familiar. Your side broke the divine law, Aradia."

"What? Kraken the familiar is in the carriage with the house witch! What are you—"

"Tamlin Ashowan's mate is a hybrid. It has recently come to my attention that decades ago, the Giong Coven offered the blood of ancient beasts to any nobility that would pay. The allure of possible power or immortality drew many."

Aradia felt her stomach roil. "They did what?"

"I believe the parents of Princess Elisara were some of these nobles, and it is my theory that her mother may have been pregnant at the time she drank the blood."

Aradia felt her jaw open as she struggled against the urge to be sick.

"Ansar should have told you who she was."

"We've been busy with negotiations!" Aradia exclaimed, though there was no anger in her response, only pain. "Wixim, please. I didn't know! I swear! You know I would never—"

"I know, Aradia. But the fates have decided which side I must fight with."

"But I didn't know! If you leave me, Wixim, I'll be… I don't know that we'll win! This… This isn't right! Please. Please don't leave me."

The golden dragon lowered his head and said nothing.

Tears of frustration rose in Aradia's eyes. "What am I supposed to do? How can I… How can I let my brother live on happily while I'm cursed? Why is it fate that I lose? What did I do? Wixim, I've tried and tried. I'm even still trying! I tried to protect humans and avoid violence, and I kept being punished and hurt! I've only been doing things the way the humans do them, and suddenly I'm the worst villain of them all. What can I do? If I do nothing, I'm hurt. If I do something, I'm evil. I'm so… I'm so tired and I just want to go home!" Aradia's voice cracked as she pressed the heels of her palms into her eyes. "I don't want to be broken anymore."

The rain continued to drench the world as the first witch succumbed to her centuries of pain and suffering.

She heard the sound of Wixim leaning forward and felt the gentle tap of his talons on her back and scaled cheek on the top of her head.

"Perhaps we try to negotiate."

"They aren't going to let Tamlin or the child die."

"That isn't who I'm talking about."

Aradia pulled away from Wixim's embrace, her eyes bright with confusion and pain.

The dragon's lips lifted in a kind smile. "Perhaps it is time everyone negotiates with the Gods themselves."

Aradia stepped backward and smiled bitterly. "I've prayed. I've sent messages with the familiars. There is nothing that can be done."

Wixim lowered his face in front of her and lightly tapped her nose with his. *"This time, you wouldn't be doing it alone. I think if we went and talked with the Ashowan family and that…* irritating *hairball that calls himself an empurror, there may be a solution."*

Aradia paused. Her body felt heavy and sore with more than just physical pain. "Will you help me?"

Wixim slowly closed his eyes and gave a faint rumble. *"Of course. I think this would also be in line with helping them end this feud."*

Swallowing, Aradia nodded, then turned to walk away. She would drink another vial of the water from the Goddess's pool and fly to Austice, where Ansar would be waiting. She'd have him draw her a bath, prepare some dry clothes for her, and brew her a cup of tea. When that was all finished, she'd start working on her new plan. Perhaps there was a less violent way to see things end.

As soon as the carriage pulled to a halt in front of the castle in Austice, Tam leapt down from the bench and hurried over to the carriage door, shouting for the physician.

He noted that his father must have ripped up his shirt to bandage the wound on Eli's neck and had covered her with her coat.

Carefully reaching inside, Tam drew her to his chest while his father guided his hands for him around the wound on her back. Once situated, Tam bolted from the carriage up the stairs and into the castle.

There already was a flurry of movement.

First there was Hannah ordering fresh towels and hot water, but when she reached his side, she matched his pace and said, "Tam! Bring her to the guest quarters at the back of the castle! It'll save you taking the stairs!"

Next, Katarina appeared, jogging down the stairs with Eric at her side.

The couple took one look at the situation and halted in their steps. Tam flew by them and proceeded down the south corridor to the room Hannah had instructed him to use.

By the time he reached the small chamber, Tam's sweat was mixed with the rainwater. He did his best not to drip on Eli as he lay her down on the bed, which only had a set of white sheets on it.

Her eyes slowly opened right as Hannah rushed in behind Tam and started working on the fire.

"I think I just am in shock," she said faintly. "The wounds shouldn't be deep, and I didn't fall that far—"

Tam grabbed her icy hand in his own and kissed her fingertips as he brought himself to kneel beside her. "When did you fall?" Tam exclaimed in alarm.

"During the fight with the archers. I jumped over the carriage, and got hit, so I fell on the carriage, then rolled to the ground."

Tam cursed and was about to ask follow-up questions about her pain when the physician arrived.

"Lord Tam, please leave the room while I— Oh."

Tam looked over his shoulder and saw that the physician's eyes were fixed on Eli's middle, which was especially noticeable thanks to the rain making her shirt cling to her.

The physician overcame his surprise swiftly and set to rolling up his black sleeves. "How far along is she?"

"Just under three months," Tam explained while forcing himself to stand and make way for Eli to be examined.

"Alright. I will take good care of her, Lord Tam. Please leave me to work."

Tam's eyes sought out Eli's, and she gave him a slow nod. "I've survived worse, Tam. Let's get on with it."

Tam wished he could've smiled at her, but he wasn't successful. He backed out of the room, only vaguely aware that a hand that appeared on his elbow was the only reason he was able to move at all.

As soon as the door closed, Tam felt his mind fire back to life with every horrible, anxious thought imaginable.

"I'll send her magic so she recovers quickly." Kat's voice sounded like it was coming from the end of a long tunnel. It must have been her that had guided him from the room. "I'm sorry, Tam… I'm sure things will be alright."

Acid and pain burned Tam's gut and throat as he turned to look at his sister's grim expression.

Somehow, seeing Kat's face after everything that had happened made him say the words that were already becoming unbearably prominent in his mind. "It should've been me. Not her. I'm supposed to die. She isn't. She can't die, Kat. I don't… I don't know what I'm going to do if she does."

CHAPTER 42

A WARY WELCOME

Penelope stared around at the growing crowd in the castle entryway.

She and Luca were standing side by side, and as news of Tam's return spread, more curious souls drifted in. She eyed them while doing her best to hide the fact that she was a bundle of nerves.

A slight squeeze of her left hand had her head snapping over to Luca, who smiled at her encouragingly. Penelope didn't even have the ability to scoff at his reassurance, and she saw the flicker of worry in his face as a result.

That was when a man strode forward, parting the crowd just with his presence.

Penelope looked at him and stiffened.

He had dirty-blond hair, hazel eyes, and a beard.

There was an air of assessment in his gaze when it landed on her.

He wasn't as tall as Tam, though, and for whatever reason, remembering this reignited Penelope's usual fury. She scowled up at him.

That is until his attention flitted to Luca and his calm albeit distant expression faded instantly. In its place there was a hardness, tinged with something that Penelope didn't need Luca's powers to know the name of.

Hate.

Penelope suddenly had the very worrying premonition that they were about to be grabbed by some of the knights that had gathered in the crowd.

She gripped Luca's hand tightly in response.

He surprised her then by turning and looking at her with an eerie calm. "It'll be okay. My dad's nearby."

"Our dad," Penelope corrected quietly.

Luca blinked, and his eyebrows rose. His stunned expression made him look like himself again, and Penelope couldn't help but smile in relief at seeing it.

He smiled back. "Yeah. *Our* dad is close."

"Who might you two be?"

The booming voice echoed out, making both Penelope and Luca turn back to stare up at the man, who watched them sharply.

Penelope frowned. "Well, who are *you*?"

The man arched an eyebrow, but he didn't seem angry or offended.

That both perplexed and relieved Penelope; her heart beat so quickly that it felt like it was choking her.

"I am King Eric Reyes of Daxaria."

The whispers that had been hovering in the air over the crowd quieted.

Penelope's steeliness hardened. "Why are you making kids announce themselves to an audience? That isn't nice."

The king balked. It was evidently his turn to be caught off guard.

A bark of laughter sounded from behind the king. "I think she is absolutely right, Your Majesty."

Penelope couldn't see who was approaching from behind, but Luca evidently did, and his face broke into an exuberant smile that had his cheeks flushing pink.

Luca released Penelope's hand and bolted around the king to the owner of the voice, who grinned down at the boy.

"Harris!" Luca wrapped his arms around his hips.

When the king turned, Penelope then saw the nobleman for herself.

"Holy antlers, Luca! You've grown at least two, maybe three inches since I last saw you!" the duke exclaimed jubilantly, which in turn made the whispers flare again.

Penelope watched Luca with the duke, frozen. A droplet of relief trickled its way through her body. Harris would protect them, right? He was a duke! A weird one with terrible fashion sense and the worst flatulence imaginable, but still!

Harris patted Luca's back and with his usual twinkling eyes addressed the king once more. "Your Majesty, might I suggest we go somewhere more private? These kids have had a wildly unfortunate time as of late, and I don't think Her Majesty, Duchess Ashowan, or I have had a chance to tell you about them yet."

Penelope couldn't see the king's face as he regarded Harris, but after a moment he slowly nodded.

"Fine. Harris, show the children to the council room. I'll send for my wife and meet you there."

The duke grinned and gave a shallow bow as the king then proceeded past him and made his way back through the crowd down a corridor to the left.

Penelope let out the breath she had been holding and allowed her shoulders to sag in relief. That is, until the whispers around her increased in volume.

Her jaw clenched as she glared at the sea of unfamiliar faces, daring them to continue being so outrageously rude.

A gentle hand clasped her shoulder, however, bringing her attention up to Harris's smiling face.

"Come along. I'll show you the way."

Penelope didn't say anything to him—even though she was thrilled that he was there and more than a little grateful for his interference—and instead looked at Luca. He also appeared a bit worried, but he spared her another smile.

There was something odd about Luca.

He almost seemed like he was a little more mature all of a sudden.

Penelope didn't like it.

So she stuck her tongue out at him right as Harris turned to guide them up the stairs.

Luca grinned in response, which only agitated Penelope further. It was probably for the better that he wasn't crying like a baby, though she did wonder why the Daxarian king already had looked at Luca as though he hated him...

It made her uneasy, and things were bad enough.

Once Harris, Penelope, Luca, and the king were all seated in the council room, the conversation resumed. This time, with Harris present, it had less of an interrogative nature. The Daxarian queen hadn't arrived yet.

"Well, Duke Harris?" the king asked, his face a mask of stone.

Harris winked at Penelope and Luca, then looked back at the king, unfazed by his apparent displeasure.

"Well, Your Majesty," Harris began breezily. "This is your new niece and nephew. Penelope, and Luca. I trust you can tell which is which."

The king drew up straight in his seat in alarm. "What?"

Harris settled back in his chair comfortably. "Luca is a surprise child Lord Tam discovered he had from a former paramour, and Penelope here was rescued from Zinferan pirates by Lord Tam and my niece, who are… What are they now?" Harris turned the question to Penelope and Luca.

"Betrothed and expecting a baby," Luca supplied happily.

"Right, betrothed and—" Harris stopped talking and stared at Luca, who merely kept smiling.

The duke opened his mouth to speak again then closed it. On his third attempt he managed to say, "Another baby? Good Gods. Fin will be living his dream life as a grandfather." The duke shook his head in awe. "Anyway. That's who they are. These two children have been through unimaginable hardships, and I think allowing them to go rest, or to see Tam, might be best for the time being."

The king raised an eyebrow but otherwise betrayed no other emotion as he looked at the children once more. He had not softened at all following the explanation.

He didn't get to say anything, however, as the council room door swung open, and in stepped Katarina, looking a bit too serious herself.

"Hey, Eric, things are looking bad right now for— Oh! Hey, kids!" The Daxarian queen cut herself off as soon as she saw the young audience in the room.

She donned a pained smile and waved to Luca and Penelope, who both bolted out of their chairs to hug her.

"Aunt Queen!" Luca called up to her excitedly.

Kat's smile turned genuine as she snorted. "Hey, kid. How's it going? I see you've met your uncle."

The sound of a chair scraping against stone made everyone turn to the king.

Penelope watched the queen's brows twitch in confusion at the sight of her husband's face.

"Hm. Okay. I'm going to ask the guards to go take you to your cousins. Your grandfather told me you all met recently, so—"

"No. I don't want them near the boys right now. Please tell the guards to put them in a guest room and to post sentries." The king's voice was firm, with no room for argument.

The queen's questioning look turned fierce, but she didn't say anything to the king before she guided Penelope and Luca out of the room.

Once outside, she knelt down and leaned close to the pair of them.

"I'm sorry your uncle is being an arsehat right now. I'll talk with him. He's a bit grumpy because I was gone for so long. Harris and I only just got back this morning, your grandmother last night, and Eric was out at the time waiting to pick up your cousins."

Both Penelope and Luca nodded slowly.

"Don't worry, alright? We'll work this all out in no time."

"Is Eli okay?" Penelope asked as she tightened her hands into fists.

Kat grimaced, and Penelope's heart sank.

"We're doing everything we can. If she weren't pregnant, I'd say she'd recover quickly, but right now… I can't say."

Penelope felt her throat tighten uncomfortably, and her nose began to drip before she could even try to stop it.

"Can we see her?" Luca asked with a croak.

The queen hesitated. "You can, but later. Right now, the physician is attending to her. I'm going to ask these nice guards to take you to a guest room for now, and one of them is going to get you some books and toys to play with in the meantime, okay?" The queen's golden eyes shifted upward to the guards as she spoke, and both bowed in acknowledgment.

"We aren't in trouble, right?" Penelope whispered. She didn't want to let on how afraid she was, but she wasn't sure she was succeeding.

The queen instantly dropped her attention back to her and gently touched her head. "Of course not! No, no! You two did nothing wrong. Just go and try to get some rest, hm? We'll talk soon."

With a final squeeze of their shoulders, the queen stood and nodded to the guards, who stepped forward.

Despite the queen's assurances, Penelope couldn't help but have doubts that they would be able to rest given how tense things were, and after a quick glance at Luca, she could tell he had a very similar sense.

For now, there was nothing they could do, though, and so they followed the guards, and occasionally shared silent looks. The wordless communication being:

No matter what, we stick together.

Upon closing the council room door, Kat placed her hands on her hips and glared at her husband. "What the hell was that?"

"That boy is the devil," Eric said darkly.

Kat felt her aura flare to life. "He is Tam's son. He was born from a human woman, and he is an absolute sweetheart."

Eric clamped his mouth shut, but only for a moment. "Kat, I know the devil. I spent a lot more time with him than any of you. He is that child."

"Or is it that you are determined to think that it's him? Gods, Eric! You could try and verify it before scaring two kids!"

"Kat," Eric rounded the table and moved toward his wife. "The devil is a master manipulator. A fantastic liar. We cannot trust that boy. He is going nowhere near our sons. And that little girl probably has parents somewhere!"

"She doesn't," Kat informed her husband coldly. "They're dead. She's actually my distant cousin. She's Caroline Levin's daughter."

"The traitors who helped the first witch?" Eric asked loudly.

"Ah yes. The traitors who obviously consulted with their infant daughter about their plots. Of course!" Kat slammed her fist into her other palm. "She was the true mastermind all along!" She dropped her hands back to her sides and stared at the king flatly. "Seriously. What the hell? She's a child who was abducted by pirates and kept in a Godsdamn cage, Eric. Why are you acting like such an insensitive tit?"

"People are dead, Kat! Our boys were abducted! Charlie is a mess, there are two covens revolting, Princess Kezia received a horrible injury, and I have not been in contact with you for months! I'm damn well going to be upset and cautious as hell!"

Kat felt her temper simmer. "That doesn't mean you terrorize *children!*"

There was a tense silence that filled the space between the couple, but it didn't last long before Kat exploded once more. "Godsdamnit, Eric. Tam is terrified right now for his pregnant partner! He doesn't need *you*, his *family*, acting like this!"

Eric's jaw flexed as his gaze bore into his wife's.

A less-than-subtle throat clearing sounded out. "So… I agree with Her Majesty, and I'd like to inquire more about my niece in a moment, but I would also very much so like to hear more about that deal you were mentioning, Your Majesty, having been negotiating with the first witch prior to our arrival."

Kat widened her eyes and her aura became tinged with red as she bore down on her husband. "You started making a deal with the first witch and you're spouting off this bullshit about the devil?"

"I'm *trying* to stop an all-out war to spare hundreds if not thousands of lives!" Eric ground out.

"Oh yeah? And other than an independent land for witches only, what does the first bitch want?" Kat growled.

Eric paused and let out a breath, but Kat already had a sneaking suspicion she knew what it was.

"The devil. I said I wouldn't stand between her and the devil."

CHAPTER 43

THE OUTSIDER'S OFFENSE

"**I**'m sorry, Lord Tamlin."

Tam felt his heart stop.

"Lady Eli is not going to have an easy recovery if she does manage to pull through. And I'm afraid the infant... While still alive right now, it is not likely they will survive the next few weeks."

Tam staggered backward.

The physician stared at him sadly. "If Lady Elisara survives the next two weeks, then her odds of making it through the removal of the child are greater."

"No... No, there has to be... There has to be a chance that they both make it," Tam rasped.

"I won't ever say never. Miracles happen. But it is not likely."

Tears blurred Tam's vision as he felt his world start to crumble around him.

"Thank you for caring for my betrothed," he forced himself to say.

"Of course, my lord. I will continue to treat Lady Eli to the best of my ability, and I have requested some assistance from one of my old teachers in Austice."

Tam nodded. "When can I see her?"

"Tomorrow morning may be best, my lord. Lady Eli needs a great deal of rest." The physician bowed.

Tam trembled. "Alright. Please, if you… If you speak with her before I do, let her know I love her."

The physician straightened and gave a sympathetic half smile. "Of course, my lord." He then turned back to the door to Eli's room and disappeared back inside.

Tam raised his hands to his eyes and slowly slid down the wall to the floor. He wanted to shout. He wanted to curse the Gods. He wanted to beg and barter… He wanted his world to turn right again.

It hadn't ever been right before her.

The murmur of the castle activity drifted over Tam, reminding him that everyone's life continued on despite his own falling apart.

But at the same time, there was silence. A silence that brought a strange groundedness to his suffering. It felt as though there should be noise and chaos. Sounds that echoed the monstrous amount of things inside of himself. How was it so… calm?

Tam stayed on the floor for a while, his head tilted back to rest against the castle wall.

They had made it home to Austice.

Yet that was when things started falling apart.

Penelope had seen Eli give birth to their daughter, but that didn't mean that either of them lived past the birth, or that they weren't going to suffer for the rest of their lives.

Tam swallowed. He needed to drink something, and he needed to check on both Luca and Penelope.

On legs that felt both heavy and unsteady, he came to a stand and moved away from the room.

He passed a maid who happened to be carrying a pitcher of water and a goblet. After quietly asking for permission, Tam intercepted it and then continued on to the main hall of the castle.

He wondered where his family was.

Where was his father? His mother? Why weren't they there? Why weren't they trying to help?

His throat tightened. His hands shook.

He arrived at the castle entryway to find all of them. His father, mother, Kat, and Eric were standing and talking… or… fighting.

"Eric, we are not handing over that boy to her! He's Tam's son! By blood!" Fin argued vehemently.

"He's still the devil!" the king shouted.

Tam stilled.

"No! He isn't the same, Eric! He isn't who you're remembering, he's just a lovely little boy who—" Kat continued, only for Eric to round on her.

"He's the one who made Alina miscarry! He tried to kill you multiple times! This is why he is dangerous! He gets reborn as a child and he—"

"The first witch has done a lot of those crimes as well and other horrible things, like creating a drug that kills people and ruins their lives, but you still made a deal with *her*!" Kat seethed.

"Because she's offering to leave! She's going to go away and it will end! The devil is still here! He isn't trying to leave! He's inserting himself in our lives," Eric enunciated, his frustration pronounced.

Tam stood rooted to the spot.

Eli and his daughter were dying.

And they were here arguing what to do about his son?

The first wave of emotions brought with it fresh pain.

Why did he think things would be different?

Why did he think that now that he'd found his place with his family, everything would work out?

He would always be the outsider, and that was fine.

But in that moment he realized it meant his family, his own children and spouse, would be outsiders, too.

I guess… I guess I have to protect them on my own.

Something tore inside of Tam. A faint hope he had clung to for a long time disintegrated in his chest. The hope that he would find his place with the family he'd come from. That he would one day be a part of them. That he would feel equal in importance with them. And more recently… that he could bring his own family into their warmth.

If it had been another day, a day when he wasn't about to lose Eli and his child, it would have brought him to his knees.

It was not one of those days.

The longer Tam stared at the faces of his family, the slower they seemed to move. The faces of people he had always done everything he could for. Faces he'd loved. Supported.

Even Eric.

The addict king.

Eric who had never trusted Tam because Tam took part in his mother's espionage work. Tam had always known Eric was uncomfortable with the unknown amount of power he held. As well as his close relationship with Kat.

Well. Eric hadn't needed to fear him before today, but Tam would show him.

A chain of control Tam had always maintained, dropped. The principles that had guided him suddenly turned meaningless.

Tam stepped into the void and stepped back out in the middle of the argument.

Eric stumbled back, his eyes widening.

Tam knew he looked terrifying. He had Eli's blood across his neck and on his hands, and he had no doubt his eyes were filled with black.

Kat was the first to splutter. "Gods, Tam, what—"

"Eli is dying. As is our unborn." Tam heard his voice echo with an otherworldly warble around the entrance.

"Tam, I'm sorry—" Finlay Ashowan began to say behind him.

But Tam didn't look at his father; he continued to look at the king.

"I see that we aren't on the same side anymore, Your Majesty. So I suggest you leave. I'll return your castle once Eli has had a chance to recover. The princes are welcome to stay, but it sounds as though you don't want them near myself or my family."

Eric's brows lowered, his hazel eyes assessing. "Tam, what the hell is going on? I'm sorry about Eli, but that child is not your son. He has manipulated you—"

"You can leave on your own, or I can make you leave." Tam felt his black aura flutter from his skin.

Eric straightened. "Tam, this whole thing involves not just you, but the entire world. The devil and the first witch are forever going to hurt people."

"Humans forever hurt people. That was what the devil always said. Yet people like you still are allowed to live."

"Tam!" Kat burst out.

Tam didn't look away from his brother-in-law. "I'm not much better, but my point is: Why do you think *you're* any better? If you choose to go against my son, you're against me. Now leave. I won't say it again."

"Tam." The duchess's quiet voice drifted over to him.

It was the only time Tam broke away from Eric's gaze. He stared at his mother. He showed her in his face his deeply felt betrayal, and his disappointment.

A slight movement out of the corner of his eye had him looking back at Eric to see he had reached for the sword at his side, and Kat had seized her husband's wrist, shooting him a warning look.

Tam didn't bat an eye at the fact his brother-in-law was willing to draw a sword on him. "Kat, go get the boys. I'll move your husband outside the grounds."

"Tam, just wait—"

Tam didn't hear the rest of whatever his sister wanted to say as he took Eric with him into the void without wasting another breath.

Predictably Eric's shock rendered him temporarily immobile, which allowed Tam to grab him by the arms and haul him in a blur through the void. He felt his way over the castle, over the lawn, all the way to the road in Austice, and reappeared with Eric there.

He dropped his brother-in-law on the cobblestones, and before the king could say another word, Tam shifted back to the castle.

When he reappeared back in the castle entryway, he discovered that knights and guards had gathered in alarm and Kat was shouting to try and instill some calm among everyone.

However, Tam's reappearance instantly cast a hush amid the chaos.

He looked over them all dispassionately. "Leave now. Or you will be trapped in this castle with me. The choice is yours."

Two knights took uncertain steps toward him.

Tam waved his hand and sent them into the void.

"TAM!" Kat appeared in front of him, her aura blazing. "KNOCK IT OFF! WE WERE JUST TALKING ABOUT THINGS!"

"I am calm. Your husband is unharmed, but he was threatening Luca, and I will not allow him to stay near him."

"I wasn't going to let him give over Luca to the first witch! I know Luca isn't bad! And neither is Eric! He's just a human processing stuff from the past!" Kat argued.

Tam stared at his sister, then looked at his parents who watched him with unreadable expressions on their faces. "Everyone expects me to just sit around while you ignore Eli's condition? While you ignore me? After I got involved in this mess for all of you? Now you threaten my son and think I should sit back. Would *you*, if you were in my position?"

"I'm not threatening Luca! I'm trying to protect him!" Kat persisted, though the edge in her voice had gentled. "Tam, I know the past few months have been a lot for you, but this isn't the way."

Tam shrugged. "Why not? No one is getting hurt. Eli is going to rest and recover, and then the kids and she and I are going to leave. You all can deal with the first witch on your own. I'm done. You've made it all very clear where I stand with all of you."

"Tam, we care about you and your kids, it's just—" Kat's words were cut off as everyone in the room vanished in clouds of black smoke.

Tam closed his eyes and pushed with all his might, dropping them all around the same place he'd dropped Eric.

The castle entryway was blissfully silent.

Tam turned toward the stairs and set to climbing. He would tell his nephews what was going on and let them choose where they would like to be.

But first, he needed to ensure his family was hidden.

Tam eyed the windows that displayed the stormy day outside. He knew what he was about to do would most likely drain all of his power. But it was worth the risk.

He closed his eyes and reached through the castle. Through the stones, through the wood, through the tapestries… He allowed himself to dissipate into the castle, scattering himself through the entire building.

And then he dragged it into the void.

Despite no longer being assembled in his physical body, Tam felt himself tremble.

He was exhausted, and pulling himself back together took significant effort, but when he did, he listened to Penelope's and Luca's voices and reappeared in their room.

He nearly fainted on the spot.

"DAD!" both Penelope and Luca shouted.

Tam's vision blurred, then cleared, but he still felt horrible. He heard their footsteps pounding across the stones to reach him.

"Dad, what's going on? It's black outside the castle! It looks like your void!" Luca asked, his eyes wide.

Tam gave a weak smile as he managed to wrap both children in his embrace. "That's because the entire castle *is* in the void."

"What? Why?" Penelope's voice was filled with alarm.

Tam did his best to steady himself as he vaguely noted the shrieks and hollers elsewhere in the castle becoming louder.

"It turns out, the king doesn't want to help us."

"I *knew* it!" Penelope declared righteously. "I knew he was a jerk!"

"Eli is…" Tam trailed off, his emotions surging once more.

Luca pulled away from him and stared at his father with open fear. "Is Mom… Is Mom okay?"

"I… Um… We… We're hoping she will be," Tam's voice cracked. "In the meantime, we need to wait here until we can travel again."

Penelope and Luca exchanged a look. "Where will we go?"

Tam did his best to make a smile, though he could tell his eyes were starting to water again as he reached up and touched Luca's face. "I'll figure it out. Eli mentioned traveling to see Lobahl, so who knows? Maybe that's where we'll go."

"Oh! Where Hamil and Bes are from?" Luca asked curiously.

Tam nodded.

"That could be fun. Could Jeong and Bong visit us?" Luca grasped his own hands and fidgeted.

He was nervous.

Well, he's nervous for good reason.

"Maybe they can." Tam forced a small laugh.

A sudden pounding on the door instantly stopped their conversation.

"OPEN UP!"

The thundering voice most likely belonged to a disgruntled guard.

Tam guessed they were about to blame Luca for the sudden darkness outside the castle.

Gritting his teeth, Tam shoved himself up off the floor to his feet. He staggered and leaned his arm against the wall to help himself balance, but he refused to faint. There was still much to do.

I'd better go set the record straight about who moved the castle, and then… I'll go talk to my nephews.

CHAPTER 44

LET'S TRY TREASON

Tam stared out over the crowd of castle occupants.

He numbly acknowledged their expressions.

Fearful, angry, anxious, uncertain…

Oddly, faces he had known his whole life suddenly seemed foreign to him.

"So you'll let us out of the castle, but not back in?" a nobleman called up to Tam as he stood above them on the stairs.

Tam locked eyes with the man, who stiffened as a result. "Yes."

"It won't hurt?" a maid asked next.

"No."

"Are you possessed by the devil?" a knight shouted next.

Tam didn't even bat an eye. "The king has had a misunderstanding, and until it gets sorted, I am keeping Elisara and my children safe."

A flush of murmurs ran through the crowd before fizzing out.

A figure stepped free of the crowd and gazed calmly up at Tam.

Hannah.

Tam felt his stoic mask slip ever so slightly as he looked at his father's friend.

"Tam, you magicked an entire castle and its people for the sake of your own family. That's—"

"No one is hurt. No one will get hurt. But if I didn't do this, people would be harmed. This was the safest option."

"Now, Lord Tam." Lord Les Fuks stepped from the crowd. His cheeks were already bright with discomfort. "It is a mite selfish to inconvenience an entire court and its serving staff."

"Are you fine with the death of my son for the sake of your comfort?" Tam asked coldly.

Les Fuks flinched.

"I saved your own son Aster days ago, Lord Les. I hate to have to ask for a favor when I would've thought this was the decent thing to do, but it seems like I must." Tam put his hands in his pockets to hide that they were trembling as a result of his anger and his weakened state.

An uncomfortable silence fell back over the castle occupants, and Tam had reached his limit.

He didn't expect anyone to be on his side, if he were honest with himself. He'd given up on that notion. He just hoped they wouldn't be actively against him.

"I will go talk with the princes to see if they'd like to stay or be with the king and queen. By the time I return, those of you who wish to leave, please be here."

Tam turned at his conclusion and began climbing the stairs.

"This is treason!"

Without looking, Tam knew it was the knight who had spoken out earlier.

He didn't bother addressing the comment.

The room was already holding its breath.

He didn't need to add any oil to the fire.

The sound of quick, light footsteps behind him told Tam that Hannah was coming up to follow him. This move most likely helped people feel a bit calmer, as the head of housekeeping behaving as usual must have made him seem less threatening.

"Hey, Tam," he heard Hannah say softly at his side.

He didn't slow his pace as he took a right.

"I understand that you are trying to protect your family, but there is a better way to do that than this."

"I had to make a quick decision. I'm sure there was a more elegant way of handling it, but for the sake of expediency, here we are," he informed her in a businesslike tone.

"Tam, you're going to get arrested for this," Hannah pointed out, her steps quickening to keep up.

"They can try," Tam countered casually.

Hannah paused in their conversation as she let that response sink in. "I can tell you've been through a lot since you've been gone, Tam. I'm glad you've found people you love. People you want to call your family."

"I don't *want to*, I do. They *are* my family." Tam ascended the next set of stairs, which would take him to the floor where his nephews most likely were. After speaking with them and moving the people who wished to leave, he needed to go retrieve Luca and Penelope and take them to Eli.

He'd left them in their room that locked from the inside, but he hadn't trusted the crowd he'd faced.

"So that's it? You're done with all of us? You won't listen?"

A fresh, sharp bite of anger gripped Tam. "And did you ever listen to me?"

"Tam! Of course we listened to you! I—"

Tam laughed darkly and kept walking.

Hannah didn't remain at his side.

When he reached the chamber where his nephews waited, he found two guards standing at attention. He approached to knock, only to have them take a step closer to each other.

He stared. Did they know what was going on? Would he have to repeat himself?

Sighing, Tam reached up and pinched the bridge of his nose before calling out. "Boys? Mind coming out? I have to talk to you."

"Lord Tam—" one guard started, but the door banged open before he could finish.

Asher bolted out straight to Tam, throwing his arms around his legs. Antony and Charlie followed closely behind.

"What's going on, Uncle Tam?" Asher asked gravely, with significantly more maturity than was usual for him, which surprised Tam a little.

With a hand resting atop Asher's head, Tam explained what was happening and the decision they needed to make.

The guards behind the children paled.

Tam ignored them.

"We want to stay with you, Uncle Tam!" Asher declared.

Tam blinked in shock. "Uh. Really?"

A corner of his heart warmed.

He looked to Antony and Charlie, expecting them to pull Asher free and tell him they couldn't stay with him.

Only the older boys were staring up at him with firm resolution.

"Of course, Uncle Tam. We protect people. That's what people with Ashowan blood do," Antony said matter-of-factly.

"You aren't hurting anyone. You're saving people," Charlie agreed with an added shrug.

Tam's lips twitched. His throat suddenly ached with appreciation. But… he knew what he needed to say.

"Boys, your… Your parents are worried about you. You should go to be with them."

"Yeah, well. They made *us* worry and we just had to wait. They can wait a little, too," Antony pointed out with an uncharacteristically curt tone. "How about we go guard Luca and Penelope?"

Tam clamped his mouth closed.

It wasn't right that his nephews stay with him and not their parents.

And yet… he didn't think he could push away the only blood relatives who didn't bat an eye at staying by his side.

"Let's go to their room."

"Your Highnesses!" one of the guards blurted. "Please return to the king and queen! This is not a safe place right now!"

Antony turned and looked at the guards, but it was Charlie who spoke first. "Of course it's safe. It's Tam. He always keeps us safe. You forget yourselves. You are dismissed."

The imperial voice he used was alarming but evidently hard to argue against, and so the two guards shared uneasy looks, but did not try to dissuade the princes again.

"Oy! Tam! My favorite godson! Good Gods, I took one quick nap in the council room and suddenly everything has gone to the pigs! What's happening? I'm hearing some very strange things!" Tam looked up to see Harris striding toward him hurriedly.

Tam sensed the guards relax with the duke's presence.

When Harris came to a stop a few feet in front of Tam, he studied him in the white light of the void that poured in through the windows.

Understanding passed through the duke's eyes, followed by stoniness. "I take it things aren't alright?"

Once again, Tam relayed the events, and this time included Eli's precarious state.

The duke's serious expression turned grim. "Ah." He let out a long breath. "If you don't mind, I'd like to go see Eli for myself. May I join you as you go pick up the children and go to her?"

Another piece of ice in Tam's heart thawed as he realized Harris wasn't challenging him, either.

He swallowed with difficulty and nodded.

Asher and Charlie each grasped Tam's hands, and the small group set off, leaving the guards stuck behind in indecision.

When they were out of earshot, Harris spoke again, though he lowered his voice. "Tam, do you have enough power to send people back through? You don't exactly look in the best shape."

"I'll manage. No matter what."

Harris was quiet for a few moments, then said, "You know, I'm sure Kasim Jelani is still here… He might be worth speaking to."

At the mention of the royal botanist, Tam frowned in confusion. "Why?"

"He has… a different understanding of magic than the Wittica Coven. He might be able to help you recharge somehow."

Tam considered this. "I doubt he will want to help me. Most of the people here are already saying I'm committing treason."

"Eh. Who hasn't? Your sister commits treason all the time."

"Yeah, but she's the queen."

Harris blew a raspberry in the air. "Whatever. Though, Tam. From what you said, your family *was* protecting you. I know you felt that they should have been there with you with Eli, but it sounds like they were holding back the king from acting immediately."

"Eric wasn't budging. And my parents are loyal to the crown, and my sister won't wage a battle against her husband."

Harris snorted.

Tam pressed his lips together. "Okay. She might."

"Tam, if it came down to it? Your parents would choose you over the crown. Especially with something like this. Of that I have no doubt."

A weary breath left Tam. "Maybe," he conceded. "But if there even was the slightest risk? I wasn't taking it."

"Fair enough." Harris turned to look at Tam as they walked. "You're a good dad, Tam."

"And a *great* uncle!" Asher contributed brightly.

Tam cast a smile down at his youngest nephew. Charlie was squeezing his hand a little more tightly in solidarity as Antony nodded in agreement.

"We'll all come through this, and next thing you know, we'll all be making jokes about that time you stole a whole castle over a couple of pints. No performance issues on your end, that's for certain! Chin up, lad." Harris clapped a hand on his back with a small chortle. "We just have to sort this all out."

Gratitude filled Tam, and while he didn't say anything, Harris's eyes twinkled in acknowledgment.

"Harris, why…" Tam trailed off, uncertain what he was even about to ask.

"I remember being all alone, Tam. I remember being alone against the world, and I remember when I found out I had people at my back. I know how much it's worth. Besides, you're practically my nephew-in-law! Embracing this new family relation with a bit of treason seems perfectly right in my mind."

Tam issued a quiet chuckle.

"Did the physician say how long it would take for Eli to recover?" Harris asked, his former levity sobering.

"In two weeks, we will know."

Harris grimaced. "Two weeks? That's a long time to keep the castle in the void. Plus there is the important matter of food."

Tam nodded. "I know. I'll have to work out the logistics of this soon. Thought if only a few people stay behind, I'm sure we'll have more than enough"

Harris didn't say anything else on the matter as they descended the first set of stairs. However, he then posed another interesting question. "Tam, what do you think everyone is doing outside the void? I remember you saying the outside moves at a different time…"

Tam's exhaustion was starting to make his steps heavy, but he tried to fathom what chaos was unfolding outside with his parents, sister, and brother-in-law.

"Rallying forces. Camping out. The first witch might even join them so that the moment I reappear they seize me."

"Mm," Harris agreed wordlessly. "Who knows? Maybe your father is diffusing the situation as we speak!"

Tam shook his head. "My father is a force to be reckoned with, but even he has his limits."

The two men and princes touched down on the final set of stairs that led to the castle entryway. A large group of people milled about, their voices clamoring in the stone space.

No one seemed to notice their arrival, so Harris helped by lifting two fingers to his mouth and letting out a shrill whistle.

The room fell silent.

Tam nodded his chin at the crowd. "The princes have asked to stay in the castle. Everyone who wishes to leave, please move to my left."

Everyone save for two dozen people obeyed. Among the group that wished to stay were Hannah, Captain Taylor, Lord Les Fuks, the elderly Lord Dick Fuks, Mage Keith Lee, and a few other faces familiar to Tam. Some knights he was less familiar with remained with their captain.

Tam took a fortifying breath and started to lift his left hand, when the same nobleman from earlier called out.

"You will pay for your crimes, Lord Tam! I always knew there was something off about you!"

Tam felt his expression turn to iron.

However, he was spared having to respond by Harris.

"Wellington, you're the dodgy end of a rotten tomato who skims off the top of what your vassals pay in taxes. Shut up."

Tam gaped at Harris.

But the duke waved his hand dismissively while turning his nose dramatically into the air. "Go on Tam, void him. Or de-void him. I don't know. Do your thing."

If it were another, less dire day, Tam would've laughed, but for now, he simply obliged, waving his hand.

It took significantly more effort than the last time he had shoved a group of people through the void, and this time, a strong headache thrummed against his skull and his gut roiled. He almost couldn't push them out the other side. Clenching his teeth, he hissed, and then he shoved with all his might.

They were out.

And he was suddenly very lightheaded.

"Ooh, now. I don't recommend fainting," Harris murmured. "The ones who stayed behind might not be here to support you. So how about I just throw my arm around you here, and I see about having Kasim meeting you up in the room Luca and Penelope are in, hm? I'm quite certain that, void or not, Kasim is still in his greenhouse."

Tam grunted in assent and allowed the duke to half carry him as he stumbled drunkenly away from the eerily empty castle entryway.

His thoughts were becoming sluggish and disjointed, but he allowed himself to relax just a fraction onto Harris.

Just until he could stand on his own again.

Then he would check on the children.

CHAPTER 45

HERE, HAVE SOME HELP

It hadn't taken long.

A full-blown battle was about to take place on the lawn, near where the castle had disappeared. All hell had broken loose in short order.

First, the king and queen had found themselves in a shouting match; the other courtiers had joined in almost immediately. Then more courtiers and serving staff had appeared, and it was revealed that the princes had chosen to stay at their uncle's side.

Things descended further into chaos, but by the next day it was even worse.

A whole slew of witches arrived.

Apparently, a number of witches Tam who had sent into the void had reappeared. Some were still recovering from malnourishment, but it soon became clear that their return to the tangible world had occurred because Tam had strained himself moving the castle and courtiers into the void.

The first witch was nowhere in sight.

Ancient beasts had started trickling in. As a result, Tak, the golem that guarded Daxaria, had moved to stand in the harbor, unnerving the citizens of Austice, who were already concerned about the hostile air.

Through it all, one thing was clear to the people and courtiers.

Tamlin Ashowan was the devil, and he had stolen away the castle in an effort to escape. The rumors had been saying as much, and now they had the proof.

By the end of the first week, the king and queen were not on speaking terms except when missives from the princes magically appeared, along with Tam's own messages informing them of Eli's condition.

As of the middle of the second week, a rebellion was brewing and demanding Tam's head.

The only ones who stood in the way…

Were the Ashowans.

Kat sat across from her parents with a cold firepit between them. The cloudy, drizzly sky above them marked the first official day of autumn, and while it usually was the queen's favorite time of year, it only felt like another day of misery and stress. A quick study of her parents showed Kat that the uncertainty and worry for their son and his children had not been kind to them; both looked pale and gaunt. It was only a matter of time before the castle would reappear and the fighting would start, and that knowledge weighed heavily on them.

"So we agree? Da, you put your shield up, I'll handle as many people as I can. Mum, you try to get Tam and the kids out of the castle to somewhere safe," the queen said in low tones.

Nearby, Henrietta the chicken witch collected sticks for a fire. The first day everything had transpired, she had quietly informed them that she wanted to help however she could.

"We have a few witches and civilians who want to help," Fin announced wearily. "I don't want to ask them to make that kind of sacrifice, though."

"I know… I can take care of a lot of attackers, but to be perfectly honest, I don't know that I'm going to be lending my ruling position any favors by harming my people," Kat pointed out, her elbows resting on her knees that were braced apart. "And I don't really *want* to hurt them, either."

The duchess cleared her throat and shifted in her seat. "It is wise to think like that. I'm afraid I, too, don't know how we can avoid a confrontation at this point without drastic measures."

"Well. We're doomed. Even Mum can't manage to think of some scheme to get us out of this." Kat dragged her eyes across the lawn, where she watched the crowd of people mill about the tents. "Why the hell did it get like this?"

"The coven's rebellion is the main cause. I'm sorry that it has gotten between you and Eric," Fin added.

Kat clenched her teeth. "I'm pissed off at him, but at the same time, things got to this point because we couldn't talk for weeks. Eric would've thought about that decision for a long time. He was trying to stop this"—she swept her arm over the brewing calamity—"from happening. I get it. He's always distrusted Tam and Mum because of their slightly illegal dealings, and this just pushed him over the edge."

A pause rested over the trio.

"I don't know what's going to happen when this ends," Kat confessed. "I don't know that our family is coming out of this without something happening. Tam is going to be arrested. If we help him escape, *we're* going to be arrested. I'll most likely be deposed…" She trailed off and dropped her head. "It's bad."

It took a while, but eventually Annika responded. "It is. We may need to disappear for a while. Unfortunately, I don't know where we can go that we will be safe for long."

A low growl sounded in Fin's throat. "I will find a place and make it safe. You have my word."

Annika reached over and touched her husband's arm.

Looking at his wife, Fin spared a softened smile.

"I know you will, love," Annika murmured warmly before turning back to her daughter. "What do you want to do about the boys?"

Kat grimaced. "Is giving them a choice fair in that kind of circumstance? They should be kept in the home they know, protected and taken care of, but… At the same time, I don't know that they will be looked upon kindly anymore."

Neither one of her parents offered a comment.

"I hope Tam's managing alright," Annika said, her eyes falling to the dead air where the castle should have been.

Fin reached out and grasped Annika's hand. "In the last missive, it said Eli's coloring was returning—and she still had not lost the child, so that was something. I feel better knowing Hannah, Captain Taylor, and Harris are in there with him."

"As soon as those traitors from the coven showed up, I sent Tam a bit of power, so hopefully that's helping him recover some magic so he isn't completely defenseless once the castle reappears," Kat said.

Both Fin and Annika nodded, then all three of them turned to look at the empty space, wondering how in the world they could possibly survive what was to come.

"Your Majesty!"

Kat turned as one of the witches who sided with her and her father rushed forward with a scroll in his hand. There seemed to be some kind of discontent waving through her husband's camp; several people meandered closer to the top of the hill.

All three of the Ashowans rose to their feet.

When the young man reached Kat, he threw himself into a bow and thrust the missive at her.

Unfurling the scroll with a curious frown, Kat's eyes darted across the page, and then her jaw dropped.

Both Annika and Fin edged closer.

A smile of disbelief climbed her face.

"What is it?" Annika asked hopefully.

Kat lifted her gaze to stare out toward the Alcide Sea.

"It would seem the new empress of Zinfera has taken it upon herself to send support to the *queen* of Daxaria."

"Deoh Rin? She sent help?" Annika didn't hide her surprise.

Kat chuckled. "Right. Things have been so busy I don't think I got to tell you… Did you maybe notice how Pina wasn't with me when I returned?"

Both Fin's and Annika's expressions fell flat.

"I was all set to leave with her in the carriage when we got to the docks and she took off. I knew better than to try and stop her from doing something but, well… It seems she's been busy."

"Are you *seriously* telling me…" Fin's voice was choked. "Pina is the new empress of Zinfera?"

Kat grinned. "Yep. It's a good thing Kraken is in the castle with Tam, Da. I don't think he'd be handling the news all that well."

Tam sat in the same chair he'd spent most of his time in for the past two weeks. At least it felt like most of his time.

He sat in the back corner of Eli's room as the physician performed another checkup and informed him with no small amount of surprise how well she was healing.

Tam managed a smile and thanked the physician. After becoming aware of the situation, and of the fact that sadly his fellow physician would not be able to come help him, the man was still rightfully quite nervous around Tam.

"Shall I allow Luca and Penelope to come say hello?" the physician asked while rolling down his tunic sleeves.

"Sure." Tam closed the book in his lap. It was one of the tomes he had taken from the Isle of Wittica. Sadly, it was not proving helpful to him in any way. "Thank you again for your care."

The physician eyed the void outside the window with a tight smile then gave a quick nod to Tam in acknowledgment.

Once he had left, Tam had a moment of quiet to reach up and rub the back of his neck. His initial panic for Eli was gradually lightening as each day she showed improvement, and their child seemed to be just as strong as her mother, clinging to life persistently.

For the most part, Eli had not been coherent when awake, so Tam kept Penelope and Luca from being around during those times. However, just that morning she had asked for some food and even called Tam's name—though it seemed to be more from a sleeping state than a wakeful one. It was still better than the random bouts of rambling about puffer fish she had succumbed to initially.

"Dad?"

Tam looked over to see Luca poking his head into the room. Penelope did the same shortly after, and then the three princes followed.

"Boys! What brings you by?" Tam pushed himself to stand as he stepped over to the group of children, who had thankfully seemed to have formed an alliance of kinds during their time in the voided castle.

"What's for dinner?" Asher asked.

Tam chuckled. He had taken over cooking for everyone shortly after his sister had sent him enough magic to recover a good deal of power.

"We're through most of the fresh food. How about something like… potato pancakes? I still have some leftover gravy from the roast."

Asher started jumping up and down.

Meanwhile Luca and Penelope went over to Eli and stared down at her.

"She's almost ready to wake up," Tam called. "She's pulling through."

Both Luca and Penelope turned excitedly at the same time.

"Really?" Luca asked, with a nervous smile.

Tam nodded. "Really."

Luca whirled back around and grabbed Eli's hand, which lay across her middle, giving it a squeeze. Meanwhile, Penelope leaned down and whispered something to Eli that Tam couldn't hear. She had done that every day since Eli had been unconscious.

Someone knocked on the open door. Tam turned around to see Harris joining the crowd in the small room, which was starting to run out of standing space.

"Just heard the good news from the physician! My niece is going to be up and at 'em soon, I can feel it! Also, love the beard, Tam!" Harris said with his usual grin.

The man had been in rather good spirits since he had realized he was trapped in the castle with his dear wife—though he worried about their numerous children, who had been left in the care of Mackenzie's younger sister back home in Sorlia.

Tam scratched at the aforementioned beard. "Thanks. I haven't had a chance to talk to Kasim yet, but did you let him know I'd be coming?"

Thanks to Kat's magical support, Tam hadn't felt a pressing need to go speak to the earth witch—not when Eli's condition was so precarious. However, with things calming down, he wondered about picking Kasim's mind about the situation awaiting them in the real world with the first witch.

"I did indeed! He's actually standing in the void, outside the door to the kitchen."

Tam's eyebrows rose. "Really? Everyone else is terrified of leaving."

"And can you blame them, Tam? You told them that if they wandered off, they could get stuck in the void forever."

Tam shrugged. "I wasn't going to let them skip off without knowing the truth."

Harris sighed.

"Are you alright staying with the kids? I'll go talk to Kasim and work on dinner."

Harris nodded and patted Tam on the shoulder as he passed.

It was a short walk to the kitchen from Eli's room, a fact that Tam greatly appreciated when he had to be away from her for long periods of time to cook.

Pushing open the kitchen door, Tam entered the familiar space, the smell of garlic and fresh bread heavy in the air. The only difference was Kasim Jelani, standing outside the open door that once led to the gardens with his hands clasped behind his back.

Closing the castle door behind himself, Tam approached the cooking table and tied an apron on. He knew the earth witch would come in to talk when he was ready. He retrieved the leftover mashed potatoes from lunch and added garlic powder, salt, pepper, flour, and eggs before molding patties.

"It's like watching your father."

Tam didn't look up from the food as he sensed Kasim seat himself at the table.

"In this case, I'd say that's a compliment."

Kasim chuckled. "It is indeed."

"So… Harris told you everything?"

"He told me all he knows. But I suspect there is a good deal more to this entire situation that only *you* know, Tamlin Ashowan."

At last Tam looked up to see the Lobahlan man, with his ebony skin, long white locs, and white goatee. Kasim stared at him with the same amount of mysterious wisdom he always had in his dark eyes.

"I have a hunch that you might have been gradually taking on a fate that was not the one you were born with."

Tam felt himself still.

The Lobahlan leaned back and folded his arms over his chest. "How about you tell me the whole story, Tam. And let's see what we can figure out, hm?"

CHAPTER 46

THE FOLLIES OF FATE

"Hm." Kasim Jelani nodded his head slowly, his arms folded over his chest, as he remained relaxed in his seat despite listening to Tam's adventure from start to finish.

He had even confided in the earth witch the dreams he had been experiencing. There didn't seem a point in leaving those out.

After taking a moment to silently sift through the long tale, Kasim's judgeless gaze met with Tam's. "You have nearly succeeded in taking on the fate of the devil."

The words hung in the air as heavy as a swollen rain cloud.

"How do I take it all?"

Kasim didn't look surprised, but he did look sad. "You cannot take a fate like that without a key piece."

"And what is that piece?" Tam pressed patiently as he carefully removed the pot of stew that would accompany the potato pancakes from the fire and set it on the cooking table.

"It needs to be willingly given to you from the one that originally held it."

Tam locked eyes with Kasim. He felt his desperation well up in him. "Do I have to tell him what I'm asking for?"

Kasim grimaced as he leaned forward once more. "I do not know, but that is not the fate due to you, Lord Tam."

"I think it is. Remember, my da was told by the Gods one of his children would help a being dear to them."

Kasim tutted and shook his head. "You are admirable, but that does mean you are about to greet Death once more."

Hearing it said aloud made it difficult for Tam to hold Kasim's somber stare, but he did. He revealed all he felt.

"I see." Kasim's voice was soft. "Your father and mother will suffer more than you can ever imagine, but… I do know in the same position, their choice would be the same as your own."

Tam managed a smile. "Thank you for not trying to talk me out of it."

Kasim uncrossed his arms to rest his hands on his knees. "Your path is not for me to walk. I only ask you to indulge me in one thing."

Tam straightened.

The earth witch smiled. "Come with me to the courtyard. I wish to see something with your power."

Blinking, Tam arched an eyebrow. "I won't be able to do much; I need to conserve a lot of energy for moving everyone out of the void."

Kasim raised his hand. "I suspect it won't cost you much at all." He then stood and proceeded toward the castle door, his hands clasped behind his back.

Before following, Tam placed a lid on the stew and ensured the bread rolls were somewhere Kraken couldn't easily access. His father's familiar had been in a downright nasty mood ever since he had woken from his nap and realized what Tam had done. The familiar had barely spent any time with him, though he did often sleep near Eli's feet as she recovered.

The two witches made their way out to the only span of grass and greenery that had survived the move to the void. With the eerie overhead light of unknown origin and no breeze to rustle the plants, the space felt like an illusion.

While Tam had expected the earth witch to take him into his beloved greenhouse, instead Kasim turned to face Tam in the middle of the courtyard.

"You described feeling a part of the forest in Zinfera when you fell apart in your void. Did you hear the life and earth you joined in these times?"

Tam balked. "Uh. Not really. It was closer to what I'd call torture, and so I was a little preoccupied."

If Kasim found this detail disturbing, he didn't relay that in his face. "When an elemental witch requires nature to shift its existence for their will, it is a conversation. When you force it upon them, it uses more magic," Kasim explained simply. "When I speak with my plants—" He crouched down next to a pink cyclamen. "—I tell them what I need and why. I hear their voices speak to me in response. Your father isn't as adept at hearing the plants in his home, but he does sense their desires, and they work cohesively to that end. I am most curious to know what kind of conversation *you* would have."

Tam glanced around at the greenery, suddenly feeling rather bashful. "Are they angry?"

Kasim chuckled. "No. Confused. Intrigued, and a bit worried. They miss the roots of the King's Forest. They all speak together through their soil," he explained, his dark eyes falling to the plants fondly.

"Does stone or air speak?" Tam wondered aloud as he stared at the walls of the castle.

"My sister-in-law, Sky, may she rest in peace, said the winds would speak to her. They were her close friends. As for stone…" Kasim trailed off, a thoughtful smile on his face. "I only hear rumblings, but I would not be surprised if you heard a word or two."

Silence fell between the two men as Tam stared around the beautiful courtyard. He wasn't entirely certain why, but he was feeling rather nervous. "I suppose I should probably try this sooner than later. Asher is a banshee when he's hungry."

Kasim chortled a little but didn't try to hurry him along.

Closing his eyes, Tam reached out with his abilities.

It was odd having the castle already be a part of the void, similar to the feeling of wearing a tunic inside out. However, it did allow him to sense the plants without the need to dissolve.

As usual, Tam felt the materials of his surroundings, the cool leaves, and rough stone… It was quiet without the wind, so he did not hear any rustling leaves, but their smell remained as earthy as ever.

Hello? he called out in his mind, already doubtful that he would hear anything the way Kasim described.

Quiet continued to reign; there wasn't even a shudder of life.

"Friend?"

Tam jolted in shock at the whispery voice that responded in the hush.

"New friend?"

"Funny!"

"Strange."

"Goddess? No. Hi!"

Tam's heart raced as the voices grew in number. He struggled to think of what to say, and the longer he took to find the words, the louder and greater in number the voices became.

"Look! Look!"

"Magic!"

"Smelly."

"Quiet human!"

"See you!"

Tam was vaguely aware that despite there being no breeze, the plants had begun to rustle around him in waves.

I hope you aren't upset, but… I'm the one who made the sky dark, he finally managed to sputter out in his mind, his disbelief bringing a tremor through his fingertips.

There was another pause among the voices.

"Sky dark!"

"Why?"

"Sun soon?"

"No!"

Tam flinched as the rush of voices echoed more loudly than before. The conversation continued to whirl around him, forcing his awareness to back away from it. When he brushed against the stone, he heard a sonorous, low groan add itself to the cacophony of sound.

Snapping himself free of the awareness, Tam found himself panting. The flood of noise had made the very air he breathed feel smothering.

"I take it you heard them?" Kasim asked lightly.

Tam swallowed and nodded.

Kasim smiled knowingly. "It is as I thought. You described your power as everything and nothing. So it stood to reason that everything included *everything*. You are the ally to all of nature. You are the most powerful witch I have ever met. In a way, you embody your coven's motto better than any other. Nature is all; without it we are nothing."

Tam recalled reading that phrase on the stained-glass window in the archive room, as the words had needled deeply into his mind...

"I still don't know that I can recharge my magic without rest, and besides... I'm not sure that being incredibly powerful with the elements and void will be as useful in this particular situation."

Kasim strode a little closer to Tam. "I don't know about that. Someone of immense power like yourself often has a great deal of options at their disposal."

"You mean like threatening covens and people into forgiving me for abducting them and taking away the castle?"

"Mm," Kasim sounded out with a look of disagreement. "More that you might offer your abilities to help the world in exchange for leniency."

"Indentured servitude?" Tam asked bitterly.

"Being indentured makes it sound as though you have no choice. You would have a choice, and you may even be able to help the world become better."

Tam considered this. It was a valid point.

As his mother would say, he needed to play the hand he had been dealt to the best of his ability. And right now, he had quite a few powerful cards in his hand. The only issue was that those cards could cost Tam what he wanted: his peaceful life with Eli and their family.

Then again, perhaps he should focus more on the matter of his imminent death before considering how to handle his legal troubles.

"I see you have much to think about." Kasim interrupted Tam's musings while bowing ever so slightly in order to catch his eye. "However, I do have one final question. Would you mind signing a letter I plan on sending home to Lobahl in the near future, relaying the details of your time with the young pair Bes and Hamil?"

At this, Tam hesitated. "Er… Why?"

Kasim didn't hide his seriousness. "They should not have left Lobahl. They did so illegally, and as a result have relayed far too much about our kingdom. I am glad it is you who has heard it, and not another, but all the same. This serious offense needs to be reported."

Tam winced. "I did coerce them a bit into it."

"Lobahlans are trained not to crack under the kind of mental and verbal traps you used," Kasim informed him sternly. "I understand you feel guilt for your part in this, Lord Tamlin, but as Lobahlans they are taught from a young age how severe a crime it is. They should have gone through the proper channels to leave Lobahl."

Clearing his throat in discomfort, Tam turned toward the castle doorway while rubbing his neck. "If you say so."

The two men gradually meandered their way back into the castle. Tam stowed his hands in his pockets as they walked. In his head, he turned over his new discoveries: that he could interact with the elements the same way elemental witches could, and that making requests as opposed to muscling the elements into doing what he wanted would consume less power.

A new question occurred to him.

"Why could I not hear the voices of the plants before? Wouldn't I have felt some pull from the elements earlier in my life?"

Kasim allowed his eyes to drift upward pensively. "I cannot know for certain, but my guess would be that you hid from your power for years. You are only now becoming acquainted with it. As all witches are advised, you would need to spend time with your element, questioning what it means to you." Kasim looked at Tam. "What does everything and nothing mean to you?"

Tam gave a wry half smile. "Pretty sure the answer is in the question."

The earth witch continued staring at Tam expectantly. His response was evidently lacking.

Letting out a sigh as they rounded the corner to the kitchens, Tam gave the question a bit more consideration.

"Everything feels overwhelming. And loud. I'm not someone who really enjoys excess. I like my privacy and space. So I guess I find nothing… freeing."

"Well, this power is rooted in who you are as a person, Lord Tam. So perhaps ask yourself: Is it possible to find joy in a life, or world, of everything? Is it possible there is an everything place you simply haven't found to center yourself in?"

A deprecating laugh escaped Tam's mouth. "I've never been in the right place."

"Says who?"

At this, Tam opened his mouth and closed it, then cleared his throat. "It's no secret that I'm the black sheep of the family. Even my sister and parents have told me to change, or try to be different."

"Is it that they wanted you to be different, or that they wanted you to feel happy and to no longer fear yourself?"

At this, Tam couldn't quite bring himself to answer. He considered all the times his parents had encouraged him to meet people, or to have friends. To talk to them about what was happening, or to stay a little longer for a family meal…

"However you leave this world, Lord Tam, I do wish that you leave it knowing you have always had a very important place here. And to see that it is possible to find a balance between answering a calling and being happy."

Tam felt emotion declare war on his throat, so it took him a little longer than normal to form his next words. "Thank you… Kasim. Can I ask why you never joined the king's inner council? Even Hamil and Bes indicated you were incredibly important back in Lobahl."

Kasim's reaction to this reminder of his past was a mix of a smile and a grimace. "I imagine you will understand me better than most, Lord Tam, when I say that at home, bureaucracy got in the way of what I wanted to do. Here? I tend to my plants. I see my family. I have the funds to do what I please. I try whatever I wish to try with my work. Here in Daxaria is where I found my own freedom."

"Do you agree with what the covens are trying to do in separating from the monarchy? I heard Lobahl isn't that different in how its government is set up. Hamil and Bes mentioned sects?"

Kasim shot Tam a rather dry look that indicated he wasn't going to be as easy to prod answers out of as the two young runaways had been, which made Tam grin roguishly and give a boyish shrug.

Still, Kasim did answer the initial question. "It's not a bad idea to have a safe place for witches to train and to examine where their talents would best settle. However, I think the coven's approach of severing their connection with the kingdoms and the people has been sloppy and has caused fearmongering and discrimination. My understanding is that the first witch is in a hurry to see this through."

Tam turned over this opinion in his mind, then went on to say, "I was surprised at how cavalier both Bes and Hamil were at the mention of the first witch and the devil. It sounded like the children of the Gods lived among the Lobahlans for a long time."

Kasim did not comment.

By this time, they had reached the kitchen, and unsurprisingly, the two men found that it was occupied by none other than the three princes and Luca. All of them were sniffing the air and watching the pot of stew with great interest. Asher was on his knees on one of the stools leaning over the table, while Antony was at his side already hoisting the lid off the pot.

Luca and Charlie stood a short ways off, watching nervously.

"I leave here for a *moment*, and you raccoons are already prepared to eat everyone's meal!"

Asher leapt out of his seat as Antony set the lid down with a clatter, and both Luca and Charlie whirled around with wide, nervous eyes. The anxiety melted from their faces, however, when they noted the way Tam grinned at them.

Luca came forward and threw his arms around his father's waist.

Tam's hand came down and ruffled Luca's silky black mop. "Where's Penelope?"

"With Eli," Luca answered before releasing Tam and stepping back.

Tam nodded and made his way over to where the bowls and plates were kept. "Alright, I need the fastest boys I know to tell everyone dinner is ready. Which of you do you think will tell the most people?"

"Me!" shouted Antony, puffing his chest out. "I'm the oldest!"

"Not anymore!" Asher shrieked in delight. "Luca's older!"

Luca blushed and inched closer to Tam. "I-it's fine, I want to stay here and help my dad."

Asher and Antony shrugged and bolted from the kitchen.

Tam regarded Charlie expectantly, but when the boy didn't take off like his brothers, he felt his good-natured expression dim. "Charlie, would you like to help Luca and me divvy up dinner?"

The prince nodded.

Tam shared a knowing look with Kasim, who quietly made his way over to the bread box and distributed the rolls.

Tam wished he could do more to help Charlie through whatever darkness he was still struggling against following his time with the coven, but unfortunately…

Tam didn't think he had much time left to help anyone.

CHAPTER 47

A PARTNER'S POINT

The castle was quiet, and most of the staff and nobles had gone to bed. Tam wished he could find a way to turn off the void's light to create some semblance of night, but that seemed to be outside his abilities.

With nothing much else to occupy his mind aside from his cloud of worries, Tam wandered the darkened corridors. He meandered past the council room, then descended to the front entrance, and from there moved to the throne room.

He gazed about the official room, thinking back to the day he had stood off to the side with Eli and watched his sister be crowned.

He could remember the breeze on the back of his neck, the feel of Eli's elbow in his ribs, nudging him to stay awake…

He remembered the day Kat had returned from Troivack a decorated hero, a wife, and an expectant mother.

Despite not having lived in the castle, he had spent a great deal of his life among its stones. It felt like an extension of his home to him. Perhaps it was because his own father felt that way, and he had managed to lace his magic through its nooks and crannies…

Tam turned and left the throne room. He eventually went to the banquet hall, the largest room in the castle. It seemed even bigger in the throes of solemn emptiness.

The haunting feeling told Tam that this stillness would soon shatter into something terrible. While the anxiety permeated the air around him, he did appreciate the quiet.

Tam was about to leave and return to Eli's room to hopefully get a bit of sleep when the sound of soft footfalls made him pause.

He waited in the shadows until a familiar silhouette appeared in the doorway.

"Luca?" Tam called.

He watched his son stiffen, then relax when he realized that it was just his father.

"What are you doing up and wandering around?" he asked worriedly.

"I was looking for you. The physician says Eli will be awake tomorrow morning," Luca explained as he blindly reached out in the darkness toward Tam.

He stepped forward and plucked his son up in his arms. "Then I guess I better be there when she wakes up, hm?" Tam moved back into the corridor with Luca. As they passed more windows, he could see the trepidation on his son's young face.

"Dad… Things are weird. Ever since we came here, everyone is angry, and scared, and… and it feels like it's my fault."

Tam's gut clenched. "It isn't your fault. I promise. A lot of people are confused about what's going on with the witches, and it's making them think silly things."

Luca's mouth twisted. He did not look convinced.

His conversation with Kasim earlier echoed back in Tam's mind… and so, having reached the castle entrance, Tam set Luca back down on the ground, then knelt before him.

"Luca, I… I have a favor to ask."

He watched his son start to fidget, so Tam reached out and gently grasped Luca's hands in his own.

"The Gods… They gave something to you they shouldn't have."

Luca frowned, and panic sparked in his eyes.

Tam did his best to smile calmly. "It's okay, you haven't done anything, I just need to do something to help. Do… Do you think you can give me your fate?"

The look of worry on Luca's face froze. Then it melted into a blank expression that was rather strange on his usually innocent and sweet countenance. It reminded Tam of the times in the past… Like the first time he had said he was glad Luca existed.

"Am I… Am I someone bad?" Luca asked slowly.

"Not at all," Tam assured while reaching up and gently squeezing Luca's arm. "Sometimes things happen to us, and we need a little help is all."

"So you… You're trying to help?" Luca's voice was distant, as though it wasn't exactly him who was speaking.

Tam ignored this, because he knew the truth. The truth was that his son deserved a happy life where he could be loved without the shadow of fate over him. It didn't matter what his past lives were; this one was the one Tam was responsible for.

"I am. It's a dad's job to protect and help his kids." Tam smiled. "And I think you've had to carry this for far too long."

A flicker of familiarity passed through Luca's eyes that made him seem himself again, but it was brief. "What are you going to do with it?"

Tam took a deep breath. This was tricky answer. "I'm going to carry it for you, and I'm going to make sure you don't ever have to carry it ever again."

Luca blinked, and a mystified look came over his face, as though he didn't understand why tears were starting to gather in his eyes. "How are you going to do that?"

"That's for me to figure out. All I want you to do after you give that to me? Is be happy. Be yourself. And I want you to play, try new foods, learn lots of new things, and know that you are loved and safe. Forever. I'm your dad, no matter what, and I will always do everything I can to be there for you."

Luca's lips quivered.

"So… Luca, is it okay if I take your fate?"

A choking sob escaped from Luca's mouth as he nodded, then threw his arms around Tam.

Tam returned the embrace, silently wondering if that was all he really needed to do to truly become the devil.

"I love you, Luca. You are a good person. Alright? Never forget that. You are… one of the best things that ever happened to me, and I am happy. *Unbelievably* happy that I get to be your dad."

Luca's cries grew louder and were filled with a deep pain. Tam's own eyes welled up with tears as he felt invisible tension and weight disappear from Luca's shoulders.

With a shuddering breath, Tam did his best to simply comfort Luca and appreciate the embrace.

Though it was difficult not to think about how he had most likely just expedited his own end significantly.

Eli's eyes fluttered open slowly.

It took her a moment to process what she was seeing.

First, there were different tones of light.

There was the warm, familiar flicker of firelight across the stone ceiling, but there was also a white light beaming in through the window on her left...

"Hey."

Turning her head felt difficult but not impossible. She looked over to see Tam.

He was holding her hand, a beard on his face, his dark eyes weary and grim.

"You look even more handsome with the beard," she remarked idly.

Eli watched Tam laugh, caught off guard. He dropped a kiss to her hand, then said, "Is that your way of telling me to shave it?"

Eli groaned as she wriggled her toes and felt her lower back ache.

Terror seized her.

"Our girl is a fighter. She's held on," Tam informed her quietly, as though reading her mind.

Eli's free hand trembled, but as it came up and rested on her protruding middle, she let out a long, stuttering breath.

She had never felt blind fear like that before in her life.

"What's happened?" she asked, noting a shadowy figure bowing out of the room behind Tam. Most likely it was a physician.

Tam cleared his throat nervously. "There's been a bit going on."

Eli lowered her brows. She slowly tried to push herself up to a sitting position.

Tam was quick on his feet and came to help her, placing an extra pillow behind her back. After a word of thanks, Eli fixed him with her expectant stare.

A lone glance out the window to her left told her that the darkness outside wasn't the night.

"I had to move the castle to the void. Eric made a deal with the first witch. He agreed to separate the coven from his rule, and there would be no fighting. Only peaceful negotiations. As long as he did not stop the first witch from taking the devil."

Eli's eyes widened.

"I moved the castle to buy us time while you rested."

Eli's heart thrummed inside her chest, prompting her to take another steadying breath.

"Tam… you…"

"I am going to be charged with treason and all sorts of other things. I know."

Eli felt the dawning realization of just how bad things were. It filled her with cold, sharp fear.

"We can try to negotiate from here," she said despite already knowing such talks would not be entered into with any amicability. "Or we can try to go to Lobahl like we jested. What do you think?"

Tam leaned forward and brushed a kiss against her forehead. "I think… You need to go back to sleep. I promise, everything is going to be fine."

Eli's eyes narrowed. She had a gut feeling that there was something else Tam wasn't telling her. "And why is that?"

Tam gazed at her sadly… lovingly…

"Oh. Absolutely not, you fucking twit."

Tam reared back.

"You are not dying," Eli bit out as certainty and rage filled her. "I didn't go through my entire life being abandoned, hurt, and helpless just to be left with another Godsdamn tragedy! So no, Tamlin Ashowan. I don't care that you most likely think you are going to go die a hero's death for our family. We are smarter than that. You and I, Tamlin Ashowan, have been inevitable despite everything, and so you will continue to annoy me with your good looks, and I will continue to tell you when you are being an idiot. Which, at present, you are."

Eli felt a primal growl start in her throat as she watched Tam open his mouth to say something, only for the words to die on his lips.

"Gods. You're going off to die and leaving me with *three* children? You selfish, lazy arse!"

"Wha— Lazy? We need to—"

A purr sounded, drawing both Eli and Tam's attention to the foot of the bed where Kraken had been curled up sleeping innocuously; however, at that moment he had an eye cracked open and seemed to be smiling smugly at Tam.

Ignoring this, Eli resumed her rant. "Honestly, of all the ridiculous things you could do! Are you obsessed with being moody and living through trauma? Are you addicted to emotional suffering? If so, get over that. Immediately. Now tell me exactly what you are thinking of doing, and I, your familiar, am going to bloody well fix it for you!"

"Eli, you need to rest and—"

"*Well, I'd like to rest, but my future husband keeps trying to throw himself on a Godsdamn sword!*" she hissed in irritation, her chest rising and falling rapidly.

Tam gaped at her, then said, "Huh… I think Kasim really set my expectation that people would understand—"

"Oh, Kasim? The botanist?" Eli asked demurely before exploding, making Tam nearly fall off his stool. "IS HE THE ONE CARRYING YOUR CHILD? DID HE JUST BARELY SURVIVE A LIFE-THREATENING INJURY? NO? THEN HE CAN BLOODY WELL STAY OUT OF IT!"

Tam held up his hands as though to stop her from eating him. If Eli were honest with herself, if she were in her beast form, she'd have been sorely tempted.

"I'm starting to suspect my sister has been sending you some of her magical energy to help you heal," Tam said faintly.

"Wonderful. Now. Get on with it. Tell me everything and let's sort this out."

"Don't you want to see the children first? They've been worried."

Eli noted the way Tam was already inching away from her. Her hand shot out, seized the front of his tunic, and yanked him with all her might down to her eye level. "Tam. If you die, I have only my own company for the rest of my life. I can do better, and I will have better."

"And you think I'm better?" Tam risked teasing.

"In this moment, no. But we'll fix that later. Now, start talking. I won't ask again, and so help me Goddess, Tamlin Ashowan, do not toy with me or I will insist we have a *large, crowded* wedding."

What little color had remained in Tam's drawn face flooded elsewhere. "Yes, ma'am."

Eli nodded in approval, then dropped a quick kiss on her betrothed's lips before settling back against her pillows to hear the details of their predicament, and how they could escape it to finally get their happy ending.

Eli noticed Kraken's languid yawn and stretch; he gave her a look that practically screamed, *I told you this would happen.*

She decided she would try to "accidentally" sit on her fellow familiar next time she was in her beast form. Certainly the empurror would be in a forgiving mood toward a pregnant woman, and if he wasn't? Well, the way Eli was feeling in that moment, she was willing to wage a war of wills with Kraken in her coming days, as long as it was the only stress she had to contend with in her near future.

CHAPTER 48

THE WEIGHT OF WAR

"Gods. This is a sight I never wanted to come across again for the rest of my life," Norman, the former Daxarian king, informed his retired assistant.

Mr. Kevin Howard nodded gravely as he, too, stared out over the camps that had erected themselves over the past few weeks. The bonfires and torches were already lit under the starry sky, illuminating the frosty clouds of their breaths in front of them.

The former king had been enjoying his retirement in Sorlia when he'd heard news of his grandsons going missing. He had then done what he could to aid search parties by coordinating the joint efforts of the knights from Sorlia, Austice, and Xava, and sending updates to Eric. Duchess Annika had joined later and added to his concerns by sharing the troubling story of what had transpired in Zinfera with her son, and the concubine. Mr. Howard had abandoned his own retirement to aid his former employer and friend in these efforts.

When a message had come that the princes had returned home, an unfortunate update followed shortly thereafter that there was about to be a civil war. Wanting to support his son, the new king, Norman had rushed as quickly as he could, but he was unpleasantly surprised to find that his daughter-in-law and longtime friends the Ashowans seemed to be on the opposite side of the conflict.

"Right. You go speak with Eric, I'll go speak with Katarina and her parents to hear what is happening," Norman ordered, gingerly patting his former assistant's shoulder.

When Mr. Howard raised a quizzical eyebrow and regarded him over the tops of his spectacles, Norman winced. "You get a bit emotional around the Ashowans, Kevin."

Surprisingly, rather than grumble or mutter about what a nuisance the family could be, the assistant wore a smile. "Not anymore, Monarch. *I* no longer have to deal with them!" He clapped a hand on Norman's shoulder as he breezed past him. "Go see His Majesty, your son. Things are different now."

Norman stared at Mr. Howard's retreating back; the flat, unenthused look the former king wore went unnoticed.

It wouldn't have been the first time the man had underestimated the Ashowan skill of annoying the sanity out of him, and he doubted this would be the last.

"WHAT DO YOU MEAN THE ENTIRE CASTLE?" Kevin Howard exploded as the Daxarian queen and Finlay Ashowan casually relayed what Tam had done.

Mr. Howard pinched the bridge of his nose. He had been smiling when he'd first greeted them, but that expression was long gone.

"Right. So now we are just waiting for Tam to bring everyone back, and then we are all going to talk?" the former assistant asked with an audibly forced measure of hope.

"Well, I'd like that, but all the witches at the other camp are out for blood," Kat retorted.

"And your husband is with the opposing camp?" Mr. Howard pressed.

"He is. The dumbass."

The former assistant bestowed the queen a very unimpressed look, and then addressed Fin.

"We leave Austice for not even half a year, and this happens?"

Fin said nothing from his seated position. His hands were loosely clasped, his elbows resting on his knees. At the sight of the house witch's drawn face,

Kat watched Mr. Howard's features still, then shift into a formation of worry. "Can this situation be resolved without an actual fight?"

The house witch shrugged.

"I've been sending Eli magic any chance I can to help her recover, and she is most definitely still alive, so I imagine they will come out soon. There isn't much time," Kat interjected before turning her golden gaze over the multiple tents.

"Have you tried speaking with His Majesty?" Mr. Howard asked through gritted teeth.

Kat rounded on the former assistant. "Oh no. We've just sent each other our best jokes and shared hair braiding tips. *Of course we bloody well tried to talk!* He's dead set against Tam's son staying free."

"Your Majesty, what compromises have been proposed?" Mr. Howard continued, with forced patience.

Kat's hands moved to her hips. "I've proposed he pull his head from his arse. We aren't handing Luca off to anyone—and the first witch hasn't even shown her face yet!"

"What do the witches want to do with the child, exactly?" Mr. Howard looked like he was ready to start shouting again at any given moment.

"Kill him," Kat bit out darkly.

"They have explicitly said this?"

Kat was just about to open her mouth to tell the assistant he was more than welcome to question her husband and the covens himself when a faint breeze brushed past her hand.

As soon as Kat's sights dropped, she backed up a step, while Mr. Howard let out a yelp and pressed his hand to his heart.

There sat Tam.

He'd taken up residence in her abandoned chair beside their father.

He looked up at his sister gravely, a three-week beard shadowing his cheeks. "Hi, Kat."

"Tam!" Fin sat up straight, his eyes wide.

"Da." Tam nodded at his father.

In a fit of relief-fueled anger, Kat seized the front of Tam's tunic and hauled him up to his feet.

"You idiot! We're about to have a war! People are going to die, do you understand that?"

"They won't. I'm going to go to the coven."

"Tam—" Fin started at the same moment Kat burst out, "What good will that do?"

"They will take me. Don't say my name. Just refer to me as the devil. But you have to tell them the devil will only be placed in the hands of the first witch."

"Yeah. Bit of a problem with that plan," Kat sounded out, her grip on Tam's tunic tightening. "As I was just explaining to Mr. Howard here—"

At the mention of the former assistant's presence, Tam glanced over and bowed his head respectfully. "Good to see you, Mr. Howard. Retirement suits you."

"Tam," he returned with a sigh.

Kat gave Tam a shake to bring his attention back to her. "They. Will. Kill. You."

"I have a plan," Tam said shortly.

"Right." Kat's tongue poked one of her molars. "Given how well your last plan worked, mind sharing this one?"

"I do mind. Let's not waste time. Go tell your husband the terms."

"Not happening," Kat said with a snort before releasing her brother from her grasp.

During this time, their father had come to his feet. "Tam, how is Eli?"

At this, the distance in Tam's eyes eased and instead a semblance of familiarity returned to their dark depths. "Better. She's awake and has started walking a little, though she is still weak. The baby is alive and fine as well."

"Baby?" Mr. Howard interrupted pointedly.

Kat bounced back and forth from her heels to the balls of her feet. "Ah. Didn't get to that part yet. Tam's having his third child with Elisara. His former assistant. Who also turned out to be the daughter of Marigold and Geun Nam. And she was also adopted by the Zinferan emperor. Though she is currently seeking to leave his roster of children. Oh. And my cat is the new empress of Zinfera."

Mr. Howard gaped at Kat, then looked at Fin, who did not deny any of the points.

Then the former assistant turned around. "I should've packed wine. What was I thinking? That was foolish. So foolish. Gods…" He wandered a short way off, but he wasn't entirely out of earshot as he doubled over with his hands on his knees and continued to take deep breaths and mutter to himself.

"He's handling it better than I thought he would, quite honestly," Kat announced thoughtfully as she took a moment to watch the poor man attempt to process the chaos.

Fin nodded. "Retirement really has been good for him."

Tam cleared his throat, drawing everyone's eyes back to him.

Blinking her distracted thoughts away, Kat felt her stern expression fall back into place. "Tam, what's the plan? How can we help?"

She watched as her brother regarded her, a flicker of the man she used to know appearing and vanishing behind unreadable eyes once more.

"Can you just trust in the fact that Eli helped with this plan?"

"Not really. I don't know her. She sounds lovely, and I mean no offense— and I appreciated her bossy moments, but can *you* please appreciate what I'm risking for you right now, and respect me enough to tell me what's happening? Tam, I might lose custody of my boys over this. So I really, *really* need you to give us some details."

At this, Tam's shoulders rounded forward and his hands found their way to his pockets. There was a beat of silence, but Kat watched the way the skin around his eyes relaxed a little in concession.

"Eli and I found a way to send the first witch back to the Forest of the Afterlife, but I need to get close to her."

Kat stared at him pointedly.

Tam shifted his feet.

"Going to need more than that," Kat said bluntly.

"After she is sent back, we are going to say the devil took over my body, making me act out of character, but the first witch took him back to the Forest of the Afterlife with her."

"No one—and I am including the idiot Lord Wellington when I say this—*no one* will buy that shit. Because how do I explain what we've done to support you?" Kat argued.

"Pretty sure they will buy it. You can just say it was a targeted attack from the devil on the Ashowan family. But just to be safe? Myself, Eli, Penelope, and Luca are going to go into hiding after this. We're going to start over somewhere else."

Kat's grip on her brother's tunic tightened. "Oh? Where?"

"Daxaria would be ideal."

"Mm-hm. Mm-hm. Da? Want to jump in here? At any time?" Kat flicked her eyes over to their father.

He looked a decade older than he had two weeks ago, and there appeared to be a large weight on his shoulders as he listened.

"I think… we all need to sit down and talk. Including with the first witch. Under a white flag. No attacks, no name-calling," he added with a meaningful look at his daughter. "And talk."

"Fin." Mr. Howard approached, once again joining the discussion. "You really have mellowed over the years. I don't know how I feel about that right now."

"We can figure that out later," Fin said with a faint trace of humor in his voice.

Despite his tone, the assistant nodded gratefully.

Kat released her brother. She was still agitated, but a little less outraged at the very least, as they discussed calmer conclusions to their dilemma. "Alright. So, Mr. Howard. You go over and have a quick chat with my husband and tell him about this meeting. We'll have it take place tomorrow."

"I'll return the castle to its original place after the meeting," Tam added offhandedly.

"Oh? The castle you stole? How kind of you," Mr. Howard countered drily.

Tam shrugged, unbothered.

Shaking his head, the former assistant turned his toes toward the king's camp. "Anything else you'd like me to pass along?"

Kat looked to Tam. "How're my boys?"

The corners of Tam's mouth lifted. "Good. Asher eats more than three men and keeps scaring Hannah with his spider familiar. I think it's growing."

"Yeah… Yeah, that spider is a bit much…" Kat said with a subtle grimace.

Mr. Howard recoiled at the reminder of the young prince's familiar. Then he closed his eyes and murmured, "I don't have to deal with this, I don't have to deal with this, I don't have to deal with this…"

"Charlie is still having troubles after his time with the coven," Tam added regretfully.

Kat furrowed her brows. "Regardless of how this settles, I'm beating the snot out of whoever tormented him."

Tam gave a jerk of his head in agreement. "He seems to really like Luca. Charlie has actually been helping him get into reading more."

Hearing that at last freed a genuine smile on Kat's face. "And Penelope? Is she keeping everyone in line?"

Tam tilted his head back and forth. "Somewhat… She stays beside Eli a lot."

The brief moment of brightened mood was once again snuffed out at the mention of Eli's state.

"Alright. Please tell *His Majesty* that our children are well—also please tell him about my intention to issue some justice on Charlie's behalf—and ask for the meeting. Thank you, Mr. Howard."

The man gave a halfhearted wave of acknowledgment, then continued to move through the shadowy grass over to where Eric Reyes was most likely still speaking with his own father.

Before Tam or Kat could open their mouths to say another word to each other, Finlay Ashowan proceeded to pull both of his children into an embrace.

Despite this move catching both Tam and Kat off guard, they wrapped their arms around their father.

"We are in this together. We all get into nonsense, and we help one another get out. I'm proud of both of you for doing the best you can to protect people," Fin told his children quietly. "Things are messy, but together we are going to work this all out."

The trio took a moment of silence to appreciate the warmth of being together once again.

"I'm…" Tam pulled away. Despite the lack of lighting, Kat's magic allowed her to easily see the gleam of tears in her brother's eyes. "I'm sorry that I assumed you were against me. That you weren't supporting me. I… I wasn't thinking clearly, and I made a decision that has affected all of us terribly. I'm sorry. Again. I'll fix this. I love you both."

As usual, Kat felt herself squirm at the show of vulnerability from her brother, and so she handled his apology—which she was actually quite pleased to receive—as she normally did. She slapped his arm firmly and said, "You've helped me out of enough sticky situations, we'll figure this one out, too, just like Da says."

After giving his sister an appreciative smile, Tam cast his gaze around the camp of Zinferan soldiers. "Where's Mum?"

"Ah. I think she's trying to get a bit of sleep. We've all been taking turns keeping watch," Kat said, displaying the uncommon weariness she felt.

She herself hadn't slept for a few days. She knew she needed to that night to be better rested for the morning to come…

Her thoughts were interrupted when a loud, screeching cry tore through the night air. All three of their heads snapped round just in time to see a large shadow landing in a span of grass between the two camps.

"Oh… shit." Kat breathed.

"Is that—" Fin started in awe, only for his son to cut him off.

"A dragon? Yes. That would be Wixim… But I don't know if he's an ally now or not. It's a bit unclear."

"Tam?" Fin's voice was faint, and mild.

"Yes, Da?"

"Please go get Kraken. I think we'll need him for this."

CHAPTER 49

TIME TO TURN IN

The two camps had gathered to stare at each other across the span of ground that had been set as neutral territory.

Katarina stood with her arms crossed, staring icily at her husband. Finlay Ashowan was at his daughter's left shoulder, his eyes scanning the crowd behind the king as though looking for someone.

King Norman and Mr. Howard were placed near Eric, murmuring together.

And Tam had gone to get Kraken.

The only figures in the neutral ground were Wixim and Aradia, who rode him.

"So," Kat called loudly enough for multiple rows of soldiers to hear across the chasm. "Nice of you to show up."

Aradia arched an eyebrow at Katarina before sliding off the dragon.

She strode down the neutral ground until she was between Eric and Kat. She looked at the king, then at Kat.

"You are the ones who made the city a nightmare of confusion and chaos. I had wanted to avoid alarming people."

"*We* made this city a nightmare of confusion?" Kat exploded incredulously. "Are you… drunk? Honestly! Did you take some drugs? Did that bloody lizard drop you at some point? *You caused all of this, you dense wench!*"

The first witch rolled her eyes upward toward the sky. "Your kingdom was going to have a breakdown between the witches and its people again. It was a matter of time. As soon as you took the throne, it began. I'd even argue as soon as your father was forced into the role of diplomat, witches started to be used as tools for the kingdom."

"We all had a choice, and we have listened to the people," Eric interrupted somberly.

Despite the fact that the king had been the one to form a deal with the first witch, there was no warmth in his eyes when his gaze rested on her.

"It is the witches who suffer," Aradia returned evenly.

"And the way you have gone about illustrating this point managed to create the most conflict bloody possible. Well done," Kat bit out acidly.

"If I may…" Finlay Ashowan spoke softly, yet all eyes moved to the house witch as he slowly crossed the chasm until he stood toe-to-toe with the first witch. "I chose my role as diplomat of my own free will. I was asking for far more from my kingdom than I was owed. It was only right that I paid a price. And for the record? I would do it twenty times over. I have no regrets." Fin stared down at the first witch, the flicker of white light behind his blue eyes causing her to go still.

A look of envy and longing overcame her features for a brief moment.

"It's true, I see. You have met with the Gods," she whispered.

Fin smiled sadly. "I have. And I will again one day. I wish you and I could have had a chance to talk sooner."

Kat tilted her head. She had never seen the first witch look so… unsteady.

But why?

"You," Fin said, a gentle smile lifting the corners of his mouth, "are craving some good stew and a cup of tea. Maybe a bit of brown bread. You seem tired, Aradia."

The first witch swallowed. "I came here to talk. To you and your familiar."

Fin blinked in surprise. "We can arrange that."

Kat made a growling noise in the back of her throat, which Fin ignored as he stepped aside and gestured to a distant fire. "Shall we?"

Aradia bowed her head and proceeded on ahead.

Fin followed, but he locked eyes first with his daughter, then Eric, before he held up his hands to keep them where they were and continued on.

Kat felt her heart start to pound, and her grip on her sword hilt tightened.

Despite the peaceful request from the first witch, she had a bad feeling about how the night was about to play out. She wished she could say that her gut instinct had been wrong even once in her life, but sadly, she could not.

Fin regarded the first witch as she sat with her hands loosely clasped in front of the fire. Mirroring her position, he studied her face while waiting for her to talk.

"I want your familiar to appeal to the Gods to allow me to go home," the first witch announced abruptly.

"By yourself?" Fin asked carefully.

Aradia leaned back in her seat. "If they will allow it."

"You do realize that because of how events have unfolded, even if you return home, you have placed a great many people in danger. Including my own son and grandson."

Aradia's eyes hardened. "Your son has made his choices. That is his responsibility."

Fin straightened in his seat and proceeded to fold his arms. "He chose to keep his loved ones safe. He does not deserve the wrath of two kingdoms."

Aradia tilted her head. "Maybe. Maybe not. He does deserve their fear, though."

Fin's brows lowered, but before he could say anything, Aradia continued.

"Your son has a power that could rival those of the Gods, house witch. In my opinion, he should not exist. His abilities? They are capable of breaking this world. All it takes is for him to learn a little bit more about them, and for him to decide one day that someone or something has angered him enough. It is the same argument I made to your king and son-in-law when he and I spoke. When a being holds too much power, the world is prone to breaking. It's imbalanced. The same can be argued for a government, a monarchy… Look at your own family. You have amassed great power, and now, as it crashes down, everyone around you is getting pulled into the chaos." Aradia gestured vaguely toward the distance, where the castle had once been.

Fin considered her words. "It was a decision made by the Gods to bestow my son his abilities, and I have no choice but to trust in their judgment. As for how power can crumble… That is life. The brightest, largest flowers wither to seeds. The tallest tree will fall. It is not for us to tell nature how big it should or should not be."

"But it should not be manipulated to be larger than it is destined to," Aradia argued.

Fin took a deep breath. "Tell me, do you know the great picture your parents have in mind for all of us? Or even just yourself?"

Aradia fell silent.

Fin gentled his voice for his next words. "As powerful and knowledgeable as you are, Aradia, there is a finite amount we can understand about how the world is meant to be. We can try, and we should continue to try. But just because you are powerful or come from power, that does not mean you know any better than the rest of us."

"I have lived longer than any other being in this world. I have seen things and know things you cannot understand. I know the secrets of the Forest of the Afterlife."

"And for all that, the future is still not yours to force into your mold."

Aradia's lips pressed themselves into a thin line. Her fingers gripped into fists, then released. "We can argue philosophy for years. As much as I appreciate your personal insights—particularly because you have met with the Gods—I'm sure you of all people understand my greatest desire: I want to go home, house witch."

Fin smiled sadly. "I do understand. But before I help you, I need my own home to be safe, Aradia. So can we think about how we can do that?"

The first witch stared at Fin, her expression and thoughts indiscernible.

However, their conversation was interrupted when an uproar broke out between the two camps behind them.

Shouts, screams, and then the clangs of swords.

Both Aradia and Fin were on their feet in an instant.

At first, nothing could be seen as a battle waged before them. But a sudden blaze of aura lit up the night sky brighter than any flame, and Kat, moving with inhuman speed, barreled forward. She held a child who wore oversized clothes and clutched a peculiarly shaped sword.

"Kat! What is happening?" Fin burst out as his daughter skidded to a halt in front of him.

His eyes then homed onto a blooming bloodstain on the front of Kat's tunic.

"It's Luca!" Kat cried out. "I don't know how he got out of the void, but he walked through my men and was heading straight for the dragon when one of those witches near Eric shot him with something!"

Fin's heart plummeted as he seized his grandson from her arms.

"Oh Gods. Is it fatal?" Fin demanded, his eyes roving over the bloody left shoulder and chest of his grandson, whose eyes were screwed shut in pain as he continued hugging the sword. "Luca! Luca, can you speak?"

Kat suddenly whirled around, cutting an arrow from the sky that had been whistling straight for her back.

"COWARDS!" she roared, her aura tripling in size.

Fin swallowed and raised his hand. His shield of lightning crackled to life, surging around himself, Luca, and the first witch.

He didn't notice until too late the way the first witch stared at the boy with the fixation of a starving man on a loaf of bread. She pulled a vial of water from her pocket and downed it.

"What are you doing?" Fin demanded, his hold around Luca tightening.

"Something many witches are ignorant of," Aradia began, her voice even, "is that I wielded all elements back when I had full access to my power. When I restore even a small measure of my abilities, I can wield magic like any mutated witch."

Fin didn't know what she was getting at until she seized Luca's injured arm, and a gold shield of lightning wrought with ancient symbols flared from her own hand, bubbling out until it hit Fin... and shot him outside of it, ripping Luca from his arms.

"NO!" he shouted right before he was launched into the air and catapulted into his own shield, both knocking his body to the ground and the wind from his lungs.

Fin dropped his shield, his gaze fixed on the scene within the golden dome in horror.

It had all happened so quickly… and there wasn't anything he could do.

The small boy fell onto the ground and gradually pushed himself to a sitting position. He calmly stared up at the first witch.

Aradia let out a long breath, tears of relief coming to her eyes as she slowly crouched down. "I guess you do truly care for this family, seeing as you are finally sacrificing yourself to end this."

The boy was pale from the blood loss, but he managed a smile. "I do. They mean everything."

"Are you ready to do this?" Aradia asked. The sounds of battle and shouts outside the shield faded into the distance as she felt time slow before the poignant moment.

Her brother nodded grimly. "I am."

There were fresh bellows of surprise from the battle that had Aradia glance up and around enough to discover that the castle had reappeared and…

Someone, an earth witch most likely—and a powerful one at that—had managed to separate the soldiers from one another, constricting them with mounds of soil and vines.

"I take it your *father* is coming for you," she noted before dropping her gaze back to her brother, who struggled to his feet, still clasping the oddly shaped sword.

"Yes. Let's finish this, Aradia."

The Daxarian queen's shouts could be heard distantly over the hum of the shield.

His small hand came out.

Aradia arched her brow at it.

She would have been worried, but the shield they were in, similar to the house witch's, blocked any magic inside —the only way Aradia had been able to use any magic was because hers was not from a natural source. It had come from the water of the Goddess's Pool. So it wasn't as though he could pull any tricks. She controlled the space. Completely.

Aradia pulled free the ceremonial dagger she had kept sheathed at her hip. "I suppose this was always how it was meant to be. I just needed to try less."

She proceeded to rest the blade against her throat, then paused. "What's with the sword?"

Her brother shrugged. "It's a good sword. I figured someone could use it after I'm gone."

That was strange.

Aradia flipped the blade and handed the knife to her brother. "In case you have forgotten, you have to say your name. Say that you wish to finish your fate."

The boy took the blade and with great accuracy laid it under his jaw by his ear.

There was a quick pull.

The sword he held fell to the grass, and abruptly he shot up, and Tamlin Ashowan stood before her.

Blood poured from his throat. He stumbled, then clamped a hand onto her shoulder to steady himself.

"Wh—" Aradia tried to back away in shock, but the weight of Tam's dying body stopped her from moving.

"I, Tamlin Ashowan, wish to end my fate," he said weakly, passing the knife to her hand. "I promise this will work. I just needed everyone to realize it was me all along so they'll leave the boy alone."

Aradia dumbly turned toward the battle where the two armies were in an uproar at the scene unfolding in the golden dome.

While Katarina Ashowan, tears streaming down her face, kept screaming and pounding her fists against the golden lightning.

Aradia turned back to Tamlin Ashowan. The light was fading out of his eyes.

"It will work," he whispered. "And if… not… you've lost nothing."

She swallowed with difficulty.

Hand shaking, she took the knife from him.

She sensed something right about that moment.

She put the blade to her own throat, much in the same way he had, and with a short move she, too, felt herself grow weak. "I… Aradia… wish to complete my fate."

Aradia watched the way Tamlin Ashowan looked at his father, who was on his knees outside the dome, crying and begging. She saw the way his dark eyes found Katarina, and how he smiled, as though to say everything would be alright. But then his expression went blank, and his body slumped to the ground.

Aradia must have cut deeper and wider than he had, because she felt herself falling toward oblivion.

"You… my brother used to look at me like that," she whispered, her bleary gaze briefly finding Katarina Ashowan's.

She half expected herself to regenerate. For it all to have been for nothing. Leaving her with an Ashowan family that would never want to negotiate with her again…

But she didn't.

Rather than the pain and rush of skin regrowing and reforming…

She felt cold.

Then her muscles gave way, and she, too, fell to the ground beside Tamlin Ashowan who… somehow… was leaving the world with her the way she and her brother had first arrived. Side by side.

Next thing she knew, Aradia found herself seated on the bench of Death's cart beside Tamlin Ashowan. Sunshine poured down over them, and peace filled her.

At long… long last…

She was heading home.

CHAPTER 50

THE DESTITUTION OF DEATH

The golden shield dissolved.

Kat was barely aware that her sword fell from her grasp.

She watched her father lunge for Tam and gather him in his arms.

Kat forced herself to move forward on shaking legs.

The ring of steel sounded behind her. The men must have been released from the hold of the earth and vines. Somewhere in the distance, she thought she heard children screaming. Thunder cracked overhead, but she couldn't move her eyes off Tam.

"Please. No." She heard her father's broken words. "No. Not my son. Not Tam. Why… No. No, no, no." Tears ravaged Finlay Ashowan's words as he reached up and touched his son's pale, still face. "It wasn't supposed to be like this."

Kat fell to her knees as she stared at Tam's lifeless eyes.

Her body shook. She reached out with her magic to feel his thread. To try to find some sense that he was still there; some hope that he could be brought back.

But there wasn't one.

Cold nausea rolled through her as she touched his hand.

Rain fell, making it difficult to discern that the sun had just begun to rise.

Warmth gathered and spilled out of her eyes.

Her twin.

Her brother.

Her brother who had always been there for her. Who had saved her life in more ways than one time and time again. Who had always been the one she could go to. Her brother who had been her anchor his whole life. Her peace.

There weren't words she could say.

Her body was heavy.

He had been… He had been the one helping them all back up when they fell. The quiet supporter that was always overlooked.

Kat's grip tightened on his wrist.

Fin sobbed, and that sound alone ripped her heart in two.

Her father who had always been goodness personified.

He cried as though his world had ended.

Though in a way the world *had* ended. Their world.

Their world where everyone they loved was safe. Where they were a part of making everything right.

There was an abrupt silence that made Kat wonder if she had gone deaf.

Not that it would matter if she did—but she distantly thought how that could not be the case, because she could hear rain and hail splattering heavily against the ground.

"My boy. My son," Fin whispered as he pressed a kiss to Tam's wetted black hair.

Kat didn't think anything else could hurt her in that moment. Nothing short of her own sons dying could make her feel anything similar to what she felt then.

But then she heard her mother's voice.

"Tam?"

The lone name was said weakly, quietly… As though there had barely been any breath used to speak.

Annika Ashowan appeared from the darkness and rain. She knelt in front of Tam's knees and laid her hand against his heart.

Fin raised his bloodshot eyes to her; the word *devastation* was too mild a term for the emotion in them.

The loud, primal cry that broke out of Annika's body echoed and touched something deeper. Something beyond loss.

Kat had never seen her mother cry before.

Never witnessed her losing complete control of herself.

And it turned out that seeing it was a torture Kat didn't know she could survive the aftermath of.

There was no doubt in Kat's mind that the world would forever carry that sound. Somewhere deep in its bones, that kind of grief had changed the world. Forever.

Eli walked slowly out of the castle. At her side, Kraken trotted grimly with his head down.

She heard the duchess's scream.

Her knees buckled.

She barely swallowed past the lump in her throat.

The Ashowans appeared completely unaware of their surroundings, not noticing that the briefly resumed fight had once again ceased at the sound of the duchess's scream.

They couldn't be aware that every soldier was staring at the scene with a mixture of disbelief and pain.

A few of the Daxarian knights lowered themselves to their knees and bowed their heads.

The king, Eric, stood two feet behind his wife. His eyes were filled with horror and shock.

Eli forced herself to keep moving. There wasn't much time.

They hadn't wanted his family to see this part. Tam had wanted to go alone to see the first witch with the Lobahlan sword Wixim had given them.

To make matters even worse, the three princes, Luca, and Penelope had beaten her outside, and were all standing a short way behind the house witch.

Eli numbly appreciated that Tam's cause of death could not be seen, thanks to the duke cradling his son in his arms.

She reached the children first and touched Luca's and Penelope's shoulders.

"Go back inside," she ordered quietly. "You can't see this."

Luca spun around, tears in his eyes, while Penelope stared blindly at Eli, her face ashen.

"Mom, he's not… Dad's not… He didn't, right?" Luca's voice was high and fearful. The threads of hysterics were already pulling tight in his face.

"Please go inside for now, Luca. We need to take care of him."

Hearing this made the princes turn around as well.

"He's dead!" Antony burst out.

Eli looked at his tearstained face as the rain and hail battered the earth. "We need to fix that. I need you to please go inside. Now."

Antony opened his mouth to argue, but Charlie stalked toward the castle first, his chin lowered. Then Asher grabbed Antony's hand and buried his face into his brother's shoulder.

Begrudgingly, the remaining two princes trudged back up to the castle through the mud, tears already carving tracks down Antony's face.

Penelope and Luca remained in front of Eli, prompting her to slowly kneel to the ground and gently reach up to touch both children's arms.

Kraken sat with his head bowed.

"Luca. We need to work quickly to make this better. Can you trust me?"

"It will be okay, though, right? You promise?" Luca asked, his hands curling into fists at his sides.

"I promise I will do everything in my power to try."

Luca stiffened at her careful wording but gave a slow, serious nod of understanding.

He looked over at Penelope and grabbed her hand. "Come on."

She didn't respond. Her mind seemed to be somewhere far away, but she allowed Luca to drag her off.

Seeing the children's reaction helped steady Eli's resolve. She came back to her feet. She had not liked this plan, but… there was no other choice. Even after talking with Kraken, it was clear. Not if they were to keep Luca completely safe.

Eli rounded the Ashowan couple and carefully avoided looking at Tam. She wasn't sure she could have faith in the next part if she did.

"Duke, Duchess, I am very sorry, but there is no time to explain. Please go back inside with Tam and keep him by the fire. If you can, start doing chest compressions. Do not stop. Kraken and I will try our best to bring him back."

Eli could feel hundreds of pairs of eyes boring in her back, along with the Daxarian queen's and king's, but it was the duke's and duchess's gaze she braced for.

The house witch's face came up first, life and hope instantly sparking in his expression while the duchess whirled around.

"What do you mean?" Annika demanded.

Eli couldn't quite hold her wild gaze, but it helped that Katarina stood up from the ground and had also turned to look at her intently.

"Kraken and I are going to go see about bringing him back. Bring him inside immediately. I am sorry you had to see this, but please hurry. Otherwise he may not be able to come back right. I can't move very quickly yet, but it is important."

She was starting to worry that they would insist she explain more, or that she would need to urge them again, but in an instant Kat dove for her brother, scooped him up with a flaring of her aura, and bolted with incredible speed to the castle. Fin rose, his jaw set with determination. Annika darted to his side, and as a unit they retreated to the castle without another word.

Eli blinked in awe.

Then, as she was about to turn to Kraken to verify he was ready to go, Eric appeared in front of her.

"Can you really bring him back?" he asked quietly.

She jerked her chin stiffly as the rain plastered her hair to her head. "I'm not completely certain, but I will do what I can."

Eric nodded, then swept his sights over to the army, which was experiencing an outbreak of murmurs. "Do whatever you can. I'm guessing the plan is to tell everyone that Tam was possessed and that his death and resurrection obliterated the devil?"

Eli bowed her head. "Yes."

Eric nodded again. "Got it."

The king lowered his head, his hazel eyes darkening as he faced down the army. "And is the devil gone?"

"If I do it right, he should be," Eli explained, though it was a much more complicated answer than that.

Eric allowed himself a half smile of relief. "Good. I'm sick of fighting against my wife."

"THE ASHOWANS HAVE RETREATED! ATTACK!"

Eli whirled around to face the army beside Eric, her eyes flashing.

It had been one of the witches.

A snarl started to build in Eli's throat, but she was startled back into silence when a screeching roar rang out, and a large, golden scaled body landed with a thud on the ground in front of her and Eric.

Wixim stood between the castle and the army.

"I'll deal with this," Eric managed after overcoming the shock of Wixim's appearance. "Go get Tam."

Eli inclined herself slightly, then looked down at Kraken who—under any other circumstances—would've been hilarious to look at given his drenched state.

"Alright. You show me how I get to the Forest of the Afterlife, and I'll remember not to change back into my human form while there."

Kraken blinked.

Eli let out a steadying breath, then shifted into her beast form. She could hear the army's alarmed shouts and clamoring at the sight of her other form, but Wixim looked over at them, his lips curling into a smile before he winked.

She gave a low purr in response.

"*LET'S MOVE, KITTEN!*" Kraken roared as he bolted across the field toward the west, where the King's Forest lay.

Kasha took off after him, easily catching up thanks to her greater size, despite being slower even in her beast state. However, just before she could ask him to describe the funny glimmer out of the corner of her eye that Kraken had said she was supposed to see, he veered right.

She followed, and as they made it around the corner of the castle, he darted left. Kasha blindly followed, but as she did… she saw it. The flicker of another scene. Trees closer than they should have been…

Did she need to chase it more?

She skidded to a halt and looked down at Kraken, who had stopped and was sitting licking his paw.

"I saw it! I think, anyway... Don't we have to keep going?" she asked breathlessly.

Kraken put his paw down. "We're here. Tam should be close."

Kasha balked.

She was in the Forest of the Afterlife? Already? It was that easy?

She looked around, and realized...

It was warm and sunny.

It wasn't rainy with hail. And when she looked behind herself, the castle wasn't there. Instead, she saw an ocean of bright-green grass spread over rolling hills with a lone dirt road that seemed to lead to nowhere.

She looked back in front of herself and noticed trees she had never seen the likes of before. They towered higher than any castle or palace she had ever seen, with bark and branch shapes that did not exist in reality.

Birds chirped peacefully, and her body felt... lighter. All aches and pains had disappeared, and she felt fully energized.

She sniffed the air...

Mint. Frankincense.

Tam, she thought, her heart fluttering.

She galloped forward, straight for the first line of trees. She bolted around trunks wider than carriages, hopped over flower clusters of the most brilliant blues and purples, until at last she came to a clearing.

Skidding to a halt, she found Tam, leaning his shoulder against a tree trunk with his arms crossed. His gaze was fixed on something in the distance.

He was whole. He was himself. He was unharmed.

On quaking legs, Kasha approached him.

He turned, his eyes widening in surprise, sparking panic in Kasha that he had had his memories taken from him by Death on his way to the Forest. Kraken had warned them that could happen...

But then he said, "I think you're even bigger than before."

Kasha couldn't even be mad over his insensitive comment; she gently pushed her head into his chest.

"The Gods are just talking with Aradia. We'll speak to them afterward."

Kasha didn't say anything, but her heart raced in her chest.

The next part would be difficult, but… it would be okay. If she was with Tam, anything was possible.

It had to be.

CHAPTER 51

A DIVINE DEBATE

Tam watched Aradia as she sobbed in the arms of the Goddess. The way her face moved… the helplessness, the devastation… It was almost like she were a completely different person. It was as though before she had been muted, and now she had returned to herself.

At the Goddess's side, the Green Man laid a hand on his daughter's forehead, his soulful eyes filled with pain and love for her. Then, after a few moments, the Green Man gently gathered his daughter in his arms and escorted her away.

Once the pair had disappeared through the thick, lush foliage, the Goddess's multicolored eyes turned to Tam, Kasha, and Kraken. Her hand rested on her pregnant middle as she smiled and beckoned them closer.

Tam felt as though he were floating, unable to look away from the Goddess. Warmth and peace filled him, and he suddenly felt perfectly content… He wondered if Kasha and Kraken felt the same way.

They stopped a short way from the Goddess, and she lowered herself gracefully onto a throne made of branches and twigs, with leaves and flowers sprouting down its legs.

Kraken sauntered over and leapt up to rest on her lap.

"Hello, Kraken," she said with a smile that seemed to make the entire world hum in pleasure. The Goddess reached up and gently scratched Kraken's cheek.

Tam's former daze of peace cleared in an instant as he stared at Kraken flatly.

It would seem his father's familiar had decided he was finished being of help.

"Goddess," Tam began, though speaking felt strange, as if his own words were foreign to himself. "I would like to return to life. As myself. In my body."

The Goddess's eyes twinkled knowingly. But she said nothing as her sights moved to Kasha, who moved closer with her head bowed.

"You may speak; I have granted you the ability while here," the Goddess informed her kindly.

Tam looked at Kasha with a reassuring smile.

"Thank you." The voice that came from Kasha was lower than Eli's. It sounded a little more mature, a little more feline somehow. "I'm sure you are already aware of the fact that Tam has taken over your son's fate."

The Goddess merely bowed her head in acknowledgment.

"But the devil deserves one happy life. He hasn't had one in the entirety of his existence, and he needs Tam to have that happy life."

"You believe you know all there is to know about my son's existence?" the Goddess asked patiently.

Tam hesitated, but Kasha was quick. "His existence has never been blended with a human child before. It is not right to make what would have been an unaffected life suffer."

The Goddess considered this. "Tamlin, you have made the choice to die in order to help bring my daughter home and protect your son. If you are brought back to life, not only will the balance of life and death be broken, but the question of whether or not Aradia should remain here presents itself."

"Not if his death is treated as the death of the devil's fate," Kasha argued while bringing herself to a seated position.

The Goddess leaned forward, like a mother listening to her child talking about their adventurous day; her smile was engaged and curious. "Oh?"

"He is not going to live with the same purpose or with his memories, if we are guessing correctly." At this, Kasha eyed the Goddess, waiting for confirmation.

She did not comment.

"His fate was to help humans be at one with their emotions," Tam interjected carefully. "No one should be privy to every emotion of another. Not all emotions stem from truth. To place that burden on a child without any parental figures to understand what was going on would create a cycle of trauma. You know this, Goddess. You've seen it." He tried to keep the traces of anger on Luca's behalf from his voice, but he wasn't entirely successful. "The hurt others give is a reflection of the hurt they've received."

The Goddess's smile faded as she listened somberly.

"Please… let Luca have a happy life with his father." Kasha bowed her head.

"You don't think a child can be happy after the loss of a parent?" the Goddess asked quietly.

There was a pang of sorrow that echoed in Tam's heart, though he wasn't entirely certain where it stemmed from.

"I think that a child who has endured what Luca has deserves the best, happiest life. Not one spent remembering a father who died to save him. This is only going to perpetuate the cycle all over again. He needs better," Kasha argued.

The Goddess rested a hand on her belly. "If I were to return Tamlin, what would be offered in exchange for the balance?"

"Are all the deaths that the devil and the first witch have been responsible for not enough? Aradia even manufactured Witch's Brew, a drug that tampered with the exchange of life and death when she distributed it to humans and then brought ancient beasts over from the Forest of the Afterlife," Kasha reminded her sharply.

The Goddess shook her head sadly. "Those poor souls who took the drug chose to indulge in the vice. That was their decision."

"My magic."

Kasha's head whipped around, and Kraken's eyes slowly opened once more.

Tam held the Goddess's stare. "I've been told I have incredible magic. The kind that many envy. I'd even say the kind that some people would kill for. Would this be acceptable as payment?"

The Goddess did not respond straightaway as she stared at him thoughtfully. "It does not change the number of lives present. Your grandmother, Katelyn Ashowan, not only exhausted her magic healing your father, but also gave her life. Even then, his return was only made possible because we knew you would help a being dear to myself and the Green Man."

It was Tam's turn to go quiet.

"If I may," Kraken said with a yawn. He jumped down from the Goddess's lap and took a languid stretch before sitting beside Kasha. "In my estimation, Tam here has helped not only your son, but also your daughter. To help the children of the Gods has been something no other mortal has done. Does that feat not warrant some leniency?"

The Goddess's eyes drifted to the trees in consideration. "It is still a life we need."

Tam felt his stomach clench.

Was this really it? Had he and Eli crafted their arguments, and tried to find a way for his death not to be permanent... for nothing?

"Pardon me."

Tam, Kasha, and Kraken looked over their shoulder to see none other than Death.

Only he wasn't standing alone. On his left was a Troivackian woman a few years older than Tam, and a young man it took a moment for him to remember.

"Thomas... Julian? Penelope called you Uncle Thomas," Tam said with his hesitancy coming through his tone. How was Thomas Julian there?

The young man bowed his head in acknowledgment, before Tam turned his confused stare to the woman. She had long chocolate-toned hair and warm brown eyes... eyes that resembled both his own mother's as well as—

"Penelope." Tam turned, his hand gesturing at the woman. "You look like Penelope, but you don't have the mark below your eye, so you can't be her."

The woman seemed to be studying him in turn. While her eyes were the same color and shape as Penelope's, a storm of emotion roiled behind hers. Grief, anger, suffering, and relief all brewed together.

"I am Caroline Levin. Formerly Caroline Piereva. I am... I am Penelope's mother. Your cousin," she informed Tam tightly while adjusting her dull-rose skirts.

"Wait, are you... Are you still alive? Or have you been here for a while? Or—"

"I died two days ago," she interrupted.

Tam recoiled "Oh, I'm so sorry. Penelope, she... she was devastated when we found her. We thought you had died a while ago. She was certain of it," he explained, his heart twisting in his chest as he thought about Penelope having to hear with complete certainty that her mother had passed.

Kasha had rounded to face the newcomers as well. To Caroline, she added, "She loves you a lot. She's such a smart girl, and she intimidates even adult nobility into obeying."

At this, Caroline's lips twitched. "Of course. She is a strong Troivackian girl. She is of noble blood, and I raised her to be well aware of it."

Tam gave a tight-lipped smile, but he nodded. "She is definitely strong."

"Why is it you have brought these souls, old friend," the Goddess called out to Death, her voice gentle.

Death removed his flattop hat, then with a smile at Thomas Julian and a kind wink at Caroline Levin, he gestured the two forward.

Thomas Julian moved to kneel, but the Goddess waved her hand, making him go still.

"You have bent yourself your entire life. Do not kneel."

The young man froze, caught in confusion as to what to do.

Evidently sensing that he may need some time—or she was simply impatient—Caroline Levin stepped forth.

"I want Elisara and Tamlin Ashowan to raise my child. She has been through enough, and I know it is because of my own choices that her father and I made…" Caroline trailed off, her voice croaking a little, prompting her to clear it. "However, she shouldn't be the one to pay for our crimes. I do not… I still do not like the duchess. But Tamlin Ashowan and Elisara, they… I think they are the only ones who can properly raise her, and she deserves to be properly raised."

The Goddess gazed in complete understanding at Caroline, and the woman's eyes flooded with tears in an instant.

"Thank you for advocating for your daughter, Caroline. I know that was not easy," the Goddess soothed while rising from her seat and pulling Caroline into a hug. "You are a good mother who put her own troubles aside for the well-being of your child. You should be very proud of yourself."

Caroline sobbed into the Goddess's shoulder. The Goddess leaned back and cupped her face in her hands. "You've been angry for a long, long time, Caroline. It is alright to put it down now. You have not failed anyone, you have not been tricked, you are safe."

Caroline could not speak, but she did nod, and through her tears choked out, "I'm so… tired."

The Goddess smiled sadly. "Go rest, child. All will be well." As soon as the Goddess released Caroline, she nodded, and after dabbing at her cheeks turned to look at Tamlin one final time. "Tell her I love her more than anything, and I know she will be a fine woman."

Tam bowed his head. "You have my word."

When Caroline had disappeared through the trees, her arms wrapped around herself, the Goddess clasped her hands in front of her skirts and looked at Thomas Julian patiently.

She did not speak, and she didn't ask him to, either.

Still, the young man ducked his head sheepishly and fixed his eyes on the grass. "I… will be the exchange for Tamlin Ashowan."

"What?" Tam frowned. "No. I will not be responsible for taking your life. I know we haven't officially met, but—"

The young man turned to him with a somber knowingness lighting his brown eyes. "My days were numbered regardless. When I chose to hide among the first witch's closest allies, I knew it placed a sentence on my head. I've watched Daxaria from afar and helped when I could. Likon, my uncle, was raised as family in your household. He… He was like a brother to you, and because of me he has been forced to stay in Troivack. I need my death to have meaning. Please let me…" The young man took a shuddering breath. "Please let me show everyone why I was doing this. So that they see I was trying to make sure I could save as many people as possible."

Tam opened and closed his mouth, unable to think of what to say until at last he managed to splutter. "But you aren't dead yet, are you?"

Thomas Julian smiled sadly. "I am near death. I have taken Witch's Brew. I've been watching from afar as Aradia's eyes for a long, long time. I was near the battle by the castle. When I saw what you did, and then how Lady Elisara disappeared with Kraken, I had a hunch that… that maybe… maybe I could finally be a hero."

"Tamlin?"

Tam was about to go on to say there was no way he could allow Likon's nephew to die on his behalf, but the Goddess's words pulled his attention back to her.

"I will accept this exchange. In light of the souls that you have saved, the light you have brought to my children, as well as a mother's final wish, I will not take your magic from you. But I will send you back with a task."

"No!" Tam exclaimed, turning back frantically to Thomas, who was smiling with a heartbreaking mixture of happiness and sadness at the Goddess. "Likon may be angry with you now, but he loves you! He's worried about you! Your mother, your siblings, they all are—"

The young man swallowed, then said with a bit more force behind his voice, "If I live now? I will be executed and die a shameful death that will haunt my family for betraying the Daxarian monarchy. Tam… This is how I… This is how I wish to end my life, and you cannot tell me how I should go. It isn't up to you."

Before Tam could say another word, the Green Man returned and placed himself on the Goddess's left side. His eyes were red-rimmed but peaceful. Death made his way over to the Goddess's right.

"Tamlin Ashowan, your task upon returning to life in your body, in a way that breaks the laws of nature's balance, is to help unite the witches, humans, and ancient beasts. It is a task my children struggled to accomplish for centuries, but this time, with your exceptional familiar"—the Goddess nodded at Kasha—"and your connections to both a normal human prince and princes who are witches, you are in a very unique position of a counselor. It will not be easy, but I'm well aware you Ashowans have a way of making things work out."

Tam was about to object again to Thomas Julian sacrificing himself, but then Death reached out and gently touched Tam's face. The Forest of the Afterlife dimmed as he swayed on his feet.

"Thank you for loving our son. You were everything we hoped for him, and more. He will still feel people's emotions, and affect them to some degree, but… the abilities will not be as potent as they were." The Green Man's words echoed in Tam's head, and next thing he knew he had fallen into a restful darkness.

Kasha barely wedged herself under Tam's unconscious body in time before he fell to the ground.

She made a low rumble of concern, but a quick look at Kraken, who was using this moment of quiet to start cleaning his back leg, told her things were not dire.

"As for you, Kasha," the Goddess said, her eyes glowing subtly in the shifting light through the trees. "We expect you to help your witch with his task. You can help him negotiate with the ancient beasts and humans. We know approaching us as a court and negotiating with us was your idea."

If Kasha were in her human form, she'd blush.

"However, when Tamlin Ashowan returns to life, and Thomas Julian makes the exchange, we expect you to document very clearly that we will not bend the laws of life to such an extreme again. With our son's fate resolved, and our daughter home, we believe it is time that the age of magic become something more… subtle. There will be a decline in witches born in the coming years. Please make it be known that while this may seem alarming, we the Gods are not angry. We simply believe that a more nuanced approach to a world with magic should be the way forward."

"What about the ancient beasts?" Eli asked, her mind already filling with possible complications of a world with less magic.

"Soon they, too, will fade. They will gradually integrate into the world until everyone is at balance with one another," the Green Man explained regally.

Kasha swallowed. "Why… did you tell me this, and not Tam?"

All three Gods smiled, and Kasha wasn't sure what to make of it, until the Goddess answered.

"Because you are a familiar. Now go enjoy your peaceful life. You will have great work ahead, but you will know great joy from here on."

Kasha lowered her head, and it was then she noticed that the weight of Tam had disappeared.

He must have returned to the land of the living.

Kraken rose with a stretch. "Right. Come along. There are going to be a lot of crying people we will need to console with our fluff. Until next time," Kraken called lazily over his shoulder to the Gods.

The Goddess laughed, sending a musical breeze dancing around the trees.

Kasha was almost too entranced to move, but Kraken shouted at her once again. "Come along! We don't have all day! I'd like to at least get a nap soon!"

And so with a final look at the Gods, and a final bow of gratitude to Thomas Julian, who waved with a smile and tears running down his face, she chased after the fluffy haunches back into reality.

CHAPTER 52

NOTHING HITS LIKE HOME

At first, it seemed like the dreams he had experienced before that had revealed snippets of the devil's past... But this was different.

Tam stared in confusion at the man standing in front of him. His black hair just brushed his broad shoulders, his hands were in his pockets, and his pale face was mostly turned away as he stared at something deeper in the Forest of the Afterlife.

Tam looked down at his body, then around himself. Hadn't he just been facing the Gods? Where was Kasha?

"Dad?" the young man's voice called faintly.

Tam startled as he looked back, and found himself staring into dark-brown eyes that had gone wide upon seeing him. For good reason, too! The young man was almost identical to Tam in appearance. The only differences were perhaps the other man's sharper chin, his ears pinned a bit closer to his head, and his leaner muscles.

Tam blinked in confusion. "Uh."

"So even with your memory intact, you feel the same way?"

Both Tam and the young man's heads snapped round to see the Goddess and Green Man standing side by side watching them. They'd seemingly appeared out of nowhere, and the instant Tam acknowledged them, his senses were nearly overwhelmed by the potent sadness and love emanating from them.

But wait… Memories?

The devil's memories?

Tam looked back at the young man, realization washing over him.

"Luca."

He watched, stunned, as the young man broke out into a smile and bolted straight for him.

Tam only had a moment to react, but that was all he needed before pulling his son into a hug.

"What is going on?" he asked with a laugh before pulling away and studying Luca's adult face. "You're just a kid back home!"

Luca beamed at him, his eyes warm as he released Tam and stepped back before looking over at the Gods. "They wanted us all to talk before you woke up."

At this, Tam turned to face the higher powers more directly.

"The devil was meant to die with his sister and to aid the humans, but the death of Thomas Julian and your own actions remove that fate. However, he will still need to enter the Grove of Sorrows upon his next death," the Goddess announced solemnly.

"Hang on—" Tam started, moving in front of Luca and pressing him even farther behind his back, only for Luca's hand to appear on his shoulder.

"Dad, it's okay," he interrupted softly. "It isn't hell. When I go… I can think about things."

Tam looked back over his shoulder, his brows still lowered as he regarded his son's partial smile.

"We still have our time together, I promise."

Tam tried to swallow past the lump in his throat, but he couldn't. "Luca, I don't know that you deserve—"

"Dad, no matter how hurt I was as a child, I still made my choices as an adult in the many lives I had as the devil. For centuries. I should face some consequences. To even get a single life with you and Eli? Our family? It will help me better understand what I did. I was not wrong to struggle with my fate, and… and you taking that from me, I…" Luca trailed off, visibly fighting against the tears coming to his eyes.

Tam hugged his son again. He didn't know what to say. Technically he had failed in dissolving the devil's fate, and instead Thomas Julian had paid the ultimate price. But… he didn't want to give Luca yet another burden to carry at the same time.

He felt Luca take a shuddering breath beneath his arms, so he hugged him tighter.

When they separated once more, Luca set to instantly wiping the tears from his face as he slowly turned to the Gods. "Is Aradia already in the Grove of Sorrows?" he asked.

The Green Man bowed his head in confirmation.

Luca's eyes fell to the ground. "Did you tell her the truth about what Tam did for me?"

At this, the Green Man spared a small smile, though his own eyes looked misty. "I did not. My thought was that the two of you might have a good conversation when you've finished with the Grove of Sorrows."

Luca nodded, his next words quiet. "I'd like that."

The Goddess stepped forward, her otherworldly gaze tracing the lines of Luca's face lovingly.

"My son," she said, her voice as soft as dandelion wisps. "I am sorry for the suffering you endured. We had hoped that if the humans named you and raised you as their own, you would be able to both feel with them and guide them."

Tam noted the way Luca's hands momentarily balled into fists in his pocket before he responded with, "I wasn't human. I couldn't sense my own feelings through the haze of everyone else's. I told you this. For centuries."

The Goddess did not move to touch Luca, but Tam could see in her glowing eyes that she longed to. "I know. However, fate cannot be untied easily, my son. You know this. Which is why…" She turned her sights to Tam, and he was once again plunged into feelings of peace and warmth. "We worked for a long time to find you humans to do what none other could."

Luca looked at Tam, his eyes red. "I… I never thought I'd want to spend a lifetime I didn't have to among humans. But, Dad, I… I really want to go home. I want to go see Mom, and Penelope. And my new sister."

Tam bowed his head with a smile. His next words were a rasp. "Let's do that."

However, before Tam could do anything more, Luca addressed the Gods again. "Rosaline Evans. The woman who… who birthed me after consuming my ashes. Bless her with only the best. The absolute best. I know I will pay for what my imp did to her once I'm here again, but she deserves peace."

Tam's stomach churned horribly at the reminder of what Rosaline had endured.

The Gods both lowered their chins, their expressions somber. "We will help the memories and pain fade for her, as well as bestowing her with as much goodness as we can. She will have great peace and favor here."

Luca nodded before reaching up with a shaking hand to rub his mouth.

Tam saw the sickness of guilt writhing behind his eyes.

He moved a hand to his son's shoulder and asked the Gods another question. "Luca won't remember his past in this life, right?"

The Goddess lifted her gaze to his own. "He will remember only small pieces. In the interest of fulfilling your request that Luca have a proper childhood and life, we will allow him to atone for his sins when he has returned to the Forest of the Afterlife. He will not understand or know the magnitude before then."

Tam nodded stiffly. "Thank you." He turned to Luca. "Let's go home, hey?"

Luca couldn't quite raise his eyes again, his conscience still visibly buckling under his remorse.

However, Tam didn't have to worry for long. By his next breath, his body felt light and relaxed, and darkness once again crept into his vision.

He was ready to wake up and see his family again, and at long last leave the heartbreak behind.

The first thing Tam felt was throbbing pain.

In his ribs.

And it kept pummeling him.

He coughed and choked at the same time.

"GODSDAMN FINALLY!"

He felt like vomiting. Though when the blows stopped the pain remained. Which told him that if he did lose whatever remained in his stomach, it would be a torturous experience.

"Water! Get him water!"

"What're those markings on his face?"

"What markings?"

"The ones under his beard."

"I can't see."

"Tam? Tam can you hear us?"

Tam's head ached, and his eyelids had taken it upon themselves to gain fifteen pounds since he'd last tried to open them.

Despite only being able to open them a small slit, however, he did manage a weak, breathy, "Yeah."

"Good!" came the unmistakable bark from his sister. "You are so damn slow, you selfish turd! I'm traumatized! Da's traumatized! Mum's traumatized! We're all traumatized, Tam! Because of you! The least you could do is *wake up a bit faster, you ungrateful shit!*"

"Kat!" Tam heard his mother's whispery voice, which came out as a croak with an undisguisable note of relief.

"He's awake! He can deal with being told what an arse he is! Actually, you know what? Me just shouting at him isn't enough. Kraken! Where's Kraken? Kraken needs to sit his fluffy arsehole down on his mouth."

"Kat... Did you..." Tam struggled to draw a clear breath. "Break all of my ribs?"

"*Well excuse me! I was trying to keep blood circulating so you wouldn't become a useless turnip!*"

The chilled edge of a ladle pressed against Tam's lips, and the next thing he knew, cool, refreshing water trickled down his parched throat.

"Where's Luca?" Tam managed once he'd taken in three mouthfuls of water.

"He and Penelope are supposed to be with their cousins, sleeping," Annika informed him quietly.

Tam tried again to open his eyes and was moderately more successful this time. He managed to raise his lids halfway up.

He found himself in the same sickroom Eli had been in previously. His father, mother, and sister sat around him, illuminated by a small fire flickering in the hearth.

Though for some reason they all went still when he looked at them.

Fin broke the tentative hush. "You met with the Gods."

Tam shifted his head on the pillow to better look at his father.

"Your eyes," Fin said as an explanation. "Because your eyes are darker than my own, it's easier to see the light and dark lights flickering behind them."

"Ah." Tam closed his eyes again and refocused his efforts on breathing. Then, when he had stored enough energy, he opened them again and regarded his family. "I am sorry I had to hurt you all that way. There wasn't any other... Any other possibility of saving Luca."

"A heads-up would've been nice!" Kat informed him acidly.

"You would've... tried to talk me out of it. Just like Eli did. Then... we realized... there wasn't another way for... his fate to die." At his mention of death, Tam jolted a little as his memories surged back. His eyelids dragged themselves back. "Thomas Julian."

Everyone in the room fell silent. Tam's gaze shot to his mother. "Thomas Julian sacrificed himself so that I could... I could come back. The Gods weren't going to let me return without an exchange. He took Witch's Brew somewhere nearby. He... He said he had been waiting for a chance to help us with the first witch. Said he... he wanted to die a hero so that his family knew the truth. He never betrayed us, he simply... spied. For years. And waited to help." The long speech was making Tam's remaining energy wane all the faster, and his eyes fluttered despite his best efforts.

Even so, he saw Annika's alarmed stare at Fin, and even Kat gaped down at him, looking thoroughly horrified.

"Eli is back... safely... right?" he asked next, hoping his family would recover enough from the shock to answer him before he lost consciousness.

His father must have sensed that Tam was fading, as he hastily responded, "She's upstairs and has strict orders from the physician to rest and not leave her bed for the remainder of her pregnancy, barring basic functions."

Tam wanted to ask more about *that* development, but his mouth wouldn't work, and his eyelids had once again taken control from him and shut themselves, forcing him back into darkness, where his mind drifted away into a dreamless, restful sleep.

The next time Tam opened his eyes, the pain in his ribs had spread throughout his torso, and he was in agony.

He wasn't even certain he *could* move if he wanted to.

"Godsdamn… did Kat hit me after I fell back asleep?" he muttered to himself while lifting an arm up to rub his face.

"While I'd like to assure you that is not the case, I'm sorry to say I'm not sure."

Tam's head snapped around. While the move made the room spin unpleasantly, he didn't care. Not when his eyes landed on Eli, who was sitting in a wheelchair like the one his sister had used years ago, with a book in her lap and a cup of tea in her one hand, while her other rested on her middle.

He smiled. "Hey."

Eli's eyebrows quirked upward. "Hello, my lord."

Tam gave a breathy laugh and regretted it instantly as the pain racked through him. "Have I… done something while unconscious to upset you, my dear one?"

Eli's flat stare in response almost made him laugh again.

"Not particularly. Though you have been sleeping for the better part of a week."

Tam watched as her one hand left her middle to join her other in cradling her teacup.

A chill claimed the tip of Tam's nose, telling him that autumn had settled its mantle over the world while he'd been recovering.

"How have you been?" Tam asked while reaching out a hand to Eli.

She slipped her warm fingers against his palm with a small sigh. "I've been enjoying the rest. Though I'd enjoy it more if my betrothed were awake and able to stop the three princes from influencing our children."

Tam allowed himself a small smile, but he wasn't brave enough to succumb to a laugh. "What've they been doing?"

"You mean aside from dismantling multiple decorative suits of armor to try them on?"

A long snort of a laugh wheezed its way out of Tam.

"Or swapping out Mr. Howard's wine with red wine vinegar?"

"Oh no."

"Or when they decided to try making a kite large enough that it would help one of them fly?"

"That one doesn't sound as bad!" Tam reasoned weakly.

"Where do you think they got the fabric, Tam?" Eli asked with an edge refining itself in her words.

"Uh—"

"Bedsheets. Tunics. Curtains."

"I didn't even know they knew how to sew," Tam mused aloud.

"*They* didn't. *Penelope*, on the other hand, does. She taught them how."

"What?" Tam couldn't mask his disbelief. "Truly? I thought this was all going on despite her best efforts!"

"At first she tried, but she thought there was merit to the kite idea."

Tam raised a hand to his face and rested it over his eyes. "How're we punishing them?"

"Well, the armor venture was harmless enough. They just had to reassemble and polish them. The wine crime, however, nearly made a grown man cry. So they are all working every morning doing chores to earn money and pay back Mr. Howard for at least one of the two bottles they dumped out."

"Mr. Howard does have expensive tastes."

"As for the kite, I'm to have a meeting with Their Majesties about it later this evening."

Tam gave a smile mixed with a grimace. "How're Kat and Eric?"

"A bit tense, but they're working on things. The king wants to speak to you at some point," Eli replied, setting her teacup down on the table beside Tam's bed and handing him a goblet of water. "I'd help you sit up, but I'm not allowed to."

Tam took the goblet appreciatively and drank what he could from his awkward positioning. It was then he discovered his torso was tightly bandaged. "At least the children sound like they aren't too shaken by the battle events."

Eli's lips pressed together. "Luca is the one keeping everyone in fine spirits. Penelope is tense, and it has been next to impossible to get her to eat anything— your father has been very helpful and diligent about making sure she doesn't miss any meals. I think she was reminded about losing her parents the first time when she saw things the day of the battle."

Tam's eyes lowered to his and Eli's joined hands. "I'll talk with her soon. It won't help when we tell her about her mother and Thomas Julian."

"No, it won't," Eli agreed softly.

Tam brought Eli's hand to his lips and brushed a kiss across its back. "We have more grief to manage, but… it's over. We're home, and we at least know better things are on the horizon."

He looked up just in time to see Eli nodding, a subtle smile warming her face in the firelight.

"Thank you for being beside me for all of this. For having faith. For trusting me," he said with every ounce of sincerity he possessed.

Eli's smile widened. "Of course, my lord."

Tam tugged on her hand with a quiet growl. "Start calling me that again and the instant I'm able to, I'll be reprimanding you in more ways than one."

Eli flushed a bright pink. "Gods. You're barely alive and you're still so base."

"You bring it out of me."

"I'm glad my wheelchair heats your loins."

"You don't want to know what I want to try to do in that wheelchair."

"Oh, for the love of—"

"Eli?" Tam interrupted her irritated outburst with a grin.

"What?"

"I love you." She stared at him until he gave her arm a small shake. "Say it back."

She grumbled, then said. "I love you, too. Just stop being so…"

"Crass?"

"I was going to say tempting."

Tam's jaw dropped.

Eli arched an eyebrow at him, and a coy smile curled her lips. "What? I said I wanted more children, didn't I?"

Tam felt his entire body burn. Did he have an infection, or was he really still able to lust after his betrothed so aggressively?

Eli pulled her hand free from his grasp, then lowered herself over him enough to brush a chaste kiss across his forehead. "Remember, *my lord*, you're the one who called me the master of torture."

It took Tam a long while to think or speak in coherent sentences after that, but at the very least when he did, despite his future wife's skilled flirting, he found himself feeling like a rather lucky man.

CHAPTER 53

HEALING WITH HOPE

Thomas Julian's funeral was small.

This was at the request of his family, though word of his good deeds had already spread throughout Daxaria. He was the young man who had gone undercover to help rid the world of the devil and first witch. He was being hailed as a brave hero. The guardian of the land.

Tam watched Likon stand with his sister's family. Thomas's mother was barely on her feet as she wept over her son's grave, which was beside Katelyn Ashowan's own. The tall, carved stone stood beside Fin's mother. Dignified. Solemn.

Thomas's father, a knight, gripped his wife's shoulders, his own tears running endlessly down his face as he stared at his eldest child's resting place. His other children were off to the side, all crying and holding one another. They all were trying to brace the storm of loss, together on the cold cliffside. The Alcide Sea churned far below on the cloudy, chilly day.

Annika and Fin stood a short way from Likon, who remained apart from his sister's family.

Kat and Eric, in their full regalia, were another row back.

Tam, Eli, and the children huddled together behind them. Beyond that, there were a handful of knights and a dozen distant family members of the Julians, but that was all.

Even though Eli still had to be transported in her wheelchair, she held Penelope in her lap as the little girl cried silently.

The former king, Norman Reyes, spoke on Thomas Julian's behalf. He spoke of how he had first met and hired him to be Eric's assistant eight years before. How, back then, at fifteen, Thomas had been bright, thoughtful, and devoted to his family. Then he described his misfortune, becoming tangled in the higher powers. How he had been braver than many knights, and his sacrifice to save Tam had been a selfless, kind act. How the world would know his name for years to come.

Tam knew that, to Thomas Julian's family, the accolades meant little compared to the pain of losing him.

It didn't matter that Thomas Julian had been right that if he hadn't died, he would've been prosecuted. His sacrifice cleared his name and elevated his family's honor. Beyond that, it removed any doubt about his love and care for them.

Tam would spend the rest of his life ensuring that the Julian family wanted for nothing. That guilt was yet another burden he would carry until the end of his days.

Eli reached out and grasped his hand, drawing Tam's attention down to her. She gazed up at him knowingly and gave his hand another squeeze.

He did his best to manage a tight smile, then returned his attention to the Julian family. They were, at present, hugging one another before approaching the gravestone and resting flowers at its base.

"Mom?" Penelope's quiet voice called out, once again making Tam tear his sights away from the scene before him.

Eli blinked down in surprise, a blush resting on her cheeks. "Yes?"

"I… I have something I need to tell Likon."

Visibly dazed at having been called "Mom" for the first time by Penelope, Eli cleared her throat and then busied her hands tucking the loose strands of Penelope's hair behind her ears. "Alright. Did you want to wait until the reception? Or should we go over now?"

Tam rested his hands on the wheelchair handles. He had only just been permitted to start pushing the wheelchair. According to the physician, Tam had re-broken one of the ribs he had fractured on the ship back in Zinfera, as well as fractured five new ones. He'd been on bed rest beside Eli for a long time.

"I want to go now," Penelope whispered. "And I want to go home after." She dropped her head against Eli's shoulder.

Tam's heart swelled.

Ever since Eli had woken following her own injuries, Penelope had been incredibly attached and affectionate toward her. As she increasingly relied on Tam and Eli, she seemed more like a regular child.

"We can do that. We'll go home afterward and have lunch there. Tam? Mind taking us over to them?" Eli added, leaning her head back to peer up at him while gently resting a hand on the side of Penelope's hair.

Tam nodded with a close-lipped smile. Penelope wasn't the only one who had become more affectionate. Eli had started doting more on the kids, though it was mainly through her actions. It made for a funny comparison with her stiff manner of speaking.

When he'd wheeled Eli over to where Dena Julian stood, her arms around two of her other children, a young man and a daughter, she looked up. Her bleary gaze didn't seem to really see them.

Slowly, Penelope pushed herself off Eli's lap, and on legs that visibly trembled, she approached the woman.

"Uncle Thomas... Thomas," she began, her voice quiet. "He helped take care of me when I lived in Troivack. I... I knew him f-for my whole life. He always talked about you."

Dena Julian's eyes homed in on Penelope, the mists in them clearing as they widened.

"He described everyone. And he would... He would tell me stories." Tears audibly choked Penelope, prompting Eli to reach out and give her arm a gentle touch. "I heard about his father, who was a b-brave, strong knight. And... And his amazing mother. He missed you all a lot."

Dena's husband drifted over to his wife's side as he, too, listened to Penelope's every word. It was as though with every sentence she spoke, she was bringing specks of light to them in complete darkness.

"The last time that we… that Thomas and I talked, he asked me to say this to the duchess or my dad, but he wanted that because he wanted them to tell you the message." Penelope finished before wiping at her face.

Tam felt his back straighten. He hadn't known anything about this. He pulled out a black silk handkerchief and leaned over to hand it to Penelope. Her small hands reached up and gently took it from him from over her shoulder. After hastily blowing her nose, she continued.

"He said, 'It's all for my family. I wanted to make everyone pr-proud. I wanted to-to show my father, and other men like me, that I didn't need to be a knight, or good at fighting… to save the world.'" Penelope's words were hard to discern by the end as she crumbled before her friend's family.

Thomas's father choked. His large hand came up to cover his mouth as his knees bent and took him to the ground. "That idiot," he managed. "I always knew that. I always knew he was just as brave. Just as strong. I never told him otherwise."

Penelope took a single step forward. "He said you were the best knight and he… he always wanted to be just like you. And that his mother… He wanted her to… to not feel bad, because he was stronger than she knew."

Tam couldn't stand it any longer. He rounded Eli's wheelchair and crouched beside Penelope, pressing a reassuring hand to her back.

"Thank you." The weak words came from Dena as she lay a hand on her husband's shaking shoulder. She offered Penelope the barest of smiles. "I… We… I am glad he missed and loved us. And I am glad he had a friend like you when he couldn't be with us."

That was all Penelope could take. She lowered her chin, turned to Tam, and buried her face in his shoulder as she cried. Hugging her, Tam rose to his feet and bowed to the family.

"I owe your son everything. Thank you for raising one of the best men I've ever met."

Nothing else could be said. Nothing else *needed* to be said. The family knew how Tam felt. They had spoken at great length before that day. Right then, they needed to be alone with one another. So without another word, Tam nodded to his sister. Kat nodded back and stepped over to help with Eli's wheelchair as Tam carried Penelope to where Luca and the three princes stood.

Luca instantly took Tam's free hand. With the Ashowans gradually gathering together once more, they all turned and headed back to the carriages that sat waiting for them.

The world was going to become a more peaceful place going forward, but that didn't mean there wasn't a price. And so they left behind the poor souls who were the ones to pay it.

Tam rubbed his neck wearily as he walked the castle hall. He couldn't stop the yawn that claimed him, nor did he see a point.

It was dark outside, and he was on his way to check that Luca and the princes were ready for bed. Penelope was going to stay in the same bed as Eli for the night. Tam was relegated to another spare room that evening, and said room was conveniently near the boys' bedroom.

He glanced outside the castle arches overlooking the courtyard as a cold wind whisked through, biting at his ears. The faint aroma of smoke rose from the many fires that burned in the castle, all of them working valiantly against the late-fall cold. Tam was grateful for his winter cloak.

In a matter of a fortnight, they could even see the first snow of the season…

The rise of voices from one of the nearby chambers pulled Tam's attention back to the task at hand.

He was already preparing the gentle reprimand about how the boys should have already been asleep as he nodded at the guards and fitted his thumb over the latch. However, just as he pushed the door open a crack, he stopped himself as the words spoken registered.

"Feelings don't have to make sense," Luca said.

Tam couldn't see anything in the room, but he heard Antony's reply. "But I know Charlie didn't do anything wrong. I don't mean to be angry at him!"

Tam felt his heart sink a little.

The negotiations with the covens, council, and Zinferan representatives had recently broached the topic of there being a wider distribution of power within a government. The question of whether or not Antony would have a leading role in it—and if so, in what capacity—had continued to be a point of discussion. Though from the sounds of things, Charlie was most likely to be named the heir to the Daxarian throne.

"But it makes sense that you feel angry. It doesn't feel fair. It's hard," Luca responded quietly.

"Yeah, but… I… I know it's just because I might end up representing the coven instead!" Antony exclaimed.

"Doesn't mean you can't feel mad," Luca countered. "Just like Charlie can still feel bad even though bad things aren't always happening."

"But I don't want to feel angry." Antony's defeated response made Tam's hand fall away from the door handle. His poor nephews were lost amid the chaos of everything that was happening. Their futures and their roles in it were uncertain.

"One day you won't. Maybe one day you just stop. Maybe one day you think of something and it helps. I used to get angry at mean customers back when I lived at the tavern. My other mom used to say they weren't worth getting mad about, but I still felt mad. But I've already stopped caring about them anymore."

"I want to stop feeling bad now, though," Antony said dejectedly.

Tam didn't hear Luca respond, but he heard some rustling as though someone had moved.

"Sometimes we just have to wait. But I'm here to help! And Asher and Charlie are, too. We can all try to wait together, and maybe we can keep trying to all feel better."

Tam swallowed with difficulty as pride swelled in his chest over his son's words.

He glanced at the guards and found that the one at his left was wearing a half smile and even gave a nod of understanding to him.

Letting out a quiet breath, Tam knocked loudly, then pushed open the door the rest of the way.

"Alright, monsters, bedtime!" he shouted jubilantly, hoping to help spark a happier atmosphere.

Then Tam took in the sight before him and faltered.

All of the boys sat in front of the hearth, circling a candle. Their beds sat empty, though they all wore their night pants and tunics.

Upon seeing his father, Luca's face broke out in a wide grin. He bounced up to his feet and darted over to him, throwing his arms around his hips.

Tam ruffled his son's hair and looked at his three nephews. "What's happening here?"

"It's a secret!" Asher announced importantly while lifting his chin.

Tam chuckled. "I see. Well. Just make sure you don't get wax on that carpet or Hannah will have a fit."

The boys all nodded seriously. They knew Hannah's temper was not to be trifled with.

"Now, as curious as I am about your secret meeting, it *is* time we all went to bed. Eli and Penelope are together tonight, so I'll be just a couple doors down from you all," Tam said while Luca released him and sidled back over to his cousins.

"Dad?" Luca asked suddenly.

Another yawn stretched Tam's mouth wide, which in turn made Antony and Charlie yawn. "Mm?"

"Are we... Are we going to live in the castle forever?"

Tam balked. He hadn't really been planning on having that conversation for a little while yet.

"Ah. Well... After all the excitement that has happened, your aunt needs my help to settle a few things, and we also need to talk with people about what is going to happen with witches and the two kingdoms. And it's good for Eli to be here with the physician given how things are with the baby."

"Oh..."

"So, after our new cousin is born, you're going to leave?" Charlie asked, his somber golden gaze finding Tam's.

Tam let out a long breath and gestured for the boys to head over to the beds. Begrudgingly they all rose and sidled over.

"I don't know what will happen. What we are looking to do is start assigning heads of government, which will diminish the power the king and queen have, but will also ideally help manage things. The covens are talking about trying the same method. In other words, there is a lot of work to do. So... here is what I *think* will happen." Tam paused his response as he slowly tucked the boys in. "I think Eli, Luca, Penelope, and I will have a place of our own that we move to shortly after the baby is born. *But,* unlike the old plan for your parents to move to Sorlia and me to stay here in Austice, for the foreseeable future, we will live close by and see you often."

The end of his speech was met with four visibly confused faces. He hadn't even mentioned how the king's council had only just recently decided that the punishment for taking the castle into the void would be an outrageous fine paid to the monarchy. Not that he cared. They had managed to prove the devil's fate had made him act out of character, which negated the threat of him being tossed into a cell.

He let out a breath and shortened his answer. "Right. You will see us all the time, but after the baby comes, we won't live in the same castle with you anymore."

"Oh."

"Aw."

"But we like Luca and Penelope being here!"

"We have to guard the new baby together!"

The four responses that came brought a smile to Tam's face. The last one in particular, which had come from Asher.

"I'm glad you all are getting along. But don't worry. You will have lots of time to be together before that happens, and even after, we most likely will stay overnight at the castle on special occasions."

The boys seemed moderately placated with that assurance, and so Tam continued to busy himself snuffing out the candles, until only the one at Luca's bedside remained lit.

"Dad?"

"Yeah?"

"Are you and Eli ever going to get married, or is my new sister going to be a bastard like me?"

Tam's jaw dropped. "Oh… Gods. We are talking about *that* in the morning. Good night, Luca, boys, I love you all, and Luca? Please don't use the word *bastard* to describe yourself, or your sister, again."

"'Night!"

"'Night, Uncle Tam!"

"'Night, Dad!"

"Don't let the bedbugs bite!"

Tam was halfway to the door when Asher's final send-off reached him, making him pause and slowly turn back around. "Asher. Do not. And I am dead serious about this. Do *not* use your magic to bring bedbugs into any home *ever*."

"Okay."

The tone with which Asher's assent was given did not sound convincing.

"Asher. Did you already bring bedbugs into this castle?"

"… Nooo."

Tam dropped his face into his hand.

"Asher. You have to tell every single bedbug to leave the castle. Right now."

"But they're really friendly!"

"No. No they are not."

Tam wondered if he should look into finding a place for Eli and their family sooner than later. As he suspected, his plans for going to bed soon were promptly dashed. But at least none of his children were bug witches.

CHAPTER 54

A BROTHERLY BECKONING

"Alright. Asher has sworn to at least five different people he will never bring bedbugs inside ever again. Antony is helping Luca learn the sword, and both Charlie and Penelope are studying together." Tam closed the door to the Austice castle library behind himself as he spoke without looking at the lone occupant in the room. "Eli just went for a nap, and I am going to sit with a cup of coffee and read my book. So Kat, don't even think about—"

"Hi, Tam."

Tam jolted and swung around to find Eric standing in front of the couches with one hand stowed in his pocket. He was clean-shaven, and his curling dirty-blond hair freshly washed. He wore a loose white tunic, with a long dark-brown velour coat to stave off the draft of the room, and tan pants.

Tam gaped at the king, then scanned the room to see if his sister or any other council members were present.

"Mind taking a seat so we can talk?" Eric asked while giving a halfhearted gesture at the couches behind himself.

Tam didn't move. "Uh. I would, Your Majesty, but my sister sent a message saying—"

"She sent it so you'd meet with me. You've been dodging me for a few weeks now."

Tam's cheek twitched as he fought off a grimace. "I haven't…"

Eric raised his eyebrows, his disbelief apparent.

Sighing in defeat and reaching up to rub the back of his neck, Tam averted his gaze. "Do we have to?"

Eric made a similar sound. "Probably."

Dragging his feet, Tam made his way over to the leather couch, while Eric meandered to the opposite one and plunked himself down. There was no kingly aura about him in that moment, signaling that this would undoubtedly be a more personal conversation.

"Do you want me to call for Hannah to get you some coffee?" Eric offered awkwardly once they'd both settled.

Tam shook his head and pressed his lips together.

Eric nodded solemnly. "Alright."

Silence bloomed between them.

"I—"

"Would—"

They both spoke at once, but Tam clamped his mouth shut again and gestured for Eric to take the lead.

The king dropped his chin for a moment, then leaned forward and placed his elbows on his knees with his hands loosely clasped. "I have had a lot of troubles trusting you because you work closely with your mother, and, until recently, you've been secretive about absolutely everything in your life."

"The work my mother and I do serves the monarchy," Tam reminded him warily.

Eric reached up to scratch his head. "I know. When I first was married to Kat, she and I had a few discussions on whether or not I wanted the duchess to stop doing that kind of thing altogether."

Tam blinked. He hadn't known that, but it wasn't a surprise.

"You see…" Eric continued, pushing himself up to lean back into the couch, his gaze turning to the crackling fireplace. "I wasn't ever told about the work your mother did for my parents. I found out about it on my own in a pretty awful way. Back when I was missing, I had started questioning a lot of things I knew about your father because I was angry with him. So all the sketchy businesses and deals with felons connected with your family seemed really duplicitous. And because I only ever learned things by dragging them out of your mother and making my own inquiries and deductions, it has been really difficult building any sort of genuine trust with her."

Tam said nothing, but he did fold his hands together in an effort to warm them. He moderately regretted turning down the coffee. Once again he was hearing things that weren't a surprise, but he hadn't heard of before.

"I knew even less about you because you didn't really talk much, and no one knew you. Even Kat, as much as I know you two care about each other, doesn't have a full understanding of you, either."

Tam tilted his head in acknowledgment of that point.

"I admit, I did not go into getting to know you with an open mind. So over the past few years I know we've danced around each other. The most revealing bit about your nature was seeing you with my boys. Though to be honest, Kat and I had our fair share of arguments about that. I just… Again. Didn't feel like I knew you. And to let your children be around someone that you only really knew was involved in shady business…" Eric trailed off.

Tam looked at the rug beneath his boots. It was a mix of red and blue with beige and leafy vines.

He tried to imagine letting someone like that be around Luca or Penelope… and found that understanding Eric's side was a little easier than it had been in the past.

"I take it my father's goodness was what won out in the end? Trusting that I came from at least partially good stock," Tam mused aloud.

Eric gave a breathy chuckle. "Pretty much. It was the trump card. That and all the times you bailed Kat out of trouble or saved her."

Tam bowed his head seriously at that.

"With what happened—with the first witch, and with Luca—I don't apologize for thinking what I did, because I was technically right that he was the devil, but I do apologize for not speaking with you before assuming I knew everything. Everything you've done over the years should've more than awarded you that much. Especially when Eli was in such a horrible state."

At last, Tam locked eyes with Eric.

He could see the sincerity there.

"Thank you."

Eric gave a close-lipped smile.

"I'm sorry that I didn't try to talk with you more about what had happened, either."

"I was pretty dead set against hearing anything you had to say, so I get it," Eric confessed.

"It was…" Tam paused as he worked to form the right words. "The whole thing was a mess. We were all emotional, and tired, and confused. What matters now is we can keep this in mind should we be in another high-stress situation and—"

"Communicate better, and with more trust," Eric concluded.

Tam bobbed his head in agreement. "And I'll try to be more open about myself. Though I think I should start off by stating I don't like crowds, or spending a lot of time with people. I like the quiet, I like staying home, and I like working on my own terms."

"Yeah, some of that has become really apparent. Though your life of quiet is going to end very soon with that new baby of yours on the way."

"I don't know if you remember, but I *did* spend a lot of time with your children when they were infants," Tam pointed out drily.

Eric grinned. "Oh, Tam. It is entirely different when it is your own kid, with your own wife who just had to suffer because of you."

"Well I guess it's a good thing Eli refuses to marry me until after our daughter is born."

"Believe it or not, planning a wedding after giving birth might not be the peaceful experience you imagine it to be."

"Speaking from experience?" Tam probed, knowing the answer full well.

Eric stretched out on the couch until he was fully lying down. "Not at all. But I do know the complete mess we were just having Antony. I can't imagine also having to worry about a wedding."

"You didn't seem to worry all that much about your wedding at all, so I'm not sure where you're getting this idea."

"It was still stressful because Kat and I got caught—"

"And we're done here!" Tam sprang to his feet. He really didn't want to hear the details of the scandalous behavior his sister and Eric had engaged in that resulted in their rushed elopement.

Eric laughed, and Tam swiveled his boots toward the door.

"Do me a favor and don't tell your sister I'm having a nap," Eric called when Tam was halfway to the door.

"I won't if you promise not to tell Eli I'm having coffee before dinner. She thinks it'll keep me up at night."

"Deal."

Tam waved over his shoulder and exited into the hallway.

Because of how cold the library had felt, Tam had seriously underestimated how bitter the air outside the room would be. He hunched his shoulders and decided he would head straight to the kitchens to get his brew.

All in all, the conversation with Eric hadn't been as painful as he thought it would be, and there hadn't been any accusations bandied about. It would also most likely help the royal couple smooth out the remaining bristles from their feud months ago.

Tam felt a half smile tug at his mouth. Who knew? Maybe with Eli helping things along, he and Eric were in for a decent relationship after all.

CHAPTER 55

A WILD WEDDING DAY

*E*leven months later...

Tam stared at the black cravat in his hands.

Did he really need to wear it?

His eyes narrowed on the fine black coat hanging on the spindle of the full-length mirror, then drifted over to the window. There wasn't a cloud in the sky, and the sun was warm. It wasn't even the hottest point of the day and Tam already felt perfectly comfortable in his white tunic, black vest, and pants.

He shrugged and regarded his reflection one more time.

His beard was trimmed close to his face, and his hair was shorter than it had been in months, prompting him to run a hand through it to make sure it lay as it should.

He turned his face to inspect his right cheek and neck, where three long black lines were mostly hidden under his beard. They were the residual marks of where Death had laid his hands on him in the Forest of the Afterlife. The ropy scar where he had cut his throat was on the other side.

The call of a chickadee off in the trees pulled Tam's attention back to the window with a smile.

It really was an idyllic day.

With a final satisfied glance at his reflection, Tam turned to the rest of his chamber. It was smaller than his chamber back in Austice, but it was cozy. Four peaked windows overlooked the rolling green fields and forests that surrounded the keep on two walls. The furniture sported an assortment of colored velvet fabrics, while the walls were decked with a Zinferan-style tapestry of the former empress in her red dress overlooking the ocean, and a Daxarian depiction of the Gods.

Well, better go see if I can be of use somewhere.

Tam crossed the room, his steps light. Upon opening the door to leave, he found himself staring down at his sister. Her golden eyes blinked wide, and her fist remained suspended in the air.

The siblings stared at each other blankly, both caught off guard.

"Were you about to knock?" Tam chuckled while taking in the burnt-orange dress his sister had donned that, without sleeves, would've been too cold for most other women to wear that time of year.

She dropped her hand, her expression sardonic. "I don't know how you're processing a day like today—and I don't want to know!" she added sharply.

Tam's eyes wound up to the ceiling.

"Oh, sure. Roll your eyes all you want, but after walking in on you and Eli that one time, I don't ever want to see your bare arse again."

Tam opened and closed his mouth with a grimace at the reminder of the unfortunate day she was referring to only a fortnight ago.

"Well, if you're finally knocking before barging into rooms, I'm glad some good came from that nightmare," he managed, putting his hands into his pockets and leaning his shoulder against the doorway. "Is everything going alright?"

Kat gave one last shiver at the memory for good measure before brandishing a sprig of sky-blue aster flowers at him. "For when you're ready."

Tam arched an eyebrow and accepted the flowers, which had their stems tied together with an ivory ribbon, then pinned them to his vest. "I'm ready. How are things coming along outside? Need any help?"

"You're not wearing the coat or cravat? Seriously? You want to fight with Mum right before getting married?" Kat asked, her smile hinting at admiration.

"It's my wedding. I get to be comfortable," Tam answered with a shrug and a grin of his own. "Eric with the boys?"

Kat arched a brow at her brother's boldness. "Yes. And I want to thank you again for saying they can wear whatever they want. After that traumatic event with the family portrait, I wasn't sure they'd come to the wedding if you said they had to wear clothes they couldn't get dirty."

Tam ducked his head and finished exiting his room, closing the door behind himself.

The siblings proceeded down the hall to the back stone stairwell. Right before they made their left turn, Tam gazed out a window at the end of the hall that looked over the wedding setup.

He paused. "Kat… Is that—"

"We all tried to tell her not to, but I've said it before and I'll say it again, your soon-to-be wife is the most laid-back exacting woman I've ever met."

Tam snorted as he watched Eli direct their footmen and maids to adjust the long tables where they would be eating to face a different direction. Without needing to ask, Tam could already tell that she was doing this to make sure no one had the sun in their eyes during the meal.

He shook his head with a quiet chuckle and resumed descending the steps. "I should've double-checked what they were doing so she wouldn't have to worry."

"In case you haven't noticed, she likes to worry. Mum loves her for it."

Tam laughed loudly as they neared the second floor of the keep. "Did Likon and the Troivackians arrive safely?"

Kat grinned. "They did. It's really funny watching Brendan struggle with the informality of this event."

"Oh? Is that why you aren't calling him 'King' or 'Majesty' right now? To help him?"

Tam knew damn well she was already doing this not to be of any sort of help, but because she loved tormenting her brother-in-law whenever she could get away with it.

"Of course that's what I'm doing!" Kat declared while resting her hand on her chest with a beaming smile and glint of mischief in her eyes.

The siblings touched down on the first floor and took a left to exit onto the back lawn of the Sorlia keep Tam and Eli had moved into that spring. The library would require another year of renovations to become the dream oasis

Eli and Tam imagined, but otherwise, the rest of the keep had been decorated and set up exactly as they wished.

Kat remained in the doorway of the castle, but Tam took the opportunity to slowly creep up behind Eli. She was about to finish explaining that the cider barrels should be placed in the shade by the keep when Tam seized her from around the waist. She yelped before he tossed her over his shoulder and rounded back toward the keep.

"Sorry, everyone, but I'll send my mother down to lend a hand!" he shouted as a number of the serving staff broke out in laughter.

"Oh, for the—I was almost finished!" Eli snapped from his shoulder.

Upon reaching Kat's location once more, Tam gently tossed her off his shoulder and into his arms so he could smile down at her disgruntled expression.

"You were supposed to be having a leisurely morning while enjoying your tea. Not bossing everyone around."

"See, I even helpfully suggested that you start drinking! That would've helped you relax!" Kat contributed helpfully.

Eli gently tapped Tam's chest with the back of her hand. "Put me down."

He arched a brow at her, then obeyed.

Once her feet were back on the ground, Eli straightened the plain, loose cotton dress she had clearly thrown on just to be decent while she directed people. She then fixed both Tam and his sister with a stern look. "I have two children and an infant that I take care of every day, a household to run, and negotiations with ancient beasts to schedule. And you expect me to know what to do with myself when you take that all away from me on a day as important as this?"

Tam and Kat responded in unison. "Yes."

Though Tam went on to say, "It's called rest."

"I sleep in a comfortable bed and have leisurely meals. I rest plenty," she argued in even tones.

"Then at least have fun!" Kat burst out. "You don't want to drink, fine! Then read a book for fun! Have a cup of tea that's a little fancier than normal! Good grief, for such a thorough woman, you are downright lazy when it comes to relaxing!"

Eli rounded on the Daxarian queen, her hands landing on her hips. "*Lazy?*"

Tam was caught between wanting to break up the fight—which his sister was enjoying far too much—and laughing, but he was saved from doing either when a familiar whimper drew their attention.

Striding up to them with a beautiful black-haired baby in his arms was Finlay Ashowan. "I think this one needs a quick cuddle with her parents before her last nap," the house witch said by way of greeting.

Both Tam and Eli moved over to Fin. Eli gently took their daughter, who instantly settled into her arms, then reached a hand out to Tam, prompting him to gently pat her head.

"Doing alright, Nova?" he asked while taking stock of her bright-blue eyes, glimmering with tears.

His daughter laid her head against Eli's shoulder with a contented sigh. Eli kissed Nova's head and with a smile up at Tam said, "Come on. We'll put her down before I have to get ready."

Luckily Eli's previous annoyance had disappeared with the comforting presence of their five-month-old.

Tam nodded happily before looking back to his father. "Mind asking Mum to come down and direct things? Your future daughter-in-law was taking it upon herself to get everything set up."

Fin rested a hand on his chest feigning a look of hurt. "You wouldn't trust *me* to do it?"

"You two could do it together," Eli suggested as Nova grasped a lock of her long black hair and chewed on it curiously.

Fin dropped his hand with a more serious nod. "That sounds like a grand idea. Where is my beloved wife, do you think?"

The Daxarian queen leaned forward. "If I were to bet coin? I'd say fussing over the last alterations of the wedding dress, or Penelope's dress."

Everyone silently agreed. Tam and Eli retreated back inside to put their daughter down for her nap, before they'd have to part so Eli could finish preparing for the ceremony.

Once the couple was alone, Tam stole a glance at Eli, who was rubbing soothing circles on Nova's back.

"How're you feeling about today?"

She arched a brow in his direction. "Fine, and you?"

Tam grinned. "Oh. Glad you're not feeling too badly about marrying me. I'm doing fantastically, thank you for asking."

Eli made an irritated noise in the back of her throat. "Tam. Despite this being a small wedding, we still have two sets of royalty attending, a former king, a man in his nineties who insists on taking all of his clothes off when he dances—"

"Lord Dick Fuks promised me he'd stay mostly clothed!"

"He can barely remember my name, so I don't have high hopes for that promise."

Tam pressed his lips shut.

"And all of this before we even mention the fact there is also going to be a dragon in attendance, and—"

"I thought it was a Daxarian custom for the groom not to see the bride before the wedding ceremony?"

Eli and Tam turned to find themselves staring at two familiar smiling faces.

"Bong! Jeong!" Tam exclaimed jubilantly. "I didn't think you'd be able to make it!" He proceeded to pull Jeong then Bong into a hug, before they did the same for Eli and complimented their beautiful new family addition.

"And where is our dear Mr. Luca?" Jeong asked, his bright smile bringing a glow to his face.

"He's with his cousins. They've become inseparable," Tam explained. "Though that isn't always a good thing. They are far too good at finding trouble when—"

A series of shouts echoed down to the group.

The adults and even Nova fell silent as they all turned toward the front entrance.

With a wordless shared look among them, they headed down the hall toward the noise until they all stepped into the wide entryway already crowded with guests and serving staff. They were still able to spot what was causing the commotion rather quickly.

There, in the middle of the room, stood Harold the donkey. He was fully decked out with a flower crown woven together with blue, ivory, and yellow ribbons, blooms tied to his tail with a yellow bow, and even flower circlets just above his hooves.

In a line in front of the ass, six children stood with their backs to Tam and the others, their postures indicating a sense of accomplishment.

On one end was the tall, lanky form of Aster Fuks; then the smaller willowy figure of Antony, with his short red hair; beside him, with his mop of dirty-blond curls, was Charlie. Then there was Luca, tall, with his black hair already styled and slicked back, and beside him was Penelope, with her hair in an elegant braid layered with flowers, wearing an ivory lace dress with a light-blue ribbon about her waist. Lastly, there was Asher, with his longer red hair in a short braid.

The guests in the room continued to clamber away from Harold, who surveyed the surroundings with a beleaguered weariness.

Tam folded his arms and cleared his throat loudly. Each child turned slowly. Tam stared at all of them with his eyebrows raised. Luca gave a wince of a smile, and Penelope pursed her lips. Tam opened his mouth to say something, but then a line of chickens, all wearing flower wreaths around their necks, bolted past.

"I see Henrietta arrived," Eli noted idly.

"Bong! Jeong!" Luca burst out, his guilt instantly forgotten when he realized the presence of his friends. He bolted over first to Jeong, throwing his arms around the man's soft middle.

"Mr. Luca! You've grown at least a foot since I saw you!" Jeong marveled, making Luca step back with a proud grin before putting his hands in his pockets in the exact same manner his father and grandfather did.

"Did we all not have a discussion about talking to a trusted adult about these kind of surprises last week?" Tam asked Antony and Luca sharply.

"Now, now, Lord Tam, all is well in hand!" Aster stepped forward, his recently lowered voice soothing. Then Tam shot him a flat look, making Aster's awkward boyish self return and prompting him to fall silent.

"I said it was fine," a new voice called over the commotion.

None other than Mr. Howard strode forward with a gleeful look on his face.

Tam crossed his arms. "Really, Kevin?"

The former king's assistant cackled while patting Harold's rump. "It isn't like the old boy can even kick anymore with his arthritis."

"You know who I'm going to have to tell?" Tam asked while rocking from the balls of his feet back to his heels.

"Oho, your father can't do anything to me now, Tam! I don't work with him anymore!" Mr. Howard looked like he could die from happiness.

A slow smile wound its way up Tam's face. "I wasn't talking about my father."

"I think my son meant *your wine supplier.*" The sharp voice of Annika Ashowan sounded from the staircase where she stood with her arms folded over her deep-purple gown. Her eyebrows rose as she stared at the former assistant, who gulped. Especially when he realized none other than Hannah was at the duchess's side, staring at him unimpressed.

The man looked dangerously close to falling onto his knees and begging forgiveness.

"Do you really not like it?" Asher asked sadly, drawing everyone's attention downward to the young prince.

Tam let out a breath and slowly knelt down in front of his nephew, whose mouth twisted in disappointment.

"Harold is fantastic, and you all outdid yourselves with dressing him up. For now, though, how about we put him in the pasture and tell people to go take a look at him during the reception?"

Asher nodded slowly, still looking a mite dejected.

Tam rested a hand atop his nephew's head. "Hey, monster. I'm not actually mad, alright? I just like tormenting Mr. Howard. Besides"—he lowered his voice—"if he realizes I love it, he might try to pull an even worse prank next time, don't you think?"

Asher brightened instantly and giggled.

Rising back up to a stand, Tam was about to announce that he and Eli needed to finish putting Nova down for her nap when a new shout echoed over them.

"FIRE LIT!"

That was all Tam needed to hear to rush out the front doors with the rest of the entryway's occupants on his heels.

He hadn't known what he'd been expecting. But Harris with his wife Mackenzie, both positioned in front of two massive blazing piles of dried kindling and logs—which most definitely had not been there that morning—along with a pleased-looking Wixim, had not occurred to him as a possibility.

"My dear daughter!" Harris roared. "Happy wedding day!"

"I'm your niece," Eli hollered back.

"I was officially named your guardian three months ago! Of course you're my daughter!"

"I'm a grown woman! It was a moot point for you to become my guardian; I just had you add me to your family for the last name!"

"Now, now." Mackenzie Harris approached Eli and Tam, who were side by side as their guests gaped at the spectacle behind them. "My dear, we adore you as our own, so why fight us on this happy day?"

Eli looked caught between a sigh and a laugh.

"Does she love it?" Harris shouted from his place—a bit too close to the fire—with his arms outstretched.

"She loves it!" Mackenzie called back over her shoulder to her husband.

Harris dropped his head back with a smile of unbridled joy.

Eli and Tam were spared from having to say anything more as Nova let out a sniffle and then an earsplitting cry.

No excuses were needed as they retreated back past the guests up to the second floor of the keep, which was significantly less chaotic.

Once the quiet enveloped them, Tam and Eli locked eyes, then let out long breaths.

"See… This is great. Neither of us has to create a diversion or bring up any awkward topics to leave early—we have a baby for that now!" Tam pointed out while winking at their infant daughter.

Eli gave her first real laugh of the morning. "You're absolutely right. Good thing you said we can start trying for our next one after today. That way we'll keep having an excuse for years."

Tam sighed happily and wrapped his arm around Eli. "Sounds like a good plan to me."

CHAPTER 56

THE END OF EVERYTHING

Music wafted through the open window of the sitting room that Tam waited in. He watched guests find their seats in front of the arch covered in white and blue flowers while the backdrop of the forest added brilliant shades of red, orange, and yellow to the scene.

He let out a long, steadying breath.

"Nervous?"

Tam whirled around and received yet another pleasant surprise for the day. "Likon!" His face broke out into a smile as he embraced the man whom his parents had adopted when they were children. "Gods, am I glad to see you!"

"You think I'd miss seeing you become some other assistant's problem? Not a chance. I'm shocked you aren't holed up in here doing paperwork." He guffawed after thumping Tam on his back and stepping away.

Likon's brown eyes roved over Tam's casual appearance, then he glanced down at his own forest-green velour coat, tan pants, and polished brown boots. "And here the duchess made it sound like I was the underdressed one."

Tam snorted. "So… are you here with Lady Dana?"

Likon flushed then narrowed his eyes. "You're more like your mother than you realize, you know that?"

Tam grinned shamelessly. "I just want to start working on travel plans in advance! I've got a few kids to take care of now."

"Dad?"

As though he'd just heard his father's comment, Luca appeared with Penelope at his side.

"Hey, Luca, Penelope, did you say hi to your Uncle Likon?"

Luca waved with a sunny smile, while Penelope shifted awkwardly before issuing a curtsy. She still was feeling a little uncomfortable with his relation to Thomas Julian.

Seeing this, Likon exchanged a look with Tam, then crouched to be eye level with the little girl. "I'm glad to see you, Penelope. You're looking more and more like the duchess every time I see you."

Penelope blushed and sidled over to Tam, taking his hand.

"Dad, Grandma says you should start heading over to the back door. Eli said we should start."

Tam's heart fluttered.

"Ready to get married?" Likon asked playfully.

"He's been bugging Eli about it for long enough," Penelope contributed under her breath.

Likon burst out laughing. "I guess we'd better let him get on with it before she changes her mind, eh?"

Penelope issued a shy smile.

Likon looked up at Tam once more, his gaze more peaceful than it had been in years. "Good luck, Tam."

Tam bobbed his head in appreciation. "You too. I think I already saw my mother speaking with Lady Dana about some future plans."

Likon blanched, cursed, then darted out of the room. Most likely to try to quell whatever cunning plan the duchess had already set into motion.

Chuckling, Tam dropped his attention to the children at his sides. "You two ready to have married parents?"

Penelope shrugged in response, while Luca pondered this. "It doesn't really change anything, right?"

Tam tilted his head. "Not much. But legally it will."

Luca sighed. "Does that mean you and Mom have *more* paperwork to do?"

Tam barely suppressed a snort of laughter as he and the children exited out into the corridor. "Just a tiny bit, but I bet you won't even notice when we do it."

Luca dropped his head back with a loud groan.

"Hey, you two," Tam called out as he approached the doorway where his parents stood waiting, along with Kat and her three boys at her side.

Luca and Penelope turned to look up at him.

"Thank you for being my kids. I'm the luckiest dad in the world."

Luca beamed and Penelope rolled her eyes, but Tam saw the blush on her face.

"You're the best dad!" Luca informed him brightly before giving Penelope a light push. "Say something nice!"

The little girl scowled at Luca, but eventually turned and stared up at Tam, though she did quickly look away as her nerves visibly got the best of her.

Tam had to strain to hear her next words. "I'm glad that you… you and Eli are my family."

Tam bent down to lock eyes with her.

"I'm glad of that, too. Now I should probably hurry before your sister starts crying."

Rising again, Tam sent the kids off to Kat, who winked in his direction and then hastily ushered them down the aisle to their seats.

Tam heard the music shift from its quick beat to something beautiful and slow as he looked to his parents.

His father was already misty-eyed, while his mother smiled warmly… until her sights landed on his throat, where there was no cravat, and then on his rolled-up white sleeves.

She raised an eyebrow.

Tam mirrored her expression, waiting for her to say something.

She merely sighed and shook her head, her smile no less loving as she held out her hand. "Come along, you."

Grinning, Tam laced his arm through his mother's, then felt his father's arm loop through on his other side.

"Thank you for keeping your promise, Tam," Fin murmured as they walked down the stone steps and stepped out onto the grass.

"I keep my promises. You know that."

"Mm-hm. I appreciate the twist of three children before the wedding," Fin added wryly.

"Would I be an Ashowan if there wasn't just a bit of madness?"

Annika gave a breathy laugh.

The trio made their way down the aisle, smiling at the many friendly faces that stared up at them. People they'd known and loved through the years. People they had helped, and who had helped them. It made Tam's heart fill to the brim with gratitude—and also awkwardness. It was weird being stared at so much.

Upon reaching the arch where Eric Reyes waited, Tam turned to his father and embraced him. When they pulled apart, tears were falling down Fin's face, and the smile he bore looked ready to split his face. Tam then faced his mother and was moderately taken aback to find that she, too, was teary-eyed.

She reached up and gently touched his cheek before leaning forward, brushing a kiss on his cheek, and whispering. "I love you, my son."

"I love you, too, Mum."

And they parted.

Tam took the final few steps to take his place in front of the king, sharing a brief nod with Eric, then rounding back to look at the keep.

The back doorway was still dark… until the music changed once more.

Then Harris appeared with Eli on his arm.

Tam forgot to breathe.

Eli wore a red gown. The straps were off her shoulders, exposing her collarbone, and they ran down into the layers of her skirt that trailed on the ground below the fitted bodice.

In Eli's hands was a bouquet of white wildflowers. Her hair was down and treated to a shine as it waved over her right shoulder. Her lips matched her dress, elegant lines were drawn over her eyes, and she wore only delicate pieces of gold in her ears and necklace.

Tam felt whole, and the world, with her in it, looking at him with a coy yet shy smile, was perfect.

When Harris reached Tam, and Tam fumbled for Eli's hands, the duke leaned forward, stopping him.

"You could have a dozen children, and I would still burn you at the stake if you hurt her."

There may have been a smile on Harris's face, but Tam could tell the threat was genuine.

"Makes sense."

Harris's smile widened as he then passed Eli's hand to Tam.

"Dad!"

Tam and Eli looked over where Luca had loudly whispered, "Remember to compliment her this time!"

Everyone burst out laughing.

However, Tam still tugged Eli closer. "I *was* going to remember, believe it or not. You look stunning."

Eli blushed and cleared her throat, then lifted her chin gracefully and looked at Eric, who quirked his eyebrows at her once in a teasing manner. "Weren't you supposed to be watching the children earlier?" she suddenly said.

"Eli," Tam whispered. "We're kind of in the middle of something right now."

Eric was already looking away guiltily. "I thought I could nap a bit before. They've been well behaved lately, so—"

A fuzzy black paw shot out from behind Eli, swatting Eric's knee.

Tam hadn't even noticed Kraken sitting behind Eli thanks to her skirts. But there he was, a crisp ribbon tied at his throat, glaring up at Eric.

Eric sighed and nodded at the feline before lifting his sights to the couple, then the guests.

"Everyone, we all know why we're here. It's to see the new ancient beast advocate," the king said, nodding at Eli, "and the new diplomat to witches," he added, indicating Tam, "get married at long bloody last!"

The crowd broke out in cheers and whoops.

"Given that close friends and family are here—and Tam isn't even wearing a cravat—"

"Oy—" Tam's exclamation was cut off as the king continued.

"—We all know this isn't going to be the usual formal affair. Lord Tamlin Ashowan, viscount of House Jenoure, and future duke of House Ashowan, and Lady Elisara Harris: Do you take each other to be lawfully wedded spouses in sickness and in health, in times of great fortune and times of poverty, in times of conflict and times of peace? To be loyal to each other and respect each other to the very best of your ability until death do you part?"

"And beyond," both Tam and Eli responded in unison.

Eric nodded appreciatively.

"Wonderful. Now, we have a small bit of paperwork to sign over here, and then we will—"

"ELISARA!"

Everyone turned at the bellowing voice. A Zinferan man stalked down the aisle. His long hair flew about untidily. His demented gaze fixed on Eli as he barreled down toward the couple.

Evidently it didn't matter that the golden dragon curled up on the lawn a short distance away was lifting its great head with narrowed eyes; the man continued surging toward Eli.

With a frown, Tam realized that it was none other than Yun Shik. Eli's brother's assistant, who had wanted to marry Eli himself…

Just as Tam was about to step forward to deal with this intruder, Luca leapt out of his seat and shouted, "FAMILY JEWELS!"

He punched Yun Shik right in the groin, dropping him to the ground faster than a sack of rocks.

Caught by surprise, Tam watched dumbly as Penelope joined Luca's side, followed by the three princes, Aster Fuks, and Kat.

"Go do your paperwork, Dad!" Luca hollered before dropping his dark gaze to Yun Shik, who lay whimpering on the ground. "We'll deal with him."

Tam opened his mouth to object, but Kat made a waving motion while rising from her own seat. She then stooped down and slung Yun Shik over her shoulders while murmuring something to Luca, who responded seriously. Most likely he was informing her who this strange person was.

At a loss, Tam looked at Eli, who turned back to Eric. The king's mouth was pressed into a thin line as he watched his sons follow their mother while she carted off someone his nephew had just punched in the testicles.

Tam stole a lone glance at Harris, who appeared perfectly proud as he sat with his legs stretched out and crossed at the ankles. His wife stared at his profile suspiciously.

After a long breath, with a very flat tone, the king waved to a small round table that had been set up off to the side. "Right… Off you go… I guess…"

Tam cleared his throat, then offered his hand to Eli. They proceeded over to the table and signed the marital contract and the paperwork for Eli to take on her new noble title as viscountess. Though they both kept stealing glances across the lawn toward the edge of their keep where Kat had disappeared with the entourage of children. Just as Tam and Eli were finishing up, the small group returned—without Yun Shik—and reclaimed their seats as though nothing had happened.

With the paperwork signed and finished, Tam and Eli returned to Eric, who was already sharing a questioning look with his wife.

With Tam and Eli blocking his sightline, however, Eric snapped his attention back to them.

"I think the only thing left to say is that we all wish you years of happiness, and we hope that you both enjoy your well-deserved peace. Now… you may kiss as a symbol of your agreed-upon vows."

Tam turned his smile to Eli and didn't waste time cupping her face in his hand. He kissed her with every ounce of love, desire, and giddy emotion he carried in him. The crowd erupted in applause, whistles, and cheers.

Upon breaking apart, Tam searched her eyes, which met his with open adoration.

"So… if Hannah is watching Nova for us, do you think I'll need to set myself on fire to get you to myself?"

Eli laughed and didn't dignify his absurd question with an answer as they turned and retreated down the aisle, hand in hand, to start celebrating.

Kat and Eric listened with undisguised disbelief when they heard how, despite the fact that Eli's birth family had been stripped of their titles following Pina's rise to the throne, Yun Shik had grown obsessive about being with Elisara. He had come to Daxaria with the muddled plan of stealing her from Tam.

Brendan Devark, Troivack's king, had managed to persuade the wedding intruder to explain his actions, and was, at present, relaying his findings to the newlyweds and the Daxarian rulers, as well as his own wife and queen, Alina Devark.

"Good Gods, you must have made one hell of a good impression," Kat said with a snort in Eli's direction before tilting her goblet into her mouth.

Eli rolled her eyes and took a sip from her own tankard.

"You know… since this affair is more of a laid-back sort," Kat began, with a forced air of innocence that had Eric looking at her suspiciously and Brendan Devark warily. "How about we start playing some drinking games? No one is pregnant, everyone is together, and we have a bloody dragon guarding us!"

Tam expected Eli to object or to say that she wanted to stay present for the other guests, who were already imbibing quite heavily. Though most of those guests surrounded his parents at the tables that were covered corner-to-corner with the wedding feast that the house witch himself had cooked.

"You know, come to think of it… I've never seen Tam drunk." Eli turned slowly to look up at her husband.

"*What?*" Kat squawked. "This is an abomination! How could you have married him without knowing what he's like drunk?"

Tam regarded the Troivackian king and queen, who normally were quite helpful with adding a note of seriousness, only to find that the two were looking all too intrigued at the notion.

"I feel like I might be in danger," Tam said, only half jesting.

Kat was already craning her neck. "Where's Likon? He's the best at getting Tam drunk."

"Excuse me, would you be able to bring Lord Tam a bottle of moonshine and some extra goblets?" Alina asked one of the passing footmen.

Tam looked down at his new wife questioningly. "Is this really what you want to see? My stumbling around to everyone talking about how much I love you?"

Eli gazed up at him serenely. "Yes."

Laughing, Tam dropped a kiss on her head and wrapped an arm around her shoulders. "I guess that settles it. Shall we all go sit so you can enjoy my disgrace comfortably? I think Bong and Jeong are waving us over."

Kat and Alina grinned, and Eli gave a dignified inclination of her head as they all headed across the lawn to one of the tables. Over the music, Eli heard the shouts and laughter of the children playing with a leather ball off in the distance.

As they walked, the smells of roasted meats and baked sweets wafted over to them in the air. The setting sun cast the world in a beautiful glow. Tam silently thanked the Gods that he had found what meant everything to him where nothing else mattered. He had found his place with his family, his wife and familiar, his children, his magic… What more could an ether witch ask for?

"Alright!" Kat roared. "Time for truth or guts!"

EPILOGUE 1

THE NICETIES OF NORMALITY

Seated at the round table in the grand council room of Sorlia's castle, Eli bounced Nova on her knee, making her daughter coo happily.

Despite this, however, her attention remained fixed on a scene on the opposite side of the bright, round room.

"My da and Mr. Howard still at it?" Tam's voice sounded in Eli's ear.

She nodded without taking her sights off Mr. Howard, who was clutching his hair and saying something to the house witch, who had his arms folded and a grin on his face.

Tam sighed. "That will probably go on for a while yet. Ready to head home?"

Eli rose from her seat, her gaze at last pulling free of the two older men taunting each other like mischievous youths.

"Almost. Would you be able to take Nova for a while? The coven sent over the book on the red thread theory."

Tam accepted his daughter into his arms easily, his eyebrows rising. "Really? They're finally cooperating?"

Eli huffed. "In their defense, their entire council was overhauled. The new curator of the records barely knows which end to open a book."

Tam lowered his face and shot her a look that said, *Was that not a bit harsh?*

Eli emitted a faint grumble in response.

With a knowing chuckle, Tam shifted Nova in his arms as she wriggled with dissatisfaction over being still. "Well, the school is almost built, so hopefully things will start to be more organized going forward."

Eli's mouth twisted. She wasn't at all convinced. Any new establishment— especially one that had not existed before—was going to take a while to function reliably. She expected this would be especially difficult since witches had not been given an annexed land or temples to command, but instead three representative witches to participate on the king's council, as well as schools with expansive grounds for their students to live with their families should their abilities need to be trained in a safe supportive environment. In other words, a community. The matter of what positions witches held in society was still being discussed, but that would take time. Tam, assuming his father's role as diplomat, was the negotiator between the three witches, and the rest of the king's council.

The schools would be run at the discretion of witches, save for the subjects of history, law, the representation of ancient beasts, humans and witches, and the Daxarian government—which was itself going through an overhaul of power distribution. That said, if the students or staff broke any core rules of Daxaria pertaining to harming individuals, treason, and so on, they would still be held to the law.

There were talks of merging the mage school with the witch school like Troivack was doing, but that was not accepted by the remaining coven members.

"I'll wait for you," Tam informed Eli, breaking through her thoughts.

Blinking herself back to the present, she straightened her shoulders. "No, no. Please head home. Remember, Harris has been alone with their own sons, Luca, and Penelope all day."

Tam blanched at the reminder.

Thus far, the extended stay of the duke and his family had gone relatively well, save for a few incidents. Three out of five had involved fire.

"Right. I'll get home, but try not to take too long," Tam added before dropping a kiss onto her head. "There's only so much common sense I can implement without you."

Eli gave a dry smile, another nod, and proceeded out of the council room, inclining her head subtly to a few of the other noblemen and councilors she passed.

As she walked down the corridor in the direction of the king's office, her eyes drifted thoughtfully to the black-and-white-tiled floors. It felt as though she hadn't had a chance to catch her breath in the two months since their marriage, thanks to the glut of work she had taken on.

Upon reaching the pale wood of the ornate double doors leading to the king's office, Eli informed the guards of her intention to speak with Eric. They knocked and announced her presence, and she was instantly waved through the door. She was surprised to find Eric alone behind his desk, with his assistant Morgan Linsey nowhere to be found.

"Ah. Eli, I didn't mean to make you stay late," Eric called while rising from his seat. He reached to his side and picked up a hickory-colored leather book with aged, uneven page edges. "You could've picked this up tomorrow."

"I've been waiting for this book for months," she said by way of explanation.

Eric tilted his head. "That you have. While you're here, how are the curriculum discussions going with the witches?"

Eli grimaced. She had been the one tasked with sorting out that detail with the coven members turned teachers. "The debate about the portrayal of the first witch and ancient beasts in history is ongoing."

Eric nodded somberly, his gaze falling to the book in his hands in a distracted manner as he moved around his desk and handed the tome to Eli.

"Thank you, Your Majesty," she said with a bow.

"We're alone. Just call me Eric," the king ordered with a casual wave as he turned toward the two comfortable armchairs facing each other beneath the tall glass windows.

Eli's boots shifted in the direction of the door, until another topic appeared in her mind. "Your M— Eric, have you heard any word from the Lobahlan government about Hamil and Bes?"

The king sank into the comfortable embrace of his faded emerald-green armchair with a quiet groan. "Aside from receiving verification of their return, and answering a few of the questions they sent us, I haven't."

Eli didn't mask her disappointment. Despite the less-than-amicable terms things had ended on, she wished the two Lobahlans a good life.

"I hear you and Tam will be leaving for Likon's wedding in the next fortnight," Eric brought up lightly.

Eli made her way over to the other armchair and eased herself down; she sensed their conversation would carry on a mite longer than she had expected.

"Yes. Though I confess, I'd hoped to have a bit more of a rest before we set off again," she lamented.

Eric grinned. "Harris is really enjoying having you in the family, I take it?"

"He's enjoying it far too much." Eli didn't hide her weariness. "I just want to rest at home at the end of a long day." She reached up with her left hand and rubbed soothing circles into her left temple.

"Mm-hm, and look into red string theories apparently," Eric added with a pointed look at the book in Eli's hands.

Her gaze fell down to the textured surface of the text. "Tam mentioned seeing us connected by a red thread when he was in his void, but only when I'm in beast form. Which makes sense with me being his familiar, but the theories I know of suggest that we all have multiple red threads to those with whom we share destinies and fates. So why wouldn't there be other threads he can see?"

Eric pondered this. "Perhaps it has to do with the soul. A familiar is tied to a witch's soul and so, in his void, he can only see what is tied directly to him."

Eli shrugged. "It's possible, but I'd like to find other answers. Even Kat says that when she turns her sights inward, she sees her connections with people as red threads. So, why does Tam only see the one?"

"Why is it… you only remember to refer to my wife informally?" Eric asked with a wry note.

Eli graced the king with a flat look. "Because your wife constantly acts informally, whereas you tend to at least act like a king for most of the day." She paused. "And because she would take it upon herself to be even more annoying if I didn't."

At this, the king grinned. "Fair enough."

"A soul bond…" Eli muttered to herself, her mind already becoming distracted.

She thought about the way familiars could share images and emotions with their witches. How they always came when their witches called them. It did suggest a connection of the soul. So why was the queen connected to so many people? Did it have something to do with the sharing and receiving of power?

"I can tell you are going to spend a lot of time on this," Eric noted with a brief chuckle.

Eli closed her eyes with a sigh. "My apologies. You know I don't like loose ends. Have you considered how Daxaria is going to plan for its long-term growth with the decline of witches?"

Eric balked. "Leave it to you to ask the hard questions out of nowhere."

She did not feel any form of guilt as she stared expectantly at him.

Seeing this, Eric shook his head with another laugh. "I'd like to explore the idea of magical items. Similar to the ones you claim the Lobahlans mentioned. But without any help from their government, I'm afraid we're at a loss. Kasim Jelani has also said that pressing Lobahl for answers and revealing that we know about the items will result in Bes and Hamil facing a far more severe punishment."

Eli eased back farther in her seat. It *was* a bit of a conundrum.

"So… how's married life?"

Eli arched an eyebrow. "You're just trying to get out of a serious conversation."

"Of course I am. I've been in meetings since daybreak. This is my downtime, and I haven't gotten to speak one-on-one with you in months."

Eli rolled her eyes but decided not to press the matter. "Married life is fine. It is nice to not have the wedding hanging over our heads. We can just get through work and go to bed."

Eric grinned as he fiddled with his own wedding band. "Your opinion on Tam hasn't changed since you saw him drunk at the reception?"

At the reminder of how everyone had joined forces—herself included—to see Tam inebriated, Eli's lips twitched. "Well, I now know we're more similar than I realized."

The king's smile widened. "You also get stuck in trees when sloshed?"

"Not too often, but—"

"You hoard pillows and blankets and make a fort, then bar anyone from entering?"

Eli couldn't stop a chortle. "The intention behind him building the fort was—"

"You also lock the Troivackian king in a closet on occasion?"

The last of Eli's composure crumbled as she burst out in full-blown laughter at the memory.

Tam truly had been an absolutely marvelous form of entertainment that night.

"I confess he is a lot better at leapfrog than I ever will be," she contributed, her cheeks aching.

Eric had crumbled into hysterics at the mention of the stern Troivackian king getting locked in in the linen closet. At the reminder of Tam playing the child's game with the Ryu brothers, he found himself leaning forward in his armchair and covering his eyes as he continued to laugh heartily.

When the two eventually calmed down, the king leaned back in his seat, a smile still lighting his face. "Gods… I would've aimed to get Tam absolutely skunked at every family gathering if I had known."

Eli gave another giggle while wiping an errant tear of humor from her face.

"I'm glad you're happy."

Eric's words made Eli blush as she met his sincere gaze.

She dropped her hand to her lap. "Me too. I never thought I'd be the marrying type, but… here we are."

Still smiling, the king's sights drifted over to the window as he took in a deep breath. "I'll let you get out of here. I'm sure you want to go make sure your keep is still standing. Hopefully the Harris family has left your library renovation alone."

At this suggestion, all joviality faded from Eli's face. "They'd better have left it alone. After paying all the fines to ensure Tam didn't go to prison after the castle incident, it was either the library or a honeymoon, and I don't want to see it be reduced to rubble."

Eric nodded knowingly. "Don't worry. Between your own and Tam's work ethics, I've no doubt you two will be comfortable again soon."

"He's not locked up and still has his titles. We are plenty comfortable," Eli assured him seriously.

Eric held up his hands in surrender while coming to his feet. He wouldn't try to placate a wound that did not exist.

As the pair approached the office door, the king turned to Eli just before reaching for the handle. "I'll see you at the family dinner?"

"Of course. It's the last one we'll have before Harris leaves and we depart for Troivack."

The king opened the door, allowing a swath of sunshine to pour in. "Wonderful. Charlie has some new books he wants to show Penelope, and Antony wants to practice his swordsmanship with Luca."

Eli bobbed her head.

"Sorry I didn't offer you tea," Eric added as Eli stepped back into the corridor.

She looked over her shoulder, a rueful smile lifting the corners of her mouth when she took in the king's teasing expression. "I'm grateful you didn't."

"I'll brew a good cup for you one day!" Eric announced with a jesting tone.

Shaking her head, Eli shifted the book in her hands under her arm. "Please, *Your Majesty*, I'd hate to hurt your feelings now that we're family."

With a final laugh and a wave, the two parted, and Eli continued to make her way to the castle's front entrance to ask for a carriage to take her home, only to find Tam and Nova still there waiting for her. He stood near the grand front doors, which were sixty feet from the foot of the stairs.

Despite the distance, Eli cast a questioning look at her husband.

Tam crossed the vast space between them and kissed her forehead. "I'm not going to leave my wife to ride alone when I just had to wait an hour."

"You're scared to go back and deal with the chaos alone, aren't you?" Eli guessed.

Her husband cleared his throat and feigned an innocent look while grasping her hand in his own. "Come on. Nova's getting fussy."

Their daughter was actually asleep against his shoulder and drooling quite happily.

Smiling, Eli didn't bother saying anything more on the matter. She was actually quite glad to have him with her on the journey home, as she knew they could then discuss her new book on the way without interruption. This idea alone was enough to make her mood match the beautiful evening they stepped out to find.

EPILOGUE 2

THE BOUNTY OF BOATS

In the depths of Lobahl's capital of Carha, a young man sat at his cluttered desk. His fists curled atop its surface; there were three deep scratches carved into the back of his left hand.

He squinted at the city map in front of him, then up at the sketches and notes that he had stuck on the cracked white plaster wall.

His breath shook as he tried to contain the anger that poured through his entire being.

All other sounds disappeared as he continued glaring, until his fury reached a breaking point, forcing him to smash his bleeding hand against his desk. A whirl of intense wind whipped through his room, sending his pages fluttering. Some even ripped off the walls. Yet he couldn't be brought to care. That was unusual for him, as he kept his room and appearance meticulous every other moment of the day or night.

A nervous knock sounded on the door to his cramped bedroom.

"D-Dyse… Is everything… Is everything alright?"

His fingernails dug into his palms as he stood. He stalked over to the door and threw it open.

"Fine. Everything is fine, Amelia. Sorry for the noise." Dyse knew he didn't sound calm, and his wide-eyed neighbor gave a weak smile and retreated in response. They were the same age, and yet Dyse often felt as though she were significantly younger than his own twenty-four years.

"O-okay, I'm going back to the school for the evening. S-sorry if I wake you up when I come back in."

Dyse forced a close-lipped smile on his face. "Don't worry about it. I'll be up late working on a homework problem for the foreseeable future."

Amelia's gaze nervously darted over his shoulder at the state of his windswept room. "What kind of homework problem?"

Dyse took a second to reply. He worked his emotions down farther into his throat so he didn't snarl his next words.

"Cats. I need to figure out how to run every cat out of Lobahl once and for all."

He watched Amelia's brown eyes widen fractionally, then blink at him.

His ire twitched in his belly, wanting to lash out at her for not having even a fraction of disdain for the creatures he loathed.

"I see… Whose class is that for?"

Dyse felt his lip curl. "I'll tell you later. Good night, Amelia."

She gave him a wary nod. "'Night, Dyse. Don't work too hard."

He closed the door firmly and stared at the pale grain for several long moments as he allowed himself to slip back into his wrath.

He didn't care what anyone thought of him. He was determined that, no matter what, he would succeed.

Even if it was the last thing he'd ever do.

"Penelope! You can't bring all of those, there's a weight limit, remember?" Eli hollered.

"Luca, they will have practice swords there, so you don't need to bring yours!" Tam called.

There was the usual response of displeasure from the children and the smattering of arguments as each parent aided a child in packing. Eventually, Tam and his family were at long last ready to board the ship leaving Austice to set sail for Troivack.

They had opted to leave from Austice as opposed to Xava in order to be able to comfortably rest at Finlay and Annika's keep following the journey from Sorlia.

Of course, the duke and duchess showered their grandchildren with gifts during their visit, resulting in the children wanting to bring along all of their new treasures—which then created the new packing conundrum.

However, with only a bit more wrangling, Eli and Tam got both Luca's and Penelope's trunks closed and ready for the voyage, then joined the others in the front entryway. Fin and Annika waited patiently by the front doors while the duchess held Nova, who gurgled happily as her husband played peekaboo.

"Alright! We are ready!" Tam announced breathily.

Annika nodded. "Wonderful. Shall we?"

The group continued out of the keep, moving toward the waiting horses and carriage. Footmen and maids bustled around them, loading their luggage.

Tam and his father first handed the ladies in, then Fin climbed in, and Tam was just about to load Luca up when his son stopped and looked up at him.

"Dad? I need to pee."

"Why didn't you go sooner?" Tam demanded, unable to hide his exasperation.

"I didn't have to go before!" Luca exclaimed, throwing his hands in the air before bolting back to the keep. "I'll be back soon!"

Tam turned and laid his forearm across the carriage's sleek black exterior before dropping his forehead and gently thumping his fist against the vehicle in frustration.

"Dad?"

Tam wearily lifted his head to see Penelope stepping cautiously out of the carriage.

"Do you also need to relieve yourself?" he guessed.

Penelope gave a curt nod, then she, too, darted off toward the keep.

Tam plopped his head to his forearm.

"It's a good thing the boat can't leave without us," Tam heard his mother say with a small laugh.

Eli poked her head out. "It's just like bedtime."

Tam managed a smile at that right as the sound of two sets of small feet crunching through the gravel drive reached his ears.

"We're back!" Luca said while jumping back into the carriage, leaving Penelope to climb after him in her usual dignified manner.

Tam clapped his hands. "Fantastic! Now we can…" Eli slowly climbed down.

They stared at each other.

"Do you also need the water closet?" he asked dazedly.

She gave a beautiful smile and patted his arm. "Be back in a moment."

When Tam thudded his head against the carriage again, he was far less gentle, and both Luca and Penelope could be heard giggling from inside.

At long, long last, the Ashowan family made it into the carriage, and all the way to the dock beside their ship. By this time, Tam felt a very strong urge to take a nap. Upon voicing this sentiment to his wife, Eli regarded him with a raised eyebrow.

"And do you think your seasickness has improved?"

Tam was silent for the span of a breath before replying. "I… I was fine the last time we sailed."

"You'd gotten used to it by then. Should I go get some ginger tea brewing?" she asked patiently.

He sighed. "Probably."

"I'll race you!"

Both Tam and Eli looked straight ahead in time to see both Penelope and Luca bolting down the dock toward the gangplank.

"DON'T RUN GETTING ON THE SHIP!" Eli roared, making both Luca and Penelope skid to a halt. Several sailors flowing around the family flinched.

The response came in unison. "Yes, Mom!"

Regardless of their contrite expressions, Eli still shot them a warning look before the two children turned and continued down the dock at a far more subdued pace.

Tam smiled down at his wife. "I've noticed since Harris and his family stayed with us, you're a lot quicker to shout."

She shot him a narrow-eyed look. He smiled and escorted her down the dock while also spotting his parents, who spoke to the captain while still holding Nova.

Gulls cried overhead and the crew bustled around them with low murmurs. A biting wind occasionally sent the ships at the docks rocking, but otherwise it was a clear, sunny day.

"Do you think we'll be able to return by Imbolsic?" Eli asked while hunkering closer to Tam as a particularly strong gust of wind froze Tam's cheeks.

"I don't know that we'll want to leave at that time," Tam confessed. "As much as I also want to get home sooner rather than later, it isn't going to be a safe or comfortable trip to make once it starts snowing."

Eli grimaced. "So… two months after Imbolsic?"

The couple reached the gangplank and began their ascent.

Tam was careful to watch his feet so as to not accidentally catch the bottom of Eli's forest-green skirt under his boot, and so he didn't get a chance to respond until they boarded the vessel. "Early springtime, yes. About four months."

Eli let out a long breath. "Well. It can't be avoided."

Tam cast a thoughtful glance down at her dejected expression. "Are you nervous to be going back to Troivack given your experience there last time?"

Eli arched her brow. "Not really. I'm curious to hear more about how they plan on peacefully mediating the witch and mage school they've started to build."

He nodded and felt a small rush of relief over hearing that she wasn't going to suffer any distress about returning to a land where she had spent time as both a slave and an indentured servant.

"Tam?"

He looked back down at Eli as she smiled serenely up at him. The tip of her nose was pink from the cold, and her eyes glittered with a hint of mischief…

"Yeah?"

"How do you feel about being four for four?"

Tam blinked. Then frowned. Then widened his eyes. Then tilted his head in silent question while briefly dropping his gaze to Eli's abdomen.

"You're…"

"Expecting our fourth. Yes."

Tam felt his mouth fall open.

His attention moved upward and he stared blindly at the horizon.

"If you comment on the virility of your family even *once* during this trip, I am shoving you overboard," Eli informed him matter-of-factly before pressing up onto her toes to brush a quick kiss on his cheek. "I'm going to get the ginger tea brewing for you, and I'll let our attendants know you'd like to sleep soon."

Tam was barely able to snap himself out of his stupor in time as Eli headed toward the stairs that would take her belowdecks. "Hey!" he shouted.

She turned around expectantly.

"I love you!"

She smiled back. "I love you, too."

With a final lingering look, Eli continued downward, leaving Tam to quell his racing heart by himself.

As he wandered over to the ship railing, his mind still stuttering along at this new discovery, he became vaguely aware of his father's presence appearing at his side.

"Eli told you the news, I take it?"

Tam slowly turned to bestow his father a dry look.

The house witch grinned guiltlessly. "The new baby was already craving oranges when you two arrived at our keep."

With a hopeless chuckle Tam braced his forearms on the ship rail and shook his head slowly. "At least she won't give birth until next summer sometime, by my estimate."

Fin nodded, his blue eyes warm on his son's face. "You're a lucky man, Tam."

Tam smiled back at his father. "I know."

The duke clapped a hand on his shoulder. "Come on. Your other children are probably finding some kind of trouble belowdecks. Luca is going through a growth spurt and is endlessly hungry. I wouldn't be surprised if he was already raiding the food stocks."

Wordlessly, Tam followed his father, already well aware that his assumption was most likely correct.

"So… Feeling excited?" the house witch asked over his shoulder upon reaching the stairs.

Tam laughed. "I am. Though I think in the future I'll make an effort to mentally prepare for boat trips in advance."

Puzzled, Fin raised an eyebrow in his son's direction.

Tam waved off the look. "Don't worry about it."

The pair continued moving, though as Tam's mind turned over the news that he was going to be having another child in the near future, he couldn't help but sink into the endless happiness that awaited him with open arms.

He hadn't even gotten to tell Eli the good news that the magistrate in Sorlia had sent word that he had accepted her as his apprentice upon their return home.

They'd be busier than ever… but it was the kind of busy that allowed Tam and Eli to spend hours together cozied up in their office with warm coffee, tea, and biscuits. Their evenings would consist of hot dinners with their children followed by comfortable beds and sound nights.

It was the life Tam had never thought he'd have, and yet… it was the absolute best one he could've imagined, and it was all his.

Other Works By Delemhach:

The Housewitch Trilogy
Volume 1, Volume 2, Volume 3

Kraken's Guide To The House Witch
This Work Is Exclusively Available On Campfire

The Princess Of Potential
Standalone

The Burning Witch Trilogy
Volume 1, Volume 2, Volume 3

The Ether Witch
Volume 1: The Casting Call
Volume 2: